OF OTHER TIMES AND SPACES

TREVOR WATTS

Dedicated to my ever-patient wife, Chris
Edited by Angela Rigley
Cover designed in association with myworldimage.com
Thanks to members of Brinsley and Eastwood Writers, and Tin Hat Writers, Selston for their help and support.

Visit the website at https://www.sci-fi-author.com/
Trevor Watts @SciFiWatts / Twitter
Or Facebook @ Creative Imagination
First Printing: March 2020
Brinsley Publishing Services

ISBN: 9798600637962

CONTENTS

PART ONE – COFFEE BREAK QUICKIES

Fourteen snappy little tales to start the day

PART TWO – LINGER LONGER OVER LUNCH

Fifteen stories to savour longer

PART THREE – WHILE HEADING HOME

Ten tales for the tube, tram or train

AUTHOR PROFILE

OTHER BOOKS BY THE AUTHOR

CREDITS, THANKS AND NOTES

PART ONE

COFFEE BREAK QUICKIES

WELL MET BY MOONLIGHT

We were sailing our little barque on a straight four-day run from Domina to Carribtown. Grandpa bought the beautiful three-master the day I was born – so we both became Adeline.

With four nights at sea, we don't trouble with harbours: it's a lot of bother to detour, and squeeze in and out, tie up, and avoid the guy who comes round for the berthing fee. Generally, we find a bay to drop anchor, but that night the wind faded an hour earlier than usual, and we were becalmed, me and the four guys.

It was hardly the first time, so it didn't worry us – it's fairly routine to drop the sea anchor over the bow and let the cable out. Fore and aft lights on, plus port and starboard, and we relaxed in the cockpit with a few rums and pinyas. That's standard practice up to midnight, yarning, strumming the guitar, chewing the fat and the jerk chicken. Plus keeping a general eye out over the water, keeping a measure of the weather before the guys bedded down. As I was skipper on that trip, I had the choice of watches, and stood the first one. I loved the tranquil warmth; the masts, sails and ropes silhouetted against the moonlit clouds.

It was the Cuba Strait; no sign of land or another vessel in any direction, even in moonlight as bright as it was that night. From what the experts said, the water there was almost as deep as it was wide – it was the Boxor Deep, a geological trench where the sea bed sank so, so far into the abyssal depths.

1

The hundreds of times I've sailed across here...
rough seas sometimes, but the nights usually fall like this
– warm and still, not so much as a murmur or slap from
a ripple against the hull.

Flying fish skipped past, raising sparks of electric-
blue phosphorescence – magical, mystical stuff. So
quiet. The moon made perfect reflections of the
scattered clouds on the black water. 'I'll miss nights like
this,' I said to myself, 'when I give up sea-faring to settle
with Rohan.'

Such a calm, soft night. Beautiful. Pace the deck,
slowly, silently, lean over the rails for a while – one eye
on the water, one on the sky, and both on the horizon.
Yes... Rohan – Gorgeous great hunk. My gorgeous
great hunk.

The fragrance of warm jasmine drifting in the air –
my favourite. A swirl in the black water: a dreaming
whale, perhaps? Or giant squid come up to feed?
Moonlit ripples spread lazily away, so calm.

Close alongside, so close... a black mass began to
rise from the water, glossed and wet. The jasmine scent
became stronger. Tiny points and patterns of light
appeared on it as the great mass drew level with me.
They moved back and forth, more and more of them,
changing colour, coalescing into circles like eyes a
metre across.

Unable to move or breathe, I stood frozen, staring
into the mind of a being from the depths, just feet away,
silently studying each other either side of the ship's rail.

Uncertain why, I reached towards it, as if for a high
five.

Something stretched back, met my hand. For long,
precious minutes an intense emotional awareness filled

me. Such feelings and thoughts... My soul took flight... and swirled through unknown depths. The night stopped, poised.

Eventually, reluctantly I sensed, it withdrew, and slipped back beneath the ripples. I was left alone with a swirl of phosphorescence as the moon slipped silently behind the clouds.

I've never told anyone why I decided against a life with Rohan, or of my continuing strange, warm thoughts about new-found kin at sea. Deep within, I treasure the memory of those long moments when we joined and shared.

I keep wondering – is that what *it's* still thinking, too?

'Horses don't talk like that, Dicky.' Miriam rolled half a dozen of her forward-facing eyes in an expression of excessive patience, flicking a tentacle towards a fly on the ceiling. 'You keep forgetting what you're supposed to be. Horses just neigh, bray and whinny; things of that nature. Refer to the guidelines; they exist so you don't make mistakes like that.' She sighed and deposited the fly in her thoracic cavity for later ingestion.

'Yesterday,' she continued, 'it was so peculiar, hearing all that coming out a pelican's mouth – er, beak. It was ridiculous. You must get in role or you'll be spotted next time you're out on surveillance. We need to get this preliminary observation report done properly on this planet. You were lucky not to be sent for dog-food – or the zoo.'

'What about you?' Dicky bristled his frilly bits. 'You have no size control. Nobody ever saw a dragonfly the size of an albatross. But, no… you have to do it. And you really shouldn't have been surprised when the kids tried to ride you when you became a sports car that scarcely reached up to their knees. Then you morphed into a cow no bigger than a hen when you were spying round that farm. We're never going to obtain all the data our employers need if you're going to keep messing things up.'

'Yeah? Yeah? And what about *appropriate*? I told you about that – you just don't get piglets wandering round an office asking questions.' Miriam's air sacs inflated in indignation. 'Can't you become a photocopier or something, and just listen in? Everybody stands and talks next to them – no need to ask anything.'

5

'Right! Right. If we're going to bring that up – who was it who decided that cats should be bright blue? And wouldn't be noticed in the dog kennels?'

Miriam's air sacs puffed up to near-maximum size, taking on a delicate shade of violet. 'I thought it was a rather tasteful blue,' she said, huffily.

'But this is Earth – they don't do taste. We'll never get any more work here if we can't get our research more accurate. This is our last chance, after what happened to those two towers…'

***

WORSE THINGS HAPPEN IN SPACE, THEY SAY

Worse things happen in space, they say.

I reckon they're right, because we are in space, just off Kirigg Hador, and we're doomed.

All of us. Every one. We have eighteen minutes. Then we'll all die.

All four thousand three hundred and eighty-one of us.

The Starship Triple Hope was doing fine; routinely steering in on the side thrusters as we drifted towards the docking bay of their little moon – Nicely called "Moon". Out the panorama windows, we watched the jagged crystal-rock pinnacles and deeply-shadowed fissures passing far below us. It's a pretty barren place, even for such an outworld location, but there are a dozen domes and about as many gully-fillers that comprise the Kirigg Hador Transfer Spaceport. That was where we were heading.

But something went wrong with our manoeuvring thrusters: they locked on, and we began spinning… more and more wildly.

The crew and officers couldn't turn them off. Our spin rate is speeding up. We're descending towards that rock-solid moonscape… Noticeably less distant now…

In seventeen minutes, we're going to collide with Moon.

It won't be a great, smashing, tremendous crash. It'll be slow and determined and cold. Two-hundred thousand tons of mass are about to collide with a quadrillion-ton moon. And nothing is going to stop it happening.

We'll hit and we'll crunch and keep going ever-harder under the thrusters. We'll be crumpled and flattened and we'll burst wide open.

And there's not a thing we can do. Even if they manage to get the thrusters into reverse, they couldn't stop us now; even if they had ten times the power. Too late. Too much momentum. We can see the pinnacles much closer now...

Lifeboats? What for in deep space? In inner-system space, they should normally have plenty of ships to get us off – but this is Kirigg Hador, light-years from anywhere. And they don't know about such things yet. No time now, anyway. We'll be close enough to touch them soon...

The captain's gone, with nine officers in his little gig; probably intending to watch from a safe distance while we all die in the vacuum. He'll have his excuses and some high-sounding reasons. But I bet he'll not have the sound on when we hit: it might hurt his sensitivities to hear us die – all four thousand three hundred and eighty-one of us.

Fifteen minutes...
Fourteen...
Thirteen...

FRIDAY NIGHT IN SOMERCOTES

'Is this Somercotes?' this guy in the car park asks me.
'I'm an alien.'

'You don't look much like an alien to me,' I says.
'But it's hard to tell round here, especially on a Friday
night.' The sights you see when you haven't got a gun,
eh?

'No, no,' he insists. 'I *am* an alien.'

'Yeah, and I'm your Aunty Flo. You know, "Go with
Flo, your local pro". It's my working catchphrase. You
interested?' I tease my blouse open a bit. No bra.

He gives me a funny look.

'Half price, if you're an alien?' I offer. Well, trade's
been a bit slack, even at my prices.

But he just mutters with this weird little mouth – like
my younger brother Joe's. 'Gottle of gear, gottle of
gear,' or something like that.

'Look mate,' I tell him, 'I seen better than you on
Stars Wars, and that must be a thousand years old. I'd
have thought modern alien suits would've come on a
bit.'

But he's going on in this metal voice. I mean – who
does that these days? Not since the Daleks and that
science nerk in the wheelchair. Only his voice is getting
screechier, like metal grating. 'Good effect, that,' I tell
him. 'You need to work on it, though. 'I mean – if you're
alien, you'd be going like, zipper-deedoodah-zipzip-
zipzip54321, wun't you? Or in binary, like 111000111.
Stands to reason you ain't gonna be talking English. I

9

mean, even Surly Sid from Newcastle 'an't got the 'ang of English, 'azi?'

'I travel through this region,' he says, all shiny and two heads. Them heads! One lurking behind the one I'm talking to!

'Come off it, Binary 001, I can see where the join is; it's all wrinkled. And your eyes! Yeah, right, you're definitely off the planet Zoggle if you think aliens have eyes like that. I've seen'em exactly the same at Partymask.com. And if you hang about till closing time in Alfreton, they get loads just like you. If you want to do the alien bit, don't talk with your mouth – Aliens got to be better organised than that. Just don't talk out your backside. Everybody does that round here.'

'But I *am* an alien; I'm passing through.' These four antennas come out of his back-facing head and swing round, like studying me.

'That's a good effect,' I congratulate him. 'Just passing through, eh? Looking for your mates in Pinxton, are you?'

Then his antenna-things grow and swing round me, like sniffing. I sniff back, 'You smell sort of acid-sweet.' I poke at one that's nudging into my blouse. Mucky little git. 'If you're really an alien,' I says, to put him off, 'You'll have a todger three foot long, bright green, with grappling hooks on the end, won't you? So show me.'

And he did! And we did! In the car park next to the Chippy. Ye Gods! This is gonna look so good on my CV.

***

EOS

I'm alone in a room. Naked. I sigh.
Unsure of who I am – I'm me, that's all I know.
There is a bed; metal and high.
A thick mattress, with covers white as snow.

A little puzzled, but not a lot. I'm simply not thinking.
I'm looking round the room and taking in the whiteness.
A room that's big and square, in which to live.
But there is nothing else in here.

But now I see a bed that's close by mine.
I don't think it was here before.
Someone lies therein, half covered: a girl.
I'm stepping closer. A radiant face, asleep.

Her eyes are closed, though I know she sees me there.
And smiles within as I sit by her.
She looks to be as young and as old as I
With exquisite breasts displayed, as though for me.

In curious innocence, I lift the cover away.
The wisp of hair looks out of place,
Her body so pale and smooth.
I carefully lay the blanket back and step away from her.

Someone else has entered now, attired in white
Asking something I don't understand.
She looks towards the other bed, and speaks again.
This time I know she asks of the girl.

'Who are you?' I think it's me who's asking that,
But I'm not sure my lips have moved to speak,
So I may not have spoken at all.
Perhaps it's my visitor questioning me.

Another in white has joined with us, looking pensive.
And soon there are more, all puzzled the same,
Standing round, looking at me, and talking low.
It might be me they're speaking to.

But I don't understand a word they say
And have no interest in what they seek.
They're looking at her, my girl in the bed
Then turning away to leave us alone.

I'm curious about the girl with the heavenly face,
For she's awakening now and sitting up.
Her big brown eyes look straight at me. She says
'I'm Aoife,' though her lips don't move, 'Néos Aoife.'

'New Eve?' I echo. 'I like your name.'
I adore this girl with soft-curled hair and lips that purse.
She reaches to me, and my hand she takes
And it occurs to me that I have no name.

'You're Néos Adamh. Shall we go?'
We leave. There are doors and corridors.
More people in white. But we are outside now,
Where a road leads away, past hedges and fields,

Towards the sunrise, far away. Hand in hand
We stand on the road and look at the world around us.
'It's ours,' we say. 'What shall we do with it?'
We smile and begin our walk towards the sun.

Me and Tarry were just weaving the webs, having a drink, checking out the new bar down Orbit Corner, where the Rocket and Kale used to be. 'New military theme for the place, eh?' I said, looking round the pictures and souvenirs on the walls... vids of alien battles and skirmishes playing on the screens... new range of drinks served in ammo containers... stools shaped like plumose antenna. 'All about the Seventh Cavalry, isn't it? I've heard about them recently. Heroes, aren't they?'

'The Seventh Cavalry? Heroes? Sure they are – like eggs in H2S.'

'Huh? Hydrogen sulphide? Y' saying they're rotten? Stinking?'

'Yep, poisonous, corrosive and flammable, too.'

'But they're the greatest force we have. Their name's carved in pride'

'Sure, they're the force behind every cock-up and massacre we've known for the past three centuries.'

'The Seventh? What about the Great Hradd Stand? They were wiped out to a man. Heroes every one.'

'Balderton! They charged onto a Deshi-controlled planet thinking they were going to have an easy time wiping out a load of civilian farmers, foresters and the like. It was intended as an example, a warning. And they did; they "chastised" four peaceful communities. "Chastised" equals slaughtered. Then found themselves locked out of their own ship; they'd left it with minimum guard. So the Deshi militia – amateur, at that – had them cornered, and took them out, one by one, without a single casualty in return. That don't get mentioned, eh? Just the hero bit, the tragic end...

'So they had to be reformed, with legend status, during the civil war on Alford. They set fire to the wrong town; burned the whole place to the ground.'

'But they were all killed themselves, by the Deshi hordes ganging up on them from both sides.'

'Sure, that's what the publicity mack reckoned: they were caught in the middle...'

'But actually?' I asked, at last managing to wrap my palps round a sipping container of 30-Proof Poison Dart.

'They all survived, and were lifted off planet. They were sent to Havos on the SN Distan.

'That's the ship that inexplicably blew up in orbit?'

'Yes. It was the sole condition of peace, and us remaining in the Federation; permitting us to land, and export their derethium – and that's essential for the new engines' core elements. They insisted on revenge on the One Hundred of the Seventh, for an estimated three thousand Deshi civilians they immolated.' Tarry wiggled a palp wisely, 'The cover story added to their legend, though.'

'Right... You noticed how this Poison Dart clogs up your probos?' I shuffled a few legs round on the stool, 'You were saying?'

Tarry sucked at his can and pulled a chelicera in distaste. 'Then there was the Namese war. Where the ground army had gone guerrilla and mixed in among the civilian population, while the Seventh gassed and blasted their way through three villages. It took millions, and a lot of promises to cover that up. In the end, though, it was the Seventh that was nuked, probably by their own illegal weapons cache being set off. It might have been an accident by their own side, or deliberate by the High Command, or the guerrillas being really good at infiltration and sabotage. Personally, I don't care. They're utter disaster wherever they've been. They get shuffled away on one side, or the innocent bystanders do. Or both. Anyway... you were saying about them? You heard something recently, you say?'

'Er, yes... their new-formed brigade's been posted here for Total Training – Hundred days. That'll be why they've re-decked this place, I imagine.'

'Foo! Ah well, I'm probably due to take a long vacation, anyway. Can you pass me the screenpad, huh? I'll see if there's any flights to somewhere warm and far away.'

***

NUMBER 16 BUNGULLA

Kori brushed the fresh dust aside. The plaque beneath
was as bright as ever, with its famous date: 4 3 0027 –
the founding of the first viable colony on Mars. The
geodesic dome that had been home to a hundred
colonists still stood, untouched for more than a century,
presiding over the inhospitable rust-red Martian
landscape. As the years had passed, so it looked more
and more like a spider's dome-web, with its silvered
struts in polyhedron patterns, and the once-clear glass
panels more greyed by the fine sand-blasting it received
in every storm that came through.

'The Fourth of Triono, the third period of the Martian
year, in the year twenty-seven,' she said, for the benefit
of the visitors from Earth, although everyone present
had that date, and the name of the colony, etched in heart
and mind.

'Number 16 Bungulla.' Her companion, Beren,
quoted the immortal name.

'Okay, we all know the colony's dome was named
after a dead spider on Earth.'

'Mmm. Funny name for a spider: Number 16.'

'Researchers studied her, and dozens of others, for
decades at a nature reserve at North Bungulla in
Australia.'

'Trapdoor?' Someone had to ask.

'They excavate a burrow straight down, and live the
rest of their lives in there, with only a little lid – a
trapdoor over the top – to keep out the desert heat and
dryness. Once they're mature, they aren't capable of
building another burrow from scratch. So they have to

19

make the most of what they have: look after it, repair it, not abuse it.'

'A lesson in self-reliance and independence, they say?' The Earth tourists were torn between the discussions, the scenery, the great original dome, and their portable info-pads.

'Exactly. Like all the others, Bungulla 16 could only leave her burrow far enough to grab any passing insects and beetles that touched her silken trip wires.'

'Then she was back down there with her food, shutting out the predators and the hostile environment.'

'Apart from those forays, she only went out for emergency repairs of the threads, such as after a foraging bird or a sandstorm.'

'And Number 16 lived safely in her burrow at least 43 years. The researchers took her survival as a life-lesson for all of us. And that's how the first colony dome was designed here: she was their role model. Sustainability was their creed: water extraction, hydroponics, surveying and monitoring, limited mining for a few gems and fossils to sell to scientists and collectors.'

'Nothing too greedy,' Beren concluded, looking meaningfully at the Earth tourists. 'Living within their means.'

'Low impact on the local and wider environment; live within your means. Keep your energy needs down... Look after your home...' Kori smiled, thinking of all the precautions and maintenance tasks that still had to be performed every day – lessons originally learned from a dead trapdoor spider.

'Keep the raiders out. That was the other big lesson that Number 16 taught us. And she managed it, with her frugal, ultra-settled ways, protecting herself, her spiderlings, and her home, and having minimal effect on her environment – for twice as long as anyone ever dreamed was possible for a mygalamorph spider.'

'But then, a parasitic wasp crept into her burrow, laid its eggs in her body…'

'And when they hatched, she was eaten alive, from the inside. A terrible death, even for a spider.'

'In a parallel irony, the colonists learned the same lesson, just as hard as she had done.'

Beren and Kori knew the wording on the plaque by heart, as did all Martians of the Modern Era. They faced the assembly, linking hands, seeing everyone else taking their lead before they began to recite the litany:

'Here stands the dome of Number 16 Bungulla, the Eternal Symbol of Mars. The people herein gave their lives to safeguard the future of all humanity on this planet. This structure of hope was invaded from deep in the rock by a microscopic, previously unsuspected form of Pre-Arrival Life. The selfless sacrifice by the one hundred colonists is forever honoured. Knowing that some of them were already infected, they sealed themselves within this dome to study the life-form, to seek a means of curing themselves without exposing others to the danger of becoming similarly infected. Their success was at the ultimate cost of their own lives. Eaten alive by Hyposoter harmakhis, it is their sacrifice in developing the AHH Serum which enables all people who follow to live and thrive here on Mars. Honour to them for all time.'

Beren stood with head bowed, as others echoed the final words, then continued, 'No-one has died of Hyposoter harmakhis since this catastrophe, 123 years

21

ago. We offer thanks each year to the memory of a long-dead spider that inspired and guided the colonisation of this whole planet.'

Kori felt tears well up, as they always did on this occasion, when she addressed the gathering. 'I'm Kori Bungulla Mars, the oldest inhabitant of this planet, and I owe that to the lessons learned from a spider that died on Earth, in 2018 – a hundred and eighty years ago. I came early today, to walk round, to remember, and to peer inside, as I often do. Through this now-frosting glass, it's still possible to make out several desiccated, eaten-up bodies in there, and I wonder which ones are my grandparents. I sometimes feel I ought to know.

'But then, I think it doesn't matter: they all made that ultimate sacrifice together, so they're all the grandparents of every one of us.'

***

PINBALL

On the long route to Aunt Persei's System, they stopped for an anti-boredom break. Grym Helaeth was relaxed about travelling, but his newly-cloned companion, Grym Newydd, wasn't accustomed to such protracted trips.

'I want to play for a while. I'm tired.' Little Newydd complained.

'Of course,' Helaeth agreed. 'We can play a game, if you like. See here... this sun and oddments system?'

Newydd's ilo-clusters twinkled in a kind of hipiric delight. 'Yes. Yes. Can we re-arrange them? That would be good.'

'That's a great idea; we could squeeze them together and build something out of them.' He flexed tenuous force fields in anticipation and gleamed like a nascent nova.

'But we've done that before. Can't we do something different?' Helaeth's clone-spring was adventurous now.

'We could flick all the planets into a different order? In order of size, perhaps, from the centre? Or in inverse size, with the biggest furthest away?'

Little Grym Newydd pulled a fassicula. 'That'd take a lot of thinking to make them stay in place – angles and speeds and things. It'd be no fun.'

'Well, how about... see all these moons round these two biggest planets?' The two Gryms swirled, wraithlike, around the two gas giants.

'Mmm. There's nearly two hundred.'

'Suppose we flick them?'

23

'Where to?' Newydd looked around.

'There's that twin planet nearer the star – the small green and blue one with an over-sized satellite companion. See?'

Newydd kulated his wavebands when he saw where Helaeth indicated. 'What? Put all these moons round that one?' He considered. 'That'd take a lot of working out, too.'

'Well, we don't have to be neat, do we? Suppose we just flick them there and see who can hit the satellite most? You have the moons from one of these big gassy planets and I'll have the other. Let's see if we can knock the big moon out of its orbit.'

'Or into the planet? Make them crash into each other, like playing bounce-ball?' This could be exciting stuff; Grym Newydd stretched and coruscated his spectral output in anticipation.

'It'll take a lot of getting right – the little planet and its big moon are spinning round each other, so you'll have to make sure your timing's spot on.'

'Suppose we each start with forty points, lose a point for missing altogether, lose two for hitting the planet, and gain two for hitting its moon?'

'Sure. You can do it. Practice with some smaller ones, then we'll start on the bigger ones.'

'Then can we go to Aunt Persei's System?'

24

A LOVELY SUNNY DAY

It was a lovely sunny day. Little boy Helios Paplova watched the ants through his huge magnifying glass. They were so big. He could see their eyes and their little legs scurrying as he followed them. 'Wow.' He breathed in wonderment. 'They're enormous through the lens. If I move the glass backwards and forwards, they shrink or grow...'

***

Helios Solaris, watching the child, understood his thoughts and interest, his amusement. So, from far, far above, he decided to help. 'I'll sprinkle a touch more sunshine for the boy.' He could see the boy liked it. So he sent more...

***

Helios Paplova loved the warm, bright sun, and was happy for the ants. He watched them grow huge or small in his great lens. And at one specific distance, the sun's light came together in a white spot that made the grass suddenly wilt.

'Wow!' He jumped. One of the ants had shrivelled, and a tiny puff of smoke arose. Being an intelligent little lad, he realised what had happened. 'I'm going to try that again,' he ventured, and moved the lens to exactly the right distance to make a brilliant white spot on the ground. Sure enough, another ant vaporised. There was the slightest of aromas. 'It's like a lemon or something,' he said in surprise. As he was a mischievous little boy, an inquisitive one, he wondered how many he could do that to? 'Suppose I could make them all go up in a puff of smoke and a nose-tickling smell?'

This could be exciting, 'Yes, that'll give them something to think about on such a nice warm day.' So he held the lens at just the right height, and played the white-hot spot through the mass that swarmed around the pinch of sugar he'd placed there.

**

Helios Solaris saw this was a good game, and sent down more sunshine for his namesake on Earth. He liked the way the child pretended to be getting too hot in the all extra sunlight he was sending – the way he sought the shade. So he sent down more and more sunshine from the great height of ninety-six million miles.

And more and more. Trees began to smoke… buildings caught alight… the lake boiled.

Oh, yes, he could appreciate how the boy had enjoyed doing this to the ants. 'Most rewarding,' he congratulated himself.

**

The Katerini Catastrophe, as it became known, involved the deaths of over thirty-seven million people, burned to death over a period of one hour twenty-six minutes.

The *immediate* cause was determined to be the most intense beam of light ever recorded – estimated to be brighter than a helix-core laser by ten-fold. It slashed across the land, and the houses and people across the whole of the Central Mediterranean, centred on northern Greece. Rivers evaporated in great bursts of steam.

Farms and villages, towns and cities vanished with no trace.

'The *root* cause is still a total mystery,' the scientific conference concluded a year later, in their final press release. 'We remain baffled by a phenomenon which had been undreamed of, and cannot be explained by any known set of factors in the realms of normal physics, quantum mechanics or quasar relativism.

***

SECOND THOUGHTS?

In the dark. In bed, thinking about Madelya, beside me, so warm and silky soft and smooth. I lightly stroke. The darkness hides her smile. Or maybe she isn't smiling; perhaps she frowns, or regrets. And me? What do I think? Well, there's a first time for everything. Or first *few* times, I suppose. A couple – at least – last evening in the euphoria. Certainly, sometime in the depth of night, when the air had been so still and quiet; not a murmur from anywhere.

And again just now as we awoke. Or had she been awake already? I have no idea what her sleeping routine is. Not that this liaison is routine for her, either. Does she usually lie in? Or sleep briefly before starting work around the home?

My hand seems to roam where it will, unbid. Am I feeling a little shy or awkward now? Is she? Why? We were perfectly open last night, and in the afternoon and evening, as things developed and we both understood more… about each other, and all manner of mutual things and interests.

'Jeems, you do have such wondrous breasts. Would you… er?'

'Mmm, yes…' Her hand – such long, delicate fingers – came to me. Her higher breasts so superbly full and rounded. The middle pair so pert and firm… the lower ones not yet matured. Her infinitely fine fur had retracted as she slept, her skin now so ivorine.

As I touch, I gaze blindly in the blackness to where her cute snub nose must be, scarce a span away, and those eyes – the front ones so green as a rule; the rear ones, more inclined to see in UV light than visible, probably monitoring the room now. The lack of external ears isn't ever noticeable, not visibly. But, as I stroke through the cascading beauty of her long, zebraic-striped hair, it occurs to me that her skin-flush aural membranes must be there somewhere.

'Second thoughts?' she quietly asks.

'No.' Sure, I'm aware of the momentousness of the occasion – a first for both of us, and much more than one night together implies. No, *implies* is a wriggle-out word. It was stated and agreed: we are committed to giving it a go – no second thoughts. After working together for more than two deccadays – nearly thirty days now – Madelya and I know each other's thinking and abilities fairly well. Very much the same vein of humour, too: we laugh at the same things, and at the same people around the complex. We work well together; and have mentioned setting up as independent operators a couple of times.

I know it seems a mite precipitous, but each of us knows the ins and outs of the business: she's bright in mind and outward in attitude, and we've been planning and preparing to team up for a decca. Actually setting it up for four days. And bed? Well, since sometime post-noon yesterday, I suppose. We'd both known we would.

Yes, this whole thing is pretty momentous: inter-species partnerships aren't unknown in business matters. They're rare in personal lives, though. Maybe a first in this part of Shiruki: it's one of the more conservative planets in this sector.

A noise outside distracts me. I pause to listen.

'Ignore them. It's just the humans across the hallway. They do quite a lot of this, too.'

I uncoil my tail, and wrap it around her body – her back responding divinely as her light down eases out of her silken skin. So delicate on the down-stroke, so arousing against the nap. Oh yes, life's good. No second thoughts for me.

Now... Which penis should I use this time?

***

'It doesn't make sense, Mrs Scapisky, when I think of how things happen around me.'

Mrs Scapisky was not happy with me, and became rather sarcastic. 'Well, we all know that things happen differently around you, Mellissa.' And she carried on telling us about different forces and objects and states of matter.

I said again, 'But I don't think that's right.'

'Do not interrupt or contradict me,' she said crossly. 'Thank you, Mellissa.'

So I listened to her telling it all again and still didn't see how she could possibly be right. I said so when we went for our afternoon wee and milk break. I thought she was going to hit me. Just for saying I saw things a little differently to how she did.

Sarcastically again, she called me Ine Stine.

I would not have understood sarcasm last year, but I'm five now, and when I told my dad what the canteen ladies had said at Christmas, he explained to me about sarcasm and how people with very small minds use it to belittle – I think he said belittle – people who know more than them and they don't want to admit it.

On the way back to class, after I'd washed my hands and face, I said, 'It's not nice to be sarcastic to small children, Mrs Scapisky. I don't think you ought to do it in class.'

She grabbed hold of me by my shoulder.

I was very surprised. It made me yelp. She was quite red and angry then, and marched me into class. She let go of me right at the front where she always stands and said, 'Alright then, Little Miss Knowall, let's hear *your* version.'

I straightened my dress and said, 'You shouldn't grab hold of children like that, Mrs Scapisky. I would have come. You only had to ask.'

So, I faced the class, 'Well, children.' They were all looking at me and I didn't know if I could explain it to them. I mean, they were only eleven and twelve – the teachers keep making me leave my friends and go up a class, so they're all older than me.

'I would like to thank Mrs Sca— Er… Firstly, there is no such thing as different forces. There is only one force in the whole universe. We can call it energy – or Fred, I suppose it could be. It's everywhere. Except where it hasn't got to yet because it can't move fast enough to have gotten to places that don't exist yet. They only exist because energy has got there.'

'Yes, but—'

'Please don't interrupt or contradict, Mrs Scapisky. Energy is everything, and it can change its form. It can spread itself out really thin and we say it's gravity. Or really, *really* thick like in black stars. It can change from one sort to another, but it might not be easy. Like light and heat can change just like *that*—' Oh, shoot! I can't click my fingers however much I practise.

'And lumps of energy can change to light and heat like in atom bomb things. Therefore, they must be able to change back. And all the states of matter – I think there must be a lot more than gas, liquid and solid – at least seven or eight or ten more. I think they can change whenever they want.' I had a sip of water before I carried on. 'And time as well. Time isn't just when we come to school or go home for tea. No – it can change and go fast

34

or slow, depending on how fast we're moving. I bet it can change into other things as well. I think time's just another sort of energy like light and gravity.'

'But time's different...'

'No, it's not, Tony Millkins. You're not listening. It's all *energy* – it just shows itself in different ways – like solid hard lumps – which are nearly all space but with very concentrated energy holding the bits together. And time and gravity change up and down together so they must be...' I wasn't sure what they must be. 'I'll have to think more about that,' I told them. 'And they make matter change as well. Yes – like time and gravity, and space-ships getting all stretched out on the way into black holes.'

Ogbo Mgbu said something really silly about his scab had matter in it and I ignored him and sniffed like Mrs Scapisky does.

I admitted I didn't know exactly how electrics and magnets fitted in – but it was obvious they did, especially with light, and so it must be with gravity and time as well. 'I expect energy shows itself according to what mood it's in – it might be feeling timely or plasma-y, or a bit gravity-ish. Like Mrs Scapisky might be feeling sarcastic-ish... Or really lovely and magnetic...' I had to say that because I saw the expression on her face. I thought she was looking a bit lumpy, like lead, actually.

'Yes, but we all run out of energy, Mellissa.'

'We don't really run out of it, Mrs Scapisky, we turn to different sorts of energy like smoke and heat; or worms and maggots. All our energy gets spread out and other people can use it, or it can even shine into space, where aliens might use it. And when the sun changes itself and blows everywhere—'

'Thank you, Mellissa.'

'But I haven't finished, Mrs Scapisky. I haven't told you about—'

'It's time to start our writing now, Mellissa. And don't tell me that time is fluid and I could change it. Hmm?'

'No, Mrs Scapisky.' Shoot! I *was* just going to say that.

'I expect the universe will run out of energy before you do, Mellissa.'

'Oh no. The universe will never run out of energy. I think it must all be changing to one sort that's spread out perfectly evenly everywhere. I think they call it entropy.

'Actually, I wonder if that's the opposite to what was before the Big Bang? Because then, *all* the energy was in a point the size of *nothing*, and there wasn't any time energy. Perhaps when all the energy is used up and spread everywhere, it like bounces back and starts going backwards towards being a nothing-point again. Then it can all start anew with another great Big Bang. And keep doing that for ever and ever.'

'Yesss... Thank you, Mellissa.'

Hmm, some of my talk had only popped into my head while I was talking, and it seemed quite exciting. That about the whole universe spreading everywhere and then shrinking back into a pinpoint black hole really is something to think about when I'm in the bath tonight.

I don't know where all my yellow ducks came from, but it's funny how, when we talk to each other, they help me to get things straight in my mind. It's like they know *everything*.

The koi carp in the big pond were getting thinned-out. It wasn't the grass snakes: I got rid of them two years ago. 'Martians,' said Polly and Percy, my twins, and started building Martian traps.

Polly saw a big swirl across the surface one evening. It was coming towards her from under the tress, across the far side.

The security camera caught multiple cats, a fox and a badger. One splash in the water could have been anything. 'Including a Martian,' the kids insisted, with their fixated, joint mentality.

The resident heron vanished, leaving a flurry of feathers. So… Alligator? Catfish? Pike?

'This is Kingston upon Trent,' Jill patiently pointed out.

'Otter,' said the zoo-man who came to see, and didn't want one, whatever it was.

'Mink,' said the HSE woman who arrived at the same time. 'Nothing is at risk as an individual, or endangered as a species.' They departed, smugly, holding hands.

'You could poison it all and start again,' suggested a blogger on the kids' "We've discovered a Martian" website.

'No you cant it cud get in the locul warter suply,' was voted most helpful response.

Then the three biggest koi went – two feet long plus tails. There were deep scratches in the shallows. 'Whatever we've discovered, it's at least the size of our Labradors.'

'Dad, we haven't actually *discovered* anything until we know what it is.'

'A baby Loch Ness Monster,' I held out for.

We thought a bit wider – the internet, the telly, the pub.

Goliath Tigerfish... freshwater shark... anaconda... mutant snapping turtles. We became familiar with them all.

'Build a Trump Wall round it.'

'Fill it with concrete.'

'Stick of dynamite.' They were particularly helpful down the Dog and Partridge late on Friday nights.

Then the Labradors vanished.

'Plenty deep enough for a Martian to hide in,' Polly'n'Percy insisted, treating me to their darkest "we-know-best" look.

The team from Harvey and Son began to drain it, but stopped in a panic. They left a fifty-metre roll of hundred-millimetre hose on the back lawn. They wouldn't come back for it, and wouldn't say why.

'Hmm,' pondered the RSPCA woman. 'I see no endangered animals here.'

'Aah,' said the council official, and ate his sandwiches on the bench in the sun.

'No law has been broken,' stated the police as they sniffed and departed.

'Underwater Discovery's our middle name,' said the volunteers from Nottdale Sub-Aqua Society, just before they disappeared in a massive thrash and splash event.

Followed the next day by two police officers and a cameraman in an inflatable boat, in an eruption of rubber and blood.

'They discovered our Martians,' Polly said.

Next day, they chain-sawed half my trees down, and erected a massive marquee over the whole pond. Floodlights and an eight-foot fence were up before dusk. Eight "government people" were poking and whispering round by then.

'They've discovered *something*,' the telly people complained. 'But they're not saying *anything*.'

'Martians,' Polly and Percy smiled knowingly.

Compulsorily moved out two days later, our belongings vanished into storage. The TV exposure programme was pulled just before it was due to be screened. Rumours abounded in the Dog and Martian.

'Midwich,' Percy says.

'Martians,' Polly insists.

'Jill… You remember that job they offered me in California?'

'Yes, Dear. Ask about their Hawaii branch; it's further away.'

***

I'm just a normal girl: they say I'm pretty and bright, with a gorgeous pair – of ankles and eyes and the rest in between. To add to the charm, I'm also blonde. Well, sort of blonde – my hair has a kind of amber sheen, and it's very attractive, some men say. 'More like a salmon shade,' said Derek, my boyfriend then, 'so unusual.' He used to stroke and caress my flowing locks, until he noticed my scent one night. 'What's that?' he sniffed. 'Is it Eau de Cologne, from Germany?'

'No, it's from further afield than that,' I said. 'It's Eau de Squid, from the Philippines.'

So it was 'Goodbye, Derek,' and 'Hello, Joe.'

But Joe was a drinking man; he'd have a few and get into rows with his mates. Then home to me he'd come, still in a narky mood, his thoughts not on love, but still on fighting. One time he decided to pick on me. My skin turns into shell, like a carapace, at any kind of threat. To his disbelief, it broke his fist. I reached across the room as he tried to flee, and grasped him with my toes. 'They're lobster claws! On the end of your feet!' He shrieked anew as I gripped a mite too tight and taught him that he shouldn't have been so cross with me.

So it was 'Cheerio, Joe,' and 'Howdy, Willy.'

My body can coruscate with patterned lights that flicker all my length from toe to crown… or gill to gut as we like to jest around the reef. I'm quite a sight in a darkened room it seems, when I nakedly stand like a Christmas tree with my body-lights on; all flashing in sequence according to mood or the music we play. And when I sway in such a way, it used to drive my Willy wild. He tried to keep up by wiring himself to a disco set, but he really wasn't as good as he thought he was, not with the dance, or the lights, or electrical skills.

My stomach tentacle has a mind of its own when I'm really starved: it snakes out, seeking food, extends itself, envelops its prey and sucks it back. It was a surprise for New-Boy Nigel when we were out for a meal at the Mexican Hat: his prawn chimichanga was just too much to resist, and my tentacle slid under the table. I saw it rise beside his plate and I had to squeal and wave to distract him as my tentacle had a quick sniff and swallowed the lot. He wondered where his meal had gone, of course, but it was safely tucked away in me. I suggested a chicken burrito instead, although he was a touch suspicious when I burped again. He said not a word, but sniffed all night, and I never saw Nigel again.

But Tony was there to help me out.

My eyes can widen up, 'Like saucers filled with milk. They're both full cream,' my Anthony said, and gazed into my depths of coral caves; and saw my shipwrecks there. He shuddered twice as if he'd hit the rocks and foundered deep. 'Full cream, that's you,' he murmured low, 'But my stomach's weak and I only drink semi-skimmed.' But I can never go for that, so I sucked him into my milken eyes, drowned him and flushed him out like cod liver oil.

Breathless once when playing with Clive, I opened my gills and waved them round for extra air; my secondary heart, of course, popped out as well to flush itself. Well… Clive was amazed but he took it well; considering the way they flapped and fluttered in time with the band on the radio. But I went off Clive when he confessed at the Ocean Grill, that his favourite starter was deep-fried calamari rings with a peppered dip. 'Yeuk Yeuk – You cannibalistic pig,' I said, and I showed him where to stick his battered rings.

'I'm an Oceanic Biologist,' my Larry says, and thinks I'm a wonderful blend of pleasure and work. 'I adore the way you can slink under the door and slide into bed.' I cuddle him there with suckers all over my arms and tentacles. It delights him when he guides my hand in bed and finds I still have another five to play with him. My tentacle pair wrap twice round Larry to keep him close, and I pulsate in time to encourage him more. When the light comes on in early morn, I'm back to me, his lovely girl, all salmon blonde and a lovely pair.

There's so much more I can share with him – like extrude my stomach out my mouth, fully inside out, and taste him all over. Or kiss him, as he likes to dream I'm doing, when his eyes are closed. My best-ever trick, he says, was when I splattered the walls in inky black that squirted out the funnel of my hypobranchial gland. 'A wonder you are!' he exclaimed in joy. 'My Melanin, my Little Miss Right.'

We said we'd bathe together tonight, in the new hot-tub in his little back yard. It's all secluded, and hung with trees like coral fronds. 'You'll feel at home in there,' he says. Yes, yes, I'm really looking forward to it – I can propel myself with jets so strong that I'll be round the tub in two seconds flat. If we toss in the fish from the koi-carp pond I'll show him how to catch and skin and fillet them all with just my teeth, and spit out the bones in a neat little sac.

But most of all, I'm wondering now, is how he'll react when I squeeze down the drain and come out the tap.

IT'S NOT MY FAULT, WHAT HAPPENED TO THE MOON.

I merely happened to be filming it, close up, as I often do. Okay, so I'm a nerd, geek and whatever else. But it doesn't make me a Moon-Wrecker, like they're saying.

There's this particular line of mountains, the Apennines, in a great curving ridge of peaks that is almost down the midline of the moon, about two thirds of the way up. As the shadow comes each month, the peaks vanish one by one. You can see the darkness race up the slopes until the pinnacle vanishes – I always think there ought to be a beep or a puff of dust to signify each disappearance. It's beautiful to watch – I try to do so, every month. It's as though I've been there: I have dozens of photographs, including from ground level – Apollo 15 landed there. And there's a deep winding valley like a canyon. It's totally fascinating.

Even more so that night. The peak of Mons Hadley Delta – which Apollo 15's rover climbed – was vanishing into its monthly shadow when it went altogether – much too quickly. It had gone totally into blackness in an instant. I took my eyes away from the eyepiece to look round for what had caused that. Looked up at the moon through the open skylight. No birds, planes or anything else blocking my view.

I peered back to watch through the lens. The mountains either side were changing, too. As if being sucked into a pit. The pit was widening. Hadley Rille – the sixty-mile valley – was distorting. I reached up to wipe the lens protector and rubbed my eyes. The whole region was swirling, as if into a whirlpool, cracks

47

spreading wider, the moon's surface layers cracking and splitting apart.

The whirlpool effect was deepening, the spiral of rock and dust speeding up. It was terrible to see. I stopped breathing. So terrible. Unbelievable. The moon, for heaven's sake. It can't happen to the moon. Like *My* Moon.

Looking through the skylight again, there really was a dark patch a little more than half-way up, along the terminator line – the sunset shadow line.

I was torn between watching the real thing up there through the roof, the subjective much loved view. Or the detail through the telescope and camera, the removed, objective view for scientists. Plus dashing to my computer to upload onto my blog live so everybody can be aware of something so momentous.

Somehow, dodging and darting round, I did all three. It's ten seconds to stream the live feed through on line, not that anyone watches my live videos. A few dozen, maybe. How momentous – the moon doing something! The first time ever, apart from the occasional little gas spouts that are probably caused by solar heating of the ground. But this was big. Huge. I mean, it's the effin moon! And there was a huge great hole, a swirling mass. So dark. The Hadley Rille had gone, and half the mountains each side of it: they were disintegrating, slipping into it, being sucked in.

It was easily a hundred miles across already, and growing. The cracks had spread so much wider. The moon was being sucked up, or in – into itself.

And it kept going, sucking in and in; massive cracks splitting across the whole sphere. I was nearly crying at the sight – my mountains gone! It couldn't be real. The

Apennines! Gone. They kept on and on, being dragged down.

Then the whirlpool – it must have been two or three hundred miles diameter by then – welled up, like a massive bubble inside it coming to the surface. Black in the middle and moving, it burst up and out. A column of dust and rock rose like a tower. And it thinned out. Stopped. Started to fall back, slowly. Collapsing back towards the surface – the all-smashed-up and cracked and split-open surface. The moon wasn't ever going to be the same again.

Maybe only a few dozen people saw my Moon Blog live. But millions have seen it since. It's had more hits than any other video or photograph in the history of the Internet. I've been interviewed dozens of times on the television, for the news and for documentaries and for newspapers and magazines.

There's even a big conspiracy theory circulating – a lot of followers, too: Obviously, I must have done it. I messed up the moon – there's this vast black pit in the middle where there used to beautiful creamy mountains and craters. Why else would I have a superzoom focus down on the exact spot where it all started? They've never heard of coincidence? It just happens to be the spot on the moon that I watch and film the most, especially when the termination line is sweeping across the mountains there. Coincidence – that's all.

What was it? There's a whole branch of astro-physics setting itself up to work that out. Initial thinking is the spontaneous appearance of a seedling black hole somewhere inside the moon, or perhaps the other side and burrowing through. They want to send a probe up to look round the far side asap. There's also the problem of where the black thing went when it exited the surface, with the column of rock and dust spiralling after it. There don't seem to have been any sensors of anything pointing that way. No gravitic anomalies monitored anything.

It appeared, and vanished. And took an estimated ten percent of the moon with it. Nobody has any idea what it was, where it came from, where it is now, where it's going – nothing. But that's a new branch of science for you, eh?

The moon's surface is settling down; it looks so different – a massive smooth depression; so dark and ominous. And cracks dozens of miles wide, hundreds long, radiating from it. Tides on Earth have diminished in height by, it's assumed, around ten percent, but it's too soon to have an accurate long-term picture – it's messing up harbours, though, with ships stranded.

I really miss my piece of the moon.

And there are still around one million people who are convinced that I did it.

Okay, so I'm a geek – I admit it. But I'm a geek with a fan club. It was started by a really cute, geeky girl with nerdy glasses like mine. She's the president, and my girlfriend. My first-ever girlfriend. So it's not all bad, what happened to the moon.

50

PART TWO

LINGER LONGER OVER LUNCH

'Thanks for coming, Alvi,' Rillan greeted his coordinator as he slithered into the lab, re-tuning his cilia to the right pitch for his voice. 'I wanted to talk to you about humans.'

'Humans? Those grubby little things living on that planet that looks like a mona crystal?'

'They're the ones. They're the dominant life-form, in the sense that they're everywhere like an itch, and bully all the others like a swagger-slug. However, they're clearly not the highest life-form; not physically, mentally or philosophically. Nor even in total numbers, bulk, planetary effect, or closeness to the Universal Being.'

'Indeed so; what about them?'

'You know Laddick, don't you? Good. He's been conducting some sociology research recently, although the concept of sociology with humans is a bit of a stretch. He has identified a specific mentally-depleted subdivision among humans. This group performs ludicrous and cruel activities, and uses the planetary communications network to broadcast them for the amusement of others of a similarly basal mental capacity. They have a complete absence of empathy with other living beings.'

'You mean they *enjoy* pain and torment as a form of self-entertainment?' Alvi was sceptical.

'In a way, yes: they relish visiting pain and terror on others, but this is certainly not an inward, masochistic, process. Quite the opposite: there is no sign that they themselves enjoy dread, pain and horror being visited upon them. In fact, it appears to be the last thing they desire.'

'Strange creatures, humans: if they don't like it themselves, why impose it on others? For mere recreation?' This whole concept had Alvi baffled.

'We're unsure, but Laddick has also observed one especially strange aspect of this phenomenon. There is a higher life-form on the humans' planet – higher in the sense of being closer to the Ultimate Being in its philosophy and understanding. It is known as The Cat; it is a kindred spirit of The Great Manitou.'

'Ahh. Almost divine, hmm?'

'Indeed so, Alvi. Many Cats live in close proximity with the human creatures. Being altruistic, they frequently attempt to raise the humans' consciousness to a basic level of understanding. So far, entirely unsuccessfully. And yet, this particular sub-group of humans finds it amusing to horrify their superiors: their closest friends and allies. Indeed, many might say humans' *only* friends and allies. In their perversion, this sub-group has discovered a quirk of a Cat's nature: they are utterly terrified by the appearance behind them of a common Earth fruit, known as a cucumber. It is shaped rather like a schlugg maggot, and is the same dark green colour. When a Cat notices such a fruit immediately behind it, its reaction is one of instant terror – its eyes widen, claws extend and it jumps six body-heights. Also frequently observed has been yowling, heart rate tripling, and running an average of fifty-two flying paces.'

'My word,' Alvi sucked in. 'Pretty extreme, that is. How awful for them. And this group of sub-humans finds the Cats' terror *amusing*?'

'To the 38th degree, according to Laddick.'

'Mmm.' Alvi flexed a couple of tentacles as he pondered. 'These humans find no pleasure in their own fear and horror, and yet they knowingly inflict it on others? Why? How do they react themselves? Has any work been done to find out?'

'It's beginning. Laddick has conducted limited tests on selected human groups, exposing them to feelings which might cause similar terror; of being burned alive, crushed, drowned, skinned, falling, and so on. All perfectly harmlessly carried-out, of course, with no actual damage caused to the individuals. He's found that, although suffering considerable mental anguish under these tests, 98.4 percent survive them entirely unharmed.'

'So virtually every human lives through these imaginary experiences?'

'Exactly. However, none has experienced the full terror reaction of the Cats – the high jump, the yowling, the claws, etc. This is what Laddick has been attempting to reproduce. Until now.'

'Ah, yes…?'

'He has finally managed to create an identical response among humans.'

'Yes? What is it they react to?' This sounded intriguing; Alvi uncoiled his antennae in anticipation.

'A cabba-gunkin. Of all things.'

'A cabba-gunkin? A child's toy?'

'Indeed. There's something about its rows of sharp, in-sucking teeth… or perhaps the fiery breath? The glowing red eyes, perhaps?' Rillan shrugged several shoulders. 'Those cute little horns, perhaps. Who knows with humans, eh?'

'I suppose it could be anything, really; the sudden forward lunges that so delight our toddlers; those adorable claws that grab and twist our babies' mandibles? They love them, don't they?'

'Absolutely. And yet, when Laddick introduced a cabba-gunkin immediately behind the humans—'

'In the same way *they* do with Cats and cucumbers?'

'Exactly. Seven out of eight die of fear.'

'At the mere sight of a child's toy?' Alvi was incredulous, 'Did they give any sign of deep internal pleasure in their deaths? Such as they experience when inflicting these responses on Cats?'

'Not so far. But the experiments have been very limited to date. Laddick has applied for a licence to run an experiment using only humans known to frequent the Cat-tormenting sites on the communication network.'

'To see if they do, in fact, derive great pleasure from having it done to them?'

'Precisely; he wishes to discover if humans of this sub-group of Cat-tormenters can learn to love what they inflict on others.'

'So what is he proposing?'

'He wishes to isolate the various factors in a cabba-gunkin, and see if he can produce that same pleasure effect within their dying panic.'

'Indeed, they must surely have some ultimate delight within their agony and dread.'

'It's a matter of discovering which exact factor they are especially sensitive to. So far, human survival rates have actually fallen with each variation he has made to the toys' features – giving them longer horns… more teeth…'

'Not a single one of this sadistic Cat-torturing group actually enjoyed their own horror-filled death? How strange.' In wonderment, Alvi flexed a different pair of tentacles.

'Laddick wishes to extend his work to more realistic grabbing with the extended claws: a more orangey-fiery glow to the eyes, the addition of sound effects, burning smells. He feels there must be some key factor that will create those final moments of amusement, akin to that which they feel when they do exactly the same thing to Cats.'

'Indeed so, Alvi. This is important, worthwhile work. Make sure his licence application comes straight to me. I imagine he'll wish to continue until the supply of human Cat-tormenters runs out, so tell him to include a request for additional funding, hmm?'

***

'Yes, Officer, George was a keen indoor gardener. It used to be orchids, but not long after Mathilda – his wife – died he became interested in cacti. "They were starting to look too much like my former wife," he told me. "So I sold them all on eBay." We were standing right here in his conservatory, where it had been full of orchids just a month or two before. He'd cleared them all out, scrubbed the orchid shelving, and bought one huge cactus at a car boot sale where an old lady was selling off her dead husband's collection. Then he bought a dozen of the finest plants he could find. "Fortunately,' he told me, "there's a top-class cactus nursery near Matlock. And I've been very selective in what I've bought or propagated since. I should have done it before – Mathilda was prickly, too."

'I came visiting not long after, and they looked pretty good already, growing so big and fast; and flowering as well as any I've seen, though I'm no expert on C&S. Er, cacti and succulents, Officer. But George certainly had a way with them: bug and disease-free, shooting up like the Sonora Desert in spring. Look round – these are huge for domestic-grown cacti. I'm sure you don't normally find these varieties growing this well – No, you're right, Officer, I'm not an expert.

'Well, I don't know if it's relevant, but you said to tell you everything I know. Thus, its relevance is surely something for you to judge in retrospect. Er, retrospect? That means looking back on it. Yes, it is a big word, Officer. He also told me he talked to them. "I do a Prince Charles," he said. He even swore that one of them answered him, like inside his head. "We commune. That one is called Mi-amiga; she's my special friend. She's from the Mojave Desert. We think wonderful things together when I've had more than a few tequilas of a summer's evening."

'Yes, I do come and visit him. Quite often, considering how far apart we live. We've been very close friends for many years. Not that it's anything to do with you, but we had been having an affair for ten or twelve years.

'He re-arranged the conservatory like this, with the big comfortable chair and a drinks cabinet and fridge and completely surrounded by his cacti. After Mathilda had gone I spent a weekend with him. He was his old self, good for a laugh and a few pints down the Horse's Hoof. The fish and chips, lounging in here – the fridge was merely a chiller for the booze. We stayed in, binge-watching manic American comedy films, with burritos and tequila, of course. Why? I expect the cacti felt at home if he breathed spicy salsa and tequila all over them. Obviously.

'Personally, I never heard Mi-amiga say anything. It just looked like a large cactus with a mix of hairs and spines to me, but George always reckoned she was communing, listening, asking. He said they felt absolutely relaxed with each other.

'Well, yes, Officer, we talked about all sorts of things, like when we used to work together; and the old haunts in Nottingham: his car; the old house; even Mathilda. But, really, he kept bringing the conversation round to his prickly friends, as he referred to them. He quoted me all their names and places of origin, their peculiarities, times of blooming. Everything. I swear he was even more keen on cacti than he had been on orchids. "I'm always getting their spines in my hands, though, Alma. They're not like orchids that way."

I said it sounded like he had his Mathilda and the plants rolled into one. "You're always stroking them; no wonder you get pricked."

"'The spines are so fine, some of them," he'd say, and keep a pair of tweezers handing for extracting them from his skin. He kept up his strict routine for watering them: intense lights, dehumidifier, heater, feeding them. I swear he really loved them. Once I said to him it was a pity his name wasn't Jack, for he could have been called Cactus Jack. But he'd never heard of it. Oh, you haven't, either, Officer? It's a sort of margarita. No, that's a kind of alcoholic drink, Officer. Mexican, I believe.

'He told me he tried tomato fertiliser last year: it's blood-based. And he said the Rebutia stellatum – that's the one over there – seemed to come on in leaps. He said he'd never seen flowers like them. "They're twice the size of anything on the net, much darker and more speckled. And so many: eleven blooms off one globe this year; eight off another."

'I asked him if he laid down in here and let them suck his throat, "Do you, George?" I once joked. Now I think about it, he did give me a bit of a funny look, then laughed and said, "Nothing like that, Alma, dear."

'After a few drinks, he said, "Actually, I did try them with my blood. I accidentally cut my hand and rubbed some of the fertiliser on it to stop the flow. Then dissolved it in the cactus water. Why not? I thought. And later, I deliberately did it more, and watered them with my blood mixed in the fertiliser every week."

61

'When he told me, I remember the way he reached and stroked down one of the soft hairy ones – that one over there, with long hanging branches.

'"George?" I once said to him – we were in bed at the time and he'd been rather rough, like spiky, you might say. "I can't help noticing your fingernails are a bit long. You always used to bite them down to the quick. They look a bit sharp, don't you think?"

'He turned his hands over, studied them on the pillow, and laughed, "I put something on them that tastes awful, and lost the habit of chewing them. They are quite long, aren't they?"

'"Like spikes, on your right hand, they are," I told him, "and I've got the scratches on my back to prove it." Then this year, I received a card at Christmas; but he cried off the New Year meet-up to see me and Alfie. No... Alfie is his child. *Our* child. Yes, he did acknowledge him. He helped with the financial side; didn't want to get involved with the personal aspects. George wasn't into personal things. Yes, Officer, except for the two of us, yes. Since you mention it.

'Then he didn't reply to my emails, tweets and texts and the Facebook messages I sent from holiday in Texas, asking if he wanted me to get him some special cactus seeds and cuttings I'd seen. But he didn't answer. I rang, but his message tape was full.

'I came down today because I was worried about him. I could combine the visit with a week's work in town, so it wasn't out my way too much. I have a key, naturally, and I found him just like he is there. He certainly hasn't moved.'

The officers scratched their noses and took out their notepads, and phones to take the pics and send their reports.

Before the police arrived, I had already taken a few pics and a vid. George was very clear then, several hours ago, so tall, very still, long spines from his fingers – two or three dozen of which were coming through his clothing, too. But while I waited, and tried to chat to him, it was obvious he was becoming assimilated into the giant cactus – or he was becoming a giant cactus himself. Either way...

Even now, it's still recognisably him – I'd know those eyes anywhere. His hair's gone white and trailing, like huge cobweb masses. Exactly how some of those cactus plants are. His arm was around Mi-amiga an hour ago, but it's completely gone green and spiny now.

There was this dead flower, with a seed pod hanging out of it. A few minutes ago, it burst apart, and scattered seeds all around the conservatory. They're being spread everywhere now, on the shoes of the police who keep traipsing through without the slightest idea what to do – waiting for "experts" to arrive, I suppose, or "forensics". I reckon there'll be lots of little Mi-amiga kids throughout the neighbourhood before long.

Gazing into his face, now, there's not much left – mostly his twinkly eyes – and I don't think they'll be there much longer. I sort of said, 'Smile for the camera, George.'

And do you know? I'm sure he did.

***

I know exactly what'll happen when I get down to the Ops Suite: I'll press the ID pad. It won't light up. So I'll press it again. And again. And eventually Zeppy'll take his finger off the blocker and the pad'll illuminate. It'll ID me automatically, but won't let me in because Ykry will be scritting about as usual on the other side, and it'll want iris recognition and fingerprints as well.

They'll all be smirking when I enter. The usual bunch'll be lounging round and contented as usual: Ykry, Zeppy and Jaya. Their eyes will light up as they watch me stride in, perky as ever. Such miniature minds. And I'll offer a slight sneer as Zeppy will call out, 'Come back, have you? Why do you keep putting yourself up for it, Drewder?'

I'll strip off my civvy gear while Ykry carries on, 'You get shot down every time you stick your head up.'

Jaya'll mock with his silly, "I'm mortally wounded" act, but by then I'll be out the rad shower and at my locker.

The door will be jammed or de-programmed and I'll say, 'Yeah, but I'm learning – about them and about myself.' I'll have opened the locker by then and Jaya'll look disappointed.

I'll pull my outside suit-unit out and check the power levels, the software dates and weaponry types. Zeppy'll shout and ask if I'm still whittling about last time when I went out defenceless, with no power, and he'll call me "Gung Ho Boy" and I'll tell him I know it was him who did the total drain. So he'll accuse me of shorting their survival suits and I'll smile and say nothing and spend twenty minutes sliding into my suit and they'll giggle.

Ykry'll come over and say, 'But it must be killing you. Nobody can take that many hits. You go for different targets every time. You're setting yourself up. You're asking to get burnout.'

'You're doing different tactics every session.' That'll be Jaya.

'Different weapons,' will be Zeppy's contribution.

'It's the only way I can learn, *tocayi*,' I'll tell them for the umpteenth time. 'I'm learning to take the pain. I get over it, analyse it and learn from it. Doesn't ever happen the same way twice – I don't take anywhere near as many hits as I used to.'

'Yeah, sure.' They'll snigger in their usual faint disbelief, and tell me I'm battered and bruised, and say I must be mashed inside as well.

Then I'll pause and give them my best arrogant stare, and remind them I'm the new guy, and I started off worst one there. Then I'll tell them, 'Not to be immodest – but now I reckon I'm faster than any of you. Every time I take a hit, it's one more place I know where to expect bother; or some other tactic the enemy's trying.'

That'll irritate them all over again, and I'll remind them of my recent status change: Permanent Volunteer for Action. The suicide code, as they called it, the PVA. 'When this conflict gets really serious, who do you think is going to survive? Come out on top, maybe?'

They'll study me all over once more, saying that's not going to happen, and asking if that's why I'm always looking for bother? Pushing myself as well as them and the Cherybs?'

Jaya and Zeppy will be dismissive and tell me I'm a permanent challenge to everybody, not just the invaders. I'll agree and thank them, and ask if they think I actually *want* to be blasted, needled and scorched every time I'm on duty? I'll put on my sneery, irritating tone and say, 'If I stayed comfy and kept my head down, like you lot, I'd get wiped over if they ever get this close. Exactly like you will.'

They'll retaliate and go on about do I expect promotion, higher pay? 'Looking out for the female officers, eh? Y' think you stand a chance, Drewy? You're a cadet.'

So I'll turn over the lapel of my uniform and show them the five silver starbursts. 'I'm already on double your pay,' I'll brag. 'I've been on live, actual, active patrol five times. That's five more than you lot put together. I've even been the squadron leader on two penetration sorties, and I've had a Mention First Class for the second action.'

Ykry'll whine about not being able to take pain, and I'll say, 'No, just the pay, huh?' And I'll tell him to carry on whinging, because I'd have withdrawal symptoms if he ever shut up.

All my gear will be connected up by then, but they'll be wide-eyed and open-mouthed as it sinks in. 'Nobody does that: from zilch recruit to five-star? And the rank status to go with it?' They'll sneer that I'm the peasant among them, the ill-accented twollop-rat from Kouru. I'm the guy who has no manners and no education in the finer matters.

And I'll inform them that it's me who's twice been invited by the women captains to their Kuiper Klub. I'll experience a warm glow at the memory of those three ladies, and the sight of three jealous fellow-officers. And I'll tell them so.

So Ykry'll ask, 'Why do you keep coming here for the SuperSims if you've been out on active patrols?'

That's when I'll say, 'Weren't you listening? To improve. I can't get sharper with only active patrols. They've been relatively minor skirmishes so far; only one major incident in five sorties. In here, I get five or six big ones every time I log in. This's the only way to improve. I love the hurt and the fire. Every pang reminds me not to do that again. I'm getting good.'

Zeppy'll sneer and I'll pick on him and take the mock and tell him I'll be the one who lives through this war, and comes out with respect. I'll also have helped The Cause; not rolled over. 'Every pain is worthwhile,' I'll say. 'It all adds up. And so do the ladies.' That'll really scab them off, and they'll call me a bighead, and I'll say, 'Y' what? Me, a bighead? Not at all, my helmet still fits me perfectly. See? And it's comfy, and it's tuned into my thinking more that I would have dreamed possible.

'Plus,' I'll add, just to chill them off one more degree, I'll say, '*I'm* not twenty percent over standard weight.' And I'll stare at Ykry and ask him when he last took a chance on *anything*? So he'll turn on Jaya, and say he's not as sluggish as him and at least he's not slower than he was ten cycles back, like Jaya is.

By then, I'll be all set up, suit checked, fully powered and weaponed. I'll be confident of coming out when it's done. In the Simulation, I'll be out beyond the asteroid belt, patrolling for Cheryb craft doing their patrols. They're getting sneakier, and some are better armed now. I'll have a terrible shift; twenty-four solid. But I'll return in body, mind and soul, and I'll be half dead, maybe killed a few times, but I'll know where to draw the risk line; and I'll be more able to take it next time. I'll have done my bit, and I'll be ready to go back to the real front after a twenty-four break.

There's no danger of Ykry, or any of them, doing anything to sabotage my unit while I'm gone. That's mainly because there are no controls or feeds accessible in the ops room. And secondly, it's a termination offence to interfere in any way with anyone on an active or simulation mission.

By the time I've told them it's mostly thanks to morons like them spurring on idiots like me, I'll be in exactly the right mood to take on the real enemy

***

'Hi. Your Eminence.' Chairman Roit always found it best to be polite and formal on first greeting with the Federation's Commissioner before relaxing. 'Have you ordered yet? Koh – same for me. Drink?' Roit briefly entwined tendrils with his companion before touching the order screens. 'I've only been here a few times. With the family, not the department. They've done it up since last time.'

Roit and Commissioner Madix gazed around at the coloured plastic and polished metal panels of the Orbital Centre's Elite Lounge. Through the panorama windows, far, far below, the view of the sunrise over Cloddah Mounts took their breath.

'I should come more often,' Chairman Roit continued as the drinks and meals popped up. 'Getting into orbit here's convenient from home; it's scarcely an hour all told, including parking.'

'I slid my ship into the members' bay – government perk.' Madix smiled before changing the subject. 'I saw some of those little spoyock creatures in the main public lot. Dead. It was messy – bodies everywhere.'

Curling an antenna ruefully, Roit nodded, 'Yes, I saw that happen. Their ship took a crushing side-swipe from some careless Rachnid crate. Maybe they don't get noticed – too small or polite to bully their way in. I expect the scuttlers'll suck'em out eventually and eject'em with the rest of the garbage.

'Hardly the first time, though. Up on Jester a couple of trips back, folk were just ignoring a bunch of spoyocks, lifeless carcasses outside their ship. That was split open, too. I couldn't tell if it was a bad landing, or died of something after. Discarded bodies crushed, getting mashed into the ground and the metalwork. Looked rather sad.'

'Mmm,' Commissioner Madix blushed orange in sympathy. 'The Board sent a ship to investigate reports of a group of Rachnids pushing a spoyock ship round last year. Too late to help: it was completely power-drained – air, water, food, power and crew. There was a scorch blaze down one side. Seems the Rachnids shot at'em with their sublasters. Enough to fry their electronix and send'em spinning. Dunno why. Perfectly valid orbit they'd been in. Scuttlers cleaned it out while the Board ship was there. Tossed the body bits in the bins, and dumped the derelict ship into refuse orbit. I feel sorry for the squicky little things – minding their own business, and then that happens.'

He hesitated. 'That's actually what I wanted to chat with you about, Roi. I've been thinking: they catch the rough end, don't they, these soft-body things? Some of the chitin-based races seem to decide the spoyocks and their ships are too small or fragile to be any use. So they bully'em, like in the bay just now.'

'I heard some Rachnids picked on a shipful near Vertex, playing with'em. It sounded like they were killing'em in turn. Sport-like. Not nice.' Roit's faceted eyes dimmed at the images that were conjured up.

Madix sucked at a mint nectar and smiled at Roit's polite effort to do the same. 'Give it up, Roi… eat your own way.'

Roit re-furled his proboscis gratefully.

'On the same subject,' Madix continued, 'Captain Ablo, of the FSS Nova, reported on a trio of Rachnid ships clearing spoyocks off some backvac heap they'd colonised for ages. Wiped'em out, he reckoned. Substantial colony, too. The Rachnids simply wanted the place for themselves. He heard they've done it a few times – exterminating established spoyock settlements over North Fringe way. It isn't right.'

'Mmm. It sounds like they're the casualty party quite regularly these days. And if the Rachnids pick on them, which of us is next? Where do they come from, anyway?'

Madix furrowed his mantle lobes in thought. 'The spoyocks? Originally? Some Outerworld in the direction of The Wisp. They're all over the place now. I quite like'em: chirpy little things. Enterprising enough; frequently arrive at new worlds first. Never heard of any trouble from them. A group of us from Fed Central pulled half a dozen off a splat-wreck last year. They seemed okay to us. We dropped'em on some planet called Raddich, where there was a spoyock colony already.'

'Raddich? Isn't there a large Luuran presence there? I heard they keep'em, like pets.'

'That's happened in the past. Not now: the Luurans and spoyocks are settled together just fine, last I heard. There're some planets where Cephlos, Luurans and spoyocks co-exist perfectly harmoniously. Not like us and the Rachnids, eh?'

Chairman Roit had another unsuccessful go at the mint nectar. 'But why are we seeing these spoyocks massacred up, down and centre? Are they regarded as vermin? Wildings? Some sort of diseased invaders?'

Madix orange-blushed again. 'I believe it's merely Rachnid prejudice against squidgy species. The spoyocks trade with anyone, start colonies responsibly, have due regard to aboriginals – all the right things. There's no record of spoyocks ever having done anything anti-Fed, or caused any disease outbreaks.'

'So... you're proposing we do something, Commissioner?'

'You know, Roit, we were looking for a unification cause? I've been thinking that maybe this is it, equality of rights for all space-going species.'

'We'd have to go the whole kekk for any major infringements of status rules. Execution of individual offenders, like the Rachnids the Board reported on; and the captain of the vessel in the parking lot here. Would you consider expulsion from the League for any species wilfully permitting or encouraging it?'

'Like making an example of the Rachnids first? So much the better, hmm?'

Their antennae pulsed in mutual understanding. 'I thought we might look into this today, Roi, while we're here? I have data on the spoyocks' numbers, their death and disappearance rates – plus causations, such as Rachnid involvements. I've already drafted a policy that sees the spoyocks admitted as guest members of the United Federation *immediately*.' Commissioner Madix touched his silver screen to illuminate the data mass.

Roit studied it. 'Cunning – that'll give them full protection during the trial period; and should quickly lead to full membership of the Fed. Think we can get that together by the next Fed Conference?'

'It's only three days to Vodonday. You want full protection for the spoyocks in place, and enforceable in three days?'

'Yes. I want it fully finalised now. The proposal is already put together, Roi. I brought it with me – *here* – the whole thing in outline. Plus detail on the vitals. We can tinker with the rationale and policy now, and agree on both before we part. We've been putting up with it too long.'

'What? Persecuting the spoyocks? Or letting the Rachnids get away with it? And others, too.'

Madix's antennae flexed slightly in guilt. 'Both; it's *not* right.'

'You starting a crusade, eh, Max?'

'No. No crusade. This must be fast-tracked. Over and done in one session – within the next half-decca. We need the Fed to sort out its principles and standards. This'll set the benchmark if we can get these spoyocks accepted, and the Rachnids reprimanded, or suspended. Sooner the better: a display like that in the parking bay brings it home, how urgent it is. I want you to get this to the top of the conference agenda, on Vodonday, with full proposals.'

'We'll need a better name for them: spoyock just means "turd-sized" in Rachnid.'

Commissioner Madix furrowed his mantle again. 'Well... how about we adopt their own term for themselves? Humans.'

***

75

I HAVE A WOMAN ON MY MIND

Just for a week or two, before I got settled – new job, new house, new town, new country – I had this Toyota Rav 4 on rental out of Phoenix airport, Arizona. I'm always a bag of nerves when driving in American cities: they are so big, and the roads multi-laned. The vehicles are all massive and wide and fast. You can turn right on a red light. And flashing red lights mean you have to stop if there's a pedestrian walking across the road. I'm moving out here, so I need to get accustomed to big-city, but in the meantime, the roads are a permanently-anxious nightmare.

Maybe that was the trouble. Although I was all eyes and ears, looking round and sticking below the thirty-five limit, I was sure I must have gone over one of those red flashing lights when the car alongside me braked hard and stopped. But I hadn't seen anyone crossing and didn't want to do an emergency stop in case the SUV behind rear-ended me. He just leaned on his horn and stopped for ten seconds or more and I was worried that I'd gone through a straight red. But a moment later he was up my backside again.

Bag of Nerves? Me? Hell, yes.

Satnav showed a left off North Stone Avenue, so I slipped into the outside lane as I approached the lights. I slowed, and the SUV was still close behind. But I signalled and didn't think I was doing anything wrong. The light changed to green left arrow and I went, sweeping straight into the slow lane along West Grant.

The SUV sailed past, not too fast, never looked at me, so I can't have pissed him off that much.

Two or three hundred yards and I was doing thirty-five, when the SUV in the third lane slowed right down and dropped in behind me. I couldn't tell why. Something I hadn't seen? Or maybe he'd picked up his cell-phone? Quick glance – yes – he was chattering away. Good – at least it wasn't something I'd done wrong.

Crossing another of those eight-lane-wide junctions, the lights were green for me, so I kept going. I glanced in the mirror at Chevvy-on-the-Phone. Too close. Still talking. Eyes off the road.

Bang!!!! The almightiest loud burst. Right next to me. Side of my Rav exploding in. I'm rocketing sideways. Glass and stuff splattering through me. I'm smashed flat across the passenger seat. Something crushing down on me. Is my car still moving? Want to stop. Another thumping crash. Jerked sideways again. *'Oh shit, No... Noooo. What have I done?'*

Another massive bang and I'm jerked forward. *'God No! I've buggered everything up... done something wrong. Shit shit shit – I'm in deep deep do-do's...'*

Faces hovering, looming close, swaying away...
A mumble of voices, bleeps and jangling pans...
Shivering, spasming and soaking sweat...
Brilliant light and gathering gloom...

Two police officers materialised over me. God. Terrified. I can't move – Keep trying. Nothing. Just twitches. What have I done wrong? Are they going to get me out? Or let it burn with me in it, save them the bother?

Serious and uniformed. This is going to be jail. An American jail. Rikers or Sing-Sing or whatever the local Pen is called. They'll tell me what a careless foreign bastard I am; and I got no rights in the Good Old US of A. The SUV driver'll testify I'd gone over a red light or something. Or I'd been talking on my cell-phone at the time of the crash. It was a crash, wasn't it? Or a bomb?

Claiming they just want info from me, plus updating me on events now they'd heard I was out of the coma.

'Eh? Coma?'

***

It was two weeks ago, and I'd been in the hospital since the crash. It was estimated that the two motorcyclists had been doing 80, minimum. A girl had been racing her club partner in some sort of rite they felt compelled to do every now and again. 'Jest ignored the junction and the lights and she can't have known anything about it – hit right smack bang at the driver-door, straight through the window and metalwork like a cannonball. Her buddy saw you coming across his path, and laid his bike down flat sideways. It slid fifty feet and jammed under your vehicle, but he bounced up and hurtled through the side window behind you. Most of him did, anyway. He didn't make it.'

They'd found me flat on my side with her on top of me, our heads splattered together. She was dead. My head was basically a severe fracture zone. It sounded rather geological, but didn't feel good.

'No, no, not your fault at all, sir. You've been exonerated of all blame. There was a Chevvy Equinox behind you and he said it was green your way. He hit your rear fender, too.'

Seems it had taken more than an hour to disentangle me and the motorbiker; especially her head and mine, smashed together. Then scraping the guy off the rear seats. And as long again to extract her Harley from my rental Rav 4. Then lift it off the guy's Indian.

The docs came in then, chatting with the cops instead of bothering with me. Except one of the juniors who was being ignored by the others, and she sidled over for a chat, face like lit-up, far as I could tell – laid out flat on my back. 'Shoot, man, you're some survivor, huh?'

I was pretty much dosed up, and strapped down, and I didn't really get what she was saying, so I said, 'Huh?' too.

'Hell, yeah, man. Godalmighty – you're a real survivor. Still alive after a collision like that – Whoa! You know what took so long to get you out? 'Course you don't.' She pulled a chair closer, leaned in. 'She wasn't wearing a helmet. A lot don't round here. And it looked like her head had smashed into yours, with a ton of reinforced glass, of course.'

'I remember... impression of somebody coming straight at me, head-first. Just a flash.'

'Took a helluvalot of doing to extract the bone fragments outa your head, even some brain matter. All mushed in together, the bone and the grey stuff. Hers and yours.'

'Bit of a mess, huh?'

'Hey, you Brits. Understatement, right? "Bit of a mess", he says. You should be up for the Award. You must be the Survivor of the Year.'

'Shitamighty, I am, ain't I?'

Bugger! That made me jump. 'Who said that?'

'Who said what?' Lady doc was looking at me like I was a nut.

'No, not you. I thought I heard something inside me.'

'Like what?'

'A voice,' I told her. But she gave me a Doubting Daisy kinda look. I tried to listen to see if it was still there... No, it was quiet. So I sort-of asked inside myself, 'Who are you? Where are you?

'Huh? This ain't right? What's going on?' The voice sounded in me again... through me. A woman's voice. Like a tannoy somewhere in my head. *'Fuckit. Thought*

81

*I was a gonna then. Did Jaimie make it, too? Who're
you? What you doing, prying in my head?'*
Oh bugger. Some woman was interfering in my mind,
poking in me. Her thinking was interrupting mine. So
was her mouth. 'Bugger, bugger, bugger. This can't be
happening. I'm dreaming. Aren't I?'
I could hear the voice saying the same thing. Baffled,
trying to make sense of it. *'What's going on? Where's
Jaimie? Who the fuck are you? You in my head?'*
I didn't say anything more to the junior doc lady, nor
the rest of the docs who came round eventually. They
were bored now they'd sorted my physical bits out.
*'And I sure don't have anything to say to them. Who's
gonna believe I took up residence with some English
guy? I can't stand Limeys.'*
'God. It can't be. It's the maniac biker. A woman! I
detest stroppy women. Like this one. A biker – terrorist
of the highways. Hateful, every one.'
*'Me? What about you? Driving on the wrong side of
the road.'*
I wasn't having that from a Yank, 'At least I look
where I'm going.'
'And the filth you eat...'
'Better than burgers and pizzas all day, every day.
Disgusting creatures that you are.'
We sank into sullen silence. I wanted her exorcised
or whatever they do with demon possessions of people.
She was grumbling under her breath, but my head was
closing down – I needed to sleep; and I wasn't going to
get any kip with her carrying on like that. 'Shurrup. Stop
whinging.'

82

But there was no rest from her: mumbling on about damn Limeys drinking cups of tea all day, and we can't spell, and we're obsessed with the Royal Family...

'Stupid moo – I hate the Royals – pack of inbred ingrates. I drink coffee. And eat Mexican and Indian food.'

'You drink warm beer—'

'Never! I drink whiskey, lager, gin, margaritas; anything except water. Don't tell me you're the only sober biker in the States?'

'You Limeys are obsessed with the weather.'

'I just moved here for work. I bought a house in Armory Park. I'm out of all that about weather. Arizona has no weather: it's just hot and dry. All day, every day.'

'You watch stupid soaps on TV all day.'

'And you call it TV, when it's the telly.'

Sometime in the middle of all this silent ranting and chuntering, one of us laughed. Or chuckled, at least.

'What?' One of us asked.

'Do you think we might go and see my parents?'

I thought about it. Long and hard. 'Okay. As long as you don't make me burst into tears and hug them. And I'm definitely not calling *anybody* "Mom and Pop."'

***

I see people coming through the waiting room, mostly with head injuries. Bad ones. Horrendous. One with half his head missing – but it looks okay from one side. Another has the front quarter missing. A lady has massive scars and a very vacant smile. I don't think she's in, upstairs. A tall man has a very broad smile but now he seems angry about sitting here. A boy near me with headphones is singing without any tune at all. One guy looks very smart in a suit and tie. I don't reckon any of his wiring's plugged into the motherboard – he keeps standing up, walking a few paces and lecturing the air or the noticeboard.

What am I doing here? I'm nothing like them. I sit here quietly. Some of them look okay. I know I do: I saw myself in the wall mirror when we came in.

Maybe some of them wear plastic moulds on their heads, with a shield and wig. I wonder if mine is. I feel my face to make sure, but I can't tell and I laugh.

People get called into the various side rooms one by one. Some with escorts. I have an escort with me – it says Laura Lamb on her badge.

Someone calls, 'Mrs Atkins.' My escort lady says that's me, so it's my turn. She lifts the tag round my neck to prove it's my name. The nurse lady who called out my name shows me her name card as well. 'Welcome back to the Queen Vic Hospital, Mrs Atkins.' She takes me into one of the little rooms and sits me down in front of the doctor.

I'm still not sure why I'm here, but I have the appointment card. I look at my appointment cards lots of times every day to see what I'm doing.

'You remember why you're here, Mrs Atkins?'

'To see you. My escort says I've been here before.'

'You recall what we spoke about last time?'

'Er... No. Something about poorly people?' I guessed.

'Suppose we talk instead of replaying the recording that explains it?'

'Mmm,' I said, but instead of telling me anything, he just keeps asking me things and saying my name. I expect that's so I remember who I am.

He pulls a large stand-up mirror round. 'Tell me what you see.'

'I see me, of course. I look normal, like most people. Except the ones who come here.' I'm becoming impatient with him. 'Why am I here?'

He reaches towards me and says, 'May I?' and runs his fingers down my cheek. Creepy.

'Why you're here, Mrs Atkins? It's so we can check how well you're doing, or if there are any problems. You know, since the operation... the accident?'

'I don't know about any accident.' I can't remember. Can I? I'm not sure.

'You're our star, Mrs Atkins. It feels as though we gave birth to you. We're so proud of you.'

He smiles, studying me. 'You were in an accident. You had severe skull damage, and it developed a deep infection, almost cancerous in its intensity. The operation was absolutely pioneering – rebuilding some of your brain. It was successful in retaining a large proportion of your brain material. Much activity was downloaded and fed back afterwards into the re-grown brain matter.'

I feel round my head. 'It doesn't feel like a re-patched jigsaw head.'

'It is inside. It's not as infinitely complex as the original, but it's still growing; you're improving every month.'

He smiles at the nurse and at me again. ''You're so much better than at any other time since your accident. New neural pathways are growing within...' He's really explaining it all. 'The new matter has the same bulk as the original, but only one fifth of it has yet been occupied by the new neural mass. It's in simplified form so far, but you're so much better every time we see you.'

I feel his fingertips touching my skin and skull again. 'That's me you're touching. I'm normal. Do you always do this? Have I been here before? Do I always see you?' I try to remember. 'I think I've seen some of the other people outside before. And some juniors in white coats and super-young serious. My head looks normal in size and shape. I have hair. All my features are here. In the right arrangement.'

'Do you want to see more clearly what's been done?' I think. 'Do I?' I ask him. 'You haven't shown me previously, have you? Have you? But I'm better than I was? Is it bad? Will it shock me? Am I like those others I see in the waiting room?' I don't know anything.

He comes and stands behind me and I watch him in the big mirror when he reaches into my hair down the back, pulling, like a Velcro zip. Frightened, I wait. Then he lifts my hair slowly, saying he'll stop if I say so, and I want to but I can't. I don't know what's so wrong that I'm here.

His face is serious, like he's making sure I'm okay about it. I look in the mirror. He peels my skin back so I suppose it isn't really my skin – it feels like it, though.

Next he pulls my face off.

I can still see me. I'm glass, and I can see inside me. My mouth is open as if I don't believe it. My teeth look real and the doc says, 'They are real. And your eyes.'

'But my eyes are different colours. One's greenish and the other more brown. I like them.' I smile at myself in the mirror. Smiling with a glass face is really weird.

The doc sits down again and puts my face over a dummy head. It looks as if it's staring at me. But I keep looking in the mirror and the nurse holds another mirror behind me so I can see inside my real head.

Deep within the glass, I can see all these plastic and metal things in me.

'They're little computer chips, Mrs Atkins. Like USB flash drives.'

They're all in rows and ever so complicated. I peer really closely in the mirror and see masses of tiny fine wires. And a pinky lumpy mess like raw sausages.

I pull a face.

The doc says the glistening part's my brain. Some is my old brain and some is new organic material they have placed there. The new matter is growing over the wires and chips. They'll all be buried soon. 'Actually, all of it's your brain – the organic and the electronic. It's all looped together in on-going feedback. That's what we'll be doing in the next hour: we'll speed the process up because you're now better at dealing with it. Then we'll download it all and feed it back into you, so you remember it longer. With extra memory cells, like backups, in the chips as well as the new organic material.

Very slowly, it all becomes absorbed, physically and mentally, we believe. All fusing together.'

I ask if they can download Wikipedia into me. Or Britannica? Doc laughs and he says, 'No. Just your own thinking. You have to read or listen or think. Then it settles in the chips and we can transfer it into the pink and it makes it spurt in growth.'

'What happens when it gets really big and grows round the chips?'

'We'll put salt and vinegar on it.' He's trying to make a joke. I get it. But it isn't very funny, so I wait. Then he says, 'Actually, we don't know. But we think... we hope, that we needn't remove any if the pink matter incorporates them. It could become a self-feedback system. Your brain is constantly growing and expanding. We estimate you're now at half original thinking power, though your memory's not retaining all of what you learn. We think that constantly downloading and reloading your memories, and parts of your thinking system, makes the pink grow bigger and more complex, as well as helping your memory and thinking process.'

'It should be grey matter.'

'It's made pink by all the tiny blood vessels inside – you have a very healthy brain, Mrs Atkins. Shall we set you up now?' He takes out a silver lurex-type of helmet and slips it on my head and he and the nurse start fiddling with bits of it.

'Just don't do a "Re-Format" command, eh?' I joke. 'And not a "Delete Everything", either, eh?' I know about computers.

A warm and tingly feeling washes over me and maybe I can remember more, but I don't know, because I've forgotten what I used to know.

While I wait for it all to happen, I ask what my accident was, and how long ago. 'Was anybody else there, or killed? Who's the lady, my escort? Do I come here very often? I've asked this all before, haven't I? Did you tell me the answers? Where is here? Do I live near here?'

It doesn't take long. I know he's told me what the accident was, but I can't remember. It's finished now, and he fits my skin back on my face and head and I adjust it. 'It feels good; it's like my skin again.'

'You can feel it?' Doc looks like he doesn't believe me. When I say of course I can he replies, 'Oh, my God,' and touches my face again and I think he might be crying. 'You can feel my finger?'

'I could before, when you stroked my cheek, and again now when you put it on. It's like wearing a living glove. Perhaps if I didn't wear the skin, I'd be able to feel even more.'

He is crying, and says, 'Oh, my... Oh, my,' shaking his head. 'Do you think you could go without your flesh-coloured skin?'

I wonder. 'You mean go out there? I don't know. I think so.'

As I'm about to take it off to think about it, and see what I would look like outside, what people would see, the doc says, 'Perhaps best not, just yet. It might be too soon. Get used to it, now you know.'

Before I go out I look at myself in the big mirror again and wonder if other people would stare at me.

Would I fit in if didn't have my plastic head on? I shall try it one day.

I go out then. My escort's there and she tells me her name. I can't remember it. 'You do look good, Mrs Atkins.'

And I say, 'I might look different next time.' She takes me through the waiting room and asks me what the doc said and I can't remember so I shrug.

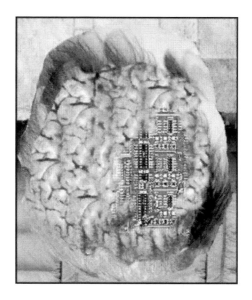

***

The simmering pits of quiet fire that pock the land
Lie stable and still for dozens of days,
Then quietly fade and die in a bubbling crust
That hardens over and joins the thousand others
That came before and did the same
And made the Silleeth Plain on Belvedere.

But now and again they burst and blast
In a mighty storm, an instant mass of plasma fire,
A towering blizzard of blazing light
That flashes to life, to rage and sear and shred
The land in a holocaust of starlike fire.

What triggers the demon that rends the land
We've no idea. When the alarms sound out,
It's far too late to see the spark
That set it off. By then the storm's a degree across,
Intensity Four, and building six,
On the Silleeth Plain on Belvedere.

That terrible time in Sixty-four when we lost three craft
In a single day when vast and blazing vortices
Of furious light and plasma formed.
Engulfed and gone as the blizzard of fire roared over them.

We watched that storm from the orbiting ship; safe enough
A thousand up. But enigmatic Belvedere, third planet in,
Round Syrus B, won't yield itself to a craven craft
Perched high above, so it's down to the ground we go
To study the storms on Belvedere.

Some clever devil who knows such things
Came up with a premise about the storms.
'The fire pits grow from a leak below,
And quietly sit till they wane and seal. But now and again,
Deep in the crust, the leak springs wide; the plasma's freed
And upwards comes as a bubble of molten flame.

'What was a chuckling pit of smouldering fire
Two hundred deep and just as wide
Explodes in fury a thousand-fold of what it was.
We need,' he said, 'an observatory to roam the land
And be on hand when a storm appears.'
And so was born The Alban Ark, on Belvedere.

We're mobile, in a way: though it takes us a day
To get anywhere.
She's designed like a tank, but the size of a ship.
We took her out on a trials trip,
And gazed down the cliffs to the Silleeth Plain
To watch for a spark or a bleep to tell us a cell
Is flexing its bowels and rising up while we sit and wait
And watch and record each pit arrayed below.

An incoming call. 'A quiet pit has warmed a degree.
'It might be the one. Is this our chance?'
We started her up and buckled in, and faced her down,
Revving hard like raths and rakes on Reggidor,
And took our observatory down
To the Silleeth Plain on Belvedere.

We waited awhile for orders to come, not fifty lengths
From the glowing edge. 'Can we closer creep
And look into the pit? Or do we stay back here

And record the warming cell from afar?
They're always warming and cooling a degree or more.
We're safe enough: there's only one in a hundred
That heralds a storm on Belvedere.

'With odds like that, we're up for it. We'll take the chance.
Let's get to the edge and peer in there,' we told our Skip.
'She's built for this, and we're paid for it.
Let's get in close and observe this thing,
For we are the Observatory on Belvedere.'

Skip checked it in, and they checked it out.
There's been no change since the first report
Two days ago,' They said, 'so it's up to you.'

We're not a democracy, but, just the same
We took a vote, and we went for "In".
It's sitting calm and quiet now, as they usually are
For days on end on the Silleeth Plain on Belvedere.

'The whole idea is to get in close,' we said.
So we trundled slow, across the hot and shattered land.
The rock crust flexed, and uneasy cracked,
Beneath the wheels of the Alban Ark on Belvedere.

Close we were, and edging in, eyes all wide and sensors on
For the least little sign of anything changed;
Of anything wrong that ticked the dials or rang the bells.
Or loomed ahead in uneasy sleep.

Ten lengths more to get to the lip
And stare into the pit of a plasma cell on Belvedere.
Just five lengths now, still crawling ahead—

It sprang! like the flash of a solar wind a thousand high.
A plasma gale in front of us, hurtling silver and solid light;
Instantly there, before our eyes, the simmering sink
Had flashed to incandescent light and terrible heat
Before our eyes in the Observatory on Belvedere.

Sudden ablaze, like the sun had come, it pounced on us
And pounded bright in a rage of light
That scorched the land and the atmosphere.
What triggered the cell, we haven't a clue,
But the vertical blast was the seed for a storm.
It triggered off, and there we sat, four lengths away
With our eyes full wide, and mouths agape.
The sensors sucked and the screens took note
Of the abyssal quakes that wracked our Ark on Belvedere.

The sky lit up in that orange glow that springs from hell.
A column of light, so solid and real,
Reaching the sky before our eyes.
In a second or so it was all around in a buffeting roar
That rocked the sensors and thundered the bells,
Locking the screens to Readout Four,
And auto-closed the airlock door
While Pete the Skip was still outside in his zipper suit.
And we all raced down to the override and forced the
levers
To manual, aboard the Observatory on Belvedere.

We dragged him aboard the Alban Ark, fried and crusted
Thick in plasma ash, and scarce alive,
As Jakkson stayed down here to scrub him free
Of the flakes of fire and algor-sleet, and scrape them off

While we four strained and prayed and pulled
The motors back from overload to Level Five.

Facing the storm as up it shot in blazing light,
And doubled the scale of volts to ninety mill.
Then the fuses blew, and blanked the dials,
And left us blind to the core of fire five lengths ahead
Of our Alban Ark, the Observatory on Belvedere.

A seedling storm, it hurled on up at rent the sky
And raged at us in our frailsome Ark on the Silleeth Plain;
The closest anyone's been and lived to tell
'We haven't a chance; we're staring at Hell,'
Young and fearful, Jaymie sobbed.
It burst on us, and over us, so live and close
Trapped down there on the Silleeth Plain on Belvedere.

It lashed us down with a howling wind
Of lightning force and algor sleet that crackled the air.
It caked us up, and tore at us, while the outside glare
Blazed our eyes and sent the tubes to overdrive.
The light tower raged and foamed in columnar blaze
And it dragged at the skin of the Alban Ark on Belvedere.

The alarms were shrill and panicking more
As the air vents gave, and a cracking sound
Split the air around, and shook us deep.
It had us down, but the Ark fought back.
The wheels screamed and the motors shrieked
As it clutched at us and we couldn't escape.

It was over us now and spreading fast,
Plasma fingers clutching round like wraiths awhirl,

Surrounding the Ark and jerking us round.
It was touch and go, though we held on tight,
All well strapped in, aboard our ship, the Alban Ark,
Our Observatory on the Silleeth Plain of Belvedere.

Writhing, heaving and throbbing beneath our feet,
The Silleeth Plain was a storm of light
That blistered and howled, and melted the skin
Of men and women and the Ark as well.

Till the for'ard bulwark splintered and shrieked
And surrendered itself to the fiery hail
That raged on past.
Sections sundered and hurled away.
The Alban Ark was breaking up.

We went for broke – 'Abandon the Ark,'
The cry went up, as into the outside suits
We crushed ourselves in the split of time,
For the circuits blew, fragmenting around us,
Billowing smoke and a shower of sparks.
Helpless there in the Observatory on Belvedere.

No other choice, we dragged and prised
The life-car out the dock at the rear,
And cranked the gates with all our strength
Letting in the fury of liquid flame that lashed at us
As our desperate hands did a dance
On keys and buttons, on settings and screens.

The power surged up, and the tracks went down
And bit the floor; and we backed her out,
In the teeth and the scream of hail and blasting light.

Ten thousand k on the temperature scale and building fast.
Already far more than the Alban Ark was built to take,
On the Silleeth Plain on Belvedere.

Scarce three lengths we'd backed away when the Ark
Split apart as we crept and defied; hugging the ground
And digging in deep with every turn of the track
And every word of every prayer we knew.
The light came in through our steelite skin,
Blinding and burning as we crept and wept
And eased her away, so slow, so slow, so wretched slow
From the power of God that burst so close
To the Alban Ark.

Four days it took to crawl away.
To find a hollow, to hunker down and pray for help.
We cowered there and grimly set the recorders anew
And waited it out, awed and parched, our little crew.
'In God and the Rescue Squad we Trust.'
Though blinded and burned and dry as dust,
We all survived on the Silleeth Plain on Belvedere.

***

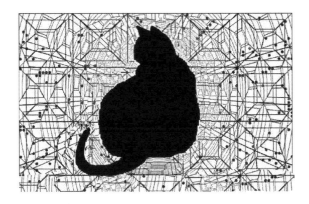

'Ah, Marty-Anna. Welcome. Sit. You've read the file on this character, Gelyn? Good. Now – what he has… What he can do…' Director Aaxon sought for words. 'You know how some people can listen to a few bars of music from a tune, and then they can play the rest of it; they just seem to know it, as though they always have?'

'Sure,' I said, shuffling to get comfy. 'Don't they reckon it's a sort of natural, universal, in-built tune that some people, er, *tune* into?

'Maybe; sometimes. But this Gelyn guy can do it with every tune we've tried with him. Where he differed, his version was considered the better one.'

'So? He makes music. What am I doing in the depths of E and C? This is official?'

'I'd have offered you a drink and asked about your family if it wasn't official, Marty-Anna. This gentleman can do the same thing with problems and procedures, solutions and logistics. And algorithms.'

'Algorithms? How's that work, then?' Algorithm is just a big word with deep hidden meanings. Hidden from me, anyway. 'They're just a way of solving logic problems, aren't they? If *this*, then go to Freddy and ask him; if *that*, go to Reece and ask her. That's one step. And they carry on in great long sequences of defined questions and instructions?

'That's about it: they analyse and organise specific sets of problems, and predict outcomes very accurately. It's automated reasoning.' He meant it about not offering me a drink, the great misery-toke. It was all business today. 'It gets more complex when there's ten "if" points, each with a yes-no division. It doubles up at each node. That's over two thousand possibilities for ten steps. To the power of twenty, it's millions of questions and answers.'

'Get to it, Aaxon. I don't have all day.'

'Yes, you do. You're transferred to E and C for now. You're mine. Right?'

There's no arguing with him in that mood. I was here till he said otherwise. I nodded.

'Good. As I was about to say, we know the enemy uses a master algorithm sequence to develop their strategic planning. Everything the Goyan Space Force does, all their attacks on our units, are governed by their master algorithm.'

I wasn't going to interrupt again while he paused for a moment.

'We latched into that algorithm sequence, just for an instant, before they snapped it down, with a huge blow-back on our systems. From the few scattered fragments, and the overall style of them, we estimate that their control system is over a hundred sequence steps long.

That's umpteen trillions and trillions of possibilities. It must have taken them decades to work it out, and refine it to how they want to analyse and respond to situations; how to predict them, prepare for them.'

'So it'll take us just as long to work it out, understand it? Replicate it? Counteract it?'

'Perhaps not. That's why you're here, Marty-Anna. Our musical analyst friend says he can see how the sequence is built – just from the fragments we have. Its purpose, its logic assumptions – he claims he can predict the whole thing.'

'I presume that's good?'

'It would be, but he's a funny'un. More than funny: the corollary to this genius part of him seems to be a perverse desire to make us earn the information. He won't tell us what he's worked out until we provide him with "Fat Cat". And he refuses to say what that is. He says we have to figure that out, and then he'll do the rest.' Aaxon shrugged. 'Basically, his genius comes with caveats. He's a weird one; a Spectrum case.'

I almost felt sympathy for him, with the "You're our last hope with this wanker" look he gave me. He was stymied. Obviously, or he wouldn't have summoned a Desperate Doris like me.

'That's blackmail,' I said. 'He's a traitor. Torture it out of him.'

'He's not exactly a traitor. He's not Allied; he's neutral; from Sarrit. Resident here almost two years.'

'He wants payment or something? For doing the right thing? Force citizenship on him, then charge him with treason.' Obviously.

'Time's getting desperate. We've begged and suggested, but he doesn't answer. It's merely a game to him, a mental exercise. He simply repeats that we need to do something to deserve it: i.e., figure out what he means by Fat Cat. Seems to think that's a fair way of doing it.'

'Does he answer anything?'

'Says, "No," now and again, so we think it's not a musical distribution contract, or an art gallery. Not a specific overweight feline, either. Or his mother, or dead sister. Or a space yacht. Or a funny-shaped island; or the life-style he wants.'

'So you want me to talk with him nicely? Or twist his dangly bits off?'

'Can you just have a chat with him? Soon. Like now.'

*

I went. The first room down the corridor. An apartment; much nicer than the one they provide me with. But aren't they all?

Gelyn smiled at me, and chatted generally, but it was like playing mental shazzy without a board. So I was immediately peed with him, the smiley little rucha. Told him, '*I* am the answer. The Fat Cat. I can provide anything you want. So either tell me or—' He smiled. Yeuk! Grease-ball smile. Cross, I walked out.

'Lock him in,' I told the guard. 'And gimme the key. He gets nothing. Can starve for all I care.'

Best not go too far away; the next apartment along. But he didn't know that.

I hung about. Battle of Wills time. It lingered, stretched. Not me. I don't bend, either.

Three times a day I received calls from senior officials at HQ. But what could I tell'em? 'He's holding out for the time being.'

'He's started demanding now,' I reported after a few days. 'Hammers on the door and the window; and he presses for the screen to light up. Wants to speak to me. That means he's breaking.' I can hold out: they probably pay me, whatever happens. 'Maybe the Allied Space Navy out there is dying in millions somewhere, but this feller knows that and doesn't care an iota, or a Fat Cat.

'And the foreign fluxtie's living here! That makes him a definite traitor on my screen.'

Then one call: someone patched through directly to me.

'What do you want?' I demanded.

'Food. Heating.'

'Go shuffle yourself, you've got water. Ring me with more demands, and I'll cut that off, too. Now, I'm overdue for a game of nabolph.' I cut the link.

He rang back. I ignored it. It rang and rang. Really shrill. I imagined him getting frustrated. Good. No more than us. He was the Fat Cat; now he could get skinnier. And drier. I cut the water off.

Half-way round to the nabolph rink, I was having a chunter to myself about him, 'Yeah, he can get skinnier. Get skinnier? I wonder...'

An about-turn brought me back into E and C, and I set about some research on the awkward schultie.

His bell kept ringing.

Eventually, I answered. Yes, it was him, 'Your people are dying. You need to—'

I cut the power right off this time. Dead. He was isolated, and couldn't disturb my delvings while he shivered and tum-griped. I had things to do, even if he didn't.

*

There was a visio call from the big chief next morning.
'This can't go on.'
'Of course it can't. He'll starve soon.'
'Talk to Gelyn again.'

*

Purely because I was ready-ish, I did. 'Right,' I said
when I vized through, 'you win. I've got your Fat Cat.
Now, tell them all about this algorithm, whatever it is.
Some way to analyse and predict enemy plans, their
thinking, whatever?'

He blustered and complained, looked desperate on
the screen, or hungry, dried-out. Definitely skinnier.
Wanted to know what Fat Cat I thought I'd found. 'You
can't have obtained what I want.'

Ah. That over-played his hand. 'If you think I can't
have done, it's because you're lying about what you
want. It's not actually a Fat Cat at all, is it? It's
something tangential, or opposite.' Ah, I caught the
blink there: I was right. And my poking into his
background might just have been in the right direction.

'Now, *Mnu-koitcher* Gelyn, you little toad-mate, I'm
going to tell you exactly what I have for you. I'll show
you a picture of it. And you're going to say, "Yes! At
last! That's it!" And you're going to be utterly delighted,
Aren't you?'

I gave him the hard stare, so he understood. 'This is
your last chance. Whatever I hold up, you say, "Yes!"
That saves face for both of us. If it's not exactly right, or
is a light year away, then you still shout, "Yes!" in utter
joy. Then, afterwards, you whisper it to me, what it
really was, over a drink and a bite. Then we'll do an
exchange, hmm? That way, we both come out alive and
fine. Does that suit you?'

106

The zilch-zipper still looked dubious, but I remained calm, checked my lip gloss, and showed him my choice. 'Here is your Fat Cat.' I held up a picture towards the screen.

He froze in mid scoff. Mouth sagging slightly open. 'Okay,' I complimented. 'Fine acting. Now the words... Come on, you can do it. Say it...'

'It... it is,' he stuttered. 'That's it. How did you...?'

'Really?' I said, 'You're joking.'

'No. No. That is what I want. How...?' Bewilderment wasn't in it. 'How did...?'

*

To be honest, I wasn't sure I believed him, but I played along. 'I followed your timeline back – last year – year before. Everywhere you've been since taking up traitorous residence here in our welcoming and hospitable, Allied haven. The people you've talked to, foods you like, drinks. I thought there might be some overweight woman you've met, called Catherine or Catelyn. Something of that nature, like Fattie Cathy, maybe.'

'And you worked *that* out?'

'Yes. Yes, alright. Now, let's get this over. You agree this is it. Then you tell them all about this war-winning code-cracking system. Then you whisper what you really wanted. Just name it. It'll just be our little secret, hmm? And you can go and get slewed and stuffed to your stomach's content.'

'That *is* it.' He looked and sounded pretty certain.

'This?' I turned the picture round to look at it again: a part-restored building from the Old Colonial Style. Perched on a promontory, bounded on three sides by cliffs and crashing waves. 'A country retreat, hotel, leisure centre, whatever it is. A year ago, you stayed there for two nights with your lady-friend.'

'We did.' He started breathing again. 'Now, can I have a drink? And a meal? I'm parched, and starving.'

'First you talk with the bods from the E and C Service to show good faith. Then a drink and something to eat. And more talk. Then I'll take you to visit your new home. Okay?'

He looked relieved that it was over.

*

Watching him talk with the Algorithm Squaddies or Whatevers, I studied the picture again. One of eleven possible Fat Cats that I'd found some obtuse, opposite or oblique connection with. Sheer luck to be right first time. Unless he really was pretending, and would get back to me later.

So, while the others are getting on with him and this damned war, I'd better go and make an offer the present owner can't refuse.

Fat Cat? All this for a dirty-weekend-type of clifftop hotel called "The Skinny Dog".

***

MY 7TH GRADE JUNIOR HIGH SCIENCE PROJECT

Grandpa suggested my 7th grade Junior High Science Project. 'Rora, my girl,' he said. 'You could investigate why the town hall clock goes faster on Sundays. It used to be Saturdays. I was its timekeeper and it drove me nuts for years. I'll treat you to a long weekend canoe-camping through Reed Lakes if you can find out.'

Now that is one gorgeous *re*-ward. Reed Lakes are the other side of Denali National Park – we'd have to fly!

I bought a new notebook, special-like, and me and Grandpa went to look at the clock on Main St. The town hall's all lapped wood, with pastel-painted fancy gable ends. It's easily the tallest building in our town, with its pointy steeple and the Town Clock with its black face and copper hands. Grandpa says there used to be a mini Liberty Bell in the steeple above it, in a space with louvred shutters instead of wall panels. 'But it disappeared a few years ago, one Saturday, maybe Sunday morning.'

I drew pictures of the town hall and the steeple, and the clock-face; and took photos and a video with the timer on so I could check the hands were moving at the right speed.

On Sunday towards midday, I went to sit up there, inside the clock loft. It was really creepy and dusty all on my own, but it was all scuffed from when they'd put the electric motor in – that was when Grandpa lost his Winding-Up job. But the new clock motor carried on speeding up just the same on Sundays, anyhow. I had six clocks and two watches with me. I spread them round in the loft, drew a sketch map of them, and waited.

Grandpa stayed outside with the video pointing at the big clock on the tower. We made sure the timer was on so we could check if there was a difference between the time at the clock and the video.

Then it happened – they all started going faster. Wow! My heart thumped like after the hockey. It was really exciting.

Afterwards, I worked it out – For fifteen minutes all the clocks went faster – some gained an hour, but others only gained forty mins. The fastest ones were nearest the big clock. So it seemed whatever made it happen was more intense in the centre. I did a diagram of the clocks and watches and time speeds to prove it. 'Now,' I told Grandpa, 'I have to refine my hypothesis, and test it against other possibilities. That's the scientific way.'

I figured it was caused by something that came periodically. It had to come *from* somewhere. I wrote it all down. Possibilities were that it might appear from another dimension. Or come up through the Earth. Or down from space. Or round in a circle that came back there every week – or week and a tiny bit, if it used to happen on Saturdays.

The following week, I borrowed all my friends' spare clocks and watches and arranged them all round – including on the roof, where I nearly fell off. Two went in the storage room, and another in the steeple where the bell used to be. I had three cell-phones and a proper video set up to film them, and I dashed round, checking them all, making notes on my list.

Some started going fast before others! Four minutes and twenty seconds between the first one, twenty feet away at the back of the loft, and the one on the plank sticking out the front. The watch in the old bell shutter-room went fastest – it gained an hour and twenty-seven minutes.

So my theory was that it – "The Event" – moved in a line. Except, if it came round every week, it would be going in a great big circle like a massive invisible doughnut, about forty feet up from street level – the height of the ex-bell and the clock. Though it could be higher. I estimated – guessed, really – that "The Event" was six feet across, and it travelled in a circles three or four hundred feet in diameter, stretching over the rooftops.

That, I postulated in my notes, was a more likely scenario than a whole series of separate events coming through. It looks best if you use big words like "postulate" in a science project.

I further hypothesised that it was a time warp that spins round in a slow circle, like the tip of a gyroscope wobbles when it's slowing down. It's called precession.

111

It should really be dead steady: it's *time*, after all, but I found that's relative – interchangeable with space and energy, for all we know. I read a lot about that.

What else might happen? Why wasn't the wood looking older? It was repainted last year, so I couldn't tell. Or what would age or rot very quickly? I couldn't think of anything, so the following Sunday I put boiling milk in the shutter space above the clock, and ice cubes. The milk cooled down really fast; and the ice cubes were all melted after twenty minutes. I had *postulated* it wouldn't only be clocks that went faster. Therefore, I ticked that as a *proposal*.

The only other thing I could think of was to sit in the empty bell room, which was very close to the centre, but Grandpa said I probably shouldn't in case my heart went five times faster – it would be doing nearly three hundred beats to the minute. So I put two white mice in there. They died.

I studied my films objectively. Acting the Devil's Advocate, as Grandpa said I should, it could seem like they had been fixed. And he said I better not tell them about those two mice that died. But at least they hadn't disappeared like the bell did.

My project went down like Maisie Zuckenheim's lead balloon project when we had to present them on Science Fair day. People laughed and said it was supposed to be a serious project, not this sort of joke.

'Them films are obviously fixed and speeded up,' they said. But they weren't. I pointed to the time counter at the bottom of the video screen; it was from the cellphone that was furthest away – so it didn't speed up like two of the others did: it kept going at the right time-speed when the clocks all rushed on. I knew I was right and I told our headteacher I was.

He – Mr Stupid Asshole – said, 'The committee should not consider Miss Fairbanks' submission because it is not a serious assignment.' Dick-Smirking-Bighead who lives across the road won again with his dad's project to build a faster Go-Kart. That was cheating. I even stamped my foot, I was that pissed with them. All that work I'd done, all on my own!

But that was last month. In the middle of the following week I was called out of Math – we were doing algebra, which I like. Miss Peroni, the School Secretary, said the Headteacher wanted to see me about my science project. I was in a stinky mood, mental sleeves rolled up by the time we got there. Mr SA was sitting there all slime and smug, not like last time we exchanged words.

Another man sat with him, no bigger than me. I'm thirteen and he's like a hundred – as old as my dad, anyway. But he stood up quickly, all smiles. 'Ah, good afternoon, Miss Fairbanks. I've *so* wanted to meet you.' He put his hand out to shake mine; and he interrupted SA, and smiled a lot at me – like that friendly, warm sort of smile – not that "he-*llo* little girl" sort of leering that Mr George the Bookseller does, or the slime-ball smile that SA puts on with visitors.

Yes, nice smile. And he ignored Mr SA. So that was two things in his favour straight away – plus the hand-shake. 'I'd like to speak, no, *consult* with you,' he said, 'about your science project. My cousin's boy told me all about it.' When SA interrupted twice, he said, 'I wonder if I might have time with you *alone*, Miss Fairbanks?'

SA said, 'No, that's not allowed.'

'Lessons finish at four,' I told him. 'I go out the West Gate. You can give me a lift home if you like. As long as you aren't wasting my time like some SA's have done of late.' I flashed Headteacher SA my darkest look.

'Oh, no, no, young lady, that's not my intention at all. May I call you Aurora?

'Rora,' I said. '*Nobody* calls me Aurora.'

So Dr Philip McKinley took me home. He was very nice. I showed him all my project stuff – the nine films I'd made, and the notes, plans and written report. I explained it and he knew huge words that I'd Googled while I was researching it, like Planck's scale uncertainties and backreactions, but he used them as if he did every day. He was genuinely interested, kept muttering and making notes, and I took him round to see Grandpa, then went for a pizza while they talked.

When I got back, they'd fixed to look in the clock loft in the morning so I could show them where I'd put everything. Him and Grandpa went for a drink, and he stayed in Grandpa's spare room so they could chatter about it all, especially the Great Alaskan Earthquake in 1964, when the land round here had risen by fourteen feet, they estimated. And could that have been what started it, or just pushed the land up to the height where it became noticeable? Like the clock moved up into its way?

After we'd looked in the loft next day he asked if he could see my notes and things again... and then if he could copy them. He took photos of all the paper stuff and I let him download all the films, me talking and my report with my theories.

He was back early on Sunday with a team – six of them, like students. They set up cameras outside as well as in the loft. I wasn't allowed inside then. 'Huh, so I'm kicked out, am I? Typical incomers,' I complained, to no avail. They had all sorts of other monitoring equipment as well, like really complicated university stuff. They were awful secretive about it all, but I bet they couldn't get a proper holometer or interferometer up there, so it was just fancy clocks, really.

Half the town stood watching them after church. Dr McKinley and his gang got super-excited when it happened and were all over the place hollering, high-fiving, laughing and congratulating each other. I thought, 'Eff you lot then, if you're just gonna ignore me,' I went home.

But he came on Wednesday after school and said he had secured funding for an observational experiment. It would be called the Rora Fairbanks Project, and they were adopting my Number One theory as their Primary Hypothesis. It possibly was a globular time warp that varied in exact position on a precessional cycle, with a diameter of approximately three hundred and fifty-six feet. They would attempt to discover if it was steady in height, position, rate of movement, gravitic intensity and half a dozen other factors that only Mr McKinley and God understood. 'And I'm not sure God is fully clued-up,' he laughed. 'If it is precessional, like a gyroscope's wobble, we need to discover if its locus is beneath us, or above, and how far.'

'Maybe it's a worm hole?' I said, and told him about the bell that vanished from the little room above the clock.

He looked at me funny and said, 'Hmm.' So I think maybe it is.

Since then – the last two weeks – the University team has practically taken over the town, certainly all three hotels, and there's a lot of Men in Black hanging around: Feds, CIA and NSA folk who wear stupid black or silver glasses like on TV, so you know who *they* all are.

Somebody said they wanted to buy the town hall as well as half the town centre, and build a big Motel 6 on the outskirts.

Headteacher SA was on CNN saying it was a school science project that had begun it all – but Dr McKinley took me on the TV with him and he said it was *entirely* my original independent work, and now it was a joint project with me and MIT and Fermilab. I told the interviewer that the Headteacher and Committee laughed at me and threw it out. 'That just shows how stupid they are,' I said, 'So it had nothing to do with school.' I really liked saying that – it was fun.

There's been an email from a TV documentary series asking if I might be available as a guest speaker for some science programmes for young people. And another email, officially offering me a place at MIT when I leave school. I emailed back to say I could leave at four o'clock if they really meant it.

Grandpa came round to see me and said, 'Hey Rora – when can you spare the time to go on that canoe-camping expedition through Reed Lakes?'

***

'You're a weird one,' I told the picture on the laptop screen. 'I never noticed you on the table. *Are* you a face?' I twisted my head round. Then the screen. Puzzling and peering. 'You look a bit like a face from *this* angle. But from that angle, you're not. And from *here*, you're a definite maybe. Couple of blobs that could be like eyes, I suppose.'

I put the computer down, and picked up the beer can, trying to recall whether or not I'd studied that specimen individually when I bought it.

No, I don't think I did. For four days, I'd been traipsing round the Great Arizona Rocks, Gems and Fossils Show in Tucson, and I'd studied hundreds of rock and mineral specimens. Bought a couple of hundred so far, for the business. This morning an Australian dealer's stall drew me in. This guy was almost sold out of his native Australian minerals, so he was selling off the rest in job lots at a third of the first-asked price. It was so he could get a cheap flight home tomorrow, not wait round paying stall and room rent for five more days.

'I must have glanced at you,' I told the screen, 'cos I took the pic.' But, actually, I don't look when I do that: one hand dragging them across the table – stop; position; click; push aside. Who looks at what they're photographing? It's purely a matter of getting the focus and the framing right.

Anyway, the pics are just for the record – to remind me over the next six days what I've bought, so I don't buy repeats; to group them by mineral types; to decide which few I'd carry home to the U.K. and which I'd have shipped back. I'd put the best one on my web site tonight, with prices about ten times higher than I'd paid. Naturally – my flights, time, expenses, etc. needed to be covered. I intended to spend a relaxing evening in my motel room with beer and whiskey, looking through the on-screen photographs of my latest purchases.

In truth, I just love them, every one. From amazonite to zircon, I drool over them. I've been known to vacantly stroke polished faces of minerals, or crystal facets when the cat isn't talking to me.

Mmm, I do remember this one. I'd moved it round a couple of times to get the light right, cleaned it with a quick spit and polish. It was a lump of tiger-eye; one of two dozen that were polished on one face, to reveal the golden silk-like fibres that seemed to be visible deep inside the rock.

I clicked through the next few photos… But that one intrigued me, so I clicked back to it. 'You could look like a face, I suppose. I must have a proper look at the real you when Ozzie brings the crate round later.'

'Fussy about them, eh?' The dealer had laughed. But they were his job lot. His choice, in effect, so I also wanted the photos to be sure he didn't substitute some before he brought them round to my motel after closing.

Yes, it had been a very good fair so far – I'd spent thousands on sunstones, opals, agates, selenites and the whole gamut of gorgeous minerals, stocking up for the year to come.

*

It's not that I forgot about the lump of rock with the slightly face-like swirl in it. It's simply that I'm a mug for supping my drink on warm evenings, the balmy scent of bougainvillea, sitting out on a motel veranda. So I'm afraid that won the day.

Thus, it was twenty-four hours later that I went through the Aussie's crate. 'Let's have a proper look at you, eh?'

It took ten minutes to find it, and I rotated the foot-long by five inches high piece of heavy rock – it has a high percentage of iron in it, that's what makes it so heavy. Between the mass of golden tiger-eye needles and the near-black base material it had an irregular triangular patch, three or four centimetres along each side, where there had been a gas bubble when the rock had been fluid and forming. Later, the bubble must have filled with the hot mineral fluids that kept seeping through the rock over the later ages; and it had created a swirl as it hardened.

Yes, the solidified eddy of mineral did look a bit like a face. Two patches could be imagined as eyes, but distortedly trapped within the rock. 'Well,' I laughed, a little the worse for the whisky, 'you can't have been in there all that time, not since the rock was formed; you're not two billion years old – the planet only had algae back then.

'Mind you, I must have been sloshed when I took this pic – you don't look quite the same now. 'But,' I checked where I'd put the bottle, 'that's enough time on you tonight, Jeannie.' I named her after a former lady-friend who had dark little eyes. 'There's all today's stuff to organise, and I can't afford to slip behind, or I'd never catch up.'

*

The following day was just as busy: buying, making new contacts, meeting a couple of customers. And a get-together in the evening with a few U.K. dealers I know. That meant I didn't have chance to look at any rocks or pics, much less have another look at that piece of tiger-eye.

*

I hadn't forgotten about her, but these are buying trips, not holidays, or *vacation*s, as I keep hearing. The day after that, I had to keep focused on the job and didn't have chance until late on, just before turning in. I'd propped the specimen up on the bedside table, 'You're different again, aren't you?' I turned the rock this way and that.

Then I realised what was happening. 'The fluid inside hasn't quite hardened. It's still shifting slightly, with the movement, and the warmth of the room and being handled. 'But,' I blearily studied the rock, 'you look a bit more like a face than you did two days ago.'

I turned it over again, suddenly imagining that I'd be making her dizzy. 'And you look worried.' Which only proves what a drunken nerdy fool I am, personifying an aberration in a lump of chalcedony fibres. I was thinking of a piece of rock as "she". But then, I often indulge in jokey-talking with superb specimens when I'm on solo buying trips, like, 'Who's gonna pay three grand for a smart piece like you, eh?' That was my chat-up line for an emerald crystal I'd seen.

But I was giving her an identity.

It, I mean.

*

Thursday evening, I went to the Longhorn Steakhouse on West Wetmore with some folks I met. They were Canadian and American dealers and miners. Nice folk and valuable buying contacts. Good night it was, too;

120

very lively. Which meant there wasn't much time for Jeannie.

But, traditional whiskey nightcap, sitting up in bed, I looked at her, sitting there next to the alarm clock. Yesss... the fluid inside that rock bubble had again shifted slightly. The eyes were better aligned as a pair, the mouth blob was small, like she was going, 'Oooh'.

I let her sit there. She could watch out for me overnight.

*

Busy all day, after a late start trying to keep up with the cataloguing and website specimens, so there wasn't much time that evening, either. Until the usual getting-into-bed time. 'Lord! Your eyes look too real. Your mouth's not right, though.' I had to laugh at myself and the whiskey glass, acting as if there was a miniscule someone trapped inside. A small part of someone, anyway – some of the head. 'Like her spirit,' I imagined. 'I should free you.'

But, a sanity-saving sip of San Miguel later, combined with further study, 'Don't be ridiculous,' I told her and Jack Daniels. 'You're merely a temporary chance growth of some treacly mineral resin. Although, this kind of rock used to be called "The Charms of Light." A beautifully appropriate name in your case, my dear.' I drank to that.

*

It almost took courage to pick her up again on Saturday, and stroke over the smooth surface where the face was buried, wiping it as if to see more clearly, staring at the thumbnail-sized visage. The mouth wasn't forming right – some pin-head beads of crystal were spreading across the bubble, where her lower face should have been.

But your eyes – it's really bizarre how lifelike they look, Jeannie.' She was staring back at me! We made eye contact, dark eyes appealing to me for help. 'That's impossible.' But there's no mistaking it when you do make eye contact, even if only for a fraction of a second, and the head is scarcely an inch across.

I swallowed, nervous. It was idiotic. I argued with myself, 'Sure… right… who gets caught inside a block of stone?'

The obvious, definite answer came straight to me: A genie.

'Don't be stupid,' I told myself.

'*Must* be, though.' My imagination was running away with me. 'But what sort of genie are you?' I addressed the gleaming piece of polished stone, and promptly looked up everything about genies. Well, half a dozen sources on Google, anyway.

'Okay.' I eventually gazed at her again, having discovered that genies come in two very distinct types. Some even mated with people, according to Google. That'd be okay – she was a smart looker. Bit small, maybe. Like some folk reckon Adam and Eve were man and djinn… genie. 'Which are you? The guardian angel type who keeps watch over people in benevolent ways; the creative and friendly type who imparts wisdom? I could do with some of that, too.

'Or… are you one of those supernatural demon-genies created from the scorch of fire and wind? The ones who haunt people and buildings – and golden polished stones?'

Whether good spirits or evil demons, they aren't all great wispy hairy monsters, it seems: they come in all sizes and shapes, including just pieces of them, like heads or tails. Women as well as men.

'Ahh… a woman's head could well be a genie's spirit.' I scrutinised her tiny face – or actually, the lower face was gone now, the mineral beads drifting across it – almost like a veil. 'Yesss, Jeannie, you might be one. But I bet genies didn't get trapped in bottles and lamps and places for no reason – they'll have been wandering round causing mayhem, mischief and trickery, pushing things too far. 'Is that the sort you are? A bucket of trouble? Is that what happened?'

I laughed, turning the smooth stone over in my hands for the umpteenth time, wondering if someone at the quarry where it was found had polished this piece of rock down to this surface by design or chance. Stopped short in fear? Or never even noticed, if the triangle bubble had only been a smeary swirl?

Stroking over the glassy surface, a couple of millimetres from her cheek, I wondered, not for the first time, whether or not I should release her. If so, how? 'Come on. Don't be stupid. It's a lump of tiger-eye rock.'

But the eyes looked so real, whichever way I turned the rock. And it was definitely like a veil below the eyes now. Suppose she really was real? And the wayward sort? Could I take any precautions? Yes, I should shut the door to keep her in. Yes, right – the massive towering evil hulk that sweet-faced little Jeannie would morph into was going to be constrained by a closed motel room door. Sure it would. Also… also… I shouldn't chisel at the rock too hard in case it gave her a headache and she got mad at me. She would have to wait: I had work to do. But… I stopped. If I kept her waiting, she might get mad about that, too. Wasn't Sinbad's genie angry about being kept waiting for thousands of years?

Too wrought up over the whole silly mess, I was actually trembling. I was going to do it: smash a fifty-quid piece of rock apart because I'd talked myself into it over a few days working and heavy drinking.

But I *couldn't* leave somebody locked up in there forever. Oh, Lord. I've just *got* to.

Ready…

It's a pity I can't keep my fingers crossed when I'm holding a cold chisel in one hand and a lump hammer in the other. 'I bet you haven't been to England before, have you, Jeannie? You'll like it.' I patted the rock reassuringly, positioned the chisel, and raised the hammer…

She's looking so hopeful in there…

Steady…

Wow!

FOUR ONZ

The uniformed officer finished his ten minin speech and handout session with a slight bow. 'Good luck.' Then he headed for the exit panels and embarked on the transporter. It hummed and hawed and trembled a mite, then lifted off. At two hundred yars high, it paused, spun slightly, and hurled itself back towards the Colony Establishment Centre at Spaceport Jenlings. We were on our own.

Koh, so we weren't on the most inhospitable planet in the Fed, but it wasn't especially welcoming, either: the data chips droned on about dangerous packs of Dirinoy birds or hounds or something. And insects... And crop diseases. Plus the high-ultra sunlight, bitter cold seasons and sporadic acid rain. But we had the shelter dome, the equipment and seed, and the livestock embryopods. It was now just a matter of deciding who was best to figure out how to use it all, and make it work or grow or whatever.

We looked around our new life-home. This latest colony settlement on Halladora was probably much like the others: a dome a hundred yars across, and all the basic equipment we need to get started. Sure, it'd be tough, but everyone was a volunteer, for various reasons that included escaping the law, poverty, abuse; wanting a new start, new ID, new anything. The situation had been made clear: half and half, men and women; no pre-pairs. Not exactly randomly chosen, but not far off. We supposedly had a spread of skills, or otherwise. No groups from the same town code, so there'd be no pre-gang culture to dominate.

We'd been dropped off thirty minins earlier, each with a bag of personals. The landing officer had explained the routine: food was supplied, enough for ten onz. That's one hundred and ten days: the moon here is called Onz, because it has an eleven-day cycle. So, first, we needed to sort ourselves out, choose a leader, decide on responsibilities and start fast: the growing season would soon be upon us.

Fifty of us. Well, forty-eight, anyway: two had skipped off before they even came into the dome. A mixed bunch we were, too, getting to know each other the first evening; a few pairing up. I grabbed a waiflike thing who appealed, with fair hair and watery eyes. She needed someone, and she now had me. We'd get to know each other soon enough. We all would: who we were and what we claimed to be an expert in, or at least knew what things were used for. Or what we had soaked in from the memocrysts. They reckoned this way was efficient and egalitarian. 'Sort yourselves out or perish,' seemed to be the watchword for colonisation, 'It's the way you build up the community feel.' There were fifty rooms. I say rooms, more like cubbies. My waif was shaking like a haapa leaf. But shugg: I'm not ugly. Didn't touch her, anyway.

A full day recovering from the travel, exploring the dome and the immediate outside; becoming acquainted with each other, the stores, and everything. Then an evening meeting to make a bid to be dome leader. No rules: someone could take it by force if he, or she, was strong enough, or had garnered enough cronies as backups. Nobody tried that. A few stood on the end table and did their speeches: extolling their previous experience, expanding their promises. Folk listened or not, intuited or had already decided.

A big guy in a ridiculously bright red shirt made a strong demand, and had four sidekicks to back him up. But it put folk off, and some posh snot called Jeremti put himself forward. He had cronies, too, and talked smoothly, shallowly persuasive. Also a little woman who perkily talked figures and quotas and targets, clearance rates, planting routines. So that put everybody off as well.

'You,' I said to the woman next to me. 'Whyn't you put up? You been muttering all the time; you understand better than them. Go on, get up there and make your pitch.' Flustered, she did. Bit of a brutey face, but she'd followed the arguments and made a good, realistic bid for it.

Seven whittled down to three on the first round. And I voted for Posh Jeremti.

She was quietly livid, 'Why? Why? You sent me up there.'

'You didn't have to go. Just let him screw it up, eh? Find the problems. Then Big Red'll take over. Folk heard you. They'll remember, and you'll be learning. Rescue us. Be happy.'

But she wasn't happy, 'I could have—'

'Sure you could. Things'll go wrong. But you won't be blamed. They will.'

'But I—'

No point listening to her, so I dragged her and Waif to congratulate Posh Jeremti.

***

Like I'd imagined, he scrugged it up big time. His head in the dome, he never really realised we were people in

127

an outback, pioneer colony unit, and tried to lord it over us. It was up to him. I kept out of it, did what I was told, suggested things that were frugging obvious. Steady, solid, average, I worked hard. So did Waif. I made sure she did: talk about a confidence-ectomy. 'You had it removed surgically?' I asked her, 'Your confidence? Buck it up. You're as good as the others and better than most. So act it.'

It didn't take long for folk to realise that Posh J knew nothing. He was a Total Unrealistic. He tried democracy, but couldn't decide anything positive. Was even eating the corn instead of planting it. Lost three people as run-offs. He was deposed by vote at the end of the first onz.

So Red forced in: all mouth, waving fists and food vouchers. He and his crookies were little better than Jeremti. Two more desertions. Things happened and he didn't know how to un-happen them, like a breach in the outer dome skin; and the water was polluted because of lack of maintenance. I did whatever I could to support them. Really I did. I worked, suggested, and took a slight pasting from two cronies, "for looking subversive".

Then I received a verbal pasting from Brutey's bunch for… for being me, I think. So I lammed into them and told'em what for. I imagine that's why a couple of her guys gave me a physical work-over, too. I'm not totally certain why, except they told me I was an obnoxious turd. Not too bad: it was more of a softening-up, really.

But I had to keep going with the mecho-planters once the first patches were cleared. Not even a day's rest, huh? But it made me appear dedicated.

Waif was growing fast and I quite liked her, so I removed the panel to the next room, and found the one beyond it was vacant, too, and so we had a triple-cubby space to spread out in. I demanded she work with me during the days.

'No, I *insist*,' I told the Fieldsman. 'I'm not having her scrugged silly by that pack in Maintenance.' He didn't take kindly to my syther blade under his chin, but the scratch didn't show if he kept his arrogant head down.

Brutey was becoming irate, seditious, wanting to take over, seeing the faults. Looking for supporters. She even tackled *me*, face to face, without two crookies and pair of tees. 'Will you back me this time?'

That was definitely not the attitude to guarantee support. 'Why me? I'm nobody. I'm second field foreman. Nope. Best to do it legal. Request a vote. No coup.' I wandered off, mentioning over my shoulder that she might try lacing Big Red's drinks with the water that *he* polluted. 'That'd be kinda poetic, huh?'

***

Purely coincidentally, I'm sure, Big Red was laid up and incapable of, well, anything, really. Everyone could see how bad the illness and the situation were, especially the gap at the top of the hierarchy.

I didn't need to stare at her, but I did. 'Your turn.' I grinned at her.

She truly hated me by then, when the spot vote was over, and she won. She didn't trust me; wouldn't consult me; or appoint me to anything. Demoted me to Third Hand. I did notice, however, that she enacted a few of the things I'd mentioned in passing. Mentioned, did I say? More like bellowing in her face when she didn't hear the first time.

'Koh, so you're knowledgeable,' she'd recovered by the next morning, 'about some things. You saw what was occurring, but you stir people against me.'

'Keeps you irritated and toesy.' I gave her my most smart-arsed grin and took Waif's hand as I led her away.

'Ireenya?' I told Waify. 'You're going to need another partner before long. You should start looking.'

'You're leaving?' Big eyes stared up at me.

'Tossed out, I suspect. I've scrawked her off too often.'

'You've been good to me. You never hurt me, or *anything*.'

'I've been good to Brutey, too. She just doesn't know it. But she's improving. She needs to: we're down to forty population. That's barely viable.'

***

Another onz. I stirred up a lot of foment, put pressure on just about everyone, irritated Brutey no end. She became tougher with me after that. When she announced the execution, I thought she meant me, but she gave me the hard, warning look and I grinned in my most superior way. Yeah, she's very capable now. She sees more clearly, is tougher, and gives realistic orders. Makes us work longer hours, harder shifts. She's taken one deserter back, and accepted two deserters from elsewhere.

It was turning round. Not enough, so I turned up the challenging a touch. Scruggit, *somebody* had to. I felt compelled to let out a few sneers about some of her ideas, uses of materials, work rosters. It was merely pushing her to think, and be tough. Totally innocent, I was.

Getting it more and more right, more harmonious, more teamworky. Except me, naturally. I had my Ireenya Waif on my back, too. She was giving me jip in public, calling me down, showing me up.

So Brutey was becoming stronger, more popular, and I saw Ireenya confiding in her, snitching on me for my machinations. So Mister Popularity, I wasn't.

That was when they voted to expel me.

***

I'm leaving. Outside the dome, escorted to the perimeter of our lands, they left me. First and last hug with Ireenya. 'You did the moaning and blabbing perfectly,' I congratulated her. 'You sure it was all an act?'

She laughed, pretty confidently, 'I wish you weren't going.'

Ten ticks later, and I was alone. I waited till they were out of sight, then turned and hefted my bag across my back, and headed down towards my pick-up point. Centralis would be along shortly.

Right, then. That worked fine-ish, then. Another dome started on the right track. My fifth. Now, I need to debrief properly: I want feedback on this one. Did I spot Brutey too easily? Does it mean I'm too casual?

Maybe not; I'd thoroughly checked the eight most likely candidates before I'd manoeuvred her into position. And yes, she's exactly and definitely the right choice. Her personality stats back that up on the four key traits and twenty-eight divisional and peripheral characteristics of personae. Experience? Nobody had any. Who runs "Start your own alien colony" courses these days?

If I'm going to stay in this role, and do it *mei instika*, as they say, *ex tempore*, then I got to be dead sure I'm right. It's nice to have the stats on my side, though.

Only took me four onz to get thrown out, too. That's a full eleven days shorter than my previous best.

***

In disbelief, Ingria sheened brightly green. 'Kaks – you *can't* go clittering off to the Outer Dolgans. Even for the promise of a commercial project.' She blinked all eight eyes in disapproval.

'Yes I can: the Dolgans is a successful colony set up by the Elder Grens, and they've asked me to help for a term. It's good money – for both of us – you and me. It could continue for up to a year, and they'll let me produce the report about it. The opportunity's too big to miss, Ing; and we always fancied going there.'

'But what about this lot? Your present project? This colony would starve in there. Surely, Kaks, you wouldn't simply abandon them? You've been on it for six wekkies – all summer.'

'Who cares? They're boring. They don't even breed any more. Nothing's happening. I'll just leave'em to take their chances, and we'll see if there's any left by the time we get back. Anyway, I'm pretty much done with them – the initial funding was for six wekkies. In their timescale, that's been around twelve years.'

'The funding's finished? You could have applied for more. They'll eat each other, trapped in there, if we don't replenish their food banks.'

'They have other animals – sub-creatures they could eat. But they haven't – because we cosset them too much.' Patronisingly, Kaks hugged his longest tentacle around her, and squeezed slightly.

'But they *can't* survive. They don't know how. Kaks, they'll all die off.'

'So what? They're a drag after the whole summer and nothing happening. Now the funding's died off, they can, too. I have a dozen other interests at the moment, and this one's had its time.'

'But, without the funding, the power'll fail. They'll freeze or boil... or run out of air. Kaks, you *can't* simply desert them.'

'Like I said – Yes, I can. If there's anything alive when we return, I'll clear them out. Now, you have twenty zin to prepare for the move. Come on.'

***

'It's definitely dark earlier. Feels a touch cooler, too.' Chakk mock-shivered as though to emphasise his words, rubbing up and down his arms. His eyes sought along the hazy horizon.

'Mmm, folk down the south perimeter say the sky's certainly a different shade of mauve these past dozen or more days.'

'Really? There's also been a report saying the northern sky's darkening over. You can see it – *look*. That's been coming on at least twenty days.'

'Something wrong, you reckon?' Pitto was always worried about something.

'Too soon to say. Maybe they're doing another Change with us, like they used to. Every year altering the physics parameters, something different every time. If not several things. Plural. Remember that year when each day was a fifteener long? Nights, too. We learned a lot, then.'

'We died a lot, too. Like the year the light spectrum altered and crops died and so did livestock.'

'And everything became sterile, including us. Food, light, water? Any of them could have caused it. The magnetics were sky-high, too. But whatever caused it, we've had five years with no births.' He waved across the fields, 'not even in livestock, or wild birds or animals.'

'If this really is another Change, maybe we'll start having children again.'

'Don't hold your breath, Pitto – we've said that every year. This one doesn't feel the same, though. The others have been abrupt and obvious. This is creeping up on us.'

'So how bad do you think this might be? You feel lighter? Like gravity's decreasing?'

'How the purple-pollock would I know? I'm Coordinator, not Diviner. Not another word. We'll meet the council tomorrow a.m. at four. Shuffle round and tell'em, hmm?'

***

'Okay, okay… Come together people. Thank you.' At the second official council meeting since the Change. Coordinator Chakk looked around the assembly – fourteen councillors plus himself and two other officers. And every other person in Honua tuned in on their molto sets from wherever they happened to be.

'It's seventy-two new-days since the first signs of a Change were noted. To summarise: we're now certain another Change has occurred. Like every other one in the past, this isn't like any previous one. The big difference is that we don't seem to be confined to the Radius any longer. We've confirmed that the twenty-kay force perimeter is no longer there. We've had explorations out since day twenty-five, when it was first

135

confirmed. Some of these expeditions have spent four and five nights away from Honua. Well beyond direct sight of home.'

'We never had sight of anything outside the force wall before, just the grey mass,' Someone butted in.

'True. But we have now. To the south we can see for nearly three radii, maybe fifty kay. That diminishes to less than one radius to the north, into the hills. We've had groups out in all directions?' Chakk looked around the circle of faces for confirmation.

'Yes. All eighteen expeditions have returned safely, except Torny's, which has a wider brief, and is carrying more electronix. They're setting up a mast as far away as we can still send and receive. So far, they're a dozen radii south – possibly two hundred kays.'

'The force barrier worked two-way,' Pitto added to the discussion. 'As you know, we've seen recent incursions by a slow-wandering flock of something that looks like orange sheep. They were patrolled by a pair of predatory reptilian creatures that fatally attacked Jimry Wads. Hence the kill-on-sight notice last Mons. Also a trio of large, lumbering creatures. Possibly birdlike – they have feathery fur, anyway, and seem to be semi-intelligent from the way they come to us and make various sounds. Miteo Jacks is working on some translation models for that.'

'A major plus,' Officer Walken joined in, 'is that we are fertile again. Eighteen women are with child. The livestock, too. Days are currently around nineteen hours, although that's still changing, which might indicate continued settling from the Change; or some new seasonal variation.'

'The other Biggy is that the appearances of food and water have ceased. Fortunately,' Pitto checked his documents, 'our stocks are fairly high, so we should manage. We're on the lookout for hunting opportunities, and monitoring the livestock to see if they breed in sustainable numbers. And if these orange sheepees breed, and are edible. Crops seem to be unaffected.

'Think back – all we adults remember twelve or thirteen years ago – it's hard to tell exactly, when the length of a day or year can vary so much – when our whole community was trapped within a force field. We had no idea who was responsible. We assumed aliens or a government research agency, but had no real idea. After a succession of Changes, we concluded this must be an alien culture and this has to be another planet, not Earth. Presumably, we've been studied by whatever has kept us here, and provided sustenance and power. The loss of the latter is a major problem: we have a few solar cells and batteries, but we do have a great deal of skill and ingenuity, as well as knowledge and experience.' Pitto looked around. 'So that's about it, in summary.'

Deafened by the instant clamour from those present and from the molto-sets, he answered, or passed as best he could. 'It's very clear where the former perimeter was, although the barrier's gone. The rocks and vegetation vary considerably one side to the other. Whilst in a few places the ground is at the same level within and outside, mostly it isn't. There's a cliff wall twenty metres high on one northern stretch. But a drop of about the same in two places to the south; where, it seems, there were valleys before we were, er, slotted-in here, land and buildings, people and livestock and all.'

'The thing is,' Coordinator Chakk took over, 'what we do next depends on what we believe has been happening in the past. Some beings have confined us, and altered our environs from time to time, for whatever reasons. Now, however, is this simply another Change? Or an ending? Are we done? Abandoned?'

'Maybe the aliens have suffered some kind of accident? Had a power failure? Lost an intergalactic war? Died of a starry disease?'

'Is this an opportunity for us? And if so, to do what?'

'Escape.'

'As far away as possible.'

'Or stay here and wait for the supplies to recommence?' The suggestions and ideas came tumbling from everyone around the assembly.

'If it's an accident, we should stay. Best not upset beings that can do this...'

The debate raged; and they argued; and bickered, mumbled and suggested, sparked and tailed off as the four-hour scheduled end came and went, and the council meeting didn't actually come to any conclusion.

'We'll re-convene at the next regular time, in thirty-four days. On the Fourth of Contra.'

***

'Kaks? Where are they?' Ingria opened her seeker-sensors to the surrounding area. 'There's nothing, Kaks. The vida-waves are dead for the extent of the field. Where can they have gone?'

'How would I know? They're not here, that's for sure.'

'Were there many of them? Couple of centurs?'

'Centurs? Ten times that. More. Monitors said four thousand, two-twenty-six at the last.'

'And they're loose somewhere on the island?'

'That, or dead in little holes, I expect.' Kaks was optimistic about the convenient wipe-out of his former project.

'How long have we been away?'

'In the Outer Dolgans? Six wekkies – you've been with me.'

'No, I mean, in their time scale?'

'Er, twelve of their years, give or take. About as long again as the project lasted with funding. They shouldn't have gotten far or done much – they didn't in the previous dozen years, did they?' Bored, Kaks delummed his trisks.

'Nothing on the recorders?'

'No. They all dried up when the power was cut with the funding.'

'Kaks? There're no heap of bodies, or skeletons or anything.' Ingria could see ominous shadows gathering around her. 'They've gone.'

Kaks didn't see a problem. 'Maybe they were all eaten by the reptovs that prowl the island: they'd keep this lot in order. There's nowhere to go.'

'They've already gone.' Kakai snifferated, and extended the range of her seeker-makis. 'I don't sense them anywhere around. They're not on the island at all.'

'So that's alright, then. No problem. Now, let's pack the rest of our gear together, and rejoin the others back on the Dolgans for the rest of the year.'

***

'Kaks? You recall those little things you did that colony project on last summer? Where they disappeared from the compound on the island?'

'Yes. The ones that stopped breeding and died out.'

139

'Have you seen this report on the Dao? Do you think…? I wonder if it's them?'

'Oh?' He corrussed closer. 'Mmm… can't be. They were on the island; they couldn't get off there. Could they?'

'Well,' Ingria tarseled through the reports, 'it looks like them. But these're on the mainland. They've been noted in several dozen large colonies. And smaller, very widespread communities.'

'Can't be. They never did anything here.'

'You had them force-fielded in a cage. Controlled everything. They didn't have the opportunity.' Tarseling deeper, she added, 'But since last summer – they had six wekkies while we were in the Dolgans, and another, what? Another forty wekkies when we went back.'

'Scrinkle! That'll be eighty years, their time.'

'Three or four generations, Kaks? They hadn't been breeding for several of their years, but suppose they could when the field went down? If this is them, then it certainly looks as if they're making up for it. You think they built ships? Migrated from the island? The mass of them by the looks.'

'Not a sign of a single one of them on the island when we looked, was there?'

'They must have been very determined to get as far away as possible. Not be trapped again,' Ingria stared at Kaks accusingly. 'It says here the authorities have no idea where they came from.'

'Good. They haven't traced them back to me, then. Trying to eradicate them, are they?'

'No, doesn't seem like it. This reports that they're "a phenomenon of geneto-origenic interest. They appear to have arisen at several loci at around the same time." Ah,

140

and this one says, "One distinct possibility is that they arrived as deliberate or accidental stowaways on ships that called in at a number of out-cluster planets."

'Well, Kaks,' Ingria smug-faced, 'it looks as though they're doing a lot more for themselves than they ever did for you.'

***

MANSFIELD WILL NEVER BE THE SAME AGAIN

I don't get gob-smacked by much I see in Mansfield. But this? Well, the place is never going to be the same.

Going round the market, minding my own business, as you do, and there it suddenly was: massive, like ten storeys high, and wide as a house. A slug. It looked just like a slug, anyroad: gigantic, it filled a whole corner of the marketplace, all rounded and organic-looking. Like slimy and throbbing. Yes, I know – I seen people like that, too.

I'm standing there, mouth wide open, looking up at it, all shiny and oozy – the thing, not me. It suddenly sends tentacles flashing down, like tendrils. *So fast.* And it's grabbing someone and lifting them up, like examining them. All these arrays of sensors popping up in patches across its surface. And it's pulsing like an elephant's heart. Then it's starting to pull him apart and he's screaming and struggling. Not for long, though, poor sod. The brighter ones among us are doing an about-turn and legging it – get some distance between us, tucking in behind columns and in shop doorways.

Some, however, just don't believe it – you know how some folks are – and they're just standing there gawping.

Next, it's sending a great long tentacle-thing out and grabbing one of the women standing there… and a few more, as well. And it's got its tentacles all over'em – typical Mansfield – and it's stripping'em… and it starts dismembering them. Some others, it's stretching or crushing; twisting them up, like wringing them. Like it's doing torque-tests on'em. I can see all this blood splurting and bursting out. And it's shaking them as if to see if there's anything loose inside – like got a screw loose. It's getting fed up then, cos it's just dropping them. Some of the lumps on the exterior starts moving, and swelling. And they goes in rotation all round it, like eyes switching on and searching.

Then, all of a sudden, it's shrinking down and swelling out sideways and longways, so it's looking even more like a slug, and slid and slurped across the pedestrian precinct. No people there by then, and it's re-raising itself up the side of Marks & Spencers. These like tendril things are flickering in through the windows, bringing people out, holding them for a moment – some shrieking and struggling – and it just drops'em to the pavement. One or two, it's chucking away, as if in disgust. I know how it feels, when I look round Mansfield sometimes. A couple of market stalls went flying – cabbages everywhere.

The big office and council building next to Marks starts falling apart. I can't see anything what it's doing from where I am, but there's these great sections of the frontage coming tumbling outwards and collapsing, and I'm seeing all these people amongst the masonry and girders and dust coming up in great clouds.

Out on the streets, everybody's running back, of course, most screaming and dragging kids. A few are stopping to watch a hundred yards away, like they've reached their own feel-safe distance.

Everybody where I'm hiding is suddenly in a panic, because it's heading this way. I'm getting knocked over in the rush and next thing I know, it's right on top of me, overlapping me with its great rounded bulk. Bloody hell – it's really slimy close up, and stinks like compost. It's moving like a caterpillar, with the front stretching out and then the insides come slurping forward inside it. Then the back end sucks into it – it's revolting. It must have had its attention on the Bentinck memorial spire because it oozed across the square and stretched right up it. It's a really complicated steeple with four corner spires round the high main one. Or it was, anyway. This slug-thing's leaning right up there, hugging the whole spire, and sending its tendrilly tentacles all up them, pulling them apart as if they're nothing.

A guy near me's saying, 'The television people ought to be here. I'm going to sell my phone footage to Sky TV.'

Some religious nut woman decides she's going to talk to it or something, and she's walking towards it, praying really loudly and calling it a demon. It was, too. It demoned her alright, all over the market place. It hardly seemed to touch her – she must have hit a raw nerve with her screechy praying.

By then, there's me and this bald guy who's covered in tattoos keeping out the way in the doorway to the Four Roses Shopping Centre. 'Somebody ought to get the negotiators in from Lambeth.' And he's wanting experts from Cambridge or some such dreaming place. He was another nutter-type trying to contact it, and wanting to study it.

I said, 'I wonder where the nearest tanks are? Do we have reserve army units down at Chilwell or Kegworth or somewhere? We don't have Apache helicopters, do we? Cruise missiles?

Then the police arrived and two of them unrolled their stripy red and white tape to cordon off the area and keep it in. 'Cordon it off with stripy tape?' I said. 'It's fifty feet high, you berk.'

The big Officer Fuzz was a bit cross with me for saying that. 'Get the other side of the tape where it's safe,' he ordered me. 'Both of you, go inside the shopping centre.' That was the last thing he did: a tendril wrapped round him. It took a tenth of a second, just long enough for him to look surprised. And he'd gone; leaving a great long red and white ribbon fluttering behind him. He should have let go.

The thing suddenly disappeared. *Potwór ślimak,* I called it. That's what my Polish girlfriend calls her big fat dad. It had vanished.

Bald Tattoo said he thought it had zipped down to nothing – like squeezing itself into a cardboard box, and then that vanished. So he reckoned, anyway. But he's from Mansfield...

***

'Honest, Boss,' Menolyptus Vee wasn't really surprised to see his boss come slithering into his office just before prinkle time. 'I simply popped out to some planet that was just put up on the "Unprotected" list. It was on the official bulletins this morning, right down near the bottom of the routine list. No details about it, so I thought, "I got nothing else on, especially." So I went down on the off-chance, just to suss it out, to see if it was suitable, you know, for vacations. It could be the next place to start pushing to the punters. We need a fresh angle: somewhere new to keep the customers happy and paying, huh?'

'And is it suitable?' Heggidorphyn sent querying pulses.

'Yes, could be.' Menolyptus Vee shrugged his elbagoyles. 'But we'd have to plan how to pitch it. The place is full of these little ant creatures. They're busy, and scurry and squeak and have lots of constructions. Everything's a bit fragile, though: I crunched a few of their erections in a cluster, like a Xerotype hive, it was.'

'What do they taste like? Any good?'

'They stick in the teeth a bit; the outer covering's a touch leathery, but if you get that off, they're not bad.'

'Maybe an acquired taste? Could we make up some ideas of local dishes? A few head parts sticking out of pies or something of that nature? Maybe take a few pots of various flavoured dips to try them in first?'

'I was thinking, Boss: we could trade on the freaky adventure angle more than local dining. We'd have to theme it in the adverts, something like, "Panic makers and lovers – come and create havoc." You know, have a bit of wreck and ruin. Fun days. Not too much or too often, or the planet couldn't keep up and rebuild as fast as we destroy. We'd need to make it expensive, limited to a few visitors per diurn, with no weaponry allowed. Make it all sklids-on stuff, up close and personal. I pulled a few apart myself with no trouble. It's easy. They squeak as they lose bits. Don't take to being screw-twisted very well, either.'

'We'd need to set a demand-pricing-sustainability balance, then?'

'I reckon so; start very high and exclusive, advertise it as a "must-have" for the rich.'

'Defensive capability?'

'None that I detected, although I was only there one sustera. That might be long enough to pitch the visits at, in case they do have other systems lurking in reserve.'

'Sounds like we could market the risk element, too. There's a come-on lure I know to boost that idea.'

'You're prepared to give it a go, then Heggy? Visit the place yourself?'

'Well, sounds like we could be on another winner with this one, eh, Meno?'

'Yep – let's shake and shoon on it, eh?'

'And shlurt all over it, huh?' They laughed, elly-ectitiously.

***

Okay, so I own Caribou Island. Not all hundred and sixty square miles of the Lake, just the island. I've been living here around fifty years – born here – and I still haven't seen any caribou. I gave up caring in my teens. Got better things to care about nowadays.

In the Thirties, the government and Northern Minerals Inc jointly carried out a massive aerial survey for copper deposits around this part of Canada. On the official maps, the area to the western side of the lake was Plot 50; the island was nominated as Plot 51, with Caribou Island in brackets. And, of course, the section beyond the eastern mainland shore was Plot 52. They didn't find any copper; there isn't any within seventy-odd miles of Lake Musquaha. So that survey was *the* big waste of time and cash in the Great Depression. Except we like to think of ourselves as "Plot 51", a bit like "Area 51" in Nevada.

We used to run this place together, but Elodie died three years ago; she's out the back in the family plot. Soon as they could, my three sons left for Winnipeg, Vancouver and Power Pine Falls respectively. I don't see them much these days. Used to miss them, but they got careers and families, and folks like that don't tend to stay hereabouts.

I manage alone now, in my own little fishing-and-boating-oriented world. Mooching round my jetty the rental boats and my diner-bar-café fills my days. I keep eight double rooms in the extension for trippers, and fishermen who don't like wobbly nights on the water, as well as days. It's pretty good: I'm the jovial host, renter, room cleaner and repairman all season. Cutting the fire timber and doing big repairs fills in the winters, between the weeks when I'm snowed-up and frozen-in. Make a mint, I do, but there's not a lot of fun out of season, and no future, ever.

So that's me, pretty much, pottering along and letting the world pass me by. And I love it.

*

One morning – cold and clear – October, it was, I watched this trail in the sky, coming from the north-east. I saw the dash cams of the Chelya-somewhere thing in Russia and I knew straight away this was the same: a meteor! Wow. It never occurred to me that there was any danger. I suppose it was too interesting, and happened too quick to think about it.

Almighty explosion. The other side of the island – the rocky, barren side.

It had hit! It was a meteor*ite!* Awesome! I'd always been interested – I'd even bought a couple of meteorite slices at a rocks and fossils fair in Ottawa one time. So this was gob-gasping awesome. I'm practically jumping up and down, going, 'I've seen a meteorite hit.' Well, almost saw it: it was over the far side of Caribou Ridge. But just the same, I count myself as a witness.

I just had to get over there. 'Must be around a mile and a half away,' I reckoned – though it would take more'n an hour over that terrain. Big rucksack and spike-end hammer, in case there were hot iron meteorite lumps to dig up.

I know every inch of Caribou, and was on the ridge by ten. Sure enough, it was difficult to miss the patch of smoke down near the shore. I hung a Larrry down the back trail, and the impact site was even more obvious down there by Beaver Knoll. I recognise blasted-over trees when I see them, especially when they're surrounding a steamy, smoke-hazed crater and a great spread of rocks.

Another half-hour to scramble down over all the fallen trees and scrub – strew me, you wouldn't believe how difficult that can be. But there it was, right at my smouldering feet, twenty-thirty feet across, shallow hole in the rock and clay. Still hot; still smoking. There was a glint of something shiny. I thought mica at first – there's plenty of that round here. But I scrabbled down the loose, rocky slope inside this crater, and something metallic was hot and steaming, and crackling.

I was a bit shaved off about that, thinking, *It's a chunk of space debris. Damn! They been having bother with Hubble again? Or a Russian one? I bet NASA'll pay handsomely for either. Wonder if there's much of it buried?*

Scratting round in the bottom of the pit with the pick, I found some bedded-in fragments. A couple were stuck solid – too deep. Definitely man-mad, not rock. Pity – I always fancied finding a meteorite.

But I couldn't do no more, I'd got the bar to attend to, and it's the night for the Poutine and Syrah Special. Two extra rooms to prepare for guests; plus one rental boat going out, assuming the ferry brings the weekenders in on time.

*

About a dozen fishers, most in their own boats, a couple of charters, all called in for supplies and bait and a hot drink – top-up fuel, enjoy the chatter, join in the gossip. Nobody said anything about this morning, not here or on

151

the TV. So I didn't mention it; I figured the angles for scrap value, or a reward if anyone came looking. My property – my reward.

That was me pretty much stuck there the rest of the day, so it was next morning when I managed to go see my crater again. It'd been disturbed.

'Now who the Blue Bugs could'a done that?' I ask myself. 'There's been nobody I don't know of on the island – if you know what I mean.' I did some digging and picking and pulling, and looked all round for footprints or anything – fat chance when every tree for fifty metres was flattened. I collected a few broken bits of metal, and cursed a fair bit. Then when I looked up, I saw something just where the first vertical tree stood. Real wary, I wandered over. Yeah, something moving... Pair of eyes – big and dark. Reminded me of a llama I saw once in the zoo in Toronto. Like big and calm and just looking at me inscrutably. Then another pair, lower down. I stopped for a mo, then thought, 'What the heck I got to lose?' and went towards them.

It was two things – like animals, two-legged, though one was sitting down – still reminded me of the llama at High Park. And a slightly purple colour. I was pretty close by then. Like long-fingery hands holding each other. And they wore clothes – also purply, and were kind of velvety-skinned – not masks or skin suits.

'You're aliens,' I said. 'Course, they didn't understand me, but they did, if you know what I mean, and didn't run. 'You're females.' I could tell that much. 'You're real, aren't you?'

It seemed like they were very weak... shocked or injured, maybe. The one sitting was touching her leg, but she shied away when I bent to have a proper look. It din't look good, so she needed transport and somewhere sheltered. Like the cabins.

'Stay here,' I said, almost calmly, and held my hands up, to sort of signify they should wait. 'I'll be back.'

Leaving my bag and toque, and woolly top and wrap-up-rainie with them so they knew I'd be back, I ran all the way over the ridge and down to the cabins. Talk about ex-bleeding-cited! And I got the launching trolley for the rescue dinghy. It weighs about six kilos, has big tyres, and bounces over everything.

I was knackered by the time I got back, but they were still there – and had put on my clothing gear. The pompom toque looked great on the sitting one's head. And I offered them water and trail mix – the sort with nuts, raisins and M&Ms in it. They understood it all when I ate some myself and waved and pointed for them to sit on the trolley's strapping so I could drag them back.

The sitting one did, after they'd looked at each other. The other one walked behind, and I took them down the ramp path so nobody'd see us. Jips, what a struggle!

By the time we got back, the trail mix had all gone, and I was bagged and knees-first in the grass. I put them in the Capricorn room – they all got zodiac names. I left them with a collection of mixed-gender clothes – it's amazing what people leave behind. And water and juices. I wondered about grass or hay, but thought better of it. Then checked back when I'd done the other cabin-cleanings.

They were scared: one was in the bed, undressed. She was female, very obviously, the hurt-leg-and-poorly one. I tried to look helpful and quizzical, but I don't think it came over very well, so I got on with the chores round the cabins and jetty and in the bar. Thinking about them all the time, just going, 'Wow... wow... awesome... hellfire... They're like real... *aliens*.' And I kept looking across to Capricorn and hoping they were alright and not going to do a runner.

I took more trail mix, and milk and beer – yeah, I know – water, too. And some cheese and Caramilk and Coffee Crisp candy bars – I provide'em all free in the rooms, so I had plenty. Plus some – yeuk – mixed vegetables.

Jeem, jeem, jeem – I bounced round like the kids used to at Christmas.

The regulars said, 'Who's perked you up, Walfy, eh?'

'Bookings up, eh?'

'Tart on the side?'

'Kids promised not to visit?'

It was busy in the bar – plus three couples in the rooms and ten more folk in their own cruisers. All that delayed me so much, I couldn't check on *them* till after midnight. I knocked, real polite, and went in. Damn – I'm a fuddled fool: it was pitch dark, and freezing cold. I almost prostrated myself in apology – one was in bed still and the other just standing there the same as when I left. I showed them the light switch, and she switched it on and off a few times.

She smiled! Wow – that was better than finding a meteorite. 'And the heater's here. Turn on, count to four, and press.' She jumped back when it blew into flame, and came back when it settled. They both smiled. Pretty faces.

I showed'em how to bolt the door – jeeps – their fingers were so long. And I heard the bolt go across when I left.

154

I had more time next morning, once the guests, fishers and rentals had left for the day. I went back and knocked, and waited, and they let me in. I took the walking one across to the kitchen and let her look all round and try things – food and different drinks – and she poked at the oven and microwave and the disposal unit and the fridge and the faucet – that made her jump, too. And smile. I thought she looked bit more human when she smiled. I mean, I could tell it definitely was a smile.

We took bits back to the room and I showed her where the spare blankets were. They zippered and chittered on about something and nodded and chirruped more – decided something. Then they pulled me over to a chair, and I had to put my hands round one of them's head. It was really silky velvety, and they both did it to me and closed their eyes.

And I got the works! I mean, I got an insight, anyway. They were *Plu-inyi* – something like that. I went really dizzy. My head spun, I felt sick with all these words and feelings whirling round.

It's not like I understood everything: I couldn't suddenly talk to'em or anything. But I did get what had happened – ish.

They were two glitz and bling girls. They'd been out drinking, and re-progged their *p'araleluri erteuli* in a fit of over-indulgence in *Śarāba atē pajanī* – I think that meant they were sloshed out their minds… paralysed as pot potatoes. They'd deliberately put random co-ords in their S-Time Unit, and kissed their asses farewell. There was an extra bit about being caught too close to the Black Spot Nightlife Centre. And they'd bounced through that – whatever it was – and there was no way back – not out of there.

They were a mite regretful now, though. But not totally distraught. Maybe more like philosophical.

You know? They made me laugh. They were entertaining – like my Elly had been – on the whacky side. Yeah, they reminded me of Elly.

*

They seemed settled after a few days – a week, maybe. I got used to'em, and took'em a heap more clothes to pick through; and they ate, and drank stuff. I just loved having them there, and spent late evenings with'em when I could. We went out along the lakeshore to talk and walk in the mornings. And on the quad bike once. Only out; we walked back.

Then one night they came into the bar.

I nearly died. Nobody said anything. Didn't seem to notice. But we had music CDs on and everybody was happy enough with their salmon and trout catches, or just the Fall colours, supping the beer and Pike Creek whiskey, chewing on the smoked salmon and Philly.

I suppose Glitz and Bling's skin was pinker, and more smooth than purple-velvety. *Maybe,* I thought, *the other drinkers aren't looking askance because fuzz-headed, everso-slightly purple girls are the trend-setters in Montreal these days? The tall one looks more like Elly every time I see her... Oh, God. Is it me who's changing? I'm seeing things differently? I been got at?*

'Do I look different to you?' I asked a fisherman with a thirty-footer and two very hard-drinking shipmates.

'Same as last night,' they agreed

'That's a bit ambiguous.' And thought, *Does that mean it's them who's changing?*

156

They were great in the bar – got bloody drunk! Like on a stagette. And sang. I say "sang" and some of us joined in, but… Oh boy, I'm not letting them loose on the Jack Daniels again. Unless it was the Cheezies with M&Ms that did it, I suppose.

*

I've noticed since then that their faces and skin are becoming more human-normal, and they smile ever such a lot. And it's *real* smiling. And Glitz, the tall one, does look eversuch a lot like Elly. Even got two or three toes now, not hooves. And boobs – real ones!

She told me, 'I like myself like this.'

'So do I, you and Ella, both.'

'Well, Walter, suppose we try to… you know… the three of us… in your great big bed?' And they had these huge drown-in eyes… and all these long, delicate, wondrous fingers touching and stroking and…

*

Oh jeeps, are my three boys going to be surprised when they come back for Christmas and New Year.

***

DAISY'S GOT HER FINGERS STUCK IN THE POPCORN MACHINE

Whatever Daisy saw, she had to poke at. The car radio packed up two days ago. Her enquiring touches with delicate fingers did something that took me ages to reverse and reset. 'Oh, Daisy, love, what you've done with the SatNav is anybody's guess – even a hard reset isn't persuading it that we're actually driving to Terrex, California. It thinks we're heading for Terrex, South Africa.'

'I've no idea, Daddy. That was yesterday. It's completely beyond me now.'

I glanced at Janey-Sue beside me, and caught Danny's eye in the rear-view mirror. We all knew there was no point saying anything more to Daisy. She really didn't know what she'd done after such unthinking, spontaneous meddlings.

Apart from that, the vacation was going great. It was four weeks fly-drive round the Western States – Arizona, New Mexico, California and three or four other states – Nevada, Colorado... That day, we drove into a railroad and cattle town and it was awesome: all the buildings displayed gigantic murals of cattle herding, vintage cars and pioneer scenes; vast trains, huge portraits of local historical characters. Some were incredibly lifelike. The town was magnificent. We wandered round with ice creams and cameras all afternoon, before finding a small motel for the night.

A mural filled one wall in the bar-restaurant we went to: a scene of the main street a hundred years ago. The large foreground figures were so real. Gerhard, the young bartender, saw our interest and told us about many others around town. 'There's a pile of maps on the bar. On Langtry Street there's a studio where they have a projector that photographs people and projects their images onto a sensitive electronic board. It creates murals like the big ones, featuring you. For you to buy the poster, of course, with any background you fancy. Some of the ones around town were done by the studio, re-projected onto the walls and painted there. Yes, some are images of real people who passed through, as well as local folk.' He was so enthusiastic about it. 'You should try it if you like them so much.'

'Dad?' Danny came up while I was chatting with Gerhard, 'Daisy's got her fingers stuck in the popcorn machine. It's pouring quarters out instead of popcorn.'

'Thanks, Danny,' I said. You have to laugh at what Daisy gets her fingers into. It's that or cry. 'Let's have a look. At least it's not another parking meter; that one in Sacramento nearly had us arrested.'

I'd only just sorted out the popcorn situation when Danny was back with news of Daisy's latest encounter with technology. The auto-electric drinks-mixer in the bar had unaccountably conked out. 'I swear she scarcely looked at it,' I told Gerhard. 'Just a couple of buttons to choose the blends that she and Danny wanted. It can't have gone all that wrong. Can it?'

I had to promise not to let her near the TV in the room, or the coffee machine, or the microwave, or the key pad on the door. I thought I'd better not to mention the air-con when we checked out next morning, and loaded up the rental car.

'Your car's totally dead,' The AAA mechanic said. 'I need to do an electronic diagnosis. It'll probably take a couple of hours.'

'It'll have been my daughter,' I told him resignedly. 'Sometimes Daisy plays with the car keys. It's a game between her mind and her fingers. There's a project called Aspero-Savant Research Inc. They say she's probably the world's only female autistic-savant with extraordinary brain *and* manual dexterity function. They call her ASEEF, but we call her Daisy. They gave up studying her when she reversed their hidden camera system and started watching *them*.'

'Hey, I'm on her side,' the Triple-A guy laughed, holding up an electronic circuit and looking baffled. 'I never came across a five-year-old, wide-eyed girl in a summer dress who did anything like *this*. Wow!'

'Never mind being impressed,' I told him. 'See if you're better than she is, and fix it, huh? We'll take a walk round town, find some more murals, and the projector studio on Langtry.'

After an hour's wandering around, gazing in wonder at building-sized portraits, paintings of stagecoaches, combine harvesters and wartime bombers, we found the Langtry Murals Studio with little effort, not far from the motel. And we could still move on before noon. And, yes, it was certainly interesting, looking round all their sepia photos and their vintage clothing to be dressed in. We could choose which of the murals we wanted as our background, and take up a similar pose. Then they would project our faces, or the whole person, onto a composite board, and fit in the chosen background. They could be printed off as a poster of any size up to A1.

161

Daisy, naturally, was totally fascinated. 'Awesome,' she said, before her mouth sagged even wider than her eyes as she studied the projector that would do the business, 'How gorgeous.'

The old guy, Mr Freska, was amiable and informative about it. 'For your poster, we can add different clothes, change the background to a wagon or a forest, or any local scenes. With your permission, we sometimes mount them on the walls around town. That way, the townsfolk get a change of scene from time to time.'

It was really weird, posing for a full minute each. Janey-Sue and Danny went first. They looked good, projected onto the screen board at the back, so lifelike up there. Of course, when it was our turn, Daisy wouldn't sit still with me. She was all fidgety and excited, and wriggled away as the projector started to warm up. I stayed still. 'It's no bother,' Mr Freska said. 'The little girl can do it on her own when we've finished with you.'

It was strange. I felt as if I was being sucked out of myself. On the mounting board behind the projector my face was appearing stronger and stronger, alongside Janey-Sue and Danny.

Half-way through, I felt queasy. Janey-Sue and Danny hadn't said anything about feeling sick, hadn't said anything at all, actually. Then I went *really* queer...

I could see the room from the mounting board as well as the booth. The impression was growing stronger, like the projector was splitting me apart, or doubling me up, as if I was becoming detached from myself. The view from up there on the back wall was clearer than in the photo cubicle. It was sinking in with me: *this is just wrong – this doesn't happen.*

162

Ye Gods! That was it: I was being transmitted to the wall board, some sort of futuristic, alien electronic storage board. I made a huge effort to force my mind back into my proper body in the stall down there, where I'm looking up my this myself here on the wall. The old guy was capturing our spirit, or something like that. If he transferred the electronic image of a person to one of the outside murals, I'd be forever on a wall, endlessly looking out over the main street or a car park. Janey-Sue would be the same. She was somewhere next to me on the wall board; I could feel her presence. Danny, too, as worried as me, was on the verge of crying as he was realising what was happening.

Losing the struggle to stay in the booth, it seemed that I was thinning out in my head, and was looking into the room entirely from the wall now. I was like in a frenzy, could see the operator guy adjusting the settings. Gerhard, the bartender, had arrived, too, looking round, talking to the me in the cubicle. I was answering, looking dazed as I stood up and went to join Danny and Janey-Sue, while Gerhard and the old man looked round for Daisy.

'Daisy! God no! Noooo. We'll all be up on the walls forever. All of us.' I wanted to scream at the other me, 'You're going to leave and never know. Gerhard... Mr Freska... Don't you two know what's happening to us? Or don't you care?'

They found Daisy and sat her in the booth. Janey-Sue and the other me tried to calm her down, but she wasn't liking it. The projector warmed up again, focusing on her. Up on the wall screen, I was screaming at her to run, tell my other self not to let them do it, warn them what they were doing.

163

Daisy began to appear next to me. I could feel her warmth, her lively mind. She'd hate it up here with nothing to fiddle with *for ever*. Despairing, I tried to scream and warn them, but I was fading, couldn't do anything about it, couldn't breathe, or move.

Frantic, I tried to scream, helplessly attempting to claw my way off the wall, but couldn't move. Just me and my silent battle on the wall screen, 'No no no Nooooo...'

Then... Is my struggling working? Maybe – I'm not getting worse, anyway. I don't pray very often, but...

It wasn't Daisy I could feel next to me any longer; the essence of the form was changing... It was a man. A male persona. Bewildered, same as me. His aura was strengthening. It was Gerhard, bouncy and smiling and friendly last night, even just half an hour ago, but not so happy now. He was rantingly angry, afraid, as well as disoriented.

He was asking, demanding something of a second mind that was forming, swimming around me. Enraged and shrieking inside, the two new personae linked together, Gerhard and Mr Freska. 'Reversed,' one said, 'The field's inverted. It's inside-out.'

'How the hell?'

'We gotta to get out. We have to stop it.' They sounded more than fraught.

I was fading again. It was frightening. My world was going black, and their voices getting stronger. They were panicking. So was I. We were all echoing across each other, fading... fading... fading even beyond whispers.

Janey-Sue was crying somewhere. Danny, too. God! I was out my mind, trying to find them, to reach them.

Everything was swirling and black and echoing. I could see the projector again, and the screen wall. Two half-formed images were there, not Janey-Sue. Not Danny. They'd disappeared from the display. Where were they? Where? Where?

Desperate, I was sinking to the floor in the projector room. Janey-Sue and Danny were crying and frightened and hugging Daisy. And Daisy was stroking her mum's hair and smiling and saying how glad she was. She gave me a huge hug as I tried to sit up. 'I do love you so much, Daddy.'

The projector was still running, and smoking. Gerhard and Mr Freska were nowhere to be seen. We searched the back room and a side store, behind all the stage sets and the booth. Nowhere. But their figures on the wall panel were so clear, so detailed and lifelike, as the smoke from the overheating projector spread more and more densely. With flames flickering, and no sign of extinguishers anywhere, the four of us fled.

***

We told the police exactly what had happened – that the projector was ablaze when we arrived, and the barman and the old studio guy were determinedly trying to stifle the flames with the dressing-up clothes, and courageously yelling at us to get out.

The police hadn't found any trace of Mr Freska or Gerhard.

It took longer to fix the car than the AAA guy expected, but that was fine – we were shaken up, so we checked back into the motel for at least one more night, and denied all knowledge of the air-con's failings.

The police took statements. We went for a much-needed coffee at the Cap O'Chino Irish Bar. A winding-down walk along the river-bank didn't make my legs feel any less wobbly. The sight of Gerhard and the old man sitting on the buckboard of a covered wagon on the side wall of Mustang Wendy's Tex-Mex Diner didn't help our nerves, especially after Danny swore that Mr Freska bared his teeth for a moment.

'Well, *I* don't know, Daddy,' Daisy told me in the bar, after the cover barman foolishly allowed her to choose some music on the juke box. 'That projector machine was working the wrong way round so I…' Her fingers twirled and inter-wriggled for a few seconds. She shrugged, big blue eyes so angelic. Ye Gods! That little face wrapped me round her little finger every time.

'Oh, yes, Daddy.' In fresh-faced innocence she gazed up at me. 'I just remembered what I did at that museum on Saturday afternoon; that super museum with all those great big trains…'

'Oh, Lord,' Janey-Sue looked at me. 'Should we warn them?'

'Maybe,' Danny piped up, 'we shouldn't go to the Air and Space Museum tomorrow, Dad?'

'Mmm, I suppose we might be safer in Death Valley.'

'Daddy! That's not fair! It's only an hour since you said I can fiddle with anything I like in future.'

PART THREE

WHILE HEADING HOME

THE LIGHT SWITCH

It began as a perfectly normal shift at the Yabanci Experimental Growth Laboratory – the unit where we re-created and raised the aliens.

On the way to the creation laboratory, I looked in on the community of developing specimens – all twenty-two of them thriving in their enclosed society. Strangely, I sometimes felt a kind of affinity with them. I think "affinity" is more than a word to them: it has a deeper meaning. Perhaps some of it is rubbing into my mind as I spend so much time with them.

Each of the alien creatures was a living tribute to our pioneering technical efforts. Perhaps they meant something more to me. I know not what, but I always linger there longer than I strictly need to. Much longer than I ever do with the two other species we had generated.

After making sure that all was well with the established specimens, it was time to make my routine patrols around the newly active vats. So I went into the R&D hall – the creation lab. Again, a new word I must have gained from them – *Favourite*. My favourite place. How can I possibly have a place that I like more than others? It's not logical: it's a work place. One unit with

169

its own functions, like all the others. And the principal item of current interest there, of course, was our latest project – Number 23. He was growing in the vat at the far end; four identical, high-shine stainless steel tanks.

Through the observation port into 23's container I could watch the mass of thick nutrient solution as it swirled infinitely slowly. Over the coming two hundred days, the gradual process of forming itself into a person would continue – a Yabanci person. A male one.

All was normal: the organs were beginning to form themselves; the mental development was proceeding on schedule; and the overall body mass was typical. I adjusted the memory-input speed a fraction, slipped a headset on, and tapped in to his actual thinking process as he began to absorb this morning's new knowledge and pseudo-memories.

***

*How did that happen? The light switch has moved.
I know it has. Absolutely certain.
If I get up in the night I know exactly where it is.
And it isn't where it should be – precisely one hand-span from the door jamb at shoulder height. It has always been there. I remember it from yesterday.
Now, it's two hand-spans away.
How did that happen? Is the light switch not real?
If something as solid and fixed as a light switch is false, what else is illusory? Could the door be unreal? Is the wall an illusion? Or my bed?
Am I an illusion?*

***

I put the headset down. My ten minins listening-in on Number 23's thinking was a little disturbing. This was very unusual. Unprecedented, in fact. Without warning, he had made a direct and original observation about the environment that we had created in his mind, and had begun to think for himself. He had noticed a discrepancy – the light switch was positioned differently – and he was deducing a great deal from it.

Ah well, I had the other projects to examine, fine-tune and update in the log... Council matters... supplies...

But, later, when I knew Nadd would be in the observation rooms, I slipped round to see him. 'About the Yabanci specimens, Nadd... I found Number 23 doing a lot more than the usual natural querying. He's suddenly suspicious of the environs we're feeding into his mind, and of himself. He's suddenly become curious, and dubious about everything.'

'What have you done this time, Coyo?' Nadd always wanted to apportion blame.

'Nothing different from any other day. This appears to be a natural development, although it's not one we've encountered with previous specimens. He noticed a very minor difference in his pseudo-environment: the precise positioning of a switch that activates a light.'

'We always said 23 would be special.'

'Not this much,' I told him. 'He shouldn't notice things like that; and he shouldn't dwell on them even if it fleetingly enters its mind. I'll monitor him more closely in future.'

***

When I climbed back into bed, I remembered once when the ceiling light moved. Okay, so it wasn't switched on, and the room wasn't very light. I had been lying down and hadn't looked at it especially

171

before. But it flickered and blurred and moved sideways, and I forgot about it 'til now.

There was no mark where it had been, I remember now.

Is this possible?

I thought I knew what I knew, but can it be imaginary? What else has been as fleeting and changing as the light switch? How much more of what I accept is make-believe? I must observe and think.

***

'Number 23 is more than suspicious.' Nadd and I passed it on to Supervisor Herry. 'I monitored him every third cycle – a hundred times since I first noticed the change in his mental processing. We need a rethink on the strategy for him.'

'The strategy for it is fine.' Herry was obstinate, even for a Supervisor.

'He's a Type 2, Herry; we refer to Type 2s as *"he"*, not *"it"*. The strategy was fine three days ago. Something profound has occurred within him, so the strategy is no longer appropriate. *He's* changed. *He's* developing faster than others; or differently. That tiny occurrence with the light switch triggered something. He's now thinking along an entirely different pathway.'

'We know the Yabanci don't think the same way as we do, but this is even more different than the rest of them.' Nadd nodded his right antenna in agreement with me.

'Alright. Let's review its genesis.' Herry reluctantly opened up the screens, and quoted directly from 23's summary banks. 'Standard starter of one hundred pin-

172

weights of correctly-mixed amorphous material, with the customary addition of genetic material from the next sample that was recovered from the wreck. Standard weight and ingredients, mix rate, cultivation, followed by very precise specifications for fermentation. With only the usual variations?'

Nadd checked. 'Yes. Mere tweaks. Well within parameters.'

'Sourcing each one from a different genetic mass takes care of the cloning issues we encountered at first. Let's see. Yes... Good balance of similarities and differences. Normal variations in set-up and continuance procedures. Adjustments based on experience.'

'So? Where do we go from here?' Nadd was impatient.

'Focus the monitoring on him,' I said. 'Full time – wherever his thoughts take him. We must be careful about what new experiences we introduce to his pseudo-environment. No completely new scenarios until the next review in six shifts. Increase the sedation a fraction – one percent?'

Herry did it. I rotated, and slid away to other pressing matters.

***

Well, maybe I do feel a bit groggy, and I can't remember what we were doing last night. There's nothing unusual there – it was crap on the vizzies. I had something really nice to eat. Oh, I remember, I had a drink. Warrha Special Reserve. It was like celebrating; can't remember what, but I was in a good mood, like everybody was. Somebody was excited, anyway.

Still, today looks like being boring.

Why am I walking this way again? I've been down here twice before. There's nothing new along here. Ahh, except that crystic knoll. Surely, this is the view of it from the other side – coming down from the house. How am I seeing that view from this direction? Is all of this false?

That's strange ... the house near the edge had green door on this side, but now it's on the front. I seem to recall that it's been the other side previously. Perhaps with a porch? Oh – it is the other side now. Did that just happen? Or is it me?

I'm going down to have a look.

Oooh, that hurts as soon as I stray. Alright – perhaps I don't want to go that way today, after all. Maybe tomorrow? I want to go somewhere new. I want to feel it; taste it; see it very close-to.

***

'He's becoming more adventurous. We can't increase the sedation – it'll damage structures that are only just forming.' We looked at the mass that was sealed in the rectangular glass vat, shaping up, collecting itself together, differentiating its internal parts.

'It's too fast. He's abnormal.'

'Maybe not,' I considered, mostly in hope. 'Maybe the others were slow?'

'Slow, maybe, but *they're* all the same, so *they're* normal.' Nadd and Herry both nodded.

'That's only our idea of what's conventional for them,' I pointed out. 'We don't actually know. Maybe we're getting better at initial mixes and subsequent care. What's the condition of the starter mass now?'

'Here, the screen. Let's see…' Nadd scrutinised the data. 'No skin yet, amorphous overall structure, but increasingly complex and differentiated internal structures – the organs. Actually, the body-mass seems to be consolidating itself into a smaller and smaller volume.'

Herry peered closely. 'Indeed, the weight of the internal mass is well below average for its length of existence. Number 23 is focusing its progress into a mass that is very much smaller than any others have been – instead of the whole mass shaping and organising itself as a complete, finished thing.'

'Thing? Call it Life, Herry. *Life* – don't be scared of the word. Even if it is carbon-oxygen-based.'

***

This not taste like last one. And I not seen that face before. I not reach to it. Something happen inside me. I not remember yesterday… I frightened… Not think so good. What happen to me?

***

'Coyo?' Nadd sought me out. 'About 23. Physical progress is going way different to all the others. I mean, look at it – it's reorganising its internals everywhere. It's a total reversion of normal trends. Utter failure. Mental processes are reverting to absolute basic – as if it had never thought anything before. We're losing it.'

'*He*, Nadd, you're as bad as Herry sometimes. *He* is a Type 2.'

I went through the banks and vizzies with him, and had to agree on what he was saying. 'You seem to be right: he's ungrowing. Taking steps back, in a

175

developmental direction he didn't even come from. The others were much larger, more nearly completed at this stage. 23's losing mass rapidly. He's shrinking physically and mentally.'

'Also,' Nadd pointed to the data blips, 'its proportions are changing – its head is still large; eyes big; arms and legs diminishing. See Number 25, two podules along? That's a perfectly standard Type 1, but it's more than twice the current size of 23, and has the regular breadth of mental processes. That's routine – start at a hundred pin-weights, add the genetic seed material, and stir: it begins to differentiate its internal existence. It gains pseudo-memories, becomes aware, thinking and awakened. It will eventually commence movement and speech. That process has been tried and tested over ten years; ninety percent success rate. We have successfully produced twenty-two specimens. They appear to *consolidate* their pre-creation awareness, and then enlarge and change after some years. This one's gone wrong.'

'The trouble,' I told him, 'is that we don't know truly what "perfectly normal" is for these creatures, Nadd. It's as though 23 is redesigning himself – gone back to the vat and started again on a fresh pattern. Perhaps an internally-driven one. Look how small the central mass has become. It's concentrating itself.'

'You mean, we may have misunderstood their basic structure, or growth progression, when we started? And now this one knows the right way, and it's re-designing itself on its own standard pattern?'

'I think that's a possibility,' I agreed. 'What's the mental progression?'

'The same radical reversion: regressive and erratic. It's totally different from the others, Coyo.'

We studied the summary data and the details. 'Number 23 seems to be rejecting the pseudo-memories we've supplied, and is creating others, much more than any others did. He's reverting to the blank template – might not even be a Type 2 any longer.'

'Ever since that simple difference in the position of the light switch triggered something in its thinking. A single artefact in its pseudo-environment?'

'Yes. I'm sure that's what made him first suspect his environment was false – the light switch, then the trees, the buildings, faces of the other creatures, the food, recent activities. It could have been anything that wasn't consistent in his pseudo-memories. It simply happened to be the light switch that started a chain reaction in his mental processes. He began to question everything – recall, conjecture, projection to past and future.'

'He's certainly rejecting the seedling thoughts that we transfer from the others. You think he could be forming his own memories?'

'To be honest, Nadd, I hadn't thought about that. Number 23 seems to be just blanking them all out, wiping his screen clean, as it were. It might be that he's now waiting for new experiences to come, so that he can begin to form his own thoughts and memories. I think we should ask the other Yabanci about this one. They seem to have a racial pattern within them. See if they can come up with any genetic-memory concepts... ideas about precedents... if they have any idea what's occurring with this one.'

'You showed Number 4 the one with two heads, didn't you? And the one with the fluked tail?'

'Yes. She knew they were well outside the standard pattern for their species, and promised never to tell anyone that I showed her: the Council would not approve, and it might not go down well with the other Yabanci. Most of my time is spent with the Yabanci nowadays, especially Number 23. No-one sees them more than I do. I know them, individually, and as a group. They're a mass of contradictions. That's why we can learn so much from them as a species. I have some basic understanding of them. Not, of course, like they know themselves.'

'They only know what we taught them.'

'No! You know better that to say that, Nadd. They interpret and project in ways we can't imagine. They intuit – they're so different, as if thinking on a different plane. I know it sounds implausible, but it's possibly a higher plane.'

'That's ridiculous, Coyo. Let's continue constant monitoring and not read too much into anything, hmm? Maintain current levels and types of input? Review in six shifts?' Nadd glowed around the base of his antennae whenever he tried to appear decisive.

***

'This Council review continues,' Chancellor Skeen said. 'We've taken views and data into account, including the costings and projected benefits. There isn't an overall pattern of consensus. Our vote will thus not be binding or final. Currently, we wish to gauge the balance of opinion within the Council before we request wider views. So, if we go to a preliminary vote, now...'

The lights showed – red, red, red, mine – a green. Red, red, red, another green. Red; a last red. This was

178

worse than I'd feared – they'd terminate the whole Programme for Re-creation of Alien Species if this went through, because Number they believed 23 to be another failure.

Sliding higher, I re-tuned my delivery pattern before addressing them. 'You know my position here i/c Practicalities and Repercussions. I was at the initial meeting 11 years ago when the vote was taken not to eradicate all trace of these things. All we possessed back then was a theory and some tiny unidentifiable scraps of decomposed organic material. It took Hoig's genius to recognise they might be the dusty remains of a form of life.' And then to propose this wonderful project. It has been an amazing success. We have created twenty-two totally alien beings! It's astounding. To stop now would be a terrible mistake.'

I looked up. They did not have a positive emanation between them. Short-minded c... councillors. I continued, 'This endeavour illuminates new ways for our own advances in knowledge. The Yabanci are a completely unknown life-form – almost purely organic, with only traces of metallic elements – around four parts in ten thousand of bodymass, of which ninety percent is iron. Our advances in studying them have been astonishing. We still know nothing of their mental processes and levels of intelligence; their reproduction techniques; continuance schedules; self-repair patterns and so on. They partake in mental digressions such as we've never encountered before – *emotions*, as I call them. Perhaps they don't grow until they divide, or vice versa, as we and the plantoids do. Organic growth on the carbon-oxygen spectrum is a closed circuit to us. We have no idea why they are divided into two variant types

179

instead of twelve basics plus variations. Possibly there's some mechanism for bi-specimen reproduction, in which each somehow contributes to the formation of a new member? Perhaps divide as they grow larger, and re-mould a new one from the two smaller masses? We have noted several morphological differences, of course, but are unsure of their significance.

I didn't pause too long, in case someone interrupted. 'With more than twenty living beings now created, and five more in the processors, we're well on the way to creating a viable, self-sustaining group, once we discover how they reproduce.'

'Are you saying they need much longer to grow, or mature?'

'Perhaps so—'

'But I understand that each of them is brought from its container at three hundred days. They are all fully formed at that time, are they not? And should be capable of reproducing themselves? Are you saying they need longer to mature?

I knew they'd be difficult about the whole matter – or about anything that involved costs. 'Eleven years is the oldest one we have at present; physically, she has changed little in that time, but mentally, she has developed tremendously. Eleven years would be plenty long enough for the plantoids, but barely a quarter of the time we'd need, of course. Each Yabanci specimen is a one-off. We have never extracted and developed more than one specimen from the same initial sample. There are clear micro-differences from one to another. Perhaps we need to keep experimenting until we find a correct pairing?'

The members were definitely unimpressed. 'I beg you not to destroy this latest specimen and the rest of the Yabanci. Their body designs are flexible, not rigid. Understanding this is of immense importance. I have an intuit about this small creature; like the Yabanci have intuits. Yes, I expect I've gained that from them.'

The council members weren't on my side. I needed to do something drastic or they would terminate the whole Yabanci project.

**

Ten days later, I addressed them again. 'I have reached a conclusion about the Yabanci. I am confident that you will agree to continue, and even expand, the project.

'I spoke with Number 4, a Type 1 Yabanci – the primary kind, conveniently referred to as a "she". Right from the commencement, I have liked them all – Yes, I admit that's a Yabanci-kind of feeling. Most especially, I have increasingly liked Number 4. Some years ago, I asked her to look at two specimens that were abnormal. She agreed they were far outside the standard pattern for their species, not some metamorphic stage; and that we should destroy them before permitting true self-awareness to develop. I trust her, as well as like her.'

'Yes, yes. What relevance is this to the present matter?' The Council Senior was probably overdue for an oilya change.

'Monitoring indicates,' I refused to be intimidated, 'that Number 4 has recently undergone various interesting changes to her physical morphology, plus chemical balances within her, and even the style and stability of her mental processing.

181

'As a result of our discussions, we both believe she is rapidly approaching maturity. This would constitute a major stage in the Yabanci's reproductive advances. We had previously believed that our specimens were fully grown when they were extracted from their original containers, although we were aware of diverse very slow changes in succeeding years. I now believe these deviations have been some kind of gradual catching-up process, as though they were indeed full-sized, but not matured. And now the actual maturation process has arrived, for Number 4, anyway.

'This would be the worst possible time to destroy them and the whole Yabanci Experimental Growth Project, after these past eleven years nurturing her—'

'So you say. You have not said why.' Senior was becoming even more impatient.

'This abrupt commencement of her maturation event; the advent of Number 23; and our discussions with her and specimens 1, 2 and 3 – who are all "He-Types" of course – were leading us to believe that several Yabanci, including Number 4, will shortly be sufficiently ripened to reproduce a copy of themselves, divide into two units, or whatever—'

'You say, "*were* leading"? You changed your mind? Do get to the point, Coyo. You become more – what is it you call it? Emotive? Every time we see you.' Second Senior interrupted again. 'You're allowing their traits to imbue you. Maybe you need to be re-programmed as well?'

'Now,' I was beginning to not-like Second Senior; I pointedly uncurled an antenna in his direction. 'We believe that Number Four's maturation is, in effect, the precursor to their reproduction, and that Number 23 would be the primary product of their normal reproductive process.

'To enquire further, I took Number 4 to the growth vats, where the containers are. I confess I experienced several moments of emotion – Yabanci-type unthinking-thinking – when I opened 23's observation port so she could see the creature within.

Within myself, I anticipated an emotional reaction on her part. I anticipated a response that we have classified as Emotion 3a – Distress. I anticipated that, in empathy, I would also experience this emotion – and also be distressed.'

'Empathy? What's that?'

'It's a thought-emotion by which they create pseudo-links with each others' minds. It was as though I had formed an emotive link with her, in anticipation of her distress. For myself, this manifested itself in a rise in my oilya temperature of one degree, and unaccountably emitted an overflow from the ducts around my sensory structures.

'Number 4 looked at the thing in the vat – Number 23 – deformed and retarded in physique. She was silent for eight beats, then produced her shrieking sound. At that point, she grabbed me, threw her arms around me and pressed at me. It was most emotive. More extreme than on any other occasion with any other specimen.

'No, not Class 3a Distress but Class 1 – Joy.'

'Joy?'

'Yes, indeed. I experienced my first-ever such strangeness – it is a contagious emotion. And one that is most... elevating. My selenoidals overheated; my circulation increased by a full eight percent; and my oilya overflow rose a further two points.'

183

'Did Number 4 say anything when it looked at Number 23?'

'Indeed. She said, in an Extreme Emotive Class 1 Joy-voice, "Coyo! Coyo! It's a *baby!*"'

***

THE SILVERSMITHS

'This workmanship is amazing,' Arianne was reaching for piece after piece. 'It's beautiful. So much better than I've ever created.' Not a trace of resentment, just admiration and envy at the skill and imagination that anyone could create such a stylish range of silverwork. So many variations, so many designs.

And the price. About half what I'd have expected. The locals hereabouts obviously didn't know good stuff when they saw it. The offer was unbelievable: Forty percent reduction if you bought five items. No problem there. I could see at least a dozen that Arianne would wear – or my sisters, or friends on the Christmas card list. Fifty percent off for twelve or more. It was ridiculous. At that rate we could practically buy the rest of their stock for tuppence.

It was our first time on this French market. Obviously: it was the first time we'd been to this part of France, right on the German border in Alsace. A sprawling move-every-day market – a trödelmarkt – with fruit and veg, tools and implements, textiles and clothing, household bits. But it had been this jewellery stall that caught our attention, Arianne and me. Almost all silverwork – bracelets, necklaces, earrings, it was beautiful. The finest, most delicate work we'd ever seen. Part-time dealers ourselves, and Arianne dabbling in silver-working, we were in the best position to appreciate it.

We sifted and sorted, put aside, dropped in our tray. At this price, we could re-sell them in our shop back in England, where we sold ores, crystals and minerals from

Britain and the USA, plus Arianne's jewellery, and some high-quality fossils that I prepped up. We'd come over with our Tranny Van full to the back windows with stock to sell on our stall, but that wouldn't be until next week, at the annual trade fair in Sainte Marie – the Minereaux Expo. Today was holiday.

Other folk were coming and going, making a single purchase, but the male stallholder was hanging near us, presumably making sure we weren't on the thieve. But we chatted about the designs and the workmanship, and the price and would he mind if we bought more to resell back home?

Although not fluent, we manage in French, German and Italian, and have a smattering of half-a-dozen others. My problem is remembering which is which, and I tend to come out with sentences that are a mixture of three or four different languages. But around here, folk are used to the mix and we all understand each other perfectly.

Except this guy and, when she joined us in a quiet spell, his good lady. And a very good lady she was, too – most attractive – Scandinavian Beauty type. They stumbled in their speech more than we did, but they picked it up quickly. Remarkably quickly, actually. And we were complimenting them on the delicacy of their silverwork, the modernity, the abstractions, the esoteric style of some pieces.

They were edging, hinting, 'How many do you want? We can make more. Same, similar, your own designs, any size.' They were hesitantly, almost shyly, eager.

We weren't looking to cheat them on the price, so when they said seventy-five percent reduction, special offer for more than, say a hundred, we felt guilty when we said, 'Yes. Yes, yes, yes.'

They could have a load ready by morning. But this market closed and moved on that night – twenty k along the valley.

'Well,' we said, 'if you're local, we could come to your workshop. That would be interesting.'

'Er, no,' they edged. Glanced at each other. 'Perhaps we might come to you tomorrow?'

***

So that was decided upon. I gave very precise directions to the campsite where we were staying but, being new to this region, they weren't certain of roads and directions. I drew a map; loaned them my satnav with the camp logged in as a favourite; the code for the gates; and the campsite's own brochure. They didn't seem too sure even then, but decided they would manage. Somehow.

Sure enough, there they were, outside our caravan, with a large travel bag each. 'Blimey,' I said, trying to pick one up to take under the awning. 'There's some weight in that.'

But she picked it up and smiled. What struck me wasn't the phenomenal ease with which she did it, but the smile – exactly how Arianne smiles. I hadn't noticed that yesterday.

She was Adelia. He was Viktor. That sounded Finnish to me, so I tried them with a few Finnish words I knew – "Kiitos, kippis. Minulle seuraava." Which means, "Thanks – cheers. My round next." Which is very useful in a Helsinki bar when someone has bought you a drink. But not on a French campsite – they looked blank.

We sat and chattered in Franglais-German-Italian and snatches of all sorts. Tending more and more to less-stilted English. They didn't seem to be in any hurry, and

187

we looked at all the stuff they'd brought – we said they must have a massive stock? They ummed and ahhed a bit. Looked shifty, and said they had much silver.

'Perhaps, if you deal in metals and ores and such things, it may be that you could obtain some unusual metals for us?' Viktor asked.

'Possibly? *Soon?*' Adelia the Platinum Blonde edged. They looked as if they had just signed their own death warrants with some terrible admission of guilt. 'Mmm? Like what?'

'I believe they are called lithium, graphene, sulfur and chromium trioxide...'

I looked at Arianne. It was an odd list. 'What for?' I asked.

They were cagey. Shuffled in their seats...

'Okay,' I took the pressure off them, 'Sulfur? No problem. Cheap. I believe Graphene is available. It's cheap as low purity powder; but probably twenty times as much for research-quality sheets. It depends what you want it for...?' Still no answer. 'The lithium? Not sure. Lithium batteries are extremely expensive. A big one, medical quality, would cost as much as fifty pieces of your silverwork. Then you'd have to extract the lithium yourselves. You could?'

They looked uncertain.

'And... What was the other? Chromium trioxide? Not one I'm familiar with.'

'Google it,' my ever-knowledgeable wife said.

Sure enough, there was a ton about it. 'What colour do you want? Green or purple? Paste or powder? Like I said, depends what you want it for, and what facilities you have for processing and purifying it?'

'You could obtain this for us? All of these?' They virtually spoke in unison.

We both shrugged, 'According to Google, yes, it looks like it. In one form or another. I wouldn't know which would be best for you – their purity, oxides, melded in with other materials – like in a battery.'

Viktor decided to be a little more forthcoming. 'It is for batteries. Ours burst – vaporised. We have stores of other materials, but we need these.'

'What you going to do? Make your own?' I was finding this hard to believe.

'It is not difficult.' He sounded more Germanic saying it like that. 'But they have to be precisely correct to our spess… if… i…'

'You can do that?' Adelia was almost as wonderstruck as I was at the idea of making high-spec batteries.

They both nodded.

This was more than merely interesting. I took my life in my mouth by making a suggestion without consulting Arianne first. 'It looks as if they're all available, but could cost a fortune, depending on the purity, and the amount you require.' They seemed relieved. I carried on. 'I could order samples of these now. But delivery? I'm not sure about timings. It depends where they're coming from.'

It took maybe an hour to order a decent amount of each of the four materials – in different forms. Then, naturally, I had to pay on PayPal. Over two thousand pounds! Sure, we had plenty in the feeder account for PayPal, but it was a bit of a risk, with strangers. 'It means staying here for at least another week, but we're in the area for another ten days or more, for the duration of the Minerals Fair in Sainte Marie, anyway.'

***

The first sample quantities of sulfur and the chromium trioxide arrived at noon the next day. That's eBay for you, with extra charges.

Adelia and Viktor looked relieved more than delighted. He hugged her. 'Perhaps we will be alright yet.'

They were back next day in the hope of another delivery. No luck. I tried tracking the orders, but it wasn't possible. 'We'll have to wait. Did you try those from yesterday?'

Yes, they had, and they could work with them, but wanted to see the other available versions before deciding on which ones to order larger quantities of.

The orders hadn't all arrived even the following week when we were due to set up at Sainte Marie for the big Minereaux Expo. That's what we'd spent months planning and preparing for. But we were feeling totally responsible for Adelia and Viktor by then, and were torn. They seemed to know so little sometimes; they never ate or drank or went to the toilet while with us; always wore the same clothes, and seemed to look a bit more like me and Arianne every time we met them.

Eventually, we had to have a deep-serious chat, not about the costs – their silver easily covered what we'd spent already. But if I was ordering greater quantities then. A - it would take time; B - it would cost considerably more; C - we would be back in England by the time some of the items arrived, and the suppliers wouldn't deliver to addresses other than the one where my account was registered; and D - I wanted to know more about them.

We resolved the problems with a fair bit of soul-searching, and Viktor opening up a little more – 'We have silver in abundance,' he admitted. 'Also of – I think you call it platinum? We use it in shielding and bulkhead plates. Perhaps you might still wish to visit our workshop?'

Next morning, they were waiting in a lorry park near Sélestat, at a huge transport container. It was enormous inside. 'It's a Tardis,' I said. And it was full of the most technical stuff I've ever seen anywhere, including on Star Wars Movies.

'The Kosmika Angeo is a somewhat elderly Morph vessel,' Adelia apologised.

'She has occasional problems. We carry spares and repairs, but it's been a long voyage. Battery problems, instead of the usual shielding breaches. So, we are marooned here,' Viktor said, 'of all things, by three exploded batteries.'

We stared all around. I ventured to suggest, 'You're not human. *Are you?*'

They managed to look sheepish. I mean – *Aliens, looking sheepish.* It doesn't happen in Doctor Who. They were embarrassed by a simple error in a starting procedure, it seemed.

'And you don't really look like this, do you?'

'You wouldn't want to see.' Adelia was very sure about that.

'I think I might.' I was mad curious. 'Just for a moment, if you like.'

They seemed to confer, and began to unform. Like reshaping. A foot shorter, reptilian at first, then more downy-feathery with huge-eyed, owl-like faces. Wow! That was just awesome. My mouth was wide open. I loved them, wanted to greet them and hug them anew. And tendrils, like fine tentacles. Like a hairy octopus. They maintained it for a few seconds while I wished I had a camera. And reformed to resemble me and Arianna more than ever.

I commented that they looked more like us. 'Going to take us over, are you?'

'It is you we see most, so your images tend to dominate our thoughts when we undergo the process. The platinum is *here*. We carry out the silverwork *here*. Our batteries fit *here*. *This* is what we eat... and drink.'

We peered. It smelled alright: quite meaty, like haggis. Though the wriggly bits were a tad off-putting.

'We grow it in vats. It is self-perpetuating.'

The sightseeing and pleasantries over, we talked Immediate Future. We'd remain at the same campsite to receive the rest of the deliveries, and commute to Ste Marie each day of the Expo. Not a lot of extra bother – we liked this site; and were overwhelmed by the thought of knowing *aliens*. The site proprietor was most entertained by the sudden flurry of parcels, especially when we decided to order more of the quick-delivery items, so Adelia and Vik could be getting on with something.

They hoped to manufacture one battery, which would enable them to lift off two, perhaps three, times, but a single one wouldn't recharge correctly.

***

For the week of the Expo, we were over-the-moon excited, selling, taking orders and renewing contacts with buyers and suppliers of our usual trade items –

192

especially some new American fossil-finds. Meanwhile Vik and Adelia checked at the campsite every day for deliveries, and prepared for battery re-building in their container.

The most unbelievable part was when we arranged to return to England at the end of our holiday-cum-expo time. It hadn't occurred to any of us how we would all do it.

Sure, Arianne and I could drive back, with a one-night stopover near Calais, as intended. But them?

It was eventually resolved by me driving back with Adelia: she would deliberately re-mould herself a fraction more to match the passport.

I was so insanely jealous of Arianne – travelling in a space ship, for Gawdsake! In a spaceship called Cosmic Angel, even if it looked like a transport container at the moment. It was out of this world – literally. Adelia and I talked and talked and she un-morphed at night at Camping St. Louis, near Calais. After an hour, I had to sleep in the awning.

It was un-nerving the first time she forgot, and turned octopoid-owlish on the P&O ferry on the way back – she'd never seen loose, sloshing, water before, and was completely awed by the sight. And again on the M25 when some twollop cut us up. I fleetingly thought she might have magical powers that would vaporise him and his Audi. Alas, 'twas not to be.

We called Arianne's phone from Trowell services on the M1, and she and Viktor were ready to join us. An hour later, immensely relieved, we arrived home, a few miles north of Nottingham. I turned Adelia loose to look around the place – including the back garden. We aren't overlooked, so there's no-one to query a container

193

appearing in the middle of my back lawn half an hour later. An over-excited Arianne was all over me with having been in Space – 'Right round the whole fucking world.' 'Scuse her language.

I think Adelia's welcome to Viktor was much the same level of excitement about all the water and waves and huge, tasty-looking, seagulls – something about 'Akwa akwa ubikwita.'

Some of the deliveries had arrived, and the rest came in the next ten days. Vik and Addy were patient, and disappeared into their container for long periods. Eventually, they were ready to test fly, and leave.

Of course, I knew it was coming. And I knew I'd miss them. Who wouldn't?

'Test flight,' Adelia said. 'You wish to come?'

'Do I? I clamoured at the container door, my best leather jacket on, and camera in the pocket.

We went round the moon!

***

All delighted, and sad – them to be leaving; us to be losing them. 'Keep the space clear, hmm?' Viktor said.

'It wasn't actually a space: it was a lawn and flowerbed.'

'With your permission, I can register this plot as a recommended stop-off. Landing charge a bar of platinum? Would that be appropriate?'

A bar? 10 kg? 300,000 US dollars. 'Er, sounds good to me. Do they want tours around the area while they're here? Included in the landing fee? There's lots of open water… if that's what you're into? King's Mill Reservoir. And trees – we have Sherwood Forest on our doorstep. Some pet shops with, er, birds and fish. Or a zoo? If they might make you feel at home?'

They both smiled. 'Perhaps we would all like a photograph together with the Kosmika Angeo, before we leave?'

***

That was in the summer four years ago. We are now incredibly wealthy, as hosts, and tour guides around Nottinghamshire, the Peak District – and even to Mablethorpe and Skegness when we found how much they craved the sight of unbridled water. And even the sound and feel of it. The beach and the sea were mind-shattering for the groups.

Apparently, we are already number 39 on the interstellar equivalent of Airbnb's list of most-sought destinations. And rising. This year, we even had two parties who weren't avian-octoids. The Arthros' requirements, with their mandibles and carapaces, were simple enough. But the invertebrate fishy lot, the ones who looked like sea anemones, were an absolute nightmare on the bus, and even worse when we got to Saltfleet.

The seals on the beach at Donna Nook didn't stand a chance.

IN THE UNLIKELY EVENT OF AN EMERGENCY...

"In the unlikely event of an emergency..."

The metal poster screwed to the bulkhead held a mass of fine print. The whole length of the passenger compartment was festooned with identical copies on the doors, the back of every seat; above all the windows. My seat in the middle of the rear passenger section was well-worn, but comfy enough. There was too much information to absorb, much less to study, and then check round the whole compartment to see what each paragraph referred to: assembly points, uniforms, location of the airlock doors, the different meanings of three blasts, five blasts... So I blink-vidded the notice to internalise later, but it was in, er, Jamet. Who the plonk speaks Jamet? Or Sortek? Ah, Standard, and even that's in the Colonial Stang version.

Unlikely event? If it was all that unlikely, why so many notices and instructions? Yes, I know – Regulations. With the complexity of them, you'd think they didn't want anyone to survive an incident.

A vessel like the Isobel Moon? She's the typical style of old space shuttle: long, tubular craft split into two 48-seater passenger compartments, divided by a snug crew-cabin in the middle. That's because people don't like to look all the way down the whole length of a 96-person cylinder. Eight rows of seats in each, with a pull-rope along the central aisle is much more comfortable on the mind. Fine on this kind of routine-schedule run – thrice a day between MoonBase Blue and Orbit Central. Nothing's going to happen, not with standardised docking at both ends, using regular berth or anchor points, depending on the other traffic.

Comfortable and convenient, yes, but, safety-wise, it's a mess: any kind of bump on a craft this size and design, and she'd pop wide open, de-air and impel herself into a solar orbit, and eventually be disposed of.

She drifted away from the terminal smoothly.

Yes, nicely done. It should be, too, with their experience.

Captain Peedy in command. He'd be in the control room at the front, or maybe the slave one at the rear, behind me. I knew Jack in the old days. He and I went in the Service as rating cadets at the same time, and ran on some of the first Wild Voyages together... Test-flew a whole range of military and civil-commercial craft... Pioneered exploration of the Celdene Cluster – where there was all the fighting, yes. We did ridiculous, risky things in hyper-traumatic bursts, and were shit-scared. In a rosy glow for a short time afterwards, we were heroes. But most of the time, we were bored silly, which was probably why we took such risks.

I peered behind and in front, thinking I might get a chance to speak with him, but there were no staff or crew around. Later, maybe...

Jack eventually left the Service as a Full SN Captain, but I had the accident, and was kicked upstairs. That's what they do with crippled half-blind has-beens, complete with promotion to Commander of the Fleet by the time I was booted out – but not even allowed to be a crew-member on any vessel since then. Gratitude, huh?

Jack's had five-plus years on this run, and oodle-years on others before that. Same with his Mate and the Docksman in the old days, too.

So, yes, they should be good at it. Slight feeling of the motor coming live as we turn... Nicely, Jack.

They still they consult me on oddments, or wheel me out as the Front Man for some new project; or figurehead at a conference, or the grand opening of something wondrous. With my kind of ancient experience, they like the face and voice of olden times for the vids, and I still have the honorary title of Commodore, after all. In truth, I do quite enjoy the attention – like the girl who settled the passengers, fetched drinks and nibbles, acted as though she knew me. Quite a few people do, especially when I wear the uniform. It's nice.

Mauteen, her name was, came to chat after everyone was settled. Both lounge cabins were practically full: several ships were up there waiting for their remaining passengers to arrive. 'Come sit through here,' she invited me, 'the central crew compartment has plenty of space during the trip.'

'Love to.' She had to be better company than the pair of overweight Sorteks next to me. There'd be a drink, and pseudo-gravity. Comfier than null.

'Best be quick; that was the twenty-second buzzer. We're just finishing positioning for WayPoint Four. We'll fire off in a mo.'

We float-pulled on the fixed rope, down the aisle to the crew room. The mini-airlock was open. We squeezed in and waited for it to auto-close off the passenger area, and open the inner door to the crew room. The sartory music was already echoing in there.

*

A slight judder.

Space ferries don't judder. They can't – they have better things to do. I slammed a hand against the emergency lock. It sealed instantly. Felt the pressure suck and tighten. Shike – that had been fast – there was already a vacuum the other side, where we'd come from, only a second before.

The inner mechanism? Huge relief when it opened. We toppled into the crew space; about spacious enough to lie down in. Yeah, it did have pseudo-grav.

'What?' Mauteen was saying, 'What?'

'We took a hit. We've de-pressured.'

She was calm. Didn't believe it. 'What's your game?'

'See?' There was a single portow. The view was black. No... a point of light... drifting vertically downwards. 'We've taken on a bit of a spin.'

'That can't happen.'

'It has. This's the "Unlikely Event". It's happened. It's trouble.'

'But the Isobel Moon is so small—'

'She's at least a thousand deadweight, and that takes a helluva lot of momentum to set her in motion. We've had a collision. She's cracked open. De-aired.'

Mauteen was bewildered. She stood up, reaching for the door handle – all chrome, plasteel, glassite. Every compartment sealable.

'You can try. It won't open.'

She did try. It was rammed solid. Held by a dozen titanium dead-bolts and the pressure-vacuum differential. 'How come you're so calm? What about the others?'

'Passengers? Dead. Guaranteed. They're the other side of that vacuum door. We're holed somewhere through there. The other crew? I dunno – depends on what the control cabin's like.

'Main one's at the front. Same airlock as this. Self-sealing.'

'Let's stay calm, then. We should be okay. They'll rad out for help.'

'Maybe not.' She looked dead already. 'They jam the door open so they can chat with the passengers, let them come up and see the instruments, take the selfies. It helps relations. Oh, looger! Look at that...'

The vast side of a ship was drifting past the portow. No sign of damage. But we could only see a fraction of it.

If that ship's damaged, there could be huge leakage there, too – really mass casualties. They're hardly going to bother with us if that's their priority. Best not mention that to Mauteen just yet.

We watched as our view slowly spun away. Drifting, our slight spin stayed the same. No idea which direction we were headed in – infinitely the greatest probability was out into nowhere space. Ninety-nine point nine percent of our spherical surrounding was empty blackness.

'The Vac Distress will have gone off,' I told her.

But without any active voice backup, they'll leave us, assume no survivors. This's only an old crate with little value.

Looking at each other in the slightest of glows from the self-lit panels, I got the impression it hadn't started sinking in with Mauteen.

'We can see into the passenger compartments – and the forward control room,' she said.

Now she tells me. 'How?'

The fore-facing airlock door had a circular iris panel about face-sized. I held her back and looked first. At least they all had their backs to us. Heads at all angles. Arms floating. A red cloud of blood droplets: the lungs of some of them had burst... leaked. Messy.

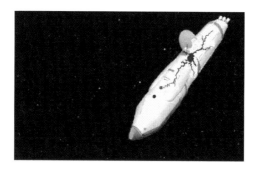

Damn, I can taste it again. Upsetting. Like the other time this happened.

Right at the far end, the open doors of the forward control room proved that there were no flight crew survivors. Two loose-floating bodies were partly visible inside, and maybe the third one's booted feet. That'll be Jack Peedy.

'You want to see?'

She did. Briefly. Turned to me and fingered the iris shut. Swallowed. 'Same at the back?'

I did the same with the rear airlock door. The two fat Soreks on my row both had blood halos and poppy eyes. Every single one was dead. Rows of ghastly faces – bloody mouths and poppy eyes. 'Yes, all dead. The two passenger compartments are connected. This crew cell would have been fitted later, separate skin. You don't want to see.'

But she did. 'The rear airlock door's open, but the inner one's closed – there'll be air inside the back control room.'

I peered... my eyes still ain't that good.

Same screw wheel lock at the far door as this one. Eight rows of seats down the length of the passenger lounge... looks a helluva long way. Not as far as the other time: but that hadn't had obstructions, like a mass of arms and legs straying across the aisle.

Reality Stage Two was beginning to sink in – we were stuck in a tiny crew room with a vacuum space forward and aft. 'The rear controls are a slave for the master set?'

She nodded.

'Koh... Should be working then. Might be worth a dash.'

Terrible thought. I'm shaking just to think about it... Like there's any choice except sit and die.

'Why not the fore one? We know those controls work.'

'They did five minins ago. But I don't know how they jammed both airlock doors open up front, or how to free them. Or how long it'd take to pressurise the whole cabin. Sudden vacuum like that – gauges could have burst, screens blanked; anything. The rear ones are backup, mostly for emergency use. They should connect directly with the motor. We wouldn't be able to access so much info, but a working rad would be enough for us.

Damnit. I'm going to have to try the dash. Must rehearse the revolving screw handle the other side. Where's the Air-In button? Confirm button? 'We don't carry internal suits, I suppose?'

She shook her head.

'You fancy sex?'

She shook her head.

'You want to make a fast-dash down there?'

Again the head shake.

So. I'm out of options. 'Tell me all about the doors, the handles, pressure sequence, timings, position of buttons. Anything that has to be clicked, locked, pulled out?'

'You're going through there? Past all the bodies? In the vac?'

'Tell me about choices, if you've other ideas.'

'But there's no big hurry: it's a long way into space before you meet anything. We have plenty of time. They'll come for us.'

'Unless you're heading towards the planet. In a tumbling, roll-over heap like this, we'd burn up, or break up, as soon as we hit the upper atmosphere. Now then…'

I was in a numb-mind non-breathing wide-awake coma by then. Merely the thought of it.

Last time had been too grim to think about. But I had to remember. The hurry hadn't been desperate then, but this time…

I kept looking out the portow. I could see the big ship we'd hit. Why the Shugg it had been there was anyone's guess. It looked like it had halted slap against the terminal. There'd be absolute mass casualties there. Our absence would scarcely have been noticed. No-one would bother to come after us; we couldn't wait here forever.

Decided. 'You must help me, Mauteen. Talk me through the layout over there. Is it a screw opening? Where's the re-pressure button? Any sequence? Yes, I know we've already said. We might have missed something. There's a Comms link here to there? The screen and pickup? Does it work?'

'Needs to be switched on at both ends.'

'How? Show me.' I felt over the pad to locate the On/Off toggle. She looked at me funny.

'I have to feel it. I don't see too good. And it'll probably worsen in the vacuum. I've... I've done it before.'

'Did you survive? Oh, er, stupid question.'

'Not intact: I got it wrong. Lost vision; lungs took a battering; guts ruptured. That adds up to me not seeing, eating or breathing so good since then. But I learned from that.'

'Oh?'

'Yeah, never do it again. Or make damn sure I do it right. I need you to tell me everything you know about that drive room, in case my eyes worsen this time.'

Can't delay any longer. She's becoming nervy. Not as nervy as me, I expect. Shuggs, I'm shaking. I don't think she realises this is simply a feel-a-bit-better way out – we're equally as dead as all the others. We've simply postponed it an hour.

She turned down my second offer for a farewell sex session, and I'd only become more confused if I learned anything else about the airlocks and rear control room, so I had to proceed with it.

We sort of nodded to each other and didn't make eye contact. I slid into the back-facing airlock. Shuggs, I was shaking so much. That was probably when I wet myself. Big mistake, that. A moment to press the cellophane across my eyes to slow down the near-instant evaporation. Sucked again on the mint chip, to create plenty of water around my tongue.

Spin the iris viewport open again. All those sightless, pale blue-tinted faces staring at me through the drifting cloud of red dots and globs.

Their arms shouldn't be too rigid yet; so I ought to manage at least part-way down the aisle. The pull-rope's taut, and straight down the centre...

'Let's go.' One last touch on the locked door behind me, and spin the unlock. Damn – the air sucked out in three seconds flat, it popped open.

Mouth wide open, I launched myself down the aisle. I've had plenty of practice at rope-pulling in null-grav – but so long ago. Hand over hand I went.

Suck the mint. Replace the moisture. My mouth's tight shut now, but dry already. Lungs drained, aching. *Shuggs – I remember that cool tickling inside.*

Heaving myself through the tangle of arms and faces. The blood blobs bouncing aside. Most of them solid. Hand over hand. Pulling...

Not too hard. Mustn't try to breathe. I can hold my breath for over a minin. But it ain't easy when there's no breath to hold. Shuggs shuggs shuggs... So slow... Too slow... Not seeing so good... Grey blurriness closing in. Need to press the cellophane tighter round eyes... Pull, pull, pull. I might last 90 seconds... Again. But that last time was in open space from a dead ship to a rescue tube that had drifted free of the airlock. Hell – one of us had to make the attempt that time, too.

Gasping on nothing.

I'm done already – no stamina these days.

Then I was there, scrabbling into the open airlock. Couldn't see much at all by then. The grey blur was darker, reddening all around. Feeling…

The door. Pull it closed. Handle? Where? So slow. So heavy. Come on, come on. come on…

I heaved, prayed and pulled, and felt the click as I searched for the air button and slapped everywhere but couldn't feel it. Where the shugg? Where? I went down, sinking on my knees and I damn knew it…

State I'm in after the last one, we didn't stand a chance.

Heard the air inlet hiss.

Too late…

*

Things were really black; except the red smears inside my head. And screwed up, really crampy in every muscle. *Shuggs. I haven't survived in this state, have I? Damnit. This's worse than being dead…*

I was breathing, sort of. Crackling inside, like one of them firecat beetles.

This's no way to live, every breath an agony. And not seeing anything. I don't want to go through the pain of standing up and trying to open the door into the rear control room. It's not worth the pain to come. Better to go now…

Dunno why I did it. My knees and other joints in my body seized up and screamed at me when I forced them to cooperate. I would'a cried if I'd had any water to spare. Flapping my hands round, I couldn't think about the inner door...

Wheel... press... spin... breathe... and falling in the rear engine compartment. No, not engine – control room – only some slave units.

Can't see a damn thing... shaking my head to try and force some sense into it and water in my mouth. Suck the mint...

Black and red was all I could see. Feeling... feeling... remembering what she'd said... *Trim... stabiliser... energy... power... heating... auto-log-on...*

I pressed them all: one had to be right. If something happened it might be noticed and they'd send rescuers. Or not.

Ah. That was the motor start-up.

I stopped it: no point sending us off somewhere unknown even faster.

Damn, I need to see... The external rad should be close... Under a flip-lid, did she say?

My breathing ragged – took as much effort as fumbling along the consoles, trying to remember where she'd said.

Maybe... maybe. Press and twist. This should open a link. These setups all have a different layout these days.

Something was warming up, or live, whatever. Saw a green-ness.

Green's for Good, isn't it? Surely, nothing with a green light would explode?

Tried to focus on it. Like swimming in muddy water. Saying things in the direction of the greeniness. Can't remember what. "Help" and stuff like that, I expect. I remember cursing the damn things and swearing a bit. Okay, a lot.

Going down again. Not enough air in my lungs. Cold inside. Cursing.

Actually, I do recall fragments after that. I remember shivering. And trying to turn over and sit against something. And peering all round as the red greyness receded to the outer half of my vision. I think I looked back down the passenger lounge; the corpses were still there. That might have been an imagined memory, though. Couldn't tell if she was there – thingy, Mauteen. I might have tried to find an internal rad to talk with her. Dunno. Don't recall any conversation particularly.

*

Noises – heavy vibes, anyway – and lurching.

We're breaking up. Must have hit the upper atmosphere. Maybe bouncing, rolling. Jerking about.

Light. Brilliant. All round.

Must be the Isobel Moon roasting on fire.

Clanking and swinging.

Come on, Come on. Get it over... Sorry, Mauteen...

'He's not crew. In uniform, though.' Somebody was in the control cell with me... slapping at me. Might have been a face...

Bit late for my eyesight to be coming back.

Somebody pulled at me. 'Shuggs, he's blue – still breathing, though.'

Lifting me. Dragging, and carrying me. Into a big echo-y place. Hurts my eyes.

Stop whinging. Must be laid down again. Can't move – strapped down. Freighter hold? Yeah. Must be. Cargo vessel grappled us inside.

Us? *Us!*

'Mauteen? Mauteen? You here?'

Mauteen survived alright. Better than me. There was food and drink in the crew's cell. Bag of nerves, though. All jangled-up inside. They got her out first. Then the passengers and Cap Peedy and the other two. Me last. Dunno why. Awkward to get to, I expect. Just another body. Seventy-eight altogether. Two survivors.

Two-ninety-four dead aboard the Crystal Bell that had a jammed side impellor and rolled against us. She was a passenger freighter. Someone had insisted on docking close-up, instead of taking the shuttle in – more fitting for VIPs in a hurry, they'd said. Taking the Ferryman now, they were.

I'm getting patched up, having lung-rebuild treatment – breathing better already. And they'll do me an eye job. 'They'll be good as new,' someone reckoned.

SNS had this televid session. It was a big docu-type investigation. History of both vessels and all that. Other incidents at MoonBase Blue... Captains and crew records scrutinised... Maintenance logs.

They realised I was me. 'Making a habit of it, are you, Comm?' and they dragged through the archives for the other incident. Vid of me pushing out the airlock of the Gunship Valiant without an outside suit or air. Steering with an airgun to the rescue tube that didn't reach across the gap. Forty-five seconds to cover the distance. Forty-five more while the tube re-pressured with me inside. Scariest thing was the pics: I looked so young then.

The TellyVee folk set up an interview with some survivors. All the survivors from the Crystal Bell were uninjured. The senior officers and engineers had unjammed the side impellors in time to prevent a complete catastrophe. But they hadn't actually felt anything: it was simply something registering on the dials. The passengers had either died at once, or been totally unaware that anything had happened. They'd had a retrospective mite-fright, as they say. Boring sods. That basically left only Mauteen and me with any direct awareness of the event, and any active involvement in its aftermath.

I was only up to the croaking stage by then. Rasping and smiling like a maniac, because I still didn't believe it. But they liked to have me there because I'm the only person to have survived two airless walks, as they call them nowadays.

She, bless Bishop Cotton's Little Green Socks, did most of the talking; recounting all of it from when she'd seen me entering the passenger cabin. 'I saw his name. And I knew him. From all the vids. And there he was, in person.'

Ha! "The Old Spacer," she called me. Just because I look a tad aged... The Old Spacer, indeed. But it's apparently a title of honour – The Old Spacer. So that was alright.

'So, of course,' she was going on, 'I seized my chance to actually speak with him, and I invited him into the crew's mid-cabin. I've always admired him. And in that gorgeous Commodore uniform...'

It was almost embarrassing. Almost.

All agog, she told them how almighty fast I'd been to seal us off. I'd calmed her, rehearsed the buttons and procedures. 'So professional, he was. So brave.' I thought she was overdoing it then, but I couldn't get a croak in sideways.

I heard her saying I was a sex maniac – I'd pestered her. Even my parting words had suggested sex, "in case it was our last breaths."

Shuggs, I tell you. My reputation! It soared. At my age. In my condition. 'I was merely attempting to keep up her spirits,' I say. 'Just trying to maintain crew morale.'

***

A LITTLE COOPERATION

I.Fine for us

'Clearly,' our leaders told us, 'the gods are displeased. Three years of poor harvests and sparse hunting success are clear evidence of their displeasure, here at Two-River Join. They have sent visions from the heavens, guiding thoughts. Our single-circle timber henge is insufficient, they say. Thus, we must build a greater henge of stone in their honour. Then the elk and the boar will return; our crops will flourish again, and the rains will come in the spring. The gods' commands are undeniable; their will is clear as melted snow.'

Some of us dared to protest that the Bow-to tribe, as guardians of the Afterlife, interpreted the will of the gods, not us. But our leaders said that the gods had chosen to speak to them, and they could not ignore their clear message.

'We need to be planting wheat and hunting for game, not digging holes to plant great stones,' we persisted. But our leaders insisted that the gods had spoken in detail and great clarity, and we must obey. So they planned our new henge: two wide stone circles of upright stones that would attract the sun, and focus its attention. Each stone would be twice the height of a man, with capstones joining with its neighbour. In the centre shall be an altar stone, our homage to the gods. We cleared the ground, sent men to find the stone quarry in Far Forest Hills, learned to move the huge blocks, and planned how we might raise them to the perfect upright position.

We realised the enormity of the task the gods had set us, but our leaders still refused to call a halt to the work, though we had neither the people nor the wealth for such an undertaking. 'If we starve, it is the will of the gods.' And so we laboured and starved, though not a single stone was yet raised in place, and our children were skin and bone.

But the Bow-to tribe had caught sounds of our work in the wind. They came, angry that we had dared to presume to know the will of the gods. Their anger erupted in violence: they demanded we cease the work, give them our plans. At first, they were sure we had spied on their earlier works, but realised the design and ambition were entirely our own, inspired by those self-same gods that they knew well. Though deeply offended, the Bow-tos saw the meaning in the plans, saw the hand of the gods therein, and admired the beauty as well as the scale of the new henge.

'Refill the holes you've dug,' they demanded. 'Replant the land with corn and crops. We have meat and milk aplenty. It is our destiny to create this henge, not yours.'

It was, in a way, a relief.

A hostage from each family was taken, to make sure the work was not restarted. From my family, I was chosen to be imprisoned in Bow-to Fort. Treated well enough, we heard their plans, watched the work on their stone henge, and sometimes laboured to dig the holes or drag the stones into place. Although the same henge we had planned, it was even larger: the circles wider, and higher. Instead of one altar stone, five formed an inner circle of capped, crystal-faced stone; a beautiful, magnificent sight. From the Higherworld of the Gods, it was an eye that looked back at them in awe.

Much of what the Bow-tos said was in admiration of our earlier imagination and plans.

'Its other-worldliness,' they said, 'is evidence of its origin among the gods. They have done this to ensure that our tribes cooperate together in this enterprise of ideas and strength, of fervour and faith.'

'This working together is fine for us,' I told my sister when she travelled through. 'I'm learning a lot here; there's a girl I like very much, and we are under the protection of the gods from this stone henge. Now, our people do not have to spend the harvest and hunting seasons digging huge holes and carrying vast stone blocks across the moors, like the Bow-tos do. Our design and their labours: we are achieving so much more that either tribe could have managed alone. It's good to cooperate, isn't it?'

***

II.   So Fruitful, hmm?

The Waterford Shipyard, in the south of Ireland, was where the master ship-wrights developed their innovative ideas for a whole new kind of fighting ship. Although only a small working company, they were keen, worked hard and had the good of the Catholic Church at heart.

'This design,' Master Devlin O'Conlon told everyone, 'will beat the English when the war looms. Our Catholic Spanish friends will see how revolutionary these craft are: how fast they are, how manoeuvrable. Low in the water, they are supremely stable, and large enough to carry great batteries of cannon that will destroy the Godless Vessels of the Protestant English. We call them "The Racing Ships". They are the future of sea warfare; a whole new kind of fighting at sea. They must remain unknown to the English foe.'

Devlin O'Conlon had a brilliant mind, superb craftsmen and wrights, master designers, the best of timbers and iron, and a huge mouth when he was drunk. The latter was his downfall.

Before dawn one day, the English raiding party, under the leadership of Sir Francis Drago, came ashore at three points along the River Suir and silently surrounded the shipyard at Ballinakill. As the workers were well into their morning's labour, the English struck, hard and fast. With little or no organised resistance, they took all the plans and drawings, burned the laid keel and skeletal ribs of the first trial craft, and threw great heaps of timber into the river. The builders of the revolutionary shapes of the three-master ships were taken prisoner, though O'Conlon and his two sons were killed when they resisted fiercely and loudly. Families of the senior ship-workers were given the choice of going with their men to England, or not.

'It was a well-carried-out raid, if I say so myself,' said Sir Francis. 'And so it should have been: for the whole strategy came to me in my prayers for guidance. The Lord God Almighty pointed me in that direction, to that precise shipyard. He showed me visions of those very ships, in *our* hands, and in action against the galleons of the Catholic hosts of Ireland and Spain. I went ashore with the first landing group, you know, to see for myself the truth in God's word and vision.'

'Indeed so, Sir Francis,' The Lord of the Admiralty complimented, spreading a set of drawings across the great table. They pored over them, tracing fingers along the raked bows and curving lines. 'These designs for racing ships are along similar lines to the ones we've been building; but theirs have improvements in the thinking of their designs at every stage and in every level. A merging of the two sets of ideas will amount to our secret weapon against the Spanish in the looming conflict.'

'Ay, Baron, the increased sail area, and this particular arrangement of sail choices, will make ours not only faster, but more able to change direction swiftly.' Sir Francis turned and signalled for three large models to be brought in, pointing out the specific choices of particular sets of sails for different kinds of sailing action,

'At the Admiralty, we've been developing new attacking strategies that these ships bring within our capability. See here...' They moved to the huge charts table where a small crew of midshipmen moved formations of model ships in previously undreamed-of tactics. 'See how we will be able to attack their mid-line with all our guns concentrating on their centre. We'll harry them close, avoid being boarded, get into better firing positions, and escape unscathed.'

'We're practising a diversity of ways of using the new cannon and ball types that you've provided.' Sir Francis pointed to the collection of cannonballs in the crates – including hollow ones that could be filled with lead shot or gunpowder. Two of the under-captains hefted the large-bore cylinder cannon shots, explaining about the thin binding that held the shots together until they were fired. 'And then they split into a hundred rods of iron that slash into the enemy. With the new designs of vessels, we have worked on strategies to use these cylinder shots in combination with fireship tactics.'

'The Catholics are certain to attempt an invasion of England in a few years, and we'll be ready for them. I don't imagine the Spanish, in their lumbering high galleons, will ever realise how much their Irish friends-in-church are contributing to our impending victory.'

'Aye, with their new ship designs and our new weaponry, these strategies become possible, and will lead us to victory.'

'Just so, Baron; cooperation – even if unwitting – can be so fruitful, hmm?'

***

III.   I'll drink to that

I was heading in for a normal Wednesday morning at The Owl offices on Whitefriars. We published the boys' magazine for the adventurous of spirit and mind in the second half of the twentieth Century. In addition to stories, true accounts and cartoon, The Owl covered everything to do with the wonders of nature, the advance of science and the inexorable spread of technology.

'We are not a comic,' I always told people. 'Although we aim at eight to eighteen-year-old boys, a quarter of our readers are girls, and another quarter are adults. Most fathers read their son's copies before they let their offspring near them. Sure, we have cartoons – funny they are, too, and some carry solid engineering or scientific messages and ideas. We're very advanced and extremely popular.'

Yes, we were the nerds' journal before nerds were invented.

218

Our most acclaimed feature was the centrefold. It was always a cutaway diagram of a real or imaginary wonder of human or natural Creation: the world's largest bulldozer; the insides of an elephant; the workings of an electric train; a racing cheetah; a tunnel excavator, or, this particular week, the internal layout of the nuclear submarine the navy was building. All our own common sense, experience, and logic had gone into the design.

Plus inspiration and guesswork on this occasion: Zack had come in one morning reckoning he'd seen it, clear as a bell, in a dream. He had sketched it on the inside of a cornflakes box on his breakfast table, with lots of details. He claimed his dream had guided him, as though walking along the length of it, inside a real one. He could remember it in overall impression, and in almost every detail. We spent a full day filling it out. It was done. In a day. A record. But brilliant. We just knew it was right. We were more pleased with this centrefold than any previous one.

But one morning, as we were ready to publish, we were arrested on the way in: gangs of police and men in black-rimmed sunglasses and suits everywhere. They ransacked our office and drawing areas. Boxes of papers and documents scattered all around, half of them carried out the door. Our two managers were locked out of sight, and so was the chief draughtsman. The rest of us were interviewed half a dozen times by different hard-faced idiots.

'You're all spies,' they informed us in various ominous and threatening ways. 'And you're staying here while your homes are searched for the incriminating evidence.'

'Evidence of what?' I kept asking. In vain.

Eventually we were given the answer: someone at the printers, or among the pre-readers, had tipped them off about a clear breach in national security. Our dreamwork, guesswork, inspiration and logic had been a little too accurate; and they thought we'd had access to their official drawings, blueprints and planning. Where our three seniors spent the night we don't know, but the rest of us were put up in a hotel with guards.

It was all cleared up fairly quickly, actually. We were allowed to produce the copy within the week, but with a blank centrefold. Nearly blank – we included the statement that, "Our diagram of an atomic-powered undersea war vessel is considered too speculative by certain arms of the government, and it cannot be published as yet." We weren't allowed to mention the words "nuclear", "submarine" or "Ministry of Defence".

It was the best publicity we ever had, and by public demand, the diagram was released for publication four weeks later, to record sales.

I heard later that our arrangement of the cooling systems and power transfer ducting and wiring was thought to be more logical and efficient than the system they had installed. Our design was incorporated into the second generation of the actual builds of nuclear submarines for the British Navy

'Pretty good, that.' Zack and I had a self-congratulatory drink together when we heard. 'Even if they don't officially acknowledge our contribution and that of our dream-giving messengers, we've cooperated in the defence of the realm.'

'Dreaming cooperation with the heavens will have to suffice, eh? I'll drink to that.'

'Cooperation.' We clinked glasses, satisfied.

***

IV.   Such a wonderful thing

'Kral. Have you heard the rumours about Ruggor?'
Humff floats into my office whenever he wants, but on
this occasion, I was expecting him.

'There are always rumours about Ruggor. Which
particular ones this time?' As if I didn't know. 'The re-
climating faction? The Independence Group? Trying to
move their moon again?'

'The starship, Kral! They're building their own
starship! My informants tell me it is more than half
completed already. Capable of a three-year voyage with
simple turnaround system. Travelling at an estimated
two-fifty XLS with perhaps two thousand passengers.'

'Yes, Yes, Humff, we do know about it. We have
done for some time.' He was even more wild-eyed than
usual – and they'd been pretty wild most of the time
since he was stirred round on Baccula. I suppose I
shouldn't chiss him about too much. He was, however,
determined to have his say before he listened to
anything.

'That's more advanced than our Seven Oh Six!
They'll be able to explore into the Riyads at around three
new planets per year.'

'And populate at least one per year; worrying, isn't
it?

'They'll outstrip us! Ruggor is supposed to be our
colony, not our rival or master. It'll be war within the
decade. They'll populate three times more planets than
we can. This is dreadful.'

221

'Indeed, Humff. I hear they've just about perfected a system of deep sleep, too. It has a near one hundred per cent survival rate – better than the deep-freeze we've been using, eh?'

'They're using some of *our* technology on their shielding. It's supposed to be restricted to our official craft, not every colony and outcamp in the region. And... and... what about the radiation protection materials, Kral? Where are they getting them from? The navigation systems are ours, as well; they *can't* have those – not the finders, locators, nor comparatives. What in Hadar is going on? They must have spies and smugglers everywhere.'

Poor Humff, he'd been perfect all this time, digging and delving, so innocent, the perfect decoy. The Ruggors had a spy on him – his Number One Lady, actually. And his total ignorance of absolutely everything had stood us in such good stead. Actually, Velvina, his Number One, had tried it on me for a time; and a most rewarding time it had been, too. But she'd dismissed me as too lowly and dim to be of use. Ahh, yes, I'm really good at being dim and low.

'What are we – you – going to do about it, Kral?'

'Nothing, Humff. Absolutely nothing. It's already been done, about, er...' I checked, 'Four hours ago, Standard Time. Our people who work there were due to hit at change of shift, with reinforcements zipped in specially. I'm awaiting confirmation of their success, but we should have taken their top half-dozen thinkers. I expect they'll be on transports here by now, and will soon be prepared to continue their work on our behalf, I expect. We already have full copies of all their plans and proposals: it was we who opened outlets for them to access materials and certain of our technologies...'

'But... but, Kral, why?' His face was a picture of non-comprehension and misery.

'Because, Humff, it was the cheapest way to get them to use their skills and dynamism to develop something we both wanted. Only they didn't know they were helping us. As far as they're concerned, the total devastation at their space-yard today will have been an accident, with all their starship technology destroyed. We will come to their rescue, offering the best we have, which, coincidentally, will be not dissimilar to theirs. After all, we have been keeping pace with them, and combining our own developments as we go.'

Humff seated himself, sighing as realisation sank in. 'You'll be telling me next that cooperation is such a wonderful thing, huh?'

'Cooperation with the Hintya Mind this time, Humff. Three of the Hintya Holy Ladies communed for an age with their Being, quite some years ago, and they came to us with this confusion of thoughts and visions, seeking understanding of it all.'

'You're telling me the Ladies of Hintya came to us – you – for clarity and understanding of the revelations they received from the Being? Isn't it supposed to be the other way round?'

'Well, yes, it is. But, as long as we are cooperating so well – if inadvertently – it doesn't much matter who initiates the mutual assistance, does it?'

'I suppose not, Kral. Let's hope the Ruggors still think cooperation is wonderful if they ever find out how much they've been helping us, hmm?'

'Not merely us – the whole Ginga Sector.'

***

V.   The best results

Astraea waylaid me by the Shoylo. I had hinted that I would be there, and perhaps be prepared to share some thoughts.

'Zod,' she conveyed, 'are you going to allow me access to your mind patterns about this new world we have the chance to create? Is that why you contacted me?'

Well, that was direct enough. But I was hardly going to tell her the whole truth on that, was I? Not all at once. As though she'd believe that the Kalimi Gods themselves had come to my mind and shown me that this was the true way forward? I scarce believed it myself: it was only the High Mystics themselves who communed with the Gods, not we Criadores. But the mind message had been absolutely unambiguous, as well as utterly unprecedented: 'Share with Astraea.' Their command had been so clear. 'Give all. Cooperate with Astraea. This will lift you and the new worlds in their forward surge.'

And that was directly from the Gods that I didn't truly believe existed. *We* were supposed to be the Gods. But, they didn't say I had to make my cooperation with Astraea easy, or too obvious: I have my own ikh to consider as well.

'And why would I let you into my thinking, Astraea? You already know how my mind works and plans, and what my worlds are like. Whether we start with a gas ball or a rock lump, I just love volcanoes. The worlds I create are nothing like your placid little havens, are they?'

She could feel the smile in my mind as I permitted her access to those parts of my thinking. Well, it was she who had long sought this interchange for her own advantage: we were rivals in this venture, after all.

'Yes... much as always, Zod.' Reciprocally, I could experience her own thinking as she searched through my wild vision of volcanic peaks, deep-frozen snow and ice-fields; storm-lashed oceans and raging rivers. Almost dismissing me, 'It has an unpredictable, ferocious beauty to it, Zod. But so inhospitable to organised life as we know it. The increasing thought is that we attempt to prepare our new worlds to accommodate developing life-forms, not,' she added pointedly, 'to wipe out their embryonic stages before any kind of civilisation comes about.'

'I merely challenge them, Astraea; I've not attempted to do another Ageris, now have I?'

'You said that was an experiment, a one-off?'

I muired my mind in mock-surrender, 'What are experiments for, Astraea, if not to learn from?'

She coruscated coyly, no doubt recalling the last time we'd rivalled for the creation of a new world from a raw orbital mass. I wasn't going to ask, but, for some unworldly reason, I really did want a glimpse into her patternings of thought on this matter – after all, this was a high-status undertaking in this particular wisp of the cluster. And I was following my new Kalimi-directed strategy to cooperate.

I let her seek freely through my planning and ideas: the regions where I was using the bulk of the terrain in positive ways to create the new formations of mountains and depths. It helped with the speed of reforming as well as the energy costings in terms of wastage. 'I'll have to create more water for the ocean, of course.'

'Ah, you want to see what I have planned?' She said it in that triumphant way that revealed she expected to win this exchange and the task that was up for the bidding. She believed I was not the sort to ever learn from anyone else. True, I went my own ways, but this Cluster Council wasn't made up of the types to approve one of my more extreme projects. This time, energised and re-adjusted by the revelations of the Kalimi, I was prepared to, er, *fine-tune* my thinking a little. As one would if you had experienced an epiphany of The Gods.

Astraea opened her pathways to my wonderings, her phantasmal non-form easing around my queryings.

'Ah, interesting, Astraea... Your usual, also? Green meadowlands, small calm seas and stretching beaches, rolling hills and a wealth of forests? Ahh, some steeper slopes, mountain peaks, I see, and deep rock-strewn valleys. An ocean, almost? You're becoming more adventurous?'

We separated, each smiling in our own way. Perhaps she'd had the same reason as I had for wanting to meet over this matter: to learn, and hone our skills and ideas. Had the Kalimi visited her, also? She would introduce some aspects of what she had gleaned from my less extreme exigencies of planetary formation. And I would incorporate aspects of her gentler visions.

I didn't imagine, at first, that there would be huge regions of overlap in our projections, but, as we compared and considered, we were progressively becoming closer in our patternings. Yes, perhaps I could smooth off a few slopes to accommodate the new kind of high flowerlands she was thinking of. I might even lower a few mountains, and calm a couple of the more violent magma masses that would lurk below the surface.

These planets were supposed to be inhabitable by civilised life, after all. It was just that I preferred to give them a little more adventure; wanting them to be less comfortable than Astraea the Innocent would dream of. 'Challenge into the future,' was my motto, not 'Cosset into stagnation.'

However, some judicious merging of our proposed environments could be beneficial for all concerned. Far be it from me to form any opinion on any aspect of the Council Judges or the Kalimi Gods, but I wonder if they may have conspired together in guiding we Criadores in their new, jointly-preferred direction.

I'm thinking several things: Firstly, I believe the council will grant me the honour because, recently, they are not wanting to seem boring. My new Astraea-assisted scheme will promise sufficient easily habitable space for colonists to set up secure bases; and just the right amount of challenge to keep them on their tips. It could be the perfect blend that the council is willing to present to would-be colonists from the Raegis Systems.

Secondly, if my proposal succeeds, I'll make sure Astraea receives equal credit for her contribution. Possibly even inviting her active involvement?

Also, if she sees that I am ameliorating my wilder extremes, then she and I might merge as one being once more. This would be good, for I increasingly believe that such ultimate cooperation is the way of the Kalimi Gods in pursuit of the Universal Life Essence. Indeed, cooperation could be the making of us

***

VI.   Equality and balance

I am the Yin.

Yang is my equal and balancing force. Together, we are the Being Supreme of All That Is – we are The Universal Life Essence. Jointly, we are the *only* being.

We are aware that our universe is reaching its end. Matter is inevitably losing its energy. Total entropy approaches – the state of complete nothingness, chaos and disorder, in which atoms themselves will lose their being and cease to exist. There will be *Nothing*.

Yang drifts godly thoughts through infinite fascinating ideas for a new universe to replace the old one that has worn thin. Yang, she who is Elkanna the Ever Perfect, dreams and plans for the better firmament to replace the dying one. Creating wonderful new rules and physical laws; understanding the implications of one, smoothing them to a wondrous scheme. Hers will be a universe of ultimate goodness and total perfection.

She gazes through the cosmos, through all time and all space. 'This shall be *perfect,*' she conveys.

As do I; for I, too, have my plans and preparations for the new Creation. We shall cooperate and compromise, inspire each other to an ever-greater Creation, Yin and Yang in ultimate cooperation.

But now – Yang presents her plan as the only possible one, for she has taken much thought in its creation. 'Such perfection is not the way of existence,' I say. 'We must cooperate, and achieve a great new Creation. For this is merely your part of *our* seedling plan for us to jointly consider at length for possible flaws, variations and improvements. We need to cooperate; we inspire each other. Together, we should arrive at the Ultimate Balance of Creation. For it is Cooperation that achieves the Ultimate Balance.

'*This* what I want and always have,' Yang insists.

'I am Yin,' I say in return. 'I am the balance for your force. We must cooperate.'

'But this is the way,' Yang emanates, 'My way. I heed you not, with your darkness and negativity; your demands and pollutions of the pure.'

'What?' I reel in disbelief. 'You refuse to seek an equilibrium of our ways? You spurn the equality and balance we jointly hold? This cannot be – to not cooperate is unimaginable. We are joint. We are We. For I am Yin. And you are Yang. A universe that was purely yours, Yang, would not be balanced. It would be the defeat of all I hold dear and close. The imposition of only your laws would wreak ruin on the miraculous plans that I have held dear for as long as the present Universe has existed. Without darkness, how can the concept of light be known? Without the negative, there can be no positive. There would be Chaos Ultima for the next ten trillion arcuates. And beyond.'

Within myself, I fear Yang will simply decide for herself. There will be no stability of force without cooperation between us.

229

Still, she utterly rejects our basic tenet that Creation is Cooperation. She is preparing to initiate the New Beginning alone.

This is not The Way. I *must* act, for I am the Yin. I am Lucifer Morning Star. I am Balance.

I say, 'Let there be darkness.'

And there is darkness...

And it will last forever.

***  ***

WATCHING THE SCURRUGS

Reju Royalty, they claimed to be; the really pretentious group that had chartered my little space yacht, The Nova Queen. All their swishing and swanking; I was very clearly seen as the working mord, and they the idle majestics. And, to prove it, they had snarls, sneers and smirks to curdle water, and had decided to be a nightmare before the off.

Then my two crew-officers cum passenger-sucker-uppers radded in. 'We're stuck in the Vapp tunnel on the Four twenty-six, and it looks like being very protracted.'

No! Not today. Shugg shugg shugg! I really can't run the trip alone. It's against everything. My insurance would be void, and I'd never be able to keep an eye on all their sillinesses.

'You'll be destitute and dead if you don't,' the most senior, self-aggrandising and regal woman informed me when I broke the news. 'We go. Or your company goes bust. Worst publicity in the universe. Compensation will sky high. Do you know how pathologically disappointed we would be? Regally so.' She had the most expressively dismissive finger I've ever seen. I suspected she was dismissing my life, not just me there-and-then.

Oh shuggeration. The doo-doos get deeper.

*

This sixsome had paid well over the odds for an exclusive small-group trip to the planet of Peris for close encounters with the life-forms there over the course of two days, noon to noon. Sure, this lot are haughtier than others, but it's good money, and it's what I do.

There're four other ships doing similar ventures. We're the best. Not the cheapest: my insurance makes sure of that. And sure not the swankiest. But we're the most adventurous – we slot into orbit *fast*. I do a perfect high-speed, spin-over approach to start them off feeling ill. She's a beautiful little craft, the Nova Queen, and I'm the best ship jockey for light years around. What we do is the core experience – "As scary as it gets" is one of our slogans.

It's what I advertise for – *"The Experience. The adventure of a lifetime for people who are young of spirit."*

The other companies emphasise safety or comfort. Not me. These folk aren't looking for luxury – they want peril: like two rough nights sleeping on Peris or in orbit; see the scurrugs close up, including at night when they fight anything and everything. After the scurrugs finish their antics, around midnight, the sky display is awesome: Peris has the best view of the galaxy anywhere.

*

I studied them. The woman was in charge – senior. Not the oldest, but acted like a princess. So shugging confident. Admirable normally, but not when you're a novice who's way out your element. Even the others sucked hers. I didn't. Big Mistake.

'No gratuity,' she told the others when I offered my hand to help them aboard. 'I don't do touching.'

232

'She's not a touchy-feely person,' the chinless wondergirl with her whispered.

It's tricky for the first hour or so in zero gravity, and swinging across from the out-bay gantry to my airlock can be dooky. But she did fine; she'd done her competent-amateur share of it. Not natural easy pro, though.

She smirked: she'd got her way; told me off; and demonstrated how skilled she was. Big deal. Or, actually, very smart, fine-looking. Yeah, a lady, alright, with that aloof look. Not that she seemed to notice me, anyway. More into casting out an order and expecting it to carry itself out. Such a condescendingly thin smile. I couldn't believe anyone's face could be so amazingly flawless. She saw me staring, and smirked. Bitch. The finest-looking lady I'd ever had aboard. Ever even seen, probably.

They were all much the same. Snooting up to each other, settling in. Having to squirt their own drinks was considered to be roughing it, part of the hazardous experience. Keit would have done that, but he wasn't there that day. I had them to myself.

I pushed the button to dilute their drinks, and set about manoeuvring out the bay at Salazar Base, sideways into position, and locking the flight data in.

'I'll fly it.' One of the men wanted to show off.

'No, you won't.' Nothing unusual with showing off, or wanting to try it. 'Not yet. Soon, koh?' I didn't look to see which of the men it was, but he'd gone when I turned, having Nova Queen heading in a hyperbolic curve that would see us into a tight orbit-ready position within the hour.

233

'There are several docking bays around Peristhese,' I told them. 'Anyone who wants can try bringing us out of them later. And if you're coping fine, you can try docking in as well. Koh?' It was pretty safe – the bays had auto-dampers to cushion against accidents.

Naturally, *she* wanted first go. In. And she spouted a heap of semi-chav techno gibberish that was supposed to make me think she knew what she was doing. She maybe did. Plus, she was paying.

'Fine,' I said. 'You can try it first, if you're that good. But you'll have to forsake the No Touching policy – I need to have hand-over-hand guidance at my disposal, in case anything unexpected comes our way.'

'You mean, you insulting creature, if I make a mess of it?'

I shrugged slightly. Big Mistake Two.

'I'm perfectly capable of...' She waved me aside as we turned for docking. So, fine... I generally let them do it sometime: it's an *adventure* trip. It's our selling point.

She did it okay, a bit stiff and calculated, but safe. She smirked. 'It's rather clunky. Twitchy. Not like our zipper.'

'You're right there, Lady... er, how do I call you when you're in take-a-chance mode?'

That took her back a fraction. An almost smile. 'Rudeness ill becomes you, Crewboy. You may call me Lady.' That was me back in my place.

'Suits me.' Sir and Lady it is, then, all round. Saves remembering who's who. *So here we have Lady Princess... Lady No-Chin... and the others down the line to Big Ears.*

*

234

Give'em their due, they all tried. Two of the others were competent, just not accustomed to Nova Queen's foibles and quirks. The other three did need hand-over-hand – the women requesting gloves first, but not objecting when I shook my head. All six managed a docking and a departure, and were moderately pleased with themselves, wanting to do it again on the morrow. 'Sure, we can make time.' Whatever pleased them. I could twist the Twitchy Dial up if they wanted more excitement.

Have to be careful, though; No-Chin almost snuggled back against me when I helped her with the docking, and Lady Princess frowned. *Keep me out of it,* I thought. *I want no bother between you two.*

The accustomed ones helped the others with zero-grav eating and drinking and probably a fair bit more, too. I went over their straps and sleeping cots – there's plenty of room on a small-group exclusive like this. We did a long-line drift out into the vacuum, with cables twice the length of any other company's; no safety officer with them; and hand-held jet packs to fly them around.

I gave them over an hour drifting and scooting out there, watching the planet below – the sunset; the darkness sweeping across, skipping the mountain ranges, re-colouring the seas. Then I had to reel them in, before their oxy ran out, or they became too tangled to ever free the lines.

'Awesome.'

'Such Freedom!'

'Jibber... jabber... need a drink... oh boy... wait till I tell...'

Yes, they were pretty excited afterwards. So far, so brill.

Next on the itinerary was a visit to the Vesi 1 Orbital Water Sphere, the only place where anyone can scuba in zero grav.

Then the first night drop onto the surface, using the gravity lift. That was new to them all. Precipitous descent, nearly twice as fast as usual. It's more heart-stopping that way. We settled onto the tower amid all the excitement and thrill of the fall – the wide-eyed, open-mouthed gaspings. I linked up the umbilical valve, pressured up, and through we went into the tower's observation bubble. Just early enough to grab a drink and a snack and another drink before the main event.

The scurrugs came, hurtling through the dark sky. They screamed – my guests – every one. A ravening face of scales and teeth and lizard frills slammed against the glassite wall, and glowed in a violet-orange shimmer. Another one came circling in from three or four hundred yars away, a snaking light-coil in the starless sky, as if prowling at speed, and homing in like a missile of light to slam into the bubble, and rake great claws down the flanks of the earlier one. Their eyes were vast, fixed on us within. Teeth snapped and slavered. The vids couldn't have done it better. My six Intrepids cowered down, all a-scream and terrified. Great! Just what we promised in the advertising – jeopardy and terror.

The scurrugs took to fighting each other, naturally. Their lighting display was unmatched anywhere else in the Humiverse – a room-sized bubble all to ourselves, encased in a mass of writhing lights and raging eyes. Hard to say how many; a dozen, perhaps. Which is pretty good, considering it's often four or five that fight and emblaze the night sky with their vividly-flashing display.

Hugely impressed, we settled with drinks, and stayed till the scurrugs were done and their lights died down.

'We can't leave just yet,' I told them. 'We have to wait till the scurrugs loosen off and slide away. They drop and glide to the forest floor, where they writhe and feed and heal themselves, and mate and sleep till mid-afternoon tomorrow when they start again. They'll fly and travel and cavort at this and that till tomorrow evening, when their lights spark up and they pick on something to fight.'

'Why do they pick on us to attack?'

'The tower emits a thousand-dee tome, and a sequence of UV and visible lights that kinda stirs them up. A thousand's the max – they'd go utterly insane with anything more. Now – special offer. If you want – no-one's got this tower booked till dusk tomorrow. After we see the Milk-view of the galaxy, we can remain here if you want, and go down among the slumbering scurrugs in the morning. So – stay here? Or lift back to the orbit slot? Up to you.'

It was kinda unofficial, but not illegal. I did it sometimes, with a full crew aboard, and it seems more excitingly dangerous than it really is. 'None of the other companies stays down here over the whole night,' I persuaded.

*

We stayed, of course. Far too wound up to sleep, they sat around, talked, drank and stared out over the starlit forest tops. They picked my brains and chatted about what we'd be doing on the morrow, the places I'd been, and where they'd been. I didn't tell'em most of mine, and I reckon they invented half theirs. They dozed in their lounger seats, and I kipped at the back, with them in sight and a power shot into my brachial artery. I clipped the sensor on my wrist for any major event, such as a breach or a temperature rise or very loud noise. It'd wake me up in three seconds flat.

I woke them at dawn. 'The adventure goes on,' I informed Her Ladyship and Hangers-on. 'The dawn down here is something else, and not many see this.'

A mass of birds and reptilian geefs rose with the sun and took to flight, circling in a mass ten thousand strong all around the tower. It really is awesome and they were enthralled: they didn't know about that.

So I was in good standing. They relaxed a bit over the fast-break drink.

'There's the special trip I mentioned last night; if you're up for it?'

They were.

'Below this bubble, there's a spiral staircase inside the tower, all the way to the surface. No other company offers this – but if you want, we can go down and walk around. I'll cook you a Triple-B, and if we're lucky, there'll be some scurrugs down there. They'll be asleep, we hope, though they have bad dreams and writhe a bit.'

Down we went and I put on the cautious act. Although, to be honest, we had only been doing this outing for the last six trips – all with a full crew – so we hadn't necessarily got it off to perfection. But it was licence-approved, and I had the registration, and I'd informed the office.

But there was something different every time. The BBB meal for fast-break down on the surface was sheer bravado, so I did it. I'd already set up the fire in the stone-ring pit, cooking pre-pack porrock burgers. They're six-legged vermin from the other side of Peris. Tasted kinda exotic-earthy, with spices and rick-shaft bread, full crusted.

It all took time – time for my clients to explore and enjoy the freedom. 'Hardly anybody has ever come down here,' I told them.

It went pretty well. Trees reaching to the sky, a cloud of insects with huge wings – multi-coloured and fluttering. I'd seen them once before, and reports said they were safe, so I was koh with my guests wandering round, making half-hearted efforts to catch a souvenir flitterwing. And then the Triple Burgers were ready.

Jeeps – they loved'em. Even Princess Snooty; it was probably high in Bragging Value among her retinue back home. Popular guy, I was; this was doing me good, I was enjoying it, and my reputation would swell, too.

We walked; overalls on, and sealed-up boots. We'd have to de-contam on the way back in, but it all pumped up the risk and zest scale. Two hundred yars away, and we found a scurrug. Just lying there. Gasps all round at the size of it: a huge coiling snakelike thing with wings tightly folded in. Body covered in armoured facets and plates, its eyes full shut. Another was a few paces away, a purply tinge – a female.

'If they're a pair, there'll be a nest somewhere close. Now that's rare. I've never seen one.' I signalled my party to stay where they were. 'I'll look.'

Ten minins, I was back through the undergrowth. 'Found the nest. Come on. Now this is a risk. I mean it. Be silent. Nobody ever did this before. So silent, hmm? And be ready to run.'

They saw the nest: eggs the size of baby-pods, in an oval patch with a raised sort of wall of baked soil and leaves and twigs; very solid-looking. We counted fifteen. Two cracked open. Empty.

I pointed to the broken shells and warned my guests, 'There's two hatchlings close by. Look round, but keep very quiet. Not a word. You'll know if you see them – like fat snakes with a mass of legs and huge facial mandibles that lurch out and slash like quick-fire sharap blades. They'd have your legs off in seconds.'

Silent they were. Crept around. Took their vids and hmmed and oohed under their breath.

'There.' A whisper. A head had appeared between the vertical leaves the other side. Eyes so big. A neck. It eased forward, head lowering, then rising again, with paired mandibles as long as an arm. Snapping. Eyes that looked around and shone with an inner gleam.

'It's a scurrug larva. Back up.' I motioned them back as it slid closer, emerging from the undergrowth, bony jaws slashing.

We eased back, fearful. Jeeps, it looked vicious. 'Back... back... It's coming this way. Go for it! *fast...*' They turned and ran like they had the trots in a space-suit.

'I'll fend it off!' I had a stazer and fired it twice. The electric sizzle rent the air with a crackling burst in an arc of brilliant light. A second hatchling's head appeared. I shouted to warn them, but they were fleeing even faster.

'It's coming!' I yelled and fired again. A hundred yars away, past the stirring scurrugs... a rippling shudder rhythming down the length of both.

In near-panic, we fled, leaving the debris of the meal and Triple-B gear behind, desperately crowding into the room at the base of the tower. I ushered them before me, all gasping and terror-eyed. Last in, I slammed the button and the doors slid to. Unnoticed, I slid the hatchling remote control into my sleeve pocket, 'It's koh... we're in. We're safe. Relax, we're fine. Try the screen. There's a vista view of the outside.' We flicked it on. Nothing: the clearing was empty of major life as far as the dense green forest with the path to the left; the flowering orange and yellow beak-face plants; some trailing vines. But no eyes and shimmering plates.

'Koh. Let's go.'

Up the stairs we tottered, and into the bubble. I made them rest, gradually calming down. They were in no fit state for anything more than a couple of drinks.

*

So, feeling quite smug, all in all, that worked out fine: the old nest we'd renovated looked fresh and real. Yesss, two thousand hej well spent. Those two mecho-larvae would have fooled anyone. Mmm, yes, very realistic scurrug hatchlings. *Must do this alone again – it adds so much to the anticipated risk value. Must be careful in future: a real one might appear one day. In the meantime, my gorgeous six have had the adventure of a lifetime, alright. Jeeps, they'll talk about this. And I reckon they'll be fine for tonight's performance, too.*

'We'll go to the old low-level tower tonight – this one's booked,' I said. *And it won't be any surprise when the glassite cracks under the scurrug attack, and we almost lose a panel, and I'll need them to bring the shutters down. They'll have to help with the emergency power and steering. We'll rocket out of there damn-near at Passout-G, into a reverse high-speed orbit so they'll see four sunrises and four sunsets before we cruise down onto the new Obs Tower at High Tide beach just in time for the daily migration of the tortuulla crabs out the waves – escaping the shovel sharks.*

That should finish mid-to-late morning, just in time for drinks and a noon return to base. Anyone feeling confident can have a go at flying Nova Queen, on Sprite setting instead of Clunky.

Maybe one of the ladies won't be in No Touching mode after that lot – it's not an unknown occurrence. The lure of null-grav, the excitement, and I'll have my parade uniform and heroic look on by then.

*

The summons arrived sixty-odd days afterwards. When I'm sent for, I do not go. Ever. Unless it's the Headline Registration and Safety Board; or the Transplant Clinic with a surgical bot with time to spare; or Royalty. In this case, it would be ill manners and ungood for my reputation if I ignored Reju Royalty – Princess Pe'a's father, High Prince Reju.

At least he'd come to Calvis and hadn't expected me to traipse to Reju. That's a full day's SP Flight, on the days when a ship's headed that way.

We met in a plush hotel suite at the Mercury Space Hotel. Very comfortable, until he turned up. Resplendent in his Reju Regal Regalia – shimmering cloak, gold braid and navy Mandar suit. *Over-dressed,* I thought. *Common.*

'I want a word with you, boy.'

'Boy?? Boy!!' I practically erupted. 'I'm the captain of my own space ship, the Nova Queen, and you call me boy? Even if you are a Regent or Imperio or whatever else foreign you are...' I calmed a fraction. 'Alright, Daddy. What about?'

That froze him. Koh, I knew calling him Daddy would be a bad move before I spoke, but nobody calls me "Boy". I own a space vacation company, for Ghirri's sake.

'You took my daughter Pe'a on one of your trips to Peris, to see the scurrugs at night.'

'Yesss? *Princess* Pe'a, we called her. She had the experience of a lifetime. That's what we advertise. Our absolute guarantee is that no-one ever forgot their trip with us. Obviously – because if they forgot it, they wouldn't be able to think about suing us for having forgotten.'

'She is a princess. And that trip was a fake... a con.'

I was taken aback, and affronted. 'It was not! My ship's real; we really went there; we genuinely planeted down to the high tower and actually watched genuine scurrugs at night.'

'And set up a fake nest, scurrug eggs as big as an armadildo. Plus mech-electronic larvae to chase after you.'

'What can I say?' I grinned. 'The real things don't come out on command. And no-one's forgotten, have they? No-one's ever asked for their money back, even at the prices we charge. Besides, the hatching pursuers were extras, not part of our advertised event.'

'She told me all about it.' He had that beady, threatening, father-protecting-beloved-daughter look. '*All* about it.' He sounded even more accusing.

'She can't have done: no-one knows all of it. Possibly two people outside this room. And two more with a fair idea. But not all.'

Jipperty Joe! What's he after? Pe'a couldn't tell all. Even her, who'd stayed with me in Salazar after her friends had gone off-planet. She'd entirely lost her No-touchy-feely attitude. 'I took a fancy to a dose of rough,' as she phrased it. Me! A dose of rough! But that's Princesses for you. A couple of nights turned into a couple of deccs together... three. Before she simply vanished.

I found she'd returned to Reju. Abruptly. *Decided she preferred smooth,* I supposed, and became inebriated for two days. Then my next trip out was due and I had to take the Soberdose.

'So now you're here for revenge for her honour, eh Daddy? Or something equally weird and stupid, like your money back?'

'Oh, no, *Boy.* Pe'a is entirely her own woman. Apart from what I pay for, naturally. No – I've come to make you an offer – an invitation. To open a branch on Reju.'

'I don't need to tout for business—'

'I don't mean an advertising office. Pe'a's accounts convinced me: I want a life-scale Peris Forest Experience, complete with scurrugs—'

'They don't survive elsewhere.'

'I'm thinking of mecho ones. Plus other attractions. I want it riskier-seeming and wilder. Bigger. You've got the skills. Between us we have the ideas. I have the money, and a planet full of people who rarely partake in interstellar travel. But there's a huge untapped element who're ultra-keen to live more ultimate lives, nearer the edge, without having to travel off-planet to get it.'

'You've got a boring planet there, then, Daddio?'

It was a really sour look he gave me, 'Hmm. Pe'a said you were— Never mind. She is keen to be involved at all levels.'

Jipperty! 'No. I can't. Not with her.'

'Thought you got on well. *Captain?'*

'She shiked off without a word. Anyway, I had both arms then. Six deccs ago. I can't have her see me like this.' Jip! I was so stupid. I blush to think how moronic I was – I mean, losing a stupid arm. Sheer carelessness. But I'm getting used to the stump and it only cost me five days' work. Hirry and Keit did fine to keep the trip going.

VC Tryja Clinic could get a replacement arm almost anytime – fresh or frozen, depending on casualty rates here and there, but they almost certainly won't be able to get a surgeon-bot to do the job. I don't want a prozzy arm. I'd feel like a mecho.

'Thanks,' I told him. 'But what you're asking isn't the kind of thing *I* do. Maybe you could talk with Hirry and Keit – they know the deal and the works.'

He shook his head. 'They don't have the skill, the nous, the ideas. The, er, charisma – as some might think of you – though I have no such feeling myself, naturally. I know what happened.'

'Eh? What do you mean, what happened? What's she been telling you?' He must know that his daughter and I were, as they say, a couple. We were coupling, anyway. Till she did a flyer that morning. She wouldn't tell him *everything*. But he'd have heard whispers and snatches, and pieced them together into a version of truth.

'You got it caught in the VM airlock.'

Oh. He meant my arm. That was a relief. 'Freak accident. I shouldn't have let it happen.'

'I know you tried to pull someone clear when the airlock was on auto-close.'

That's what he thinks, huh? Did I, shugg. Actually, two trips later, we dashed for the tower chased by Hirry with his larva mecho gnashing and squickering on our heels, and I ushered this shrieking pack of dorkheads inside in front of me. I turned to check on the larva. Ten yars away. I courageously waited one more second and leapt into the base-room behind the others. Except somebody had pressed the Never-Touch-Me panic button, and the door was already closing. I tried to reach in to cancel it, but it just kept coming, and crushed my arm a hand's length from the shoulder. I'd forgotten the door absolutely insists on fully closing when it's operated via the panic button. There's no over-ride for obstructions, such as my arm.

And that, of course, left me trapped outside, with a very realistic mecho larva clawing at me. Hirry was either over-enthusiastic or not fully in control, and its claws were really sharp. He thought I'd stalled there for extra show, and got it to maul me before Keit fearlessly drove it off and was able to attend to me – feeling so stupid standing there, held against the airlock door by a slice of skin and ligament, covered in razine claw rips bleeding into my boots.

They cut the skin and tendons free, and I sagged and sank while they searched for the spray-on skin. Last thing I said was something like, 'If one of them shikers on the other side does anything to my hand I'll kill'em.'

So now the High Prince of Reju wants me to do it all over again on his own planet, with the daughter who dumped me? 'Sorry, Daddy. No. Can't do it. I've been traumatised quite enough lately, without being dragged to Reju for your Pe'a to have a laugh at me. She sniffled at me quite enough when I had two arms. It'd just be a laugh too far now.'

'She's in the other room, watching. Ask her.'

*

Yes, Pe'a was all smiles and charm then; full of persuasion, lovey dovey, enthused.

I was supremely suspicious, but, with extra chat-up, the proposal sounded exciting. I'd have the freedom to design and build, with plenty of cash to be spent, and much more to be made.

Not seeing any better options, I went along, threw myself into it and practically worked my other arm off. I promoted Hirry, and he brought his brother in to help. Then we full-hired one of the designers who made the larvae in the first place. This time, he worked on real-looking scurrugs – not screen simms.

We put a pitsofalot of time and effort into them; and they did look incredibly real. The big trouble, I realised, was that I was doing all the managing work. 'What's happened to the partnership?' I asked. 'The skilled workforce... workshops... detail designers? Unlimited budget? Nine-star accommodation?'

I wasn't even being paid – they'd slipped a commission-only clause into my contract. So who was the mug here? Especially with Daddy or Daughter arbitrarily over-riding my designs and orders. They seemed to be intent on adopting their own pre-designed avenues instead of the experts' ones – i.e., me and Hirry and his brother and Lazlo the larva specialist. But: they controlled the money. We were treated like mere employees, or subjects. And I was chasing my butt off, all hours Kotusha sends. I hardly ever saw them to argue with, persuade, discuss, or, in Pe'a's case, couple with. And the latter had been rather prominent on the promised list when I was talked into this.

Pe'a would sometimes come, all smiles and assurances, but she always sported that "Peasant Creature" look, exactly how she'd been when we first met. If I wasn't so wrapped up in the project, I'd have time to loathe her. As it was, I sighed, shrugged and brooded. They'd had their wicked way with me during their promise-time. One of the more-than-insinuations had been me and her, together. That was never going to materialise again, was it?

Then she turned up out the purple. 'I'm pregnant. It's yours. From when I was with you in Salazar. We must be wedded.'

She was insistent. They all were. Daddy included. Deathly insistent. They couldn't have made the alternative clearer. So, one little but lavish ceremony later, I became part of their family. A slightly removed We-don't-talk-about-him part of the family.

Then I discovered it was only so the child could be a legitimate heir. And, I overheard, it's okay to ditch Captain after the birth – once the child's a year old.

Now, don't get me wrong: he's a fabulous little kid: he reaches, and holds my fingers; and smiles at me when we pull faces at each other. Plus all the other baby-type things that are smelly and messy. But, if I'm going to be ditched when my year is up, I need a plan.

*

So it came about that, come the grand opening of the Para Peris Wild Park, we went into the rugged terrain and the dense forest under the full glare of the cameras. We were all interviewed, me in my ultra-smart, upgraded space uniform. I stressed how genuinely dangerous the place really was. 'These things are real. They can turn just like that. We *should* be okay this time of day, but you never know.' I warned the cameramen and the sound lot and the hangers-around several times: 'I mean it: it's dangerous… this is a high-risk pioneering venture. It's in its infancy… supertech stuff…'

Just into the third bend, by the very realistic boulder-group and cave, they attacked. Two huge, fully-grown scurrug males.

It was messy. One cameraman thought everything the other side of the lens was unreal, and never moved a brad. He caught some beautiful close-ups. Princess Pe'a succumbed in a flash of non-realisation. Daddy Reju expired in a gory version of what he probably had planned for me.

Naturally, I fought the scurrugs with unparalleled ferocity, and was severely slashed and battered, but too late to save them. All that practise and re-programming was so worthwhile.

A rogue fault, it was postulated, probably caused by cosmic rays, power blips, High Prince Reju's own re-alignment of the scurrugs' claws and actions. Something unpredictable of that nature, it was eventually decided. I truly regretted the death of Princess Pe'a, but it was her or me. She said as much.

Thus, filled with sorrow, I inherited the business and the title of High Prince, with my son, Ceddie, as the natural heir. Lady No-chin was acceptably high up the aristocratic chain, they informed me, with deep meaning in their tones. Thus, we were wedded on Ceddie's first birthday. Just in time, they said.

*

The Park does amazing business. That opening day created a legend. Several legends, actually – the fearsomeness of the scurrugs, the tragic death of my wife and the High Prince, the awesome creatures that this magnificent park is home to, the very real dangers herein, and the sheer courage of the park's owner – me. The non-interstellar-travelling population of Reju love the whole thing. The cameraman's fantastic close-ups were a hit on seven planets.

The only fly on the windowpane is that I was wearing the ultra-smart Captain's uniform with all the star flashes and gold braid when I fought off those two scurrugs. It's very much become my trademark. Now I have to wear the bloody thing all the time.

Obviously it was a space ship. I used to read SciFi, so I know. It was silver, like brightly galvanised tin; just like one of the old-style dustbins. Sitting there, scorched grass all round it. My beautiful Medallion lawn was ruined.

I pulled the bedroom curtains right back. Yep – *ruined.*

Okay, so a space ship wasn't the most likely option. But then, kids having a fire in my back garden wasn't, either. Especially bringing their own bin; and no trampled ground. Besides, there's no way in: my garden's very enclosed.

So I wondered: maybe it had blown in during the storm last night? It had been really windy, with hail, late evening. I thought the conservatory roof would come in at one time.

I couldn't tell from up there, so I went down for a closer look.

Yep, it was a posh-looking dustbin, without any handles. Cylindrical, with corrugated sides and a rounded top. I was pondering about it: perhaps I was half-right first time. I didn't know exactly what it was, but it sure looked like a piece of space debris. A NASA dropout, or a Tesla escapee. The top of it was scorched black as the lawn. So, I figured, it was a fallen bit of space litter, come down in the night. But must have been under some kind of control, or it would have smashed up and made a massive crater, and woken me up. So, the top had to be its heat shield, and it must have flipped over and fired rockets underneath to slow it right down.

Probably automatic systems; Tesla are getting good at that. Right: it made a soft landing.

There'd surely be a reward, a finder's fee? I'd found it, alright – right in the middle of my precious lawn, my centimetre-high magical perfection lawn. I was due an awful lot of compensation for this.

'Hmm. What am I to do?' I asked myself. 'Ring Tesla? Or NASA? Or the UFO Society of Nutters? And tell them it's an ILO, because I've identified it, and it's landed, not flying.' No, they'd trample all over my garden and sensibilities; and pontificate like a pack of wan— Thingies. They'd cart it off and tell me nothing and keep the reward. I tried to move it – it weighed a ton. I couldn't budge it a millimetre. Too heavy to be a space craft of any kind. A dustbin full of concrete, by the feel of it.

I decided to wait, and watch the news on the telly and keep an eye on the internet.

*

Nothing. Not that day, not the day after. Nothing about space debris or anything getting lost, going astray. *Maybe they're frantically searching,* I thought, *and keeping very quiet.* Yes, it's probably worth a fortune, and they won't want it found by the competition.

Yes, I'll wait and see. No hurry – there was plenty of clearing up to do after the wind – the side fence looked wobbly.

But still nothing on the news, and internet searches got me nowhere. So I decided I'd keep it. It looked a right sight in the middle of my garden, though. I wondered if I could make a feature of it, with a flower bed round it, or a circle of block paving. Best not, they might come and root it up when they pay my finder's fee

– and wreck my lawn even more. They'd owe me even more compensation for that.

At least no-one else could see it: panelled fencing down both sides. Everything covered in clematis and wisteria and suchlike climbers. My neighbour on the left is a bungalow – Silas and Enid with their twin cockadoodles – something like that. All of them as old as Arthur Askey's jokes. Years ago, I bought the double plot on the other side, all one point one-five acres of it, just to prevent anyone else building a house overlooking my garden. Or maybe if the kids or my mum wanted somewhere to build later in life. They didn't. Well, they might have done, but the crash of Flight VA4641 put an end to that. They'd had a great time on the beaches, though – while I tidied up last-minute problems with the GR1 project in the U.K. I sold the firm not long after that and sort of dedicated the empty plot to the family. But that's private, just in my thoughts. I didn't tell anyone.

There's no-one to bother me from over the back, either: my rear boundary is a high, solid sandstone-block wall with a bricked-up archway that once led into the Church Estate field. I own that plot, too, ever since I engaged in a fit of retail therapy when the developers were sniffing round, and I had spare cash from the sale of the firm. I never had any intention of doing anything with it because the far section might have been a graveyard at some distant time past; and I'd have to apply for permission to interfere with such things.

I like to look over "my domain": the church field is eight point-three-six acres, complete with big muddy duck pond, or "lake" as I like to think of it. The only access to it is from my next-door plot. And the only way

253

into that is either via a chained-up five-bar gate from the road, or a small doorway from my garden.

The only thing I do with either plot is let some environmental group send me a mushy sack full of seeds and manure every year, and I pay Fred Gillington from across the road to spread it over both plots – for a summer mixed-flowers meadow. In return, I let them harvest all the seeds they want, and then Fred can mow both fields, and gather a ton of free, high quality hay for his livestock. It's okay if he turns his animals loose in there late on, too.

*

For a few more days there was still nothing on the telly or the internet. I carried on pottering round the garden, weeding, pulling the rampant campanula out, on-going pruning and dead-heading. Then I usually sit in the afternoon sun with a shandy and a book, and a handful of floating stix to toss in the pond and watch the fish swirling round; plus the camera for the birds on the feeders; or the squirrel that sometimes visits, too. And JoeTheCat, of course. He's a smooth grey Siamese-cross, who will miaow for something or nothing, then stalk off or curl up under my seat. Plus, of course my NASA Dustbin plonked there. I could get used to it, with a background of the pond and the rockery and the overgrown sandstone wall.

Or perhaps not.

Half-way down my second shandy a few days later, I noticed a dark mark on the side of NASAD, low down. So, idle devil that I am, I picked up the camera, focused in, and took a shot. Oh, yeah, course you did, I hear you say – camera there, convenient that, innit? Well, yes, it was convenient, but I *always* have the camera with me.

It's a compact Canon SX270 HS, with a 20x optical zoom. You should see the shots I've had of the squirrel and a heap of birds, including a sparrow hawk, wren and heron just lately, plus all the usual farm and field birds. "Superb close-ups" according to Bird magazine, and the same from the RSPB and Nature Life monthlies.

That was a bit of a puzzle: a little hole in NASA's finest throwaway. I couldn't make it out properly, so I sipped my shandy and took three or four more pics on different settings. I didn't know it then, of course, but they were the first pictures ever of aliens – real, genuine, living-breathing ETs. Tiny little things, from twenty feet away on the max zoom. Blowing the pictures up on the camera screen, I estimated that hole was about an inch across, hexagonal, with a clean metal rim. Definitely part of the metalwork of the bin – not a rust-hole. On max, I could expand the hole to a life-size one-inch across on the little screen, and it was still nearly in perfect focus.

And it was obvious, even with my eyesight, that things were moving around the hole: just inside it – there were four or five little things, like beetles standing on their back legs.

I watched for a time until they came out. I thought at first – obviously – they were insects scavenging for rotting food, laying their eggs or something. But no, these were upright, and organised; about a quarter-inch high. Less than a centimetre, anyway. I set the camera on movie mode, and there they were! Fantastic! Living little things. I watched them through the camera. Absolutely amazing. I was gob— you know – everything. Enthralled is probably the best word.

A tiny ramp came down. 'You're lucky I cut the grass this morning,' I told'em, 'or you'd be lost.' The ramp opened out to make a rounded area, like a drinks coaster a few inches across, and it pressed the grass down. Then some of them dropped off it. Must have gone exploring, I imagined. And some of the left-behind ones set something up. They probably just pressed buttons. Imagine the size of the buttons – like a tenth of a millimetre across, at most. These miniature structures resembled tiny moon landers or Mars rovers, an inch tall. They grew like self-assembly inflatables while the little beetle-guys busied themselves all round.

'So,' I said, mostly to myself, 'you're either doing the ET bit and phoning home, or monitoring your new environment, eh?'

See how quickly you come to accept aliens colonising your back garden?

They spread out, going on little sorties to the edge of the lawn – freshly edged into the flower beds, hiking round the perimeter. They even came within four or five feet of me sitting there with my drinks. Then they all retreated: two minutes, and they were all back inside and the hole closed up. That was it. Settled. It was getting late, so I figured they were either preparing for take-off, or they were bedding down for the night. Their sudden departure would be disappointing, but spectacular – I even practised panning the camera upwards to follow its flightpath.

But it was the latter. Next morning it – they – were still there. The ramp and marshalling area were out again and I told'em, 'If we have a shower today, you'll be in bother – you'll have to take it all back in smartish.'

There was, and they did. But later on, when it started spitting again, they raised an umbrella. I say umbrella, but remember – this was about three inches across, more like a circular gazebo for them, the size of a parasol in a pina colada. It just seemed to appear instantly – I reckoned it was from a pole they erected in the middle of the pressed-down area.

That was when JoeTheCat decided to sniff round them. Consternation was written all over them. But they stood their ground, give them that, perhaps warning any groups who were out exploring. See how I call them "who", not "that"? I must have been thinking of them in terms of people, not animals or things already. JTC had his head down sniffing at their base, and dabbed a paw at them. He jumped back, very nervy. Waited, went in again, cautiously. Managed to creep in slowly, close again, and leapt back with a yow and miaow. I met him half-way and picked him up, a little burn scratch across his nose.

I tried to think from their point of view, and it seemed pretty reasonable. I consoled JoeTheCat and I don't think he went near them again. Mostly, I kept an eye on them from not too close up. I saw them tackling insects like ladybirds and ants; even a mouse. I suppose it was a stupid mouse because it was dead later on: they must have felt threatened by it. I saw them along the paths each side of the garden, past the three-foot flower border to the back wall. Easy way for them to explore without the ruggedness of the rough soil, or the rockery, or the dense clumps of aubretia, saxifrage and phlox – they'd never get their little moon-rover through them.

The squirrel was very nearly their undoing – it picked the garden-rover up and they spilled out and it turned the little vehicle over as if trying to decide which bit to bite first. Then it jumped around and was pawing at its face. I never saw it again. They had to walk back.

A short while afterwards I noticed their outpost. It looked like a taller rock on the rockery, built against the highest and biggest stone, extending a foot or so higher. 'Good tactical place,' I congratulated them, taking a few more pics.

The pond was even closer to being the end of them, brave little souls that they were. I was weeding under the Virginia creeper at the time, keeping an eye on them. They gathered on one of the flattish rockery stones that made a semi-natural edging for the pond. Suddenly, they were panicking round all a-buzz. There was this buzzing in the water – like a bee whizzing round... then another. I thought, 'Silly sods – one's fallen in and the others are going in after him. In a koi pond!' I have about thirty fish in there, including six koi – Kohaku, Ghost and Showa – that are about two feet long and permanently peckish. So up they came for the buzzing whirligigs. Three of the little buzzers were in the water by then. Double whammy: they were about the same size as pond-stick food, and the koi always go for buzzing insects that land in there. I nipped round with the skimmer net and swept them up. I don't know how many fell in, but I netted the three I saw, and dumped them on the rock. Maybe the koi swallowed a few – the Gin Rin is around thirty inches long.

Would you believe it? They tried again a couple of days later – in a boat the size of a TicTac box. That didn't last long – a pair of koi nibbled at it and almost capsized it. Lord knows where they thought they were going. They went round the edge of the pond after that and I didn't see the boat on the water again.

I didn't mind them in the garden: they and their little machines were as interesting as a dozen Emett whimsies all going at once. Fascinating things.

But. Not near the house – I didn't want them in the walls and under the floorboards – like that song "Those DDD are everywhere." I started by painting a white line right across top of the garden. They came straight over it. I dug a little trench – like a seed drill line. They built a bridge, would you believe. I threw it in the pond, dug the trench four inches deeper and put a line of bricks alongside it, like a tiny Roman defence earthwork. I'm sure they laughed as they brought up a longer bridge. Not for long. I poured oil and petrol into the trench and laid concrete slabs on their side, so I'd have a clear view of any of them coming across it in my direction. They'd feel exposed before coming to the drop into a petrol-pit and the high single-brick wall. Pretty formidable from their point of view. I saw them looking at it a couple of hours later, and they didn't scootle off. They just stood and waved. Well, I thought they waved, anyway. So very slowly I bent down and took some pics. It was like sussing out the opposition before a launching a major attack across No Man's Land.

The grass was growing. I didn't like to get the hover mower on it, but I wasn't going to start doing it all by hand with the old mower. So I started it up one dinner time, began cutting in the corner closest to the house, and worked my way round, slowly… carefully. Closing inwards in big circles, so they'd know. And they did. I didn't see a single one. I even did their scorched part in the middle where the new shoots were coming up

259

through the black ash. I put the mower away and left them to it for the rest of the day.

They were out again next morning, on one of the slabs. 'Ah,' I thought, 'a delegation.' Don't we think stupid things? I mean – they're beetles, for Lordsake, like better-organised ants, that's all. I had no idea what they were doing with their little apparatus that made weird noises. I gave up and watched from my seat in the sun. Then something pinged right between my eyes, just on the top of my specs bridge. It was them! Little buggers! I went to look in the mirror – a tiny burn spot. *Right*!

Out I went, grabbed the yard brush and swept the lot away, off the slab. Their little machine thing was there and I picked it up – size of a cigarette lighter – vicious little thing. I tossed it in the pond, stepped over the fire trench and stomped up to the NASABin and gave it a mighty thwack on the side with the yard brush. I bet that rocked'em. The vibes must have carried on for ages.

The grass mowing wasn't due until the day after, but I did it then – from the outside working inwards again. I saw a little cluster of them cut off under the aquilegias. Ha! Talk about panic. I left them there, backed off and finished the grass. The rockery needed sorting out, too, I decided. I took a trowel to a few weeds, the mini-shears to the over-spreading dianthus, and the spade to a few rocks that had slumped down. I had a close look at their outpost base. It was pretty good; fabulous, in fact. It could easily be a Stars Wars castle, except it was only three feet high, with a couple of turrets rising higher. But that's pretty impressive, considering it was built by beetles on my rockery. It put me in mind of a fairy-tale castle bristling with technology – dull grey metal with mica-like bits that caught the sun. I shoved the spade in a few inches away, and tried it out... levered it back a fraction. Yes, their structure leaned a degree or two. Good – it wasn't invulnerable. I left the spade in and went to see if my between-the-eyes burn needed a dab of Germolene. It didn't.

I think that was lesson learned: they weren't telling me where I could go in my own garden. Setting up *their* perimeter line in my garden indeed. That was my line for them, not theirs to keep me out.

To make sure they understood the situation, I made a habit of stepping over the line every day – as I always did before, to check around, keep an eye on weeds, do some dead-heading, look for any deceased or dying mice or birds – JoeTheCat's a little devil sometimes. I left the spade there for a few days – I imagine the implicit threat was clear enough. Then I carefully eased it out the ground, trod the soil back firmly, and put the spade next to my chair. Let'em ignore that at their peril.

One day there was this tinny, whining noise coming from their bin. It was awful – screeching. I thought, *I'm not having bloody music on, especially not like that.* So I sorted out the battery-op radio, dumped it right next to their foot-of-ramp base – which was a foot across by then – and put it on Rock 404 for an hour while I went down the shop.

That put a stop to the musical disturbance.

Then, of course the drone came over *again*. Highly illegal over residential properties, but when did the police ever want to disturb their tea breaks for anything less than an easy-to-persecute speeding offender? And there it was, low – hundred feet or so, hovering right overhead.

The fuzz redeemed themselves by also not bothering to look into some moron's complaint that his drone had crashed, and therefore must have been shot down. I don't know how my tiny visitors did it, but if upright beetles ever had a smug demeanour about them, it was that lot.

I say "again" about the drone – it was up there a couple of weeks ago, same height. And the nosy toad put the footage of my garden on YouTube, complete with dustbin and rockery castle, claiming it was some Gamer fanatic. YouTube? Huh – refused to even answer my complaint about an invasion of my privacy. Fuzz didn't want to know about it, either. I'd have to get a solicitor. Oh, forget it.

So, I joined the blog and said it was a good job they'd airbrushed my half-naked children off the on-line footage, the ones who were playing the fantasy-gaming in the sunshine in the privacy of their own garden. But had he retained the original for his own pleasure? That got him taken off within an hour. And banned, I gather. I expect that had something to do with the fuzz not troubling themselves over the crashed drone. They visited, slightly amused, I think, and said the drone had obviously over-heated. It hadn't been shot at all; the motor was entirely melted. It had crashed about a kilometre north of where I live. Thus, equally obviously, nothing to do with me.

As I was pruning the clematis on the back wall that Sunday, I found two things: The first a stairway to heaven – or their equivalent, like a mountain cliff path winding its way up and up, round the wall blocks, digging into the mortar. Some of them were even up there doing it. I watched – they were slow, but it didn't

262

put them off, me watching. I let them get on with it and left the clematis as cover for them. The other thing was a heap of mortar dust, a miniature spoil heap – they were tunnelling through the wall! 'Twin escape bids, eh, guys?'

Well, if they were that desperate... I took a 1.5 cm masonry bit to the wall and drilled a hole almost right through – it's only a 300mm-long drill-shaft. That necessitated a visit to Screwfix on Monday to get a 600mm one and finish it – or actually, I drilled a separate one next to it, in case there were any of them inside, trying to finish off the first hole. Then another one, for two-way traffic.

That gave them access to the rest of the world, in effect. They could widen the hole if they wanted – I'm no jailer. The holes led into the Estate field, which had the hundred-year-old hedge and sort-of fence round it. It was hardly a barrier to anything: foxes came through regularly, and so did a badger sometimes. And I've seen weasels, or whatever the littlest ones are called.

I saw *them* using the bigger holes, coming and going. And I sat back in the sun and wondered if the world would be able to cope with them – my precious little drone-saboteurs. God bless'em.

They seemed to meet their match in the ducks. There was this enormous commotion one day – early morning. The ducks in the Estate field were really upset about something. There was all this flapping and quacking, and that beetle-generated high-pitched squeaking split the air as well. I figured that meant they could defend themselves, though not too well against ducks, perhaps. Maybe an honourable draw.

Whatever, the holes were covered with neat little doors next day. Maybe they'd come across a snake? There're grass snakes around the area, though I've never seen any on my plots – that's the only thing that would stand any chance of getting through the drill holes. Mice, perhaps.

That was pretty much how things remained for a time – although they finished their stairway up the back-stone wall. They've built another outpost up there, like the one on the rockery, but taller. I imagine it's a spy-out point rather than an antenna to the stars – three metres closer to the heavens wouldn't make any difference, but three metres above the surrounding landscape would. I could erect a flagpole if they wanted, I suppose. Or a tree. I bought a silver birch, a slender variety. The bark's rough, and they seem to be managing to climb it. I fitted a bird table up there, with my ladder at maximum extension to get it as high as poss. It's just a board with a wooden rim to stop seeds and metal-looking beetles falling off. And I put a Perspex top on it so the birds couldn't land and peck them up. I don't go up there to see, but I bought a Lumix camera with an extension lens that gives me 180 x zoom – and I can watch them up from my bedroom window. I've even taken pics of Jupiter and its moons with it – so it can get terrific pics of alien beetles, as long as I use the tripod.

*

We did something for each other last week. They started it with that infernal noise – they use it to get my attention these days, so I went over to see. They were spreading out another flat clearing area on the grass. The burned part has mostly regrown, and they were all lined up. I say "all" but there were about two dozen of them on parade; and my latest estimate is approximately a hundred, all told. They brought out these tiny things, the size of grass seeds, and laid them out on the sheet in three neat rows, twenty-one of them. And then they just sort of hung about. Yeah, right, fab ceremony that one, laying seeds out in the sun. It didn't even look like they were having a barbie and booze-up, but they started to go up and down the lines. I thought they were squirting something on them. They looked wet when they'd done, anyway. And they did it a few times. Watering them, I thought.

And after maybe a half-hour in the sun, they seemed to swell; the seeds, I mean. And then I was sure. Bigger and bigger. More water, sun still very warm. And my beetly friends dashed along the lines doing something. It might have been shouting or tapping.

One of them hatched! They were eggs! Bugger me! I was gobbled. I thought it was a party, but it was the outside maternity ward! Awesome. I was absolutely… *everything'd.* Couldn't think or breathe or say anything. I just watched – they'd invited me to the birth! 'Bugger me,' I kept saying. 'Bugger me.'

When I'd recovered, I went back for my camera and a can of John Smith's and sat there with them for ages. I couldn't bloody get over it.

So it was my turn. I fetched a notepad from the house and took it to them and did a drawing of the beetle-and-seed event, so they'd get the idea of 2D representation of real events – i.e., sketches and maps. I did it really small so they could see it without walking all over it. And in a series of picture maps, I did the baby unit again, next to their NASABin and on the lawn. And then expanding it to the whole garden, with the fences and back wall and house. I don't suppose they were nodding, not really, but I imagined they understood, and were probably becoming impatient with me. Then I added the adjacent plot that was just a slightly sloping meadow. They probably didn't know much about that one – although they had the silver birch perch, I suppose. Anyway, I drew it, and put extra lines round it; and rubbed out a bit of the fence between the garden and next-door. That would be another little hole. I tried to emphasise the double lines round the field – they would have access, but it would be secure for them.

They understood! They became all excited. Or maybe it was panic, not delight at my baby shower gift. Whichever, they were understanding it.

I rang FenceMeIn in the morning for a quote on a decent boundary fence all round my double plot next door. Five grand! Give or take, depending on the ground conditions, with concrete lower panels – they called them "gravel boards" – and larch-lap upper panels. One point eight metres high. But five grand? So what? Money schmunny: for my little oppos, nothing's too much. I'm probably a Godfather now. With my own family again – I can't get over it.

I'll have a solid gate through from my garden, and maybe a double one onto the road. And I thought, *If they're still here next year, I'll fence the big church field in as well, and there must be something I can do about the ducks. Soup, maybe.*

But winter's coming up, and my Littlies didn't like the heavy rain the other week. God help them with hail and snow and high winds. Maybe I could rig up a timber shelter for them, over the top of the NASABin, something like a wooden gazebo. I'll fill the fire-trench in, or drop a paving slab across it. Plus, perhaps, a hole through my back door, so they can get indoors if it turns really cold.

I'll do some drawings tomorrow and ask them. I wonder about the squeaky shrill noises they make: perhaps they're asking something. It sounds to be a complex, modulated FM sound that might be comprehensible with some effort.

I wonder if they like sugar? Or WD40? I could get them some fruit or mushrooms, maybe? Or a sample box of mineral and ore specimens?

And something special at Christmas... Ecclefechan tarts, perhaps.

Yes, it'll be wonderful to have a family again.

Stabbing pain. Awareness from nothing in an instant.

I gasped – or tried to. Mouth and nose blocked with slime. Eyes, too. Can't breathe… or scream. Choking, drowning in heavy gripping mud.

I'm sinking; trying to scream. Something foul writhing in my throat. Gagging, clutching for it. Fingers can't reach it. Retching on the taste… the stench. Sinking more. Struggling… so weak.

Exhausted. Can't carry on. Making it worse. Collapsing back. Need to stop – wait. Rest, not fight. Must stop – not sink further. Wait… *'Kyre hresh…?* What's happened? Where am I?'

Wait… wait. Let the pain ease… strength return. Crawling things against my skin. Near-buried in mud. Wait… wait…

*

Shuddering with cold; scarce breathing. I'm in a world of glooping mud. And zipping shrill insects. 'Who am I? *Ky-toin?'* What the fryke has happened to me?'

A single weak, choking cough. Not enough to rid myself of a finger-pinch of filth, never mind the thing that squirmed. Confused whirling in my head… What am I? I have a mouth? Hands? Face? I'm pain. As much pain as there is mud. Think back; can only be a few moments ago. I must know who I am… what I am. What is this place? Where am I?

Why am I here?

Wait… wait…

*

A voice! Loud and close. Raucous. Crashing into my head. Splitting me. 'Wha's app...?'

Grasped and heaved through mud, branches and leaves. *Kuit!* – my naked body, trailing legs, slimed and bloodied. Trying to struggle. Dragged out the mud... dumped onto a rotting log.

This is me? This convulsing body? What am I? Can't stop the shudders. Blood pouring down my chest and my arm. Can't cough... scarce breathe. Men hitting my back. Shouting, laughing. So loud. Black mud spurting out my mouth; blood splattering down me. Kuit! My side's split open in a huge rip, flesh straining out, blood pouring, mud-worm squirming, sinking back within.

Panic fading. Gasp a breath. Look round at hard faces and drawn swords. Men in muddied, dull-green uniforms. All so wrong. The whole stinking place reeking of decay. 'You're soldiers? Who are you? You *odiousi* creatures?'

In some awful guttural language, they demanded and sneered; laughed and poked at me, asking something, pointing up into the trees, at broken branches. Huge splatters of mud adorning drapes of grey lichen.

'Me? I fell? Through the trees?' Couldn't shake the dullness away. 'Where the *kuit* from?'

A pair of troopers closed round me, peering and prodding at my head, muttering. 'What's wrong up there? *Kyre rej?*' I asked. No answer. I reached up, *'Fryke!'* A jagged split.

One of them, a scar across his face, grunted, and jerked my hand away, and splashed swampy water over my head. He picked, teasing fragments away, showing me splinters of bone. And wood. I had fallen through the trees. Our eyes met. We both grimaced.

270

'*Yye froik.* That doesn't look good.' I stared disbelievingly at the bone fragments. My head's shattered? I was finished before I started. Started what? *Why am I here?*

Some of the men jabbered, pointing at my eyes.

'My eyes? What about them? *Gahi Kyre?*'

One forced into my mouth, fingers clawing, tugging out a flat-headed worm. Another prised two more from my skin. Vile things. Poking, digging into my side, deep inside, working another writhing creature from within.

Forced the pain to wash away... *'Na Kyre?* What do you want? Who are you?'

No-one answered. A baffled shrug. More incomprehensible muttering and head-shaking. One raised a sword over me. Scarface pushed it away, rapping orders. A rope slipped round my neck. I grabbed at it, *'Kyre hruuki...?* What are you doing?'

Too late. No strength. Dragged upright, swaying. Tried to resist, but I was forced away with a sword thrust and jerk on the neck rope. So that's where I'd been – in a splatter-pit, a crater of mud. Filthy brown-green water oozing back into it.

*

The faint, twisting trail was a torment, staggering through sucking mud and ensnaring vines, compelling me to keep going with incessant curses, sword stabs and jerks on my neck tether. Equally vicious little creatures snapped at my ankles, and swarms of insects plagued everywhere I bled – and that seemed to be everywhere.

'Hateful *maluki:* that one – called Scoppo – just loves using his sword. And that one who laughs so much. Him, jerking the rope. Not one of them understands a word I speak. *Voitugs!* They die.'

271

'Grallator! Grallator!' Yelling, the troopers were scattering into the swamp. I was alone. Mud-caked and naked. My tether hung free. Nowhere to go.

A dozen paces ahead: a crouched creature, covered in armoured scales, with a mouth to chew a man in half. Legs widespread, straddling the way, swaying slightly. My heart drooped into the mud with the troopers. 'So, you're a grallator, hmm?'

A whipping, barbed tail twanged like a straightening spring. I dipped; a trilth of a beat before it zizzed through the air where my neck had been. *Fryke! It was fast.* I crouched lower, trembling, and watched it bite down at a uniformed corpse, now headless. It growled, raising its head, as though fixing on me. Double rows of yellow-brown teeth, a killing system, backed up by a mass of writhing worm-like tongues. It glowered back across the trampled trail between us. Its tail lashed again, mouth opening in a silent roar, shoulders tensing, readying to come at me.

'You want me, do you? Not if—' I threw myself at it, half-rolling, grabbing a fallen wayside branch. Off-balance, the branch out in front of me, hurling myself at the beast.

So *fast* – hardly aware of my own movements, I was ramming the splintered end into the open mouth, deeper and deeper. Ranting at the monstrous *retilja,* forcing the branch inwards with all my weight and remaining strength. *Kuit!* I was shot through in searing pangs.

It bellowed and flailed, the hot stench of rotted stomach breath buried me, dagger-teeth snapping into the branch, raking along my arm. *'Ky-yack!!* – my hand!' Deep score-marks spurted blood.

Half leaping half-thrown by a swing of its thrashing head, I was spinning over backwards. Scrambling away, hardly aware of what I was doing. Beyond the range of the frenziedly-lashing tail, I knelt low, reaching to a second part-buried branch. *Careful... fingers grasping.* Crouched, watching the grallator as it raged, head waving wildly; long, taloned legs clawing at the protruding branch in its jaws, until it fell free, heavily bloodied. A moment more of fury and tail-whipping, a final, blood-spraying bellow, and it stamped howling into the swamp, raising clouds of insects and noxious vapours.

'Skoig oiff!' I cursed as it vanished, and I sagged. 'Where the Jebem did speed like that come from? In me? *Kuit!* I was fast.' And shocked at my own sheer violence.

Still on my knees, absolutely exhausted. The pain, effort, lost blood. Barely aware of the drab uniforms floundering back from the quagmire and root entanglements. Shaking, I breathed again, but couldn't even attempt to stop one of the troopers retrieving the neck tether, and adding a second one.

'Kyre vai? What am I?'

They pushed the mangled body of their former comrade aside. Dragged to my feet, the trek restarted.

'Yordy,' Scarface said, as we trooped past the abandoned remains, dark blood seeping into the sucking ooze – the first wriggles of hidden creatures already homing in.

'Kyre yu? These *vaahtos* left me here to join you, eh, Yordy?'

I detested them. Scarface was probably the only one who was not swamp-born scum. Our eyes met again, for a beat. Perhaps fellow-feeling, before the rope jerked, and I was dragged onward.

'Shu gustya.' I spat a mouthful of gunge and blood at the trooper gripping the rope, and bared my teeth at the one who held the new tether behind me. Both men flinched. That was better – my victory; my first smile.

*

The pace was more urgent. The mass of gashes and grazes brought me more pain. Ducking under low-hanging branches, constantly tripping over tangles of roots, I staggered through the mud and clutching vines. Unending, foul-tempered yanks at the neck leashes forced me on; plus the hilarious jabs from Scoppo's delightful sword. More and more, my hate concentrated on the ugly-grinning little *voitug*. 'Just give me one chance, you *vaahto*.'

He grinned, full of confidence. Swung his vicious blade…

*

A piercing two-note sound stopped us. The troopers listened and conferred – *that* direction. The brutal speed picked up again. A two-beat pause when the peal of notes sounded again, closer. Feet stumbled around the umpteenth chaos of creepers and hanging mosses, the ground seemed firmer, drier.

A clearing... Ahead, a high tower loomed, rising from a timber and wicker stockade wall. The troopers' shouts were answered by sentinels atop the tower.

My neck jerked forward; Scoppo grinned.

'You die. Definite. *Voitug.*' I snarl-smiled at him.

Another wrench. Another curse. Heavy wooden gates swung menacingly open.

'Need to get my head clear... gain strength.' I didn't know who I was appealing to, but I really needed help from somewhere.

*

The gates closed behind us, seeming to seal my fate. The air seemed suddenly darker in the settling gloom of evening, as heavy beams dropped into place. Hauled across a bare clearing, into the clamorous, stinking disorder of an army camp. All around were troopers and animals, smoking fires and fluttering banners, high tents and sheaves of stacked pikestaffs.

Taller than all others, I stared over the throng of drab uniforms and eager faces that crowded around us. A confusion of demanding, scowling troopers, egged on by the jeering Scoppo.

The evil little *vaahto* poked at the gaping split in my side; pointed at my eyes, between my legs, and the wide-open head wound. They seemed to be jabbering about every part of me, as I swayed in their midst. Yordy was mentioned, the men imitating the swing of the grallator's tail, pointing at me.

Dulled by the numbing pain, legs buckling, I mumbled, '*Kyre shoit?* Who are you rabble? Leave me be – I need to think.'

A broad, dark-uniformed trooper, three silver stripes on each shoulder, pushed through. Glaring red-faced up at me, his rasping, spittle-flecked interrogation meant nothing. They were all increasingly angry, shouting and arguing, until something was suddenly decided. They shrugged, waved at me dismissively.

'Hric cui...? No further interest to you, am I?' That much was obvious. I wasn't sure if that was a relief. Or more ominous.

*

In a beat, I was stumbling away – pushed and dragged through the horde, to a stake where a dozen coarse-haired animals rose, growling as we approached, needle fangs bared, back hair erect. One of the troopers said something about *hounds*, forcing me to the ground. He knotted the rope to the same post as the animals. Laughing, he kicked at me, swaggered away.

After the horrendous slog and stink through the swamp, the rich warmth of animal reek was almost comforting. Naked and shuddering, I sagged, befuddled. I don't think I ever felt that way before. It was... what? Humiliation. I didn't like it.

'Kyryck...? So, Fanged Ones, what do I do when you attack, hmm?'

But, as the moments crept by, and they didn't move, I began to believe they weren't going to attack, and I didn't feel so afeared, nor as shudderingly shocked by the whole thing. 'You're accepting me, are you?' I reached to the nearest one, let it smell my hand. Briefly, it licked at the blood. Strange – it didn't worry me – I wasn't getting any feel of death-lust from them. 'You'll share your warmth, eh?'

Couldn't think – a swirling red mist covered everything. But I had to sort through my mind – the tangling thoughts – think back. *'Kyre reck?'* I appealed to the hounds. 'Who am I? What is this body I have? It's damaged? Badly? And who are these vaahto-men yelling at me like skacks on heat? If that sadistic little Scoppo fryker sticks me once more...'

I raked into the fur of the closest hound. *'Kimji Kyre voi?* Do you know what they're planning, eh?' The teeth-baring beast answered with a low growl. I growled back. *'Mie ti...* Come closer, Warm One.' I pulled at it, feeling it resist a moment before shuffling beside me and accepting my arm around it. It didn't growl any more. I felt better.

The gloom deepened, and I sniffed a rich aroma of spiced food from the camp fires. Another of the hounds came snuffling uncomfortably close to my groin. *'Jresh...?* Getting restless? We're all in the same javola, are we?'

Slumping against the post, I waited, and the minins stretched. Tried to relax my tensed-up muscles, and slow down my spinning mind. Two dozen paces away, the flame-silhouetted mob of soldiery stamped round, stoking the fires up, voices raised in laughter.

'Ahh, the drinks are out, hmm?' The hounds didn't answer. 'Well, whatever they plan for me, I'm more rested now; and I'm not shaking so much.'

'Come.' I dug my fingers into the neck fur of the beasts on either side of me. 'You'll share your strength with me, won't you, my *killi* friends? I suspect I may need it before long.'

*

277

The wait stretched gratefully out; the men were settling; more wood went on the fires; a group began chanting. Eventually, two gloating troopers headed my way, jabbering together as they towered over the hounds and me. I managed to smile back. 'You voitugs speak in the tongue of worms for all the sense you make. *Kyre inik?* My turn for dinner, is it?'

Twisting the tethers free, they hauled me up, and dragged me towards the main fire before I could get my balance. Staggering into the middle of a circle of baying soldiers, I stood alone, still the tallest there. They were readying themselves for something... something to do with me. Ritual execution, I imagined.

'So, I'm the *oyin kulji*, am I, the entertainment? One of these *vaahto* creatures is readying to attack, hmm? Which one?' Alert as a goyat mother, I studied them all, tried tensing and untensing my muscles: some felt unweakened. Others were gone. The stocky soldier with silver stripes stood slightly alone, prominent among them. They didn't like to crowd him too much, hmm? He would make a clear target, should I need to attack.

Take the advantage – with all the flamboyance I could muster, I spat at the nearest tormenter, flexed my fingers in anticipation of how I might retaliate when he launched at me. Perhaps, just perhaps, if that swamp-born speed comes to me again, I might survive longer. The trooper was considering his choices. Carefully, I coiled the tethers around one forearm. Swaying, stumbling without even moving, I tensed, ready to burst into movement when he – or another of them – pounced.

A shout! A commotion. Two people pushing closer: both so different from the weather-beaten faces and forest-green-and-mud uniforms of the soldiery. One was

278

a tall man in a dark uniform, gold braided. The other was small, in scarlet apparel with black cording, and a face that was smooth, with pale cheeks. I stared down as the smaller one came close. My mind blanked. What are you? Slender fingers reached to me. I flinched as they trailed across my body, where the open slash still trickled blood. '*Hruish*?' A strange shock as I realised, 'You're... a woman?'

Turning, she berated the troopers, ranted at Silver Stripes and argued with her companion; turning to prod at the blood-crusted split in my side, pointing up to my head, and the equal split up there. Angry, she demanded something of me. I had no idea what, and silently stared back. She renewed her argument with Gold-Braid, pushing the jeering troopers back, her arms waving more urgently. Silver Stripes argued with her and Gold-Braid; all asking and demanding; troopers gesturing skywards, arms dropping in a sudden fall, and great splatter.

'Kyre ti? That was me again, Hmm?'

Another decision. The woman raged at the two decision-makers, and fought against the muddy green uniforms who held her back. She didn't look too happy with me, either. 'Perhaps you're averse to blood-and-mud cloaked monsters?' I wondered. 'You had your own plans for me, eh, woman?' But she hadn't had her way – the circle re-enlarged around me. Cheering and chanting, they were ready to continue.

Radiating confidence, it was sword-sticking Scoppo who stepped forward, twirling his blade with well-practiced ease, clearly expecting an easy and amusing triumph. A bragging jest, accompanied by deft whirling of the blade in the direction of my groin.

'Good of you to tell me what you intend, hmm?'

The troopers' impatient yells sparked in my head, added a sharper edge, and I sank into a defensive crouch. 'You gruesome little voitug. You mean to slice bits off me, hmm? Nai mie.' I fixed a rock-smile on him.

Focusing on Scoppo... increasingly aware of everything around me: the fire's heat; the tang of smoke and burned food; the uneven ground. Scoppo's teeth reflected the fire, red and ugly, bared in a confident snarl. The changing hand-grip; the light footwork, over-playing to his audience; stepping close, reaching down to me. Down... down... He was so slow...

So much time... In a dozenth of a heartbeat, I had him. Rigid fingers rammed straight through his eyes, destroying the arrogance. I clutched, cartwheeling over, ripping out the middle of his face; hurling him back. Staying on him, I crushed him down, smashed a fist into his throat. His neck bones crunching most satisfyingly.

I spat into the dead and ruined face, 'Visco, Shirick – Riddance, Accursed One.' And tore the sword from his failed grasp. 'Remain calm; stay on the corpse. There'll be more. This sword hilt feels good.' I adjusted my grip, and spat defiant blood at the nearest troopers as they recommenced their chant, and clattered swords on their scabbards. Faces lit up from within as well as from the fire. *'Kyre rashi?* Who's next?'

A low growl behind me. Stupid to warn me. I dropped aside. Rolled to my feet. My newly-acquired sword lancing of its own accord. Straight through the gaping mouth of the trooper launching at me. I side-stepped. A wrist-flick, and his brains were stirred as he toppled face down into the fire.

'Not so entertained now, are you, *moi kytterlings?'* Inside, I shook, but found grim pleasure in disposing of two of my tormenters. I treated the rest to a challenging, bared-teeth snarl, and waited.

The mass of shouted advice from his encrowding supporters didn't make the next one any less careless, confident that I was tumbling off-balance. His face a sudden picture of disbelief as the steel blade sliced into his guts, and his bowels slurped, glistening, by the fire, as he descended slowly among them.

'*Kyre ruti?* Who now? Wait, wait,' I ordered myself. 'Wait, see.' Swaying badly, I could scarce stand. But needed to watch them. Which next?

They quietened in the flickering firelight. The sword was slipping from my grasp; fingers numbed. 'Strength, Ti Kyre – I need strength. Come to me.' The troopers edged, shuffling, undecided about their amusement now.

That *riuff* woman was still close by, still screeching and yappering her protests. Glancing, yes, *there*. Watching us. I stared back at them. 'Braided Uniform's annoyed – keeps shushing her. *Ti mie voi...?* You still want me, do you, woman? It'd stir you up if I could get to you, eh, *Uniform*? Ah, these two on my left – they've agreed their tactics? All their nodding and eye-flicking? Coming... Now!'

The instant they leapt forward, I side-stepped – no thought, no plan. As though of its own accord, my sword cleaved straight down through one trooper's head, splitting it in ghastly halves. I rammed his over-fleshy comrade backwards, crushing him flat on his back in a heartbeat. Tubby gasped something fear-filled, face a mask of amazed horror.

Silence shrouded them all... breath held. Blood dripped into Tubby's left eye from the point of the sword I had poised over him. He was down and out. I hesitated… '*Kyre huig?* You concede?' He wouldn't know the words, but he knew what I meant, alright. They all did.

A loud shout. Commanding. Braided Uniform was demanding something of the woman. She nodded repeatedly; eagerly. He hesitated… dismissed her to the shadows with a wave, and stepped forward.

'So you've agreed something with the woman, have you? What this time?' I kept the blade hovering over the fat one's face, splitting my attention between him, the advancing Uniform, and the edging-closer troopers.

'Captain,' Uniform said, patting his own chest, 'Captain Briand.' He was afraid. Of me. Visibly trembling, he gestured for me to surrender the sword.

'What do I do? *Ria voi?* I should trust you?'

Uniform – Captain – gestured again for the sword. What else to do? Attack them all? Carry on like this? Not realistic. Deeply untrusting, eyes wide, I started to rise.

A too-fast movement from Tubby. His blade sliced up. I twisted away, '*Kaka!* Fool!' He died instantly, Scoppo's sword slamming through his right eye, spiking his head tight to the ground. 'You treacherous bakho creature.'

He'd slit me across my belly. A stinging, biting pain and yet more blood. How could I trust them? The sword sucked out Tubby's eye socket, and I raised it slowly, to within a hand's width of Uniform's belly. He stood his ground, shaking more than I was. '*Soiking Vaahto.* You're fearful, aren't you?' It was almost amusing. He barked orders to the soldiery, waved them back, and stretched out a hand to me for the sword, speaking again in quiet tones.

'The entertainment's off, is it, *mi kuik?* Trying to reassure me?' The same debate inside. What do I do? Attack them all? Frykit! I had to risk him again... lowered the sword a second time. '*Kyre rashi?* You know you're dead if that happens again, Uniform... Captain? *Tio Theron.*'

'Kyre?' The captain repeated it, and beckoned Silver-Stripes forward, rapping orders to him. Both said Kyre several times. They knew not what it meant. I told them, but they had no understanding. Pointing at me, as though calling me Kyre. Then telling me the broad silver-stripe one was called Mink. '*Bannerman* Mink.' Patting his own chest again. '*Captain* Briand.'

I tried to stand. Couldn't. Raised the sagging sword again. '*Nai Kyre...* Kyre's not my name. It means Question – I ask a question.'

But it was obvious Captain and Silver-Stripe Mink didn't understand. They repeated it. 'Kyre,' pointing at me, 'Kyre.'

'So, I'm called Question, am I?' I tried to think, 'I'm not Kyre. I'm... I'm...' It was blank. I had no idea who I was.

Ky-oh, what to do? Accept it? I half-nodded to them, knowing I couldn't keep the sword – they'd attack me, all at once, if I refused to give it up. '*Kiri hagg.*' In a last burst of defiance, I thrust the long blade into the fat one's rounded chest and rammed it home. It had the required effect on the surrounding troopers, and afforded me the opportunity to slip Tubby's dagger inside the wrapping of corded tethers around my forearm.

Standing next to the two Uniforms, I gave the assembled soldiery a long stare, and growled like a

283

hound. I know it was stupid, but they got the idea. And I got a smile out of it while I wondered what was next to come: 'I've killed five troopers at what should have been my execution. What now? Back with the hounds, am I? While these two consider more entertaining ways to kill me? That woman, too – where's she gone? *Troi gasri?* Given up, has she? Or up to some malign scheme of her own?'

It was comforting to feel the dagger's hilt, buried in the coiled tether. I turned to the higher uniforms without one iota of trust. I tried to keep what tiny advantage I had, and summoned up enough arrogance to deliberately irritate them. Straightening, looking down on them all, I sneered around, waved them to lead the way, to whatever they had in mind for me. *'Hoi! Vaahtos...'*

*

They escorted me through the mob of gawping troopers, the captain rapping out his orders again; the bannerman arguing. A small enclosure with high wicker walls was what they had in mind. Large animals were tethered to rails outside.

The two uniforms continued to argue: Silver Stripes demanding and loud; the captain calm and insistent. I watched, 'You want different things of me, hmm? One wants me dead; the other has plans for me... and the woman? I expect you'll take turns with your own schemes.'

Pushed into a dimly-lit compound, a motion across the throat conveyed the idea that I shouldn't attempt to leave. Behind me, bolts grated into place, and the arguing continued: they seemed to have a fondness for bolts and arguments. I stared into the dung-reeking darkness, nervous of what might be there, but feeling

284

slightly more secure with the dagger clutched tight. *'Kyrith ki?* What's in this place?' Movement. Four men were sitting together in the near-black corner, staring my way. A couple of water pails by my feet. A heap of loose pelts and blankets filled the opposite corner. 'They'll do. At least I get a rest.'

I stumbled across, and reached down to the furs. Fryke! Pain bit through me! Plus the powerful stink of wet fur, on top of my own swamp and blood stench. The mound moved. *'Toi gaic* – someone's in there already. Damn!' I sank to the ground next to the heap, readjusting my grip on the knife, and leaning back against the heavy wickerwork. 'I need to retch. Did I swallow some of those vile worms? Or just mud? What the kroit is happening? Kyre moi? Who am I?' I shivered, chilled by the cooling air, the slaughter of five men, the incubus trek to this ghastly place, and desperate to know who the fryke I was.

Very tentatively, I touched at patches of numbness, areas that oozed and ached. *'Liru kyre?* Am I still alive?' I felt at the wounds across my head and side... my belly. 'Oh, *Kroitit* – Tubby's knife-slash's feels worse than I imagined. Be lucky to make it to first light – too much blood lost; too much mud and mould taken in. Then the noisome threesome'll be fighting over my scraps.' I almost managed to laugh at the prospect, 'Give me rest... some sustenance... and we'll see.'

A movement among the furs, *'Kyre ets?* Who's there?' Heavily shadowed eyes peered at me. 'I watched warily as a slender hand appeared. It beckoned. I hesitated only a beat, and shuffled sideways under the raised kurk. Grateful to whoever... whatever, I let the long coarse-haired pelts envelop me, half-expecting another knife in my stomach. *'Keetai,'* I muttered in thanks, gradually settling, with an awareness of welcome body warmth, less alone in the darkness.

A touch on my upper arm made me jump. Smooth fingertips caressed my skin, exploring me. *'Jebem!* Why would...? The woman?' I checked the dagger again. 'I know nothing about such creatures. There's something worrying about them? They're an unknown peril? Kroit! Is she *that* woman?'

Fingers stroked... pressed delicately at my skin, paused at a crusted, bloody patch; then slithered onward. *'Hoi-tu!'* she triggered something in me. 'What does she intend? Is this some dreadful mistake? Dare I reach to her? Surely can't be worse than my experiences with men.'

A harsh, strident voice! Above me. Two men. Wrenching at the furs that covered us. I raged upwards. Tubby's dagger slashed into one's face, tearing a great flap of flesh away before plunging to the hilt in his throat. The man had no lower-body clothing, something protruded like a baton. His partner was slow. The dagger tore him apart in five raging beats. Panting with tension, half-crouched, I took a final rent at each corpse, 'What now? Damn, it's all ended now.'

My furs-fellow strode across the open compound, bending briefly over the two survivors. A blade flashed momentarily. *'Shai chi!* She really is a she – the shape, the way she walks. Yesss... she's the captain's irritant. So what was it that she wanted me for?'

Unspeaking, we struggled to heap all four corpses in their corner. She pulled at their clothing, gathering a selection of coats and trews, shirts and boots, and tossed them to the pile of furs we had just vacated.

Whatever she'd intended, my encounter with her was finished, wrecked by these frykers in the corner. For some reason, I was immensely disappointed, 'Fryke them. Just when something was about to happen.' I wasn't sure what, but – *Svecki!* – it had felt good. Furious, I slashed at their faces, rage taking over from the memory of that warm-body near-experience. 'Though perhaps not completely,' as I looked down at my nakedness.

She was back beside me, dismissing the corpses with a curling lip and a shrug, 'Brigands... Bandits... *Come.*' The words sounded familiar. That's what Scarface, in the swamp patrol had said, and Silver Stripes.

Gesturing, she pulled me beneath the dim entrance lights. Pressed me onto an upturned wooden pail, and began to wash me, slowly and deliberately, using water from a second, leather pail. For an age I suffered the rubbing and poking, both of us grimacing as she pulled wood and bone splinters from the gashes in my head and side. I shuddered with the cold and unending pain, gritted my teeth, and forced myself not to jerk away from fingers that determinedly pried and picked and probed at me.

She turned to the long split across my stomach, where the fat little fryker's dagger had sliced. Holding up a bone needle and a length of thread, she asked something. I didn't understand, until she pulled the sides of the wound together, and forced the needle through the brought-together flesh. Screaming inside, I clamped my eyes shut, tight-balled my fists, and endured an eon of fiery agony as she crudely stitched across my stomach.

Sinkingly miserable and disappointed, I attempted to divert my thoughts from the injuries: *'Kyre rash va yoi? Who are you? Kyre hirimi? What is this place?'*

Her interest focused on the deep, bursting-out swamp-split in my side. Splashing water around it, she initiated a new age of agony as the needle dug into my flesh again and again, probing and pulling, pushing flesh inwards and sealing it with a ragged cross-line of thread.

I forced my mind to think of other things, words: Captain, Mink, sword, dead. I was covered with threads the thickness of cord, certain that my own words should feel clearer in my head. Maybe this gash is really serious? I reached to feel at my head, but she shushed me, and pushed my hand away.

A vision to bathe in, I knew I'd remember her quiet smile in the faint light as long as I lived – 'Perhaps even as far ahead as dawn.' I almost chuckled as I said it. A sharp word from her stopped me, and her hands pressed to each side of my head. She chanted a rote of mysterious words over and over, 'Strength... Power... Rua... Wellness... Unity...' Intermittently, she picked more embedded bits out of my hair, tutted about the skull wound, and repeated the words slowly, over and over, as though I might remember them better.

Caressing my skin; murmuring. I caught the meaning of that, but she returned to washing and digging into the head split, and didn't sound so positive. 'Mould,' she said several times, pulling faces and shaking her head. 'Swamp fungus.'

Whatever that was, it didn't sound good. But she patted and poked and spat into the wound; rubbed deftly. At long last, she bound up the split with a length of sleeve. *'Dreshi* – I feel freshly pained in all places.'

'Kyre?' she asked, then pressed my hand against her face. 'Li. I am Rua Li. Of the Rua Sisters. Now *drink.*' I took the clay vial that she proffered, and swallowed the contents; a sour-sweet taste with eye-smarting aftertaste. Two more followed, each accompanied by, 'Drink.' Plus another that she poured onto the head binding.

Seemingly finished, she sat and faced me, held my head and stared into my eyes. Again, she chanted, and repeated the same meaningless words, 'Strength... Safety... Loyalty... Rua.' I spoke the words with her, trying to understand their meanings.

'Hui lut? Why do you help me?' I knew there would be no answer. I scarcely knew what I asked, though more of their words came to me – Rua. Li. Welcome. Warm. Help. Body. Drink. Come. Give. Some have a reassuring sound to them, but others are harsher: Scoppo, die, hate, kill, blade, bandit, trooper, Captain, Bannerman. 'What a dreadful language they speak.'

That soft one-sided smile, and she urged me back to Furry Corner. Her mutter sounded warmly promising as we pulled the skins over ourselves. 'Whether it's the scrubbing or the medyky... Or the words, or the smile, but something's making me feel good.'

She shushed me, and settled close. Her fingers trailed excruciatingly along Tubby's long, newly-stitched split across my stomach; and then the other one. She said something – about the wounds, perhaps. Then repeated it slowly as if I might understand better. I didn't; but it didn't sound wonderful.

By then she was caressing elsewhere. Her murmurs sounded considerably more approving, as her fingertips delved, and stroked me softly.

Straightway, my... my *something* was rising uncomfortably again. *'Shoh!'* Her fingers curled around me and massaged. My breath taken, I sucked in abruptly as she pressed closer. Unsure why, I tried to find a way through the furs and covers to reach her body. It was a dream of warmth and refuge and delight at the unknown. Uncertainly, I explored... and probed into her softness and intimate places... a smooth curve... a tuft of silken hair. In moments, we were sharing low gasps and murmurs, warm clutches and gentle touches, bodies pressed together, legs intertwined.

'I... I don't know what I should do.' I realised I had no idea what this was about. I burned in shame and regret for being there, for doing this... whatever it was. 'Kroit! I wish I'd never started, not had today in my life, not had a life.'

But she knew, guided me, and I was grateful for her dominance, and calmed as she delicately eased and gripped at me, leading me to enter her. So carefully and gently at first, and I was overcome and then I knew... powerfully, and driven. Feeling her tighten and dig her fingernails into me.

'Jeemo! Kyre. Slow... slow.' She urged me, softly massaged and eased. And she wriggled and writhed back at me, impaling herself. We each sighed and thrust back.

*

The exigencies ended, we sank into a torpor, arms entwined. Through the night I tried to ease my agonies in body and mind. 'What have I been doing? How can I not know? Is there some terrible aftermath to this? What will the dawning bring?'

Sick inside, I tried to sleep. At one time, I was aware of troopers at the gates, peering in, talking briefly in ominous tones. '*Ti liuk*. I fear I'll need to be rested for the morrow.'

Somehow, I found her presence deeply comforting, warmly asleep beside me. Occasionally, she nuzzled closer and pressed her forehead against mine, as though passing her inner thoughts into me. Her hands nestled round my head as she murmured the words – perhaps to heal me, or for me to remember, 'Strength... Realm... Loyalty... Rua.'

From time to time, her delicate fingers strayed, and lingered over my muscles and injuries. 'Jeemo, Kyre,' she said, many times, as she stroked me.

As the sky lightened, her warmly naked body stirred again, her hands on me, coddling and demanding anew, her voice persuading, encouraging. Her body so supple and smooth, and it aroused me as the night before. My breath came in forced gasps as I explored her inviting softness again, finding she responded to some touches, and to others. And to yet others, as did I, with more urgency.

I believed I knew what to do now, but she surprised me, sliding her nakedness over mine, and pressing intimately together. I had so little understanding of what was happening, permitting her to ease me back, mounting me as she adjusted her position, spearing herself. I adored her, her words, her body, her movements. Welcoming her softness around my hardness.

Lost in the power of the experience, I let it happen, encouraged where I could, and responded as best I might. I stroked at the tactile vision that rode me, eased the furs back and gazed at the unsuspected beauty of naked breasts as she writhed and gyrated on me.

We both gasped and strove in increasing urgency for a dreamlike age, until I burst into her, completely lost in awe and release. That face of splendour, body of utter wonder… ecstasy for mind and body.

'Li,' I said. 'Li.' Knowing there was definitely something infinitely more splendid about women than men.

*

Easing free of each other, I lay still, momentarily sated, my mind wandering over new things. 'I've been dragged out a swamp… butchered seven men… entwined with a woman twice. *Yuaka!* So much going on; all so baffling. My big trouble is *kiri-ya* – I don't know *anything*. I'm filled with confusion; strange people, and words with unknown meanings – Strength… Li… Rua... Safety. She means me to remember these things. To believe them? Live them? Why? What do they mean? Realm… Unity… Loyalty?

'Why am I here? There must be a reason for being in this world. But it's lost to me.' My head wound panged and stabbed, as though awakened by my uncertainty. 'Did someone, or something, have a purpose sending me here? Did I truly fall through the trees into the mud? Where from? For what purpose?'

From somewhere very close came that same piercing two-note sound that had led the swamp troopers to the gates, now repeated three times. The gates to the compound were pushed open, and four scruff-coated troopers stepped in. 'So,' I wondered, 'what do you plan now?'

Li waved them away. They hesitated, conferred, and turned to the corpses in the corner. Although grimacing, they didn't seem to be greatly concerned about the ravaged state of them. One trooper searched through the pockets, removed a few pieces of something, and collected the remaining boots and other clothes.

She murmured, and pressed me back down, holding and cuddling me for a moment. I squeezed back, but she was rising, wanting to check the wounds beneath the red-stained bandages. Her expression conveyed a sense of, "Ah well, such a pity." That faded smile. A regretful gaze, perhaps, as she stood and pulled a karakul pelt around her for warmth.

The darkened bruise that stretched from ankle to my neck caught her attention. She touched along it, pressing tentatively, before moving onto the red-stained bindings across my side and stomach, peeling them off in a time of skin-ripping, crusted blood and deadened flesh. I poked delicately at the stark and sticky slashes – laced with Li's thick thread to hold them together. Felt sick.

It took long moments to pour something sticky and stinging into the wounds, and to replace the bindings with less-bloodied ones. And then to manage three more swallows of the oily drink as she held my head, endlessly murmuring the same few words, staring into my eyes, as if the message would sink into me and be understood later – 'Strength... Loyalty... Rua... Realm...'

Then brought me the salvaged clothing. I sniffed at each piece dubiously, and struggled to pull them on. Li sliced the tethers from my neck and coiled one round my waist. It was almost hidden by my newly-acquired too-tight shirt. The needle dagger seemed to meet with her approval, and she pushed it into my tether belt, putting a finger to her lips. That was clear enough. So wondrous, her bearing seemed less tense now, with bounce in her movements.

'Captain Briand,' she said. And repeated it several times, nodding. Make sure I understood. I nodded back, Captain? That was the tall one in the braided uniform. What about him?

She led me to the open gates. A thing with wheels stood outside, two of the large beasts beside it, a cage on the back. Around it stood a dozen troopers, their uniforms the same dark green as the Captain's, though theirs had no decoration. Waving towards the distant hills, touching my chest, 'Kyre,' she said. 'Captain Briand. Great House. Kyre Go.' With all her waving and pointing and touching, I gathered I was to be taken somewhere far away in the thing – the *wagon*. Uniform's orders? These are his own troops? He has plans for me?' Not a welcome thought – A more ritual, public execution, perhaps?

The swamp-mud-and-green troopers already in the compound snapped a few words to Li, pushing her through the gates, blocking my way when I tried to follow. She stepped away, pausing at the threshold. 'Kyre,' she said. That part-smile again before she turned and in two beats was lost to sight in the assembled ranks of the bannerman's soldiery.

'Rua Li, *Kyrisha*.' I said, feeling more alone and desolate than I had in the swamp. 'You have whatever you fought the captain for? Leaving me to... to what? Captain Gold Braid with his wagon or Silver Stripes with his massed troopery?'

The nearest troopers shared nods, and turned to me, grinning. One jabbed a goad into my back – Another Scoppo! I whirled in an instant and had the runty little black-haired vaahto up in the air by the throat. '*Noiya dammi.* Touch me once more and your throat will be gone.' I tossed him away, suddenly aromatic in his fear.

I paused for a moment, watching him snivel away. 'Might as well face this like a – whatever I am.' And stalked through the gates, stopping again for a moment to glower around the massed soldiery, sliding a hand inside my tethers for the dagger.

'Whatever you have planned for me, I'll give you a kroiting good run for your trouble. *Hoi, vaahtos!'*

THE TWELVE DAYS OF CRYSTAL-AMMAS

This is so exciting! We are leaving Erith for a new life at a planet called Yeniev! It's fantastic! *Us!* It's a very long way away.

'We'll be three decca-days getting there,' Mum and Dad say.

It's amazing. We're on this space ship. It's called the Boldly Go. This is the first time we've been up in space. Though we've seen lots of pictures, of course, and films and sims; and games on the vids and tellyvees. There's even been some vids of the very place we're going.

'That's the exact same place we're going to, Crissy,' Dad said. He always calls me Crissy. He says Crystal-Ammas is much too formal for a twelve-year-old girl for every day.

'We can build our own new house there, and I'll have a job as a machine operator at a new mine that works Carbonous Beryl Idium.' I think that's what he called it.

Me and Jenny, who is my little sister and my best friend, are allowed to play in the Vista Lounge where there are big screens like windows, and we can see outside at Space and all the black, and the stars.

I've already counted nineteen other children. 'And I think there's lots more,' Jenny said, 'because Dainty Fourn told me it's a very big ship with loads of other areas.'

**

Something is ever so wrong today. All the grown-ups are looking really worried and talking in whispers, though all they tell us children is, 'Things are alright and

297

will be fine.' But Mum and Dad look more scared than I've ever seen them. Me and Jenny are strapped into the big comfy seats, in a lifeboat that's called a landing podule, and I'm so frightened. I'm shaking all over and somebody's saying we'll all be killed. And that's making people really upset. Mum and Dad are in the same podule. And some of the other passengers, too, like the Wilyons with Bazzy and Freddy and Desmy, who are my friends.

'It's only while the crew try to fix what's gone wrong,' Mum says. 'They say there's a planet we might be able to reach and get help.'

I think it's a magnetic something but I don't know if it's inside the Boldly Go or in space outside. I hope we'll be—

***

The Boldly Go has crashed. We don't know what happened, but Daddy says it must have broken up in orbit.

'Or been shot at,' Mr Wilyon thinks.

'They released all the lifeboat podules so they could land on their own.'

It was really terrible and frightening for all of us. We were shaking about all over the place, juddering and jumping, and people were screaming and praying. Like me and Jenny. They said it was white hot and we were burning up and breaking up. But we bounced and rolled and there was all this crashing and banging and being thrown everywhere, and Dad was shouting.

'It's splitting up,' somebody yelled, and it was.

The wall down the side has split wide open and we can see dark outside.

We're all shouting and trying to get out.

'It might catch fire,' one man keeps saying. He's a crewman. The men are telling him how brave he is and how he got us down alright. So now we have to sit outside because the smashed-up lifeboat might catch fire. It's cold and dark and we don't know where we are.

Dad says people are trapped inside but we can't see them in the dark. Somebody's screaming, but that's getting quieter. A lot of people are scared and sobbing. We can hear them.

****

We still don't know where we are. It's morning and very grey, and a lot of people were killed in the crash. Our lifeboat is all crushed and crumpled and smashed. Some of it's missing altogether. We can see other parts of it a long way away. And big scratches and holes. 'All that wreckage is just ours,' one of the crewmen said. 'We don't know what happened to the other lifeboats – if they escaped. Or if they crashed.'

'We lost contact with the Boldly Go, and the other lifeboats when we cut free.'

They told Dad and Mr Wilyon there were twenty-eight lifeboats. 'They can't all be lost.'

'Not with all those people on them.'

'They must be scattered everywhere.'

'What happened?'

They're looking at me and Jenny. 'Well, *I* don't know. It wasn't me,' Jenny said.

'They said about magnetics-something trouble, then the Boldly Go couldn't slow down enough. We had to launch the podules at too high a speed.'

They're counting up now. 'We think there are only forty-one people still alive here,' another crewman says. 'Lifeboat Two-zero was full to capacity – one hundred and twenty souls. And twelve crewmen. There are only four of us now.'

I work it out. 'There must have been three thousand, three hundred and sixty people on the space-ship,' I whisper to Jenny. 'As well as the crew.'

We can see people who are dead. They're like broken and twisted in their seats in another compartment where there's a lot of blood. And some're charred, like scorched. Mr and Mizzy Joynes are dead. 'I don't mind that too much because he was always telling me off for making a noise,' Jenny whispered.

Ah, the men are excited and waving. There's a floater coming this way. It's a big wide one, and it's going slowly. 'It's searching for us.'

'It's found us. Look.'

'It's not easy to miss a craft the size of a lifeboat,' someone's saying, waving at all the wreckage. 'There must be debris for miler after miler.'

'And massive scrapes in the land.'

We're everso pleased and happy but a bit worried as well because we don't know which planet this is, or who lives here. Me and Jenny are dancing up and down because we're saved.

*****

We're in a place like the livestock market at Ryetown. It's so awful and horrible. Everybody is hugging everybody else. It's noisy and loud and these horrible creatures are all round and they look at us and talk with the big ugly horrible thing that was in the floater. It found us and brought us here. Not like a man, it's an alien with four arms like tentacles – and suckers instead of fingers. One of the crewmen – the one with the grey edge on his working drags – says they are Urigs. So this must be the planet called Urig. 'They don't do much space travel,' he said. 'I've seen a few. Bit backward. Brutal. Speak a dialect of Stang – might be able to communicate with them.'

But it didn't want to communicate when it found our lifeboat podule. It came round, stomping and kicking like we'd smashed up its best fields, going mad and throwing things. And people. Dad was in its way and it just ripped him up! In pieces. Dad's blood was everywhere and Mum screamed and hit it but it picked her up, shook her and threw her. I hit it and screamed and it picked me up in its tentacly arms-things and threw me through the air into its floater – like a big open wagon. I was really hurting and I couldn't see Mum, and my dad was killed. Some of the others were dropped in there with me – Jenny and the Wilyons and three crewmen and others…

301

It brought us here to this place like a market and we can't get out because there's an electric wire all round and it goes Flash! And Sizzz! if anyone touches it. The Urig pushed Crewman Dave against it and he yelled and smelled of burning. We're all together near the middle, and Crewman Dave can't move. He's choking and there's smoke coming from his clothes.

I'm on my own now. In the middle of this electric pen and I ache all over and haven't had anything to eat or drink and the Urig thing lashed a tentacle arm at me when I had a wee. It put a bowl near me after that. Then another with water in it.

It came in and it killed Crewman Dave. Just like that – tentacle arms round his head and body and twisted and it ripped Crewman Dave's head off and took him away. It talks, like our Stang, but different. I can understand it some of the time. The grown-ups said the Urig was selling us to the other Urigs coming past – for novelty slaves, live bait, ornaments... collectables... pets... *sex things*. It quivered its upper armicles whenever it said "sex things" to the others, and its eyes glittered and sparkled.

The last Urig he did that with took Mr Wilyon and Mizzy Wilyon.

Bazzy, Freddy and Desmy were crying and hugging each other with me and Jenny. But then others came up and pulled us apart and they were like laughing when we struggled and kicked, and they dragged Freddy, Desmy and Jenny away. We were all screaming, and Jenny tried to get back to me but the thing wrapped its armicles round her and I saw her carried away.

Our Urig is called "Boiko". It's clunkier and bigger than anybody, especially in the leather-smelling and metal-shining clothes it wears.

A different Urig was here a few minins ago. It had skin that was purply, and frills. Thinner and taller, it was looking at us and talking with our Urig. I think they are the men ones. He came in our pen and his armicles crept all over me! It was horrible. Slinking inside my clothes and stroking my skin. I mean – *everywhere*! And he was feeling at me, like to see if I was plump like we do with Blotefish. It did it to Bazzy as well. And he didn't like it, either. Some other purply ones came in as well and looked at us and talked about us. Then they went away with Bazzy.

Which leaves just me on my own here now. And not so many Urig people. I can see some other pens with animals in them – some with long necks, and some really hairy ones. And I can see the two crewmen in a pen with things like lizards with huge long teeth and claws, and the crewmen are dead and the lizard-things are eating them. They had been alive. The lizardy-things did it. "Live bait," Urig Boiko says. 'And live food, as well.'

'Are they eating Bazzy?' I wonder. 'He's fat.'

They're packing up now. The floaters are coming in, the electro fences wrapped away and all the equipment loaded onto the float-backs. A lot of soft-looking bird-things are put on them as well. I can see Mr Fourn. He has a tether round his neck. I wave to him, but he mustn't be able to see me. Two Urigs have him tied to the back of their floater. I don't know if they've forgotten he's there, or if they think he can fly, but it's taking off – rising with no sound. And swinging away towards where the sun is going down. And Mr Fourn is hanging off the back of it. He's stopped kicking now.

Will they do that to me? I'm really scared and I haven't got anybody to cuddle me, and I want another wee. I'm cold and don't know where Jenny is or what she's doing. She'll be everso frightened.

Big hosepipes and brush machines are going round and picking up rubbish. My Urig is just going to leave me here. I'll be swept up and thrown in the big bins.

'Nobody wants you,' he says to me. 'I don't have storage for you. Anybody can have you.' I can understand nearly all of that.

'I'll see if Monigo the Tinkra'll take you if I drop the price – or he can just have you if he'll take the rest of this stuff off my tikkari.' Something like that, anyway.

He calls another Urig across, tentacle-twisting – I think that's my neck he means. They're laughing; they laugh a lot; and get grumpy a lot, too. The new one's bending down and his armicles come round me so fast I can't scream. He's going to rip me in half and I swing up and land in the back of his floater. There's some bird-things in here with me and they're flapping and clucking and as big as me. I think they might be called avians.

Now the tinkra has come in the back. He's moving things round, and putting a tether round my neck. I hope he doesn't forget and put me over the side. And there's eggs and fruit, hunks of meat and bundles of vegetables... a lot of big packages and tools and pipeline... bags and a lot of smelly stuff. And just all sorts.

******

We were all pushed off the floater last night. Into this place like a yard with a cover at one end with a high fence all round. The birds are in here with me. No other people – not human people, anyway. The bird things are from a planet called Quale, except they say it really funny, like 'Ker wai-ull.' That's because they can't talk like we do, with their stubby little beaks: they can't make the sound. Anyway, they talk something else mostly. I don't think they're very clever. But they don't say much to me. I suppose they think I'm stupid.

This is, we think, at the back of an old house. It's made of wood! We don't know why we're here. There isn't anywhere to sit down or lie down and it's cold. We all tried to sleep together in the night. I wasn't the only one who was crying. I put my arm round a little one who has lovely soft feathers.

Now we're all just wandering round this pen with nothing to do and not very much to say. It's everso scary.

Another Urig – a lady one, I think – tossed food out a few minins ago, and I'm still grabbing at some of the bits on the floor and I drink water with all the others from a bubble-pond in the corner. She looks over us, and I wonder if she'll put my collar and tether back on. I took them off this morning – where would I go?

She comes across and talks. The avians understand bits and they seem worried, but don't say anything. She just grabbed at one, swings it round and leaves with it.

I think the Urigs eat them, but I don't know if the birds know that. And I'm in here with them. I think they're saving me for a special day. Like New Year Day dinner.

I try to hide under the hay every time one of the Urigs comes in the yard.

****

The little Urigs found me after I'd been with the avians in the yard for four or five days. They put me in this separate space and give me different food, keep looking at me. They stroke me. It's like me and Jenny used to look after our pet rinabbits. I don't like it, though.

The food's better, but I wouldn't eat anything as smelly and fishy if I wasn't so hungry. I don't know about these little Urigs – I suppose they are children Urigs, but I can't understand what they say – it's so fast and squeaky.

I sleep in a separate little room like a box, with rags to cover myself. I can see into the yard with the birds, but I don't have anywhere to run round. And I'm cold.

I'm terrified all the time.

****

This morning, just when I was wondering how many more days I'd be there, they pulled me out, put me in a box on the back of a little floater, and brought me to this place where there's another Urig. He has purply patches, and orange, as well. He keeps looking at me and poking me. He says things in a slimy voice, and he's giving them money. They're selling me to him!

I'm really cross and sad and scared.

He pretends to examine me, like he's making sure I'm plump enough. I'm not. I'm much skinnier now. His armicles are inside my clothes, feeling all over me. A lot. Like stroking me. It's horrid. He won't stop. I try to persuade the little children Urigs to keep me. But they laugh and take the money cards and leave me. I shout after them, 'You're poigs and horrible, and I hate you.'

My new Urig feels all over me again and says, 'You are soooo smooooth...'

****

306

He does that a lot to me, touches me and dresses me in all different clothes. His armicles touch me everywhere and I have to stay still, but sometimes he makes me wriggle, then undresses me. I hate it and his horrible dressing-up clothes. One long dress is red and gold, another is blue and white like a uniform. I think his favourite is a black set with buckles and studs and his armicles creep through and undoes them all. I never feel clean.

It's been ages and ages. He keeps me in a room on my own, and he takes me where other Urigs put different clothes on me. Some of them have the orange and purply patches, and they get drunk when they eat, and drink a lot, and they wibble and wobble.

They often eat birds like the ones I lived with; and sometimes they bring other aliens called kefflows like I used to see on Erith. They were nice on there: slender with no real bones. They have to do tricks and dance. I talked with two of them at one place and they're everso sad and can't do anything. Their names are Harley and Quinn.

****

I saw Jenny today.

Hanyu, my Urig, took me out for some of his friends to stroke me in different clothes, and there's always one who wants to hurt me and make me cry. But I make myself not cry any more. Other peoples will be here as well, having to do things, like the kefflows; and perhaps the avians. I think I'm fourteen now.

We went into this hallway and Jenny was there! I shrieked and shrieked I was so happy. and ran to her. She had different clothes on, too. Of course she had. It's been a long time. But she just stood there, didn't move when I grabbed her and hugged her and we nearly fell over. She was all hard and stiff and her eyes didn't see anything and the Urig men pulled me away. They were very cross.

Jenny wasn't My Jenny any more. She was dead. And cold.

I screamed, and hit at them and they wrapped their armicles round me very tight and squeezed me hard till I couldn't breathe. Hanyu had his suckers in my throat and in my mouth and said I must carry on like always or he would rip my face off and stuff it down my throat. His suckers pulled and stretched my mouth and I couldn't do anything.

I'll never see Jenny again.

He's angry and hurting me and I tell him it isn't fair. 'You're not nice. We're real people. Not like *you*. You're horrible and you should let us all go.'

He's everso mad because the other Urigs are watching. It makes his face go all twisted-up and his neck frill's quivering. His purple bits have gone yellow-like and suddenly he screws me up in a temper and it makes me scream because it hurts so much.

****

I don't know where I am. Except I've been in a little room on my own a long time, really cold, shivering and hurting everywhere. I'm covered in red patches, bruises and bandages.

It's even more painful when I try to sit up.

I'm really worried what they're going to do with me. I must have had some bones broken, like my ribs and my leg and my arm. Some Urigs keep coming in and muttering about me in a different sort of Stang. I think they're going to do something with me when my bandages come off, so I try not to go to sleep. They keep touching me and making me swallow things. I don't want to, but they hold me down tight and make my mouth open. It's horrible. I hate them.

One brings me food, drinks and clothes. I don't know if it's a man or woman Urig. It says things like, 'Eat your food.' And 'It will do you good,' And 'Put the clothes on.'

I don't put them on because I know what they'll do when I put on their dressing-up clothes. I just wear a white long smock that comes down to my knees. And I don't eat all the food. It's probably poisoned to make me sleep or get fat. One of the men Urigs tells me things will make me feel better. But I know what that means.

There's another one, definitely a lady Urig – her frills are much shorter and there's more of them. These two Urigs both keep asking me things like, 'Where do you come from?' And, 'What's your name?'

I won't tell them that – it's *my* name, not theirs. They'd use it if they knew it. So I just shake my head and don't say anything.

I hear them saying things about humans. That means us Erithans. And kefflows and others called kites, and, 'Do you understand? How did you get here? What are you called?'

I shout at them and say, 'You're all horrible and nasty and you'll be sorry if you don't let me go, and take me home.'

That stops them. 'You understand? You can speak.'

'Of course I can – I've been here a very long time and I really don't like it, especially when all you horrible Urigs do nasty disgusting things to me. And you keep the kefflows with chains like prisoners. And you eat the avians, as well. We're people as much as you. More than all you Urigs put together. You're horrible *things*, not peoples.' I'm really mad, crying and hitting them. I know they're cross at me.

They go out.

I sleep underneath my bed. It's better there.

One of them came in one night, saw I was crying and held me for a long time. I was waiting for its armicles to come inside my dress. But they didn't. I managed to sleep a little. They put like a tent on my bed so I could sleep in that. But it's a trap. So I don't.

They make me go out some days. I never know if they're going to put me in another room with men Urigs; or in a box on a floater. I try to push them away, but they make me go.

We walk in a park that's down a long corridor outside my room. Perhaps it's a zoo park. I think they are deciding which cage to put me in. I see other peoples here – kefflows – except they're called Russels, after their home planet. And two other sorts as well. Perhaps three different sorts of alien peoples. They say I'm an Erithan, after my planet. But my dad always said we were humans, after our body sort. That's like the kefflows are called that because of something about their heads. I haven't seen any other human people. I really miss them. I want Jenny back and I know I can't. I remember all about her in my bed at night when it's dark and I'm on my own.

I think they're going to get rid of us all. They look like they're embarrassed having non-Urig people on their awful planet. Actually, they have nice sunrises and sunsets. But that's all. I want to go back to the sky; and all of us go to Yeniev like we should have done before the magnets went wrong.

The Urigs say I must stay here. Some try to be nice to me. But it's just like the men Urigs used to pretend to be nice with me. I hate them all – what they did to My Jenny, and the kefflow next to her, and the other peoples with her, like preserved in an exhibition. They ask me about those things some days, but I shake and mustn't think about it and climb under my bed where I can be safe. I want it all to go away.

****

Something's happening today.

I'm really frightened by it all. Two of the Urigs removed my bandages and cleaned all my skin, but nobody tells me what for or anything. They haven't taken me to the park for three days, and there's been a lot of muttering and looking dire. I can tell they're going to get rid of me because I know too much about Urig people who they think are important. But I told them. *'I don't know their names or where they are. Just leave me alone.'*

They want me to behave how they tell me, so they can dress me up and do things to me again. I'll scream and fight if they try to make me do things again.

I know it's today: *they* keep coming in and wanting me to put their clothes on, saying it'll be alright. But I know it won't. I'm never putting them on again. I don't care. Not after what they did to Jenny.

Someone else has come in. On her own. It's a person. A *human* lady! She can't be real; they're trying to trick me. I'm so frightened I can't move. I'm just sitting on the edge of my bed and looking, but I need to crawl under my bed.

'You're not real. You can't be. You're not real. Go away.'

It's smiling at me. Like my mum did. I hate it.

My eyes sting and fill up, but I don't cry any more, and I can't get my breath and I don't know what to do. I'm just sitting here and shaking my head to make the tears go away because I don't cry any more.

She sits in front of me. 'I'm Carolyn.' She tries to smile, but she's not very good at it.

'Crystal-Ammas,' I try to say. That's the first time I ever told anybody here. I can't look up at her now I've told her my name. 'Crissy.'

She waits. I don't know what she wants. She's not real.

'Would you like to show me the park, Crissy?'

'No. It's a trap. You'll make me put the dressing-up clothes on.'

She reaches a hand towards me. And waits. Her fingers wiggle. 'Hold my hand? Show me the way?'

'I'm not putting the dressing-up clothes on.'

'You're fine in whites. You look very nice.'

'They say I look nice when they—'

'You can change clothes with me, if you like?

'No.' It's like a uniform. White and green. With a badge. Sometimes I had to wear one like that. 'I want knickers. I don't have any. I just want my knickers.'

It's a nearly-proper smile now, and she looks in the clothes they brought for me to wear. She lifts up something. 'These do?'

They're white. With a pink edge. I used to have some just the same. I nod a tiny bit. I don't want her to know I really miss them. They're still in a see-through envelope. New, clean and untouched. I love them. My fingers can't open the packet. She wants to help. I won't let her. 'I can do it.' And I do and I go in my corner and pull them on.

So now... She stands there, looking at me in my white long smock, then puts out her hand for me again and I can't stop myself walking to her. My legs are wobbling eversuch a lot. I can't walk very well and she holds my hand and opens the door, saying, 'If you show me to the park, we might find more people there – human people. Perhaps you might like to see them? And talk with them?'

We look down the long wide corridor. The outside light floods through the doors at the far end. I'm shaking all over. I *can't* walk down there.

'It's alright, Crissy. It's alright. We found the Boldly Go. Other people who were aboard her are still alive, too. And they're here.'

I'm afraid. I can't meet people now. I want to. I don't dare go – it might not be true. My eyes are hot and wet and stinging and I'm crying. Tears going all down my dress.

I think Carolyn's crying, too. 'The Urigs have to let everyone go free,' she says. 'And the chitins, and avians, and kefflows.'

I'm all weak, and can't say anything. Want to wee and can't stop crying.

'It *will* be better, Crissy. Shall we do it together?'

She holds my hand and we both cry as we walk down the long corridor to the park...

313

DISCOVERY

... was the day *that* appeared.

How could a day that had begun so typically miserably become so momentous? Yet another day without a fast-break; slit-eyed after the alarms in the apartments had been ringing all night; the corridors and stairs down to the basements were cold and unlit – for a change; and the snack-stall was closed again. So, in a crabby mood with this world and every other, I had sat in my work-dungeon, as I generously called it. Ever hopeful, turning on the screens and pads and datacubes, never dreaming that could happen...

My research project was to classify the findings of a host of survey probes that had been operating more than a hundred years earlier, towards the end of The Wars of Rights. This particular one had worked its way through a small double cluster of stars almost two hundred light years distant, transmitting its jewels of data back about each planet it discovered in turn. I was following its route, cataloguing every world as a whole, and then classifying the detailed data. And generally enjoying the first sight anyone had ever had of a whole new planet. But one like *this*?

So far in this cluster, there had been two dozen inhospitable gas giants, molten blobs and barren-rock worlds. This was the sixth habitable planet: pleasant, I loved them all, each and every one, even stroked the screen sometimes, as though it would take me there. 'Beautiful... Oceans and islands, mountains and plains,

315

rivers and lakes. Maybe there'll be a decent holopic I can use as the cover pic for the cluster...' I was flicking through them on the screen. 'Nothing exceptional,' I muttered to the keypad. 'Zipps! How can I be so blasé so soon?'

I stopped. What was that? Went back a couple of holos. '*That* is absolutely impossible,' I said, and stared closer at the hologram on the screen. Part of a planetary surface, taken from orbit. Like all the others. 'That can't happen. Never. Not on an uninhabited planet a hundred and seventy-odd light years from the nearest known population. It can't.'

There had to be someone I could tell. I stood. But who? I was alone in the depths of the college's astrophysics buildings. The supposedly finest college on GeeCee – the Empire's capital planet. No-one close by would be interested.

So I sat down again, looked back at the screen, and focused in. It was *a straight line* across the planet's surface, not a graphic flaw. I could make out a river along a section of it, a gorge where something had furrowed through a low range of hills, cutting through a forest. Ragged-edged, but unswerving in its course, it didn't look like a tectonic junction – the landscape either side matched up, they hadn't shifted sideways. Hmm... this line hadn't formed itself. Something massive had ploughed along there. What in the Pit could be that vast? With so much momentum to keep it going for – I followed the groove – for a hundred milers or more? It ended in a rock-and-undergrowth-filled bowl, bedded against a high ridge.

Taking the zoom in really close, I thought it might be a meteorite crater, but there was sign of high impact: no extensive debris or damaged fields. 'Ah… what have we here?' The data banks registered a particularly localised pocket of metallic minerals. Something had come to a halt right there. The readings showed incredibly high-grade material, and in varieties not normally found together. 'Can't be natural. But that's far too great a mass to be the original probe… And I know it continued transmitting back from the whole of this cluster.' And anyway, the river pattern, erosion rate and regrowth features put its formation at possibly ten thousand years ago, not a hundred or two.

I didn't breathe. 'Shuggs! It has to be an enormous spacecraft.' I checked all the data for long minins… sat back. 'This mass weighs approximately eighteen million tons, is at least a miler in diameter, and is virtually on the surface.' There was no visible metal: rock debris from the surroundings had settled on it, and it was largely overgrown with trees and undergrowth in the pockets of soil, and contour-hugging mosses on smooth surfaces. 'You are, aren't you? A ship? Hiding under all that tangle?'

By lunch, I was far past the intrigue level, well beyond fascinated, and up to absolute thrill. I'd found something *totally* different to anything else in the known universe. Discovering a long-lost twin brother must be something of what I felt. I desperately wanted to tell someone about it. But at the midday break, I couldn't bring myself to share it. Not yet, so I cut my break short, fled back to my cell, and began to work through the other holograms and data packs for the same planet, studying and analysing.

Before I finished that day, I knew nothing would ever be the same for me. I felt different, simply looking at the holos, thinking about the vast ship, and imagining the far-distant world. 'The discovery of the miler-wide wreck of a spaceship must be the most momentous discovery ever. And I'm the only person in the known universe who has any knowledge of it – happily spinning out there in the distant wilds of space. Wow!'

Thus, I decided several things: firstly, I would give the planet a name instead of the next code number in the listing – 1376/06. So I stood, and formally announced its new designation, "Discovery". Secondly, I would record its early history, beginning with its new calendar, 'I hereby nominate today as Day One, Year One on my new Discovery Calendar.' It would be a welcome change from thinking in terms of Empire Date 4707, Day... who cares? – they all merge together.

And thirdly, I would not tell anyone else about this awesome spacecraft, hidden away on a gorgeous little planet, tucked in the middle of a small double cluster on the far side of The Gap, way beyond the main stars of The Strand, largely hidden by dust clouds. I called it The Ship... Discovery, and The Wisp. And it was all my secret.

*** Day 2 ***

The following day, my research supervisors were called to a meeting, so I was free to re-examine the planet and its hundred-miler long scratch. Utterly enthralled, I worked through the other holograms and data packs for the same planet – *my* planet – *Discovery*.

I craved to tell someone, but all morning I was constantly re-determining to keep it secret. It was *my* catastrophe from before the dawn of the Empire, and well beyond the Empire's bounds. 'You are mine.' Over a cup of double scottie, I actually said that to the datacube, as well as the holo on the screen.

But how to keep it mine was another matter: erasing the whole cluster completely wasn't possible: the probe had already been monitored and catalogued as number 1376, containing 269 stars in this sprinkled little cluster. But no-one else knew that half the stars had planets, and three dozen of the planets were "inhabitable without major adjustment to flora or fauna". 'On the other plate, I'm the only one doing this monitoring, so I don't have to make that information public.'

*** Day 3 ***

After another day of inner and outer turmoil and sheer excitement, I concluded that my problem was that I was merely an off-world student with no status to do anything about a planet one-seventy-five light years away, with a vast space-wreck on it.

And I had mixed feelings and loyalties here…

The Wars of Rights had staggered to an end fifty years ago, leaving half the settled universe devastated by the Empire, or the Falkans, or the Booker Group, or whoever fancied wiping out a few planets at the time. Three decades of ruin followed, before interplanetary movement restarted on any scale. Outlying communities, remote planets, former enemies were still in the early stages of recovery. That was when the Empire's Great Reconciliation began. Pure guilt: inviting bright young souls from the ruined colonial and rebel planets to attend the great colleges of the central empire planets. Trying to bring us together, to think their way, as goodwill ambassadors for our home planets. There were plenty of us in the same pudding mix at the College of Original Thought on GeeCee. Original Thought? That was a laugh.

We used to drown our complaining in the student bars. Statements like, 'The Empire reduced the civilised universe to isolated wastelands,' usually surfaced after the third drink.

'Hard years, Kell,' I remember agreeing with a friend before he ranted on about growing up in the Dead Time on his own planet. He disappeared not long after that.

The Empire cindered Linkin, my original planet, simply to deny its facilities to the Falkans, in case they ever invaded our way. In Imperial mythology, as explained by the Commander of a visiting Battleweight Cruiser, 'This is a great victory over your treacherous rebellion.'

'Happened the same on Colline...'

'And Foster...'

It could have been rough, surrounded by a morass of former enemies and ill-wishers among the other students and staff, as well GeeCee citizens. But for me, The Wars had petered out before I was born. 'Let it all rest,' I said, when some fellow drinkers wanted to raid an itinerants' hostel. 'Nowadays, they're only trying to survive the same troubles as we are.'

I fostered a new accent and appearance to be as much like a GeeCee homer as possible. I did okay, I settled, and completed my treatise on the varying styles of thought process on different planets.

The Empire was glad to retain bright, well settled, off-world students such as me, so I was offered a research programme for a Higher Award. 'You've always fitted in well, and worked hard,' the College Dean told me.

'He means you're a walking showcase for our humanitarian, peace-seeking policies,' one of the less toe-the-line tutors told me.

Just the same, I accepted. 'There's no future for me yet on Linkin,' I said to them. 'I want to learn whatever I can, anything that might help my home planet.' They liked that – it demonstrated good attitude.

None of us was desperately fond of the Empire, so, having made the most incredible discovery in the universe, why would I tell GeeCee about it?

I wouldn't. And I didn't.

My research programme turned out to be accessing and organising thousands of data transmissions from hundreds of unmanned survey probes that were sent out long before The Wars, and continued to explore the distant reaches of the spiral arm throughout the conflicts. All knowledge of them had perished, until a professor complained that all the resurrected data banks that were newly allocated to him were already full. Some bright spark investigated, and eventually realised the banks were stuffed to the outlet ports with data... from probes... of original survey records... of thousands of stars, systems and planets. The closest were dozens, if not hundreds, of light years away. All long-forgotten.

'This,' they told me, 'is basic data about thousands of distant planets – all we have is a near-infinite mass of dots and dashes. Take your time. Find out everything you can about them. Sort them out. Analyse them. Come back in two years with a massive and unreadable report, and collect your HA Certificate.'

So I started, the first day of this year, 4707. For days and deccas, I toiled with my computers, processors, recorders, and half a ton of data. My senior tutor had no interest, and never looked at any of my narratives, so I stopped reporting to her after a few deccas. At first, no-one had any idea which probes had headed in which direction, how far away the planets were, or even which stars and planets were close to each other. 'It's *your* job to find out,' she slammed the door on me. 'Not mine.'

I made one last attempt to keep her in the poop when I eventually worked out which coding language they were in – that allowed me to group the planets from each probe in a separate cluster. She still didn't want to know, so, as the deccas went by, I stopped sending her anything, even when I did work out which direction each probe had taken; and how far away they were when they began their data transmissions. And I was the only person who knew anything about them.

'Exactly the sort of excitement a dashing young student craves, eh?' My friends took the Dick when I told them how fascinating some of my findings were proving to be.

'Pull the one with bells on,' I'd tell them. 'This's an interesting project that might lead somewhere. There's a holdful of information about every single planet hidden somewhere in all the dots and dashes. Besides, I never dash anywhere.'

I'd been struggling for around six or seven deccas – yet another dirty grey morning routinely fiddling and manipulating settings. My screenful of blips and bleeps suddenly swirled, and sorted themselves out into digits and letters. 'Now this,' I stared at the raw data, 'is something I might be able to understand.'

Within the hour, I had it figured, and could morph all the stored data into readable statistics of planetary size, mass and gravity; length of day and year; surveys of minerals, landforms and atmospheric conditions. This was *the* breakthrough. Except, that same day, post-noon, came the next, equally massive breakthrough: hologram pictures! 'This's more like it!' I shouted it out loud when I laid eyes on the first one. 'You're an unknown planet a hundred and forty light years along the spiral arm,' I told the gas giant with rings and moons. 'I love you, Nine-eight-seven Oh-one.'

There were dozens of 3D images for each planet. Thousands for some planets that the probes must have found more fascinating than others. I lost myself in them – absolutely awed, trawling among whole new worlds. Specific, identifiable planets in all directions. I spent deccas fixing the precise coordinates of hundreds of them.

Then came the first time the Empire and I came into direct conflict: as part of the ancient peace agreement, they needed an integrated policy for re-development of the known galaxy. Several members of the Independent Planetary Cooperative were pushing for my probes' far-flung systems to be included in the Expansion Policy, more to embarrass GeeCee than anything else.

That was the day I was locked out my workrooms while a team of officials tried to discover what I already knew. My much-loved flat was raided that evening while I was playing cards with friends, all of whom liquidly sympathised with me and helped to stoke my outrage at the injustice. Five days later, two security guards came up behind me with a stunner, and I woke up in my own computer workroom, looking into the pale blue eyes of a small, benign man who apologised profusely, and denied all knowledge of my raided flat. 'I'm Officer Consder. What do you know about the probes?'

'You might have asked that last decca,' I complained, feeling head-delicate. It was a bad start on their part, so I stalled and misdirected, being devastatingly helpful, explaining new ideas. Nobody knew enough to be impressed or otherwise. But, as I clearly knew more than they did, they allowed me to continue with my labours.

Every half-decca, they contented themselves with asking about progress in general terms, and I'd furrow my brow, suck breath and shake my head. 'Going slowly,' I'd say. 'But I can have all the data arranged in little groups and clusters for you to develop a policy on.' They had no idea that there was now much more than mere screensful of binary data.

So, when my tutor woman and Officer Consder weren't there, I spent half my time numerating the stars and planets and putting them into discrete little clusters for the policy-development team. And the productive, enjoyable half of my time studying new planets. Most were airless rocks, molten blobs, iceballs, or methane mediums and giants. Enormously awe-inspiring, but useless for colonising. A few held deserts and jungles, mountains and plains, seas and moors. And a few looked enticingly habitable – perhaps one planet per dozen stars.

I was careful to keep them all a complete secret, until, one morning, right in my ear, 'Where's that?'

324

It was *her*. Come up behind me. My heart stopped. I mumbled, totally shocked to be found out, 'I dunno, it suddenly appeared. But... but...' I was desperate, 'It's the breakthrough! It's it! We've done it!' She tried to push me aside, as though she knew what to do, but I was enthusing recklessly, cursing my carelessness, expecting to be thrown into some deep hole if she didn't believe me. Almost panic-stricken, I tapped keys, manipulated screensful of dots and dashes and freshly rediscovered all the data information I'd been looking at for the past ten deccas.

She and Consder believed me, and I kept my research job: the day could have been worse.

A decca or two later, we received the news that the government's Expansion Policy Development Team proposed to auction all the newly discovered planets the probes had surveyed. That was their galactic development policy – to sell my Wisp!

'This is a generous, forward-looking policy that will open up the middle systems towards the rim,' said a few sycophants.

'No,' came the opposing and more realistic view, 'merely a crafty way of raising cash with nothing in return. Most of these stars are at least a hundred light years the far side of unfriendly or uninhabitable territories; or hidden by dark dust clouds.'

Doing exactly the same work as previously, and still captivated with it all, I became super-enthusiastic, hiding more information than I exposed, but creating concise reports on groups of stars that could be auction lots, along with distance to the nearest Empire system, the total spread of each star-cluster in light years, and a list of all the planets circling their stars.

For each probe, I assembled the planets in groups, simply type-listing the uninhabitable ones and black dwarfs, but including details and pictures of the possibly-inhabitable ones – holograms of the surface and atmosphere; deep probe geological surveys; whatever there was. It made attractive packages of planets for would-be purchasers to peruse before bidding for them at the proposed auction.

'They're a hundred or more light years away – it's not as if anyone alive today will ever go to any of them,' I told Consder and the woman, and they passed the same message onward and upward. It became the accepted wisdom.

*** Day 73 ***

The first details of the proposed auction filtered down. For ease and speed, each of my report blocks would be sold as a single lot. I was catatonic to think that someone would steal my double cluster, with its scratch, space wreck and three dozen other habitable planets.

With the confirmation came the instruction that we must be prepared for the auction early in the new year. It would include all rights to the planets: land for colonisation or mineral exploitation, trade… whatever. The Imperial Government in GeeCee guaranteed their complete autonomy forever. It was a cosmetic exercise: they were selling planets that they only knew of through a series of data recordings. There was no way that anyone could possibly take up actual occupancy of any of them – the nearest were around fifty light years distant, and The Wisp was almost a hundred and eighty. The guarantee of non-interference was bound by a series of provisos and conditions that the Government slipped in, concerning non-aggression and stipulations that preparation for colonisation had to be established within "a reasonable time".

That seemed like it. Finished. Nothing I could do. I was silently, ragingly distraught. I used to gaze into the night sky and imagine I could see my planet through the dust nebula in The Gap. That planet lived for me, as though I'd been there. I knew every possible detail of its surface and geology, its major ecosystems and weather, its stellar orbit and companion planets. The probe had been unusually protracted in its examination; presumably because it had been programmed to look for anything artificial or beyond natural parameters, such as a straight line, or intense metallic readings. It had done its job so well. Discovery, indeed.

I wandered, schemed, plotted and thought of nothing positive that I could do.

*** Day 101 ***

The day when the seeds of hope began to sprout. Drinking with my usual crowd, I overheard the tail of a remark by one of the fringe drinkers. Something about her uncle "had one of them", and someone else laughing, 'Nothing can go two hundred times faster than light. Three's the absolute limit, and one point one is the norm.'

My ears pricked up instantly. *How fast!?* I heard a word or two – the Dee drive. Now that, I'd heard of – the Dorling Effect Drive, the magical secret weapon that was always on the horizon at some hidden establishment on the next planet. It was one of the myths of The Wars, along with true force fields, anti-gravity, regeneration of all body parts, rebirth, pocket-sized planet-busters, matter transmitters, time machines, invisibility... They'd all been discovered or invented, and, 'Shuggs! Would you believe? – they've all been lost again.' The only ones that had ever materialised had been nuclear fusion, longevity at a price, and instant voice transmission up to about two light years distant. Further than that required relay stations. So at least communications systems had improved during The Wars of Rights, but they had nothing to talk about, and not many people to talk to.

It was a girl student called Derika Brambling who'd been doing the talking: tall, neatly-built and dark-haired, with flashing fun-filled eyes. She'd shut up when her two companions began ridiculing her, but I reckoned she was only keeping quiet because she thought she'd said too much, not because it was a ghostale. I waited and watched, and happened to join her at the bar when she went for another drink.

I didn't have anything planned to say: I didn't know her particularly well, and couldn't think of anything subtle to start with. In the end, I bought her a drink, and simply asked, "Is it true? There's an enhanced Dorling Effect Drive? In a ship? Does it work? Where is it? Can I see it? And oh shit is there, really?"

Derika, of course, was immediately on full defence. 'Why?' was all she'd say.

I recognise a standoff when I see one. After about five self-tormenting seconds, I said, 'Because I have a space ship a miler across, on a planet two hundred lyres away and I can't get at it without an extremely fast ship, one with a Dee Drive. Do you really know of one? Your uncle?" I was young then, impetuous, and couldn't think of another way of extracting the information from her – getting girls drunk never did anything for me.

Half an hour in my data cellar at the College in the early hours convinced her that the mile-across ship existed, over a hundred and seventy light years away. Effectively a hundred and fifty years away by the standard speed of passenger travel, not counting the best and newest military craft that could do it in half that.

'Okay. You know of a ship and it's not here. I know of one and it's not here either.' Eyes laughing, she beamed broadly at me, 'You're so serious, Hal. But mine's a lot closer than yours. What are you doing over the deccend?'

*** Day 105 ***

Derika's uncle turned out to be Dom Corstar, a scrap merchant who lived in the Istrimic Garden suburb on the southern continent of GeeCee. Not that there was any sign of a garden or the continental limits beneath the unending mass of buildings, but I was impressed with an address like that. He – "Uncle Coz" to Derika – was non-committal but listened to everything we said. I hadn't dared bring a hard copy of the scratch and crater on Discovery, but Coz was intensely interested.

'Alright, Derika... IngHal... I'll be in touch.' Ahh. Nobody calls me IngHal nowadays; not a name I miss. *Halberr* suits me fine. We all swore each other to melodramatic secrecy, and waited.

*** Day 111 ***

329

The trivid sounded in the middle of the next decca. We were requested to kindly join Dom Corstar for a long deccend. 'And bring some proof of this Discovery.'

We lifted into orbit on Dom Corstar's private shuttle, and transferred to his private yacht that effortlessly whisked us to Broober, GeeCee's sister planet. A hot little place, it was mostly populated by mining and manufacturing communities. Our craft drifted high above, manoeuvring gently towards The Ring – the reputed-to-be million or so derelict ships and part-ships that circled the equator as a vast orbiting junkyard.

'This section's mine,' he proudly announced, running a finger over the screen. 'One seventh of the Ring. And we are... *here.*'

Coupling the screen with the observation viewer revealed a vast panoramic junkyard all around us – an endless selection of wrecks silently hanging in space; large and small, some brilliantly clean and others dusted and glazed; some apparently intact and undamaged, others in various stages of dismemberment; some blown apart with extreme violence; and some merely scattered pieces and fragments. The appearance of a few was familiar – fast yachts, spacious liners, heavily-armed orbital peacemakers, pods and lifeboats. One vast tanker looked hopelessly ravaged, merely one more write-off among the thousands that Dom Corstar owned, part of the bright Ring around Broober.

He pointed. 'It's the tanker we want. We need to be in the pod to see it properly.'

It was a tight fit for three of us, and I was more than a touch dubious as we moved closer. The tanker was absolutely twisted and blown apart, the inside a cavernous blackness. 'Worry not,' he laughed. 'It's tucked away inside.'

In the depths of that tanker there was a jumble of mining and ore-processing machinery. Buried among all of that was a small, slightly crumpled spaceship; but it was intact, and its power unit was the original working Dee Drive. It looked like the sort of innocuous customs shuttle that pottered round, checking from ship to ship; until it upset some big-time smuggler, of course, and had come off second.

We nosed around it in the pod, with Uncle Coz assuring us it wasn't a customs shuttle: 'It's a genuine Dee Drive prototype ship. And it worked last time I tried it. What could happen in twenty-eight years? In space?'

Hovering round the little ship, bathed in arc-lights, he told us how he had come to own it – 'Towards the end of all the strife, I worked on the drive, member of a team that investigated all kinds of unlikely avenues of research. This was one of our smaller and cheaper failures. When I started, the research principle was well-known, the FOTAS – Filaments of Time and Space... Strings. We used to think of energy and matter being composed of miler-long strings, knotted a thousand times, then tangled up and dropped in a heap with a billion others; just to make one atom. Anything trying to work along such a rope would be exceedingly slow. Feeding power into a Dorling Field straightened the filaments – though not perfectly, the best we could manage was an S curve, like a lightly coiled spring rather than a fully taut line.

'It was good enough to create a working communications system – the distal rad, which is virtually instantaneous over a two-light-year distance – but we wanted to transport matter as well as energy – a ship as well as an electronic voice.' Uncle Coz kept talking, even though he was delicately manoeuvring to gain a closer view of the undamaged motor section. 'We couldn't tighten or strengthen the Dee effect enough, nor undo all the knots, as it were. It doesn't matter if a voice breaks up after two light years, or if it's spread over half of Creation, but it upsets people if it happens to them personally, or the pod they're in. We calculated that the S curve would allow travel at about two hundred times the speed of light. Not perfect, but pretty good.'

He must have seen our baffled expressions, 'Anyway,' he smiled lamely, 'It works. We eventually tuned the beam tight enough, and strong enough, to carry matter. The limiting factor then was how fast the Dee Drive could produce the field, and suck itself along it.'

'How come it's here?' Derika asked.

'You know what it's like in a War... Or you probably don't, but we were top secret, and quite small, and we had a series of, er, *setbacks*. Unfortunately, they always involved politicians during demonstrations, or our beloved lab leader, or an exceptionally expensive new cruiser. Sometimes ships disappeared, or they exploded, or didn't do anything at all. That was worst because we didn't know what had gone wrong. One that we thought wasn't doing anything was disintegrating; going all powdery.' He smiled at the memory. 'Another one, the High Hope, vanished and reappeared spread over half

332

the space between Curtain and Ravine. It was only there for a few hours, extremely tenuous, before the Stellar wind took it. Pity, that. But it was obvious something was happening: we were getting somewhere. Or, in the case of the High Hope, everywhere.

'The fighting was probably dragging to an end, so our funds were cut.' He edged us in, uncomfortably close to the outlet of the Dee Drive. It didn't look much; a black exhaust pipe big enough to fit a gyrocopter in. 'They told us we literally weren't getting anywhere; but they obviously hadn't read any of our reports, or understood them. A couple of us were left to wind it all down. Me and Aconto were told to clear the debris away, destroy the records and protos. No chance – we came out with this little beauty and all the records.'

'Little beauty? Are we looking at the same thing? It's a wreck, a shambles. It's been chewed by something especially big and nasty.'

'I told you it works, and it does. Aconto and I went over the figures again. It only took a couple of deccas to discover and correct the final error, simply an adjustment that was needed, that's all. We had four of these at one time but we didn't know how to control them; crashed them all, but they worked. We used the standard engine for starting and manoeuvring, and the Dee drive for the straights.'

'What happened to this one?'

'We were unlucky.' He pulled a face. 'We hit some sort of debris, maybe a spanner or a pebble, but it went through us; through Aconto, anyway. I managed to shut the drive off, but it took me four deccas to shunt back – it's basically a shuttle, remember. I was near starved – we'd only popped out for the morning. By the time I recovered, this had been scrapped, and the project terminated. All our recent data gone.

'It took me a year to find her. I call her the Black Angel – and I bought her as scrap. There was so much total rubbish, and some good stuff floating round this system. I bought quite a lot of it to cover myself for wanting this particular item. There wasn't anyone to actually sell it. Nobody cared about it, or space, or anything, so I offered a few creds to the Broober PA, and they took it without even knowing what it was they were selling. So I bought more and more. It's damn high-quality stuff, this. Fortunes are locked up in this lot. The only condition was I had to tidy it up into a fairly tight orbit parameter, and not leave it all drifting anywhere.

'I only dismantle things now, or my crews do – I do the buying and I arrange contracts, fix things. Lots of people like to keep a private spacer of some kind, and need cheap spares and free advice to keep it on the charts. You've seen my place.'

Dom Corstar made money, alright, we agreed on that. 'Koh, what's the deal?' I don't recall which of us said it, but we all looked at each other.

In his capacity as bored uncle looking for a dream to come true, he said he'd played with the Black Angel, servicing and tuning it, for years, and even taken it out, wrecked as it was, a few times. But had never dared, or had time, to properly fit the craft out, 'I merely kept it here, as well hidden as possible. No specific cause to chase after, but now? I recall what I pined for, all that time back. Perhaps I can achieve it through you two.

'So how about I let you have the wreck with the Dee Drive system? There's also a stately old tub – a bit wonky, but sound – ex-admiral somebody-or-other's military yacht. She has working weaponry, but she's sedate; under-powered. Suppose you remove the drive from this one and fit it in the yacht? On condition I go on the first journey to Discovery.'

I hardly needed to confer with Derika before agreeing to the best offer I'd ever received on any subject. This was too good to think about.

'You do everything – it'll be long and difficult. Around two years," he estimated. He was the only one who had any real idea how vast a task it would be. The Dee drive wasn't a small, detachable unit. It was heavy and cumbersome, and had appendages and leads spreading throughout the craft, especially through the skin. 'It all needs to be disassembled, checked, moved into the yacht, reassembled, powered up, rechecked and finally tested. I'll provide technical advice, and spares, but I haven't done any work in a space suit for twenty years, and I'm not re-starting now.'

*** Day 123 ***

We drew up a list of things to do, and in all kinds of confused order, we leased a dilapidated in-system freighter; enlisted help among college colleagues and friends; began to strip the Dee drive; considered the forthcoming planetary auction; wondered what we needed to get ready for a long voyage; and kept it all secret.

***Day 200 ***

'It's impossible,' We agreed, in the aftermath of a nasty encounter with the scrapyard watcher that had us trembling for a decca. 'The work's scarcely progressing.' A tiny craft had come buzzing round us, inside the tanker. Its noise overrode all our communications channels as it closed in. Grapples and drills festooned its nose, rotating and flexing slowly. It looked ominously ready for action. We were petrified, and retreated fast.

'Sorry about that,' Dom Corstar apologised, and handed us a tiny circuit board. 'I forgot. You need one of these. Clip it onto the rad. It sends out the coded whistle that the watcher recognises, and it'll leave you alone. They're fitted to all our standard pods.

Derika lost the fingers of her left hand when an engine mounting gently drifted against her and trapped her hand as it neatly slotted its ten-ton mass into the bay, surgically removing all the fingers. She considered herself remarkably lucky that it hadn't killed her: working alone in the tanker's interior. She lost air quickly and had almost passed out by the time she reached the pod's airlock. It was a decca before all the little blood spheres vanished, and we never did find enough of a single finger to stick back on her hand.

'It's all it takes: a second's inattention, or a fractional mis-judgement, hmm?' Dom Corstar had words with us. 'You need to be properly organised. It's a destiny, not a hobby. You need to treat it seriously. You, IngHal, ought to be at the College more, to arrange for the auction. You might as well own the planet as well as occupy it. You need to recruit more colleagues to help. Can't have a one-handed girl working alone up there.'

We took in a third member as a partner – Colin Berner. He fringed the wilder side of our circle. A physics engineer, he drank like a squabble-fish and played cards like a tortinsh – with subdued flair and great success. He was wild, bored, and reckless. 'Not reckless,' he'd argue, 'creative.'

Derika and I approached him jointly, with a theoretical problem about possible flight and navigation problems at one hundred and ninety-eight times the speed of light. He rattled on about red and blue shift, regressions, blank spots and stretch patterns. Then he decided that one hundred and ninety-eight was too specific to be an abstract question, so he wouldn't say anything else without being cut in. 'I don't play cards for the money; it's a challenge to see what I can get away with. What are you offering?'

He was hooked. Shortly afterwards, he and Derika announced that they intended to suspend their respective research to prepare for a long study trip to document the effects of sudden new contact in a long-lost colony after two centuries of complete isolation.

They hinted to likely-to-be-useful people that maybe it was to be something far more exciting than another newly-contacted planet, and, 'You might possibly be interested in an unofficial, top secret, five-year trip to a non-civilised Out-Empire planet?' As the summer wore on, I did the same in my circles, and concentrated on the Planetary Probes Auction. We gradually built up a core of three dozen students, staff and others who we thought could be trusted and invaluable.

***Day 300 ***

Dom Corstar called in, 'Pilst Puncter, the Auctioneer, is tasked with selling the data, the planets, suns, systems – all the rights to everything. I know him well – bought a

337

planet through him once. He can't fiddle the auction itself, and unfortunately, neither of us has any idea what kind of interest there'll be in the sale. GeeCee government doesn't regard it as anything serious – much like when they sold billions of creds' worth of space hardware to me. They're being pressured into carrying out a PR exercise, so they're leaving the details to the professionals – Pilst as Auctioneer, and a high official called Rhagfarn – from Tessard – as Adjudicator. Plus your team as Preparators.'

Derika protested that we didn't need to buy the charter. 'Nobody else's going there for a hundred and fifty years, at least.'

'Don't count on it. A bit of inspired R and D, and everybody'll have a Dee Drive next decca, and we'll be overtaken on the way there by a gang waving their charter at us.'

The four of us discussed a thousand possibilities. None was fool-proof, but we held them in reserve – like making The Wisp seem ten times further away; or filled only with worthless gas and lava planets; or having someone arrive dressed as the president just as The Wisp block came up. That would divert attention, and we'd blip the computer to accept our bid. Or I could interrupt the process with false bids, block incoming bids, or ignore them. Or... well, we had a dozen new ideas every day.

Kidnapping Prince Willkin-Garney and holding him to ransom backfired because he enjoyed the excitement and wanted to join the venture. We agreed, but even his substantial contribution didn't guarantee our bid being successful: some big multi-planet concerns had expressed an interest in the auction for long-term markets, and so were some of the war-ravaged systems looking for new homes.

Alpino Kreuz wangled us a grant from the gullible College Colonial L-Fund. That helped our financial situation, as well as Alpino's. So did an unusually large sponsored game of cards that he organised. That was what we called it, but the victims in a private room at the Imperial Star Casino on GeeCee called it robbery. Nothing was ever proved, and our funds swelled. Plus, Uncle Coz promised any provisioning help we might need, and, he winked, 'I'm not without a marigold or two.'

While the others worked on the ship, the instruments, the engines, power sources and drives; the shielding and quarters; the gunnery, stores and their cover story, I pored over the data, both of Discovery, and of all the other systems.

***Day 372 ***

It occurred to me while I was making a security copy of the files: I would create one lot with hardly any stars in it, perhaps with only a few gas giant planets.

Later on, I'd say that it didn't seem to be worthy of being a single group – so we'd amalgamate it into one of the adjacent blocks, leaving that lot-number vacant. I couldn't scrub it from the auction – that'd look suspicious – so I'd merely let it remain as an empty lot. The Wisp would fit into it nicely when the time came, and I'd bid for a supposedly vacant lot-number – merely for the kudos of owning a set of digits. As I was the only person involved in this mundane allocation processing, there was no-one to check or argue.

After deccas of worrying and conniving and labouring over hot screens, that was exactly how easy it was. I bid one thousand creds for the pleasure of sticking an unused lot-number on the wall. Pilst accepted my bid, I tapped the key to insert the Wisp's ID code – 1376.269. And the Wisp was mine – Ours. No other bids made it in time.

That was it: the sale had come and gone, raising precious little interest among the fifty billion population of GeeCee. Lots went for small amounts, a few hundred thousand credits, others for several hundred million, but it seemed to make little difference how much was bid. Some colonies and businesses were successful with negligible bids, whilst several Multis with massive budgets failed.

It appeared to be arbitrary, unless one knew the background of the government official who was co-ordinating the bids and the conditions. Pilst ran it, but Rhagfarn was in total charge of the decisions, and whimsically allowed his personal preferences to dictate the proceedings, remembering which colonies had come to the aid of his home planet, Tessard, and which had scorned them; which companies had sponsored relief efforts, and which had refused to help; which wealthy planets had democratic systems, and which were repressive. He settled many old scores that decca. And there was nothing anyone could do about it. He was the senior official in a semi-autonomous department in a solidly bureaucratic government that didn't particularly care about a rather pointless sale.

The furore over the large unsuccessful bids attracted all the attention. Our subterfuge wasn't even noticed. Neither Rhagfarn nor Pilst Puncter knew exactly which of them was interfering with the process as they each had their own agendas. My bid had gone through; fully accepted and registered. The computer said so, and carried smoothly on.

'So that was my contribution,' I bragged as we sank a few schvimms that night. And, during the celebrations, we finalised the details for dropping out of college. It wasn't exactly unexpected, the college thing – Col and Derika were told there were punitive penalty clauses if they weren't back on their courses and research studies within the decca. And the Colonial Fund expected its money back.

***Day 444 ***

That was when we had the explosion to kill us off. I thought I might as well join in and get my death over with as well. My relatives were still on Linkin and I hadn't seen them since I came to GeeCee, seven years before. Col Berner was the same, and Derika had only two relatives – Uncle Coz, and a sister, A'arka.

Ahh... A'arka. I was never close to her, emotionally – if only. But what a great girl she was. I ought to look in on her descendants someday, see if any are as striking as she was.

Uncle Coz arranged our deaths with consummate ease. The highly localised thermic blast in the college astrochemics laboratory was proved to be Derika deliberately overriding the safety cores during an experiment into the collapse of atomic particles in the

341

cores of blue-white stars. Colin Berner had evidently been explaining his research to his two friends when there was a row over another girl, probably A'arka. The badly corrupted trivid tapes proved it. Our bodies were completely destroyed, and A'arka was, of course, devastated.

The highly respected, and visibly sad, Dom Corstar, gave a generous donation towards rebuilding. He withdrew it when he discovered that the college authorities were willing to accept it. 'This,' he said, 'shows how guilty you must be, in your failure to enact proper security arrangements. I will sue you for the loss of my beloved heiress.'

So our funds swelled again.

We hadn't given much thought to our new identities, though. 'All we need do is change our names,' we decided. That made us feel different when we set out for Broober's Ring, as full-time spaceship converters. Becoming Halberr Blissen instead of IngHal Varrnanachter Dal Intracho Dai Linkin, was a relief – the gateway to a new personality; new responsibilities, new freedoms. The committed full-time rebel with a vision, undercover worker and hero, all in one. Instead of a colonial youth with a dream. Shuggs, those were the days – all excitement, the future, the unknown, the possibilities...

I remember my passion lasted well into the first shift on the drive transfer. My new Blissen name came from a chance mis-hearing whilst working in suits inside the tanker. Derika asked me what I was going to call myself, and I thought she'd asked if I was enjoying myself. 'Bliss, nn?' I'd replied, sweating and straining with the unaccustomed effort.

Derika contented herself with adopting her uncle's family name, Corstar. They were both pleased. Colin reversed his names, reckoning he would never become accustomed to anything completely new, so he became Berner Colline, which he quite liked, of course: his home planet being Colline. 'Most of my friends call me Bernie, anyway.'

'This's still a time of incoming workers and students,' Dom Corstar told us, 'passing traders, troop movements, itinerant populations, refugees and temporary business dealers. No-one'll be concerned when you three drifters turn up without IDs, wanting to become registered; it's routine.'

Papers and crysts and fingernail IDs were easy to arrange after we erased the entirety of our former identities in an illicit deprogramming den that Uncle Coz knew about.

A day later, 'Please take your nominations from the slot below.' Thus spoke the oily voice of a machine in an outer office on Broober. That was the only occasion any of us went down to the surface – scorching place, almost glowing and airless. The air stank of burning metal – but that was something we were accustomed to in the Black Angel and the tanker.

A simple transfer of funds to our new identities completed the formalities. The emptying of our old accounts, a couple of days before our deaths, was commented upon, but as there was no trace of the money, there was nothing anyone could do.

'It's assumed that one of you had been up to something, and all had been lost in the intense heatball at the lab.' So reported one of our clandestine colleagues ten days later.

Fifteen deccas of unrelenting labour saw the Dee Drive fitted into the new craft. We tested it over two days, and had a one-day rest and slosh-party to celebrate, then got back to it.

Staying away from former haunts, A'arka was our main contact with the outside. The work proceeded better once all three of us were on it full time. Especially when three others joined us permanently, and others came in regularly to assist.

We set up camp inside the tanker and lived on the breadline for deccas at a time. Appealing to Uncle Coz for more help, he refused, 'It would raise suspicions if I began to work on scrap personally. I hardly ever operate a mechano-handler, and certainly not in a spacesuit. And no – not my own workforce, either. They're a suspicious lot, and wouldn't take kindly to doing amateur work with a bunch of kids. Sorry, but that's how it is.'

Fair enough – he had given us two space-ships, and had recently acquired a small lifeboat we could use instead of the hired freighter. 'It's full of desiccated bodies,' he told us. 'It found its own way back from the Major Dependencies, where the Colony ship Master Clipstone had been abandoned, for reasons unknown. Unfortunately, it took ninety-two years to get here. Who would want such an unlucky craft? But it'll serve you well between GeeCee and Broober's Ring for now, and later down to the surface of Discovery.'

The deccas passed, the work continued, sometimes slowly as overhauling jobs were laboriously slogged through; sometimes rapidly, like when we invited a gang of fellow conspirators to vacuum barbecues and sleepovers, when a major manpower task was looming. Great deccends, they were.

*** Day 3 ***

Someone was too suspicious for their own good. We were working deep in the cavern of the tanker, and Derika piped through, 'Hear that? It's that *kahrolasi* Watcher again.' We chilled and froze. That raucous rising and falling tone sounded like death coming up on us. We panicked, nerves in shreds, crap in suits, checked the key was in place and working. So it had to be something else. We turned the beams on and swung them around, 'See? Down in the aft – the triangular shadow patch?'

'Yeah, it's a pod, quietly hovering, watching us. The occupants can't be aware of it.'

'They'd be gone by—'

'Too late.'

The auto-guard closed in, nuzzling up against the curving flank of the pod. 'Oh, Shuggs; look at that!' Grapples clicked around steps and handholds, tightened, and clamped close against the bare metal. A single drill extended its bit fully four spans across, and hollow. It spun, and began to eat into the pod.

'They must have realised: their engine's started up.'

'She's swinging sideways…'

A puff of air gouted from the drill hole; a flickering of lights from the interior. The Watcher detached itself and departed with calm determination.

The crippled pod was left suspended there, slowly rotating end over end. Reaction to the air-blast, I suppose. 'Come on, let's go see.'

Two bodies; a man and a woman, faces frozen in horror, their mouths exploding with the blood that had crystallised around them. We didn't stay long.

'They work for Mewton; this is one of her jobs,' Dom Corstar told us when he examined it. 'They should know better than to come out here. She does freelance espionage, detective work, industrial, commercial, private, anything, and won't come looking. Scuff off the ID plates with the grinder and I'll retrieve the disc from the auto. You can weld it back on. Nothing too important there on the hull. Then you've acquired a spare pod for nothing. I'll see if we can fit some grapples, and you won't be such suities any more, will you?'

We really were better organised by then. Everyone had an assigned area of responsibility once we were restructuring the admiral's yacht – which we renamed Black Angel, after the Dee drive's original carrier.

Others planned for the journey, acquiring stores, sensors and navigation holos. There wasn't much to find out about the regions we would pass through: only the probe had been that far, and it hadn't transmitted until it reached its target destination. Yet others planned for the landing on Discovery, and how we would live during half a year's travel, and at least three years of exploration and excavation, survival and living, wonderment and despair – whatever Discovery threw at us.

Food and defence, travel, communications, medicines... Experts in geology and interpretive geography, climate and agriculture, weaponry and mechanics. We needed everything and recruited whoever seemed appropriate.

*** Day 751 ***

'Have you heard about the auction?' Dom Corstar radded through with the news.

'What?' My stomach and heart changed places at the thought that someone had crumbled us.

'We thought it wasn't like the big corporations to lie down. There's been a simmering furore over it, so Rhagfarn demanded to see the specifications of the auction data. He intended to hold a mock review of the procedures, and conclude that it had all been above board, maybe alter a couple of results – to spite them even more. So Consder and the woman supervisor logged in to the program, gave IDs and access codes—'

I could guess the rest... 'Then watched in horror as the whole series wiped itself in less than a minute?'

'Ah, so you do know something about that, Hal?'

'Me? Er... Might do,' I had to confess. 'My booby trap worked, then?'

'Something sure did. They were shocked beyond belief when it dawned on them that *everything* was lost, all the records, everything. They frantic-ransacked the drive records, the cube bases, the old backup files, the holding systems, the processing boards—'

'Let me guess... To the Gods be Thankful, they found the Subitis Dumping Plot with a full copy of the entire proceedings?'

'Yes.' Dom Corstar was realising I was involved. 'They copied it several times into different banks, onto solidos, cubes and crysts, plaspaps and iridium plates.

Nothing will ever be lost again. Your bid and purchase are enshrined in something better than plascrete now, along with everyone else's.'

'Complete with our new identities,' I pointed out.

'Rhagfarn's happy that the records have been so well broadcast. He brazened it all out, "Too late to change anything now: the sale stands. Any further complaints will result in severe Government Sanctions against the protestants."'

Dom cut the link, and I lolled back, relieved that it had worked – the only possible fly on the window that might have spoiled things – apart from a thousand GeeCee troopers blasting their way into the tanker, I suppose.

Thus, the new me was formerly recognised and confirmed as senior owner of a block of a 269-star system with three dozen inhabitable planets – almost two hundred light years away. Including one planet that had a vast space wreck on it. And no-one outside our group knew anything about it.

The conditions imposed by GeeCee were minimal, as a concession to the spirit of the sale, to encourage private colonisation, granting independence, and general support of individualism. As befits officialdom throughout the galaxy, there were idiosyncratic passages such as GeeCee accepting no responsibility for delivering the goods to the vendee; and would not escort the vendee to the goods. Failure to pay for the purchases within one year… No responsibility for the accuracy… No complaints about ships arriving at planetless stars. Once sold, the lots belonged to the purchasers. The registrar had to be informed when any expedition had begun active preparations, or actually set off. 'This is all wonderful,' we decided. 'We'll draft a note out to the effect that we're "proceeding with preparations". And tidy up our partnership contract while we're at it.'

Our agreement was for only the three of us – Me, Derika and Col Berner – to have shares. Should one of us die, they would pass to the survivors: we didn't want to dilute ownership to a mass of unknown relatives back in Empire Territories. Nor to all the others involved: they had other rewards to look forward to – when I look at the properties that the Grand Old Families own across Discovery now. Alpino Kreuz had a pitsofalot more about him than his current-president grandson; same with a few others, including Garney. It happened to be me who lived longest, and I outright own it all, and have done for well over a hundred years, since Derika and Bernie died.

The preparation task that we imagined would be most difficult and time-consuming was to attach the lifeboat and the storage pod stuffed with provisions and equipment to the Black Angel. We managed it – stupidly easily – with flexi-cables and bolts. Our calculations and sort-of-testing indicated that the Dee field would encompass a much larger volume than the Black Angel alone. It took three days to manoeuvre the shuttle and lifeboat onto the back of the Black Angel, nestle them onto Uncle Coz's brackets, and cable-bolt them together. Sure, it looked like two male hog beetles humping a female, but it was all securely rigged up and ready. Two more days to complete the loading. And one to try it out and summon up the courage to decide there was no more to do.

*** Day 843 ***

The Great Set-off day. Not a wild fanfare and fruggle-party, simply a perfect feeling inside ourselves. All the quiet testing done, we were ready. We assembled the last of the people, equipment and stores, and took everyone on board. Our story was that it was merely a summer field trip together, thirty-eight of us in total. With supplies for five or six years, but we didn't mention that. Then it was a matter of steering the Black Angel beyond Broober's orbit on the old main motor, then pointing her in the direction of the Wisp, aiming, we hoped, for the centre of the larger of The Wisp's two clusters. With luck, Discovery would be somewhere close. Then I pressed the button.

It was as laid-back as that. We had programmed it for several course changes, to take an angular course – the long way, over the Rift dust clouds. There was absolutely nothing to see on the occasions we came out of Dee drive for a few seconds while the Angel adjusted her direction. That was the worst thing – not being able to see anything for fifteen deccas. We simply timed it for the distance we calculated to Discovery, and the speed we gauged the Angel would go at.

*** Day 996 ***

After a hundred-and-fifty-one days she switched herself off, and we gently came to a stop over the next two days – we weren't too good with the braking effect back then. It was weird that first time: light streaking past us, red, blue, stretched. Then completely black again, until we gradually made out a few stars. We felt like dying – so far away from anywhere. We prayed to the Gods of

350

Castavan – because we had a Castavani with us – and decided Discovery must be *that* one down that way.

It was a crude way of doing it, but it's not much more scientific nowadays: it's all Point and Go. The processors guess now, instead of us. And Dee effect travel is common for some of us.

*** Day 999 ***

We arrived here, in orbit around Discovery, parked in orbit and took it all in as we drifted over the continents, and marvelled that we had actually arrived at *our planet*, in *our double cluster*.

*** Day 1000 ***

Seven of us came down to the surface in the lifeboat. Beautiful sweep in, delicately performed, as I recall. And it immediately became Year 1, Day 1, Discovery Time.

*** Year 153, Day 93, Discovery Time ***

Hoft lifted the memocryst set from his head, still half-immersed in my memory chronicles. 'I've practically lived that with you, Hal,' he shook his head as he waited for the pseudo-reality to fade a little. 'Hectic days, pre-arrival… the earliest times. It takes some absorbing.'

I sipped at a glass of meluta spirit. 'We landed right over there, where the park is now. Of course, we should have spent a decca running final checks on the microscopic and macro life on the surface, but we couldn't wait. I went out first – to claim First Man Status, to my great honour; and just dessert. In a lightweight suit as a precaution. Ten minins later, everyone was out, and I made the formal announcement, standing on the crater rim, overlooking the wreck, "This Landing Day is hereby designated as the First Day of Discovery Time: Day One; Year one. Long may Discovery and The Wisp prosper and thrive." The memocryst of the event is preserved for all, and, naturally, it's played every year on Discovery Day.'

'It doesn't look a lot like you, Hal. Not after all these years. No wonder a lot of people don't believe it is.'

'Best to keep it that way, I think. The three of us – me, Bernie and Derika – stood, looking down at the wreck, or, at least, at the veneer of vegetation that covered it. So massive, that first sight of it. It took us about ten seconds to decide – suits off and all seven of us slid and rolled down the Overlook Cliff to see it properly... to touch it... feel and taste and smell it. Hoft, you've no idea how immense the whole concept had become for us. It was *everything* to us. We simply had to get right up to it, asap.'

Hoft looked bemused, and fiddled with his finger ring, probably still lost in the depths of my memories.

I waited, but he wasn't about to say anything, so I carried on, 'Once we were right up close, it was breath-taking to touch huge expanses of raw metal, some part-buried; some towering and overhanging us. A lot was still bright satin silver. It was more mind-numbingly vast than we had ever imagined. We walked round the whole thing. It took the rest of the day to get through all the undergrowth, but no nasties lurked in it, and when we returned to the boat, we had a celebration toast before radding up to the Black Angel in orbit that all was *supremely* well.'

'Bit of an understatement to say you've done well, Hal – all this in one-fifty years.' He glanced at the readout at the base of his thumb, Year 153 Day 93. It flicked to the time, 04.99. 'Should we be going through for the Board Meeting? It's time.'

'They can wait. I told them there was nothing for The Board to discuss, but they insisted on meeting us. Let'em stew. Have a drink yourself.'

I knew that'd be sufficient for Hoft: he touched the pad for another drink, 'I wish I'd been there instead of my brother.'

'Instead? Not as well as?' I reached for a second drink, too.

Hoft pulled a face, his more usual self, 'Not really. Bernie was twenty years older than me when he left for the college. Mostly, he ignored me and my sisters, so we didn't have much of a relationship. I always felt... I dunno... bullied. Too small and quiet, I expect; where he was big and confident.' He tapped the memo-set, 'And the Board think you're prepared to negotiate it all away? Thirty-seven planets supporting well-established populations. We're at peace and thriving—'

'Apart from a few local difficulties,' I had to laugh at the thought of perfect unity among us, but it was pretty good.

'You created it, Hal, The Wisp. The Board and the Council merely give the appearance of democratic unity.' He summoned a faint smile.

'The appearance is all it needs; the two of us manage the real work.'

'Well, you decide the policies, and I manage the operations. You still own every single planet, even if that's largely nominal nowadays.'

'I'll have to insist on full Owner's Rights if the Board try to force their own way over this latest affair. Ha! Empire ships heading this way, and the Board thinks they intend to talk? I'll take over total control and do what's necessary.'

'You don't think Arena Xye, Garney and Kreuz will try to stop you? The others on the Board?'

'Of course they will, but they have no idea what happens behind their backs most of the time, and I'm sure that *my* security forces will see things *my* way.'

Hoft's been my right hand since... when? A hundred and thirty years now? We both have extensive families and associated responsibilities with them, so he and I have never been brotherly close, but we're the perfect working pair when it comes to whole-Wisp matters. I govern Discovery, and let the other thirty-six planets rule their own internal matters.

Before today, his knowledge of the early settlement times had been gleaned from official records, parkland statues, legends and dropped words throughout his rapid rise to the top. And he'd been deeply involved in everything for well over a century. But, with this biggest-yet threat from the Board and the Empire, I wanted him to know how much all this meant to *me* – how far back *I* went.'

I couldn't tell if he was enjoying the talk and the drinks, or feeling a mite restless at making the Board wait for no particular reason. There was a reason, of course: to irritate them, let them know who's in charge. They can't leave the conference room once they're in, not until I release the lock. And no, I wasn't ready to put the Board in their place quite yet...

'We had so much to do in those first days and deccas after landing: setting up the self-sufficiency aspects – the agriculture, mining, forestry, exploration to the coasts, communications networks, all based around here, at the wreck. It all took so much doing: the incoming craft had first touched a hundred-odd milers to the east and gouged The Ditch as far as here. It was pretty well destroyed by the time it hit here, dug in and spun over, tubes-first into the Crantor Hills. Crushed everything with the impact. Most of the ship's internals were forced down to the rear, and made a nearly solid mass of metal buried into the cliff and the crater. No chance of any survivors after that. You koh for another drink?' I poured myself one and passed the spig to Hoft.

'A combination of our survival needs, and the sheer difficulty of cutting through a solid mass of bulkheads and floors, all twisted and crumpled into each other, meant it was impossible to do much real exploration inside the wreck for years. I was desperate to find wonderful things in there – the first totally alien ship ever encountered. But whole stages were compressed into a hand's width – girders, panels, pressure hulls, equipment, wires... And the metal, well, you know how tough the metal is. 'We were three years finding the first section that was even remotely intact. I think the sense of adventure had worn thin by then. Finding the control room was the huge leap... Wow! So small, right in the heart of the thing, with a few dusty organic remains all jumbled up. And beyond it, we came across the cylinder, *The Unit,* buried under a heavy shielding section, intact, undamaged, and live. You've seen it often enough since; not humming or anything like that, just *live*.'

Hoft tried smiling – he's not too good at it. 'It's a Wisp-maker, alright. Everything here stemmed from the discovery of that cylinder. I use it when I need to; but it's not a form of travel I'm keen on. Purely the thought of what it does to my molecular structure during transmission.'

'Same for me, really, although nowadays, I fret that some vengeful underling will tap in the wrong coordinates, and put me in orbit round a brown dwarf somewhere.'

'You must be pretty confident that won't happen – we have too many safety and security checks.'

'True enough, Hoft: I worry for nothing. Right from that first view on the screen in GeeCee, I knew there absolutely *had* to be something wonderful out here, something worth all the time and trouble. We spent a year theorising what the cylinder did, commissioning it, and another year's effort simply to move it to its present position in the Communication Hall, and begin testing it as a transmitter of matter, people, anything…'

'You were still learning all its little quirks when I arrived – I was on the team for a time, while we were fixing target points on each planet. And now, of course, it's The Unit that keeps The Wisp together.'

'Not exactly: we keep the planets united, the two of us, and The Unit's our tool. Instant communication and delivery within the cluster. Koh, so it's small-scale with only the one cylinder, but, whether it's high-level, routine or emergency, we can contact every single planet in moments.'

356

'And the other matter in the early years was sending the Black Angel back to Broober for more volunteer colonists and supplies?'

'Indeed it was. It only took three deccas for Dom Corstar's workforce to piggy-back a patched-up passenger freighter to it – the size of a village. Then we started to bring whole societies from derelict planets out here, a few thousand people each trip. Nobody with any love for the Empire. Isolated, destitute communities that wouldn't be missed too much when they vanished. We started giving them the invitation for a new life well in advance, and they were out there waiting – equipment, stores, seed and livestock when the BA arrived.'

'And seeded every inhabitable planet in The Wisp with its own populations. Remarkable, Hal. Remarkable.' Hoft knows how to grease me up.

'We also carried on searching for experts in anything and everything to kidnap, along with technology, high-value material, equipment of all kinds. The Empire had too many rich planets and not enough defensive forces to protect themselves from us. We were always small scale; still are – absolutely specific on who or what we snatch.'

'That's how you found me, of course,' Hoft nodded, 'The best move I ever made, coming here. Shame that my brother died before I arrived. And you didn't tell me for years that he'd even been here.'

'We've been over all that, Hoft; so many times. You know we didn't simply come across you by accident: Bernie sent us looking, wanted to surprise you and all the rest of your people from Colline. He shouted your qualities often enough – young as you were. He wanted it to be a huge surprise for you to find him here, still alive. But he was killed a few deccas before you arrived. It didn't seem right to tell you, after you'd thought he was dead for so long. You settled, and never mentioned him.

I wanted you to rise by your own skills. So... I watched you, put a few things your way. You maxed them. And when you made it – Secretary of The Wisp – I did tell you about Bernie. You rose to the top on your own merit, not his shoulders.

So now, it's you and I who hold the power, and we choose to share it with the others.'

'No: it's you who decides everything; I set matters in motion and manage them; then we convince the Board and Council it was their idea – allow them to believe they have some influence and power.'

'You make me smile, Hoft. Okay, so that's the way of it, but no-one has risen higher than you, even with the Grand Old Family connections they parade.'

'I suppose so,' he nodded in slow agreement. 'And we carried on bringing more and more communities here, united in mutual distrust and dislike of the Empire. All of us living long and breeding like ratifers must make The Wisp the greatest population explosion in galactic history, what with all the land and natural wealth, and the large-family bonuses, incentives. And now, after all this time, we have five warships from the Empire heading straight for us.'

'I guess it was our turn, Hoft. I presume they've developed a propulsion unit with about a third the speed of our Dee Drive. It's still an enormous step up for them.

'You're not intending to negotiate with the Board or the Empire, from what you said to Kreuz?'

I had to smile – Hoft only says things like that to check on me. I treated him to a mock-withering look, 'Certainly not: President Kreuz isn't a shadow of his great grandfather – he's clueless, as well as gutless. The Empire's concept of negotiating is to annihilate anyone who isn't them. They fought The Wars of Rights on exactly that basis. They haven't sent a fleet of Battleweights here to carry out discussions.'

'So how are you intending to let Kreuz and the Board know they won't be having it their own way?'

'Let's see how it goes, eh? I wonder if we've kept them waiting long enough?' I looked out the panorama windows, thirty floors up, directly above The Wreck. It always renewed my desire, inspired me, that view straight along The Ditch, across the plains to the Eastern Hills, towards the coast. Studying the present view from there, and remembering the past, is a ritual with me. I motioned Hoft to go through first, into the inner conference room.

The five Board members were waiting. Impatiently. President Kreuz silently, coldly despising me and Hoft for being Ancients who had outlived our time, clinging on to power they rightfully deserved, in the name of The Wisp. The same was written all over the other members.

Chairman Garney red-faced, made rash by his anger at the delay was all set to blurt out his true thoughts and scuff the niceties. 'What do you think you're doing? Keeping The Board waiting? Most disrespectful…' Mmm, he really was wound up, probably seeing the Empire fleet's arrival as his opportunity to fulfil his destiny.

'They're worked up,' I muttered to Hoft as we took our places at the mahon wood table. 'Let's listen to these also-ranters for a while. They're seeing this as their big chance to take control.'

'Made bold,' Hoft quietly quoted Kwahan the Poet, 'by this wine and great love for ourselves.'

The meeting quickly settled – or unsettled – into the five of them badgering, insisting, persuading, pointing out that the Empire was around a thousand times bigger and more powerful than us. 'And if they've despatched a fleet of five Heavyweights in our direction, they're serious about the matter.'

'We're also serious about the matter, President Kreuz,' I agreed. 'But it's everything to us, not a mere far-distant prickle like it is to them. I've lived there, remember, and the Empire's not changed.'

'We are The Board... The High Representatives of the Grand Council. *We* represent the will of the peoples of all the planets. Not some clingers-on to a history that's far gone.

'We need to negotiate, get the best deal we can—'

'Thank you! I saw your memo; your demand for this meeting. For our advance surrender at the first long-distance contact with them. They're three deccas out and you want to hoist the flags out already? We've successfully dealt with them before—'

'Stragglers; mere wandering craft that didn't know where they were, not expecting our attack.'

What a shugg-brain Kreuz is... constantly interrupting. Tall, thinks he's magnificently handsome; wears a semi-uniform as though it means something. All mouth and self-importance. 'No. They weren't stragglers—'

'We wouldn't stand a chance an Empire fleet!' How wonderful – Senior Council Rep, Arena

360

Xye, was slinging her cred's worth in, Big Miss Ignorance. 'They're expecting trouble. We need to show we're not going to give them any reason to fear us.'

I let her rant on, Garney and the others nodding, mumbling their agreement... conferring.

'Okay, gentlemen, lady,' I interrupted their babble. 'You won't know all the details of their previous approaches. We've had three, over the past sixty years. Two in the last ten, and *they* weren't wanderers; they were on a mission here. They attacked at first contact, fired on our ships and populations. To avoid panic, I never released all the details of our losses, or how we dealt with those aggressions. We defeated them with some difficulty and a considerable amount of planning and calculation.

They will have learned from their three losses in this cluster. These new ones – five together – will be fully armed and ready to take all kinds of attack and avoidance tactics the instant they come out of the Dee-style drive—'

'Exactly...'

'We must disarm...'

'Scatter our populations...'

'Broadcast our messages to them...'

'We must be completely clear that we're no threat...'

'We *are* a threat, you fools. They know it. Why do you think there're five of them? They'll spread; they'll wait and observe; they'll identify target centres – certainly here on Discovery. Battleweights carry planet-busters – racks of twelve in each, the last time I saw one. You really want to take that chance?'

'We can't beat the Empire...'

'We'd be wiped out if we resisted...'

'We'll take it to the Grand Council...'

'The Council? A hundred-strong pack of vote-catchers and appointees who believe in peace, plenty and unity with no cost. Gentlemen!' I demanded quiet. 'We have negated Empire craft before. We can do it again, even against five of them. We have The Unit. We can use it as a weapon – negotiate in the only way they understand—.'

'To do what? Transfer one of our people aboard their vessels to talk with them? Arrange our capitulation?'

Imbeciles, I thought. *Why can you not see?* 'If we can put people aboard, we can just as easily send them a thermic detonator, set on, say, two seconds after arrival – no time to do anything to it, or initiate anything against us. We've been practising with rapidly moving targets, and we can lock onto them for delivery.'

'Think, Blissen. Think! You're prepared to take chances with all our lives?'

I'd talked enough by then – I'm a patient person; I wasn't angry. I merely needed to let them stew a little, allow them believe I was re-considering the situation... the options... their demands. 'Talk with me a moment, Hoft,' I said, and we politely excused ourselves, and returned to my private suite, poured ourselves a drink.

He knows me too well, does Hoft. 'You want me to set the thermic option in motion, Hal?' He motioned towards the internal rad unit. 'We're basically ready.'

'Not yet, Hoft. There are cheaper and equally effective ways to neutralise the incoming ships, rather than matching speeds and locking on to them, wasting thermic bombs. What we've mostly been practising recently is sending large pieces of rock or metal via The Unit. So far, we've successfully locked on to four

362

unmanned drogue craft, and put rocks aboard with zero relative speed.'

'Zero speed?' he echoed. 'And the effect is…?'

'What would you imagine? An object with zero spatial speed encounters the insides of a ship travelling at ten thousand megs per second. No contest. The momentum impact is enormous. Even if it's only a piece of metal the size of a zorc spanner, or a glass of Finest Reserve, the arriving item remains exactly where it is. But the ship continues with such a vast difference in momentum that it rips the guts out the ship. Actually, the ship fillets itself, regardless of its size, in around a millionth of a beat.'

'You're sure about this?'

'That it works? Yes – we've tested it. That I intend to do it? Yes, certainly. The trick is in locating their exact whereabouts after they come out of Dee-effect travel: they'll scatter. We'll need to re-find them, then calibrate to each one's precise position. Lock on; press the button.

'I came here to escape the Empire, not prepare a garden patch for them. I'm the only person left in The Wisp who remembers the aftermath of The Wars of Rights. And it's not going to happen here. If the Empire wants to follow me, and restart The Wars on my territory, it's at their own risk.'

'And if President Kreuz, Garney and the rest of the Board object?'

'Ah, yes. I was coming to that.' I finished that drink, poured another one each. 'I reckon that a mass the size of President Kreuz would be plenty big enough to take out the insides of a Battleweight Cruiser. Don't you?'

Hoft pondered that for a moment, digesting the idea. He smiled faintly, 'And they have five ships…'

'And we have five Board members, yes…'

* oOOOo *

∗∗∗ Davvy Six-Four-Six ∗∗∗

'Hmm?' The ignorant skyker eventually looked up, the same as a year ago – tattered uniform and a face like run-over giblets.

'I was summoned,' I said. 'Name's Davvy.'

'Where from?'

'Digsby.'

'*Unit.* Not planet, Davvy from Digsby.' He sounded like he was up to his teeth with idiots. 'Like Compound Four-One... Section Three-Oh-Three.'

'Hill Six-Four-Six.'

'There! You *can* do it. Let's see... Davvy Six-Four-Six. Ahh, yes. On your own now? Come for partners, have you? Stock? Equipment?'

'I don't know. *You* sent for *me.* Mind-memo code Zero H 646.' Actually, I had a pretty good idea what my first sending-for was about, and there was no way to avoid it, not with a chip the size of a fingernail in the back of my head.

'Ah yes... *You,*' Criminal Colony Supervisor Huldrik murmured, really ominously. 'Your End-of-Year-One Review.'

Four of us had been allocated Hill Six-Four-Six when we arrived on Segotta a year ago. No experience. Just the chip implanted, and we could access the instructions. 'Sort yourselves out,' he'd said. 'Clear as much of Hill Six-Four-Six as you can. Come next year with a decent plan for the future, and maybe you get "Settle and Farm" rights to it.'

We soon managed to lose one partner to insanity: Aldri was a danger to us and the machinery, so I had to "let him go" one dark night when he wasn't looking. Then I forgot to warn Bendax I was turning the timber masher on while he was clearing a blockage – thieving idle toshcan that he was. But they were two hundred days ago. Surely, Huldrik wouldn't have waited this long? Unless he was letting us finish the clearing before shipping us out somewhere?

He can log in to our head-chips anytime he wants, so this summons shouldn't be about me and Chorky's recent amicable parting. Chorky was magical with the machinery, and operating it was all he wanted to do. It was like the chip had found a brother soul in him. Central would allocate him another hill or flatland, and he'd continue with fresh land clearances to work off his sentence, buy the worn-out machinery, and eventually make a profit. That was the dream, anyway.

Me? I was intending to keep the land we'd cleared: farm the whole of Hill Four-Six-Four till I broke even on my sentence

Perhaps Huldrik really meant it when he sent the last mind-memo requiring my action plan for The Hill to be more precise than my reply: "Farm it".

I mean, how would I know what my exact intentions were? I'm no farmer. 'Send me lots of seeds and I'll plant them and work another year off my sentence, possibly with the help we were promised last year?' That should have been sufficient for him, surely?

'For those who survive the first year,' he told us, that first day, 'it takes an average of twenty further years to clear your sentence. Plus any added years you've borrowed against. The more land you clear and farm, the more profit you'll make; and thus pay off the loans and the time faster. Up to you.'

I took it to heart. I'm not a criminal by birth – I could have been re-aligned, but I preferred to do real, meaningful time. I earned it.

I've no idea where Segotta is. It must be one of the In-cluster planets not too far from Digsby – my former home. It really doesn't matter: they'll never allow me back.

Now Huldrik's sitting here wanting my action plan in person? 'How you going to farm it? What crop? Where's the seed coming from? Tools? Equipment? Three partners short, aren't you? Where's the helpers you were supposed to adopt and train up during the year? It is not easy for eight workers to farm a hill that size. Very hard with four; impossible on your own. You should have amalgamated with a few others, hired and trained helpers. You'll need to obtain quick-growing Palma Fruit: profit within the first year. Not a task for one man alone.'

In sheer relief, I didn't speak. Thank the stars, it wasn't about Aldri or Bendax; nor the partnership split with Chorky.

'And the chemix for growth and weed-killing? Irrigation system? You figured it out?'

'I think I am doing. Never give a Crim an even break, huh?'

'Nothing's free, Davvy Four-Six. It's all added to your sentence and debt. The two things are interchangeable.'

'I imagine you have a suggestion, Supervisor?'

He went all devious-smiley on me. 'I do happen to have a consignment of helpers in the Pen. Their feed allowance is exhausted, so I have to dump them, probably into the Wildlands on Farside.'

I suspect it's impossible to be more suspicious than I was, so I just stood and waited, still relieved about Aldri and Bendax. 'We had some humans in last dodec,' he was saying, 'but they were snapped up straight away – four women among them.'

'And what do you have lined up for me? Mechoes?'

'Come see. They're Crims, of course, but they do have human genes.'

He took me out the back, to the Pen – glass screen. Must have been twenty of them. They looked somewhat like women, but definitely not human ones. Their necks were twice as long, and they had huge eyes and lashes. 'They're Highraff Folk. From somewhere called Raffery. These adults are all female. Workers, so the notes say. Pick a docile one, smart looker, and who knows, eh?' He was grinning at me. 'Or the strongest, most thick-looking one.'

I stared. Skyke! They looked more than a mite pathetic – standing or sitting round in shabby one-piece canvie dresses. Seven little ones. Several could be male. Three very small; just kidlings. 'What is this? Family clearance somewhere?'

'Probably. It'll be a rebel thing, or criminal family gang. Whatever; they're being clearanced. You want one, or not? Go in. Talk with'em: they do speak Empire…ish. You're the only chance for one of'em. Take a couple – some of'em look strong; guaranteed disease-free. You'll need to decide now, though: feed's all gone. Any you leave'll get dumped'

So we went in the Pen, and they stared at me, all suspicious, distrusting, like I was the specimen. 'Yeah,' I said, 'maybe I could get used to one being around; do the pruning and weeding.'

'Sure; you should be able to afford one's food allowance out of the increased profit prediction. How about *her* – looks strong. Tell her.'

I did.

She hit me! A right smack across my face. Skyke! It knocked me flying and I belted her one back. We both said, 'What did you expect?'

I stopped. Skyke-it! Bad situation for both of us. 'Hey, hey, lady. Quits, huh?' I retreated a step or two – she had a long reach and a mean right hook; a bit of a snarl, too.

Huldrik told her the score, but she was still all fiery looks and blazing temper.

'Koh, forget it, Huldrik. She'd turn the fruit sour.'

'You *need* someone, Davvy Four-Six. I'm *telling* you. You can not cultivate that much land alone. The Fed says it must be put to use. Waste of the land if it reverts, plus the machinery's wear and tear.'

'I'm having one of these, like it or not? '

'If you don't, I'll offer the land to someone else when the next consignment is transferred in. What about the planting, fertilising? Irrigation? Pest control? You'll need to keep the chucker population to a minimum –

369

them little vermin are everywhere. Repairs, cleaning, food prep? You'll need more'n one helper.'

'Oh, yes? How much will it cost me?'

'You catch on, Davvy. I'm in a good mood, so how about a year added to your sentence? Per person. That's cheap. Think of the raised efficiency levels, the increased profits from fuller use of the land.'

'They'd have to be skyking good to be worth that. Three are hardly old enough to stand, much less walk or work.'

'I tell you what – I'm fair. I'll charge you only for the adults – fourteen of them. You get the little'uns free. Can't be cheaper than that.'

I was aghast: I was buying people? Children free? 'It'd add fourteen years to my sentence.'

He laughed. 'Go on then, half price – only seven years added.'

So – he was up for bargaining, was he? 'Call it two years for the lot.'

'Four years.'

'Three.' I must have been mad to barter for lives I didn't even want. But... we could farm The Hill together. They'd have no chance on Farside. I'd heard about the heat and insects and diseases and no food or clean water.

I tried to explain to the pugila one, but she was still snarling and growling, fists raised. I gave up, 'Let's call it off, Huldrik. Please.'

He explained to them: 'Stay here and I'll dump you at an Eramaa Station on Farside, where you can become One with Nature. That's a three-day survival prognosis. Or, he buys you, and you go with him.'

Load of crying and ranting and foul looks, but five foul-mouthed mins later, they went trooping out.

'Thanks, Huldrik. How to dump me right in it, huh?'

'Y' didn't want it easy, did you?' The baster grinned. 'Show'em who's in charge from the start. Like strangle *that* one with the bendy neck and big mouth. Anyway, come through and we'll fix the data-pod.'

They *all* have bendy necks, I thought. And pearly skin.

'What have I done? What am I supposed to do with'em?'

'Negotiate,' he said.

'Negotiate? They're furry creatures with mobile ears and huge eyes. They're a pack of Crims.'

'What do you think you are, *Lifer* Davvy? Besides, they're not furry – it's officially "a fine velvet down".'

I took a walk through my fingers, and came up zilch on ideas. So I had a chat – no, not a chat – a surrender – with Huldrik. My only card was that I was taking them off his hands and it'd save him the expense of feeding them.

'Feed them? Don't be ridiculous. Their food ran out days ago.'

He had me under the wheels: I fingerprinted left, right and down the middle, and tottered out.

*** DayMia ***

The Highraff were packed aboard the trailer I'd just bought – at a cost of two years. 'Don't think about it, Davvy,' I kept telling myself. 'It'll look better by morning.' I needed a drink, but I hadn't had one for over a year, Empire Time.

371

By the time I climbed back into my cab, I couldn't have told you which planet I was on. I stared at the slap-handy one on the passenger side. 'What have I done?' I asked myself, but I knew: the gruesome details hadn't sunk in yet. I stared at her: fine-looking, strong face – for a semi-human. Cheeks and jaw carved by an artist. Negotiate with her? Podge of a chance. Especially while my mind's absent, and her slapping hand's flexing.

'Y' with me,' I told her, 'Koh?'

She looked hating, plus defiant, and started mouthing off before I'd even settled and switched on. Threatening non-cooperation... conditions... would run... refuse... 'Nobody owns *us*.'

'I'm just trying to survive, lady. Same as you. Gimme a rest, hmm?'

Her skin had this slight velvety sheen when she blazed, like milky opal. 'You need us. You must look after us. *You* have no choice,' she told me.

'Hush it, Creature.' I started the motor up, letting it warm through. 'You were going to be dumped.'

'Bluff,' she sneered.

This was getting worse. I looked back at the trailer, full of them, all bedraggled and wrecked, the jetsam of the Fed's latest policies. Plus all the equipment and sacks... and just everything. I was a nut in a pressure crusher set on Max. 'Lady, neither of us has a choice—'

'There's always a choice for me, Scummy.' Dark surly eyes with lashes long enough to scour your skin away.

'Yeah, and yours is to shut up or get out. Skyke-it, Lady, I'm not arguing with a geeraff crossed with a Spanyol.' I thought she was going to swipe my face again, but she resisted the obvious urge. 'I'm trying to rescue you. I'm praying we can help each other – you know – *mutual*? And all I'm getting is grief.'

'My mother's there,' she pointed. 'And my young sister. You better take care—'

'*Shurrup*! Everybody works. Farside was no bluff. They don't want you. I do. I can—'

'You expect gratitude?' She was off again – snub little nose twitching like a doraker's backside. And we hadn't even started moving.

'You bought us?'

'You know I did, with years added onto my sentence.'

'We're not property.'

'We all are. The Fed owns us. No! Shut it. I'm not Charity Chaney – this's a work offer. It's the same for me as you—'

She was off again about not being a bargaining chip or a prize or a slave…

'You think I was asked? The Supervisor gave me a screwing over; said I'd lose my plot if I didn't have a viable number of helpers to farm it. You were all he had on offer. Yes!!! I accepted. So just shut up about it: it's probably his idea of mutual reprimand.'

'Starting your own zoo, are you? Slave camp? Your own pervy fuck-farm?' She had these long, slightly pointed ears with a tuft of hair growing up. They jiggled.

I threw my hands up in despair, 'Lady, you're just what I need, aren't you? I'm throwing my life away on you lot—'

'You're figuring on dumping us, Scummy?'

'Why would I pull you out the Pen just to dump you?' I stared at the cab roof. 'What do you want I should call you?'

'Oi.'

'Just tell me your name, title, addressance... whatever you'd prefer. And make it decent, respectful, not stupid or piss-taking. We're stuck together, so make it something you're comfortable with.'

'Your Great Ladyship.' I felt her smirk, didn't need to see it.

'You feel like that?' I slammed my fists on the drive bar. 'Get off now, and I'll cancel all these contracts, be happy again – at the cost of just one day instead of the life-time I owe now.' We sat there in raging silence. She didn't get off. Nobody moved.

'You're staying? It's on my terms. Here, earn your keep.' I swung the bar across to her side. 'Drive. *That* way. The screen'll home us in.' I needed to pow out after the previous night driving and the day I was barely surviving.

I laid back in a power-kip of torment and stared at my perfidious hand that had just committed me to tools and minimacks. And enough seeds and seedlings and chemix for growth and weed-kill for the whole skyking hill. The trailer, fuel cells, irrigation system... water rights. A year's feed for us all in three types of Basic, plus an extras selection. Clothing and workwear guaranteed for three years. Amounting to eighteen years added to my twenty-year sentence. What the skyke have I done?

As Huldrik said, 'You cleared more than I thought all four of you would manage. You sure you want to risk farming that much? It's a Pits-of-a-Commitment.'

'No, of course I'm not sure, but it looks like the only chance they've got, and what've I got to lose?'

'Everything, if you skyke it up.' He had that smug told-you-so look that he most likely reserved for corpses. 'You'd forfeit the past year's work clearing nearly a thousand heck of virgin land. Someone else would have it for nothing.'

'Am I permitted to die in this place?'

'Only when your sentence expires.'

'DayMia,' she said. 'I'm DayMia.'

I tried to sit up. It was a stiff, reluctant struggle. Time had jerked and bounced by. I looked around – back at my place. The Highraff all looking about as skyked-up as me. 'The Fed's had its wicked way with all of us, huh?

Yi-zack! I deserved my sentence. But this lot? I looked'em over as they climbed out the back of the trailer and stood dazed – just kids and women. They've done nothing. Collateral. Conned. Clearanced. Whatever. But… It's not up to me to buck the whole system. We have a better chance of surviving if we stick together.

'DayMia? That isn't some gormy name where I'm taking the skyke out myself every time I say it, is it?'

She shook her head.

'Cos I'd rip your head off if it was. Koh?' She nodded. 'Right, Shall I tell them to unload the trailer, or do you want to be foreman?'

'They're people, for Drun's sake. They hear you.' Boy, had I skyked her off.

'Koh.' I pulled the covers off the stores. 'Let's get the trailer unloaded. Seed sacks into the shelter there; the small boxes onto the shelves; the food packages on that side; one into the housing unit over there. Before the rain. See the cloud? It's imminent.'

They just stood. Vacant. She came close, 'They haven't eaten for four days.'

'The seed sacks need to be unloaded straight away. We *can't* leave them out here in the rain. Come on – Unload.'

'We eat first.'

'No, you don't. We must get the seeds undercover.'

'Food.' She was rock-still. That was when I knew I had signed my life away on a useless pack of skyke-knows-what.

'I hate you,' I told her. 'You destroy me. I *need* that stuff unloading before the rain. It really *can't* be left out here. You can eat all you like when it's in.' I went to the trailer and dragged a sack down and lugged it across to the shelter. 'Come on, help,' I told them. 'You all do it.'

They looked. She shook her head a fraction. They didn't move.

I practically begged, and dragged another. The rain was spitting down. Another sack. 'The seeds have to be covered...'

They stood under the shelter and watched me struggle. I ranted at them. Ordered them. Begged them. Skyking Puddings. The rain was darkening up... 'You gotta help do it.'

Inspiration! Re-cover it. Yes! I had to get the cover back on. It was blowing, flapping wildly in the rising wind.

Too late. The Black Hole of Heaven opened and the rain was suddenly belting down. The cover lashed and refused to be controlled. After ten mins, it was too late. The seed stock was saturated... ruined.

These pearl-skinned, unmoving creatures had beaten me so easily – just by not moving.

I pulled out a crate of Finel Basic. 'Help yourselves. Sure as Shufflers, you haven't helped me.'

Out in the yard, the rain was cataracting down. 'I'm dead. It'll be confirmed soon. Huldrik'll blow my head up. *The seeds are wet.* They'll germinate. All at once. All two million of them will need to be planted on the same day. Instead of batches ten days apart, spread over six onz.

'You shredded my life,' I told my traitorous hand. 'I should'a left'em there... This's all my own fault, not theirs.'

Jipps – The Hill looked so bare and grey and soddened. My hill. Ripe for planting. 'It's not gonna happen now. A whole skyking year's work with Chorky thrown away, and another eighteen years on top.' Fruggs! I felt sorry for myself.

The planting all needs to be done *now*, immediately. A thousand hecks to plant in one go? To tend and prune? To irrigate all at once. To harvest within a few days? Totally unmanageable. 'I'm dead. I belong to Huldrik and the Fed. I'll never buy myself back.'

I wandered towards the base marker at the foot of The Hill. I could see it all so clearly now... 'Pack of parasites; they'll be always demanding, never doing. I'm dead.'

After only four days, the weeds were already starting to come through. The chemix were waiting to be unloaded. The tools were still on the trailer. 'Yeah, great, they're happy – having their skyking food.'

What could I do? I was drenched and semi-liquid. And the rain continued to torrent down. Wandering across the hill, I slumped. Terrace One, Area Two, row

377

nine six – I know every brad of The Hill. We'd left a huge Jessmina tree there, with a colony of cunyuk birds living in it – very smart with their bright plumage. Me and Chorky'd left half a dozen on every terrace – all of them, actually. We didn't feel rapacious enough to root them out. The trunk was comforting; soft and furry. It was the only comfort I could think of. Huldrik was so skyking right: I must be mad.

As the sun eased down on my first nightmare day, I practically crawled back to the shelter yard. Lethargy itself, they were sitting around, looking at me. Like I wanted to know. I needed sleep right then, not fresh confrontation. 'Aren't you going to tell them where they sleep?'

'Nope. They don't listen to me. I need to be up at dawn to start the planting. On my own, if you're not going to do what you get sheltered, protected, clothed and fed for. I should be able to get ten thousand in. In five days, the rest'll be too delicate to plant and I'll have to throw them away. You lot might as well go with'em.'

'So. It's going to be like that, is it? Us against you?'

Skyke me backwards, she was going to be an utter pain – for the few days of life she had left to her at this rate. I restrained myself, 'Only if you're intent on it, DayMia. Only if you insist. Meantime, *that's* my sleep corner. You lay where you wish.'

*** Sylfi ***

Terrace One beckoned as the sun rose next morning. I powered the pup motor on the dibber and set off. And had to stop: they were all there. Well fed. Their new canvie workwear on, same as mine. All as ill-fitting. I'd bought five dibbers. Showed them how to charge them, start them, lubricate three times a day; check the over-heater. It was all on my head-chip. They split themselves in pairs, with a child each, and stuck in.

We almost completed Terrace One by dark. And weeded T Eight as well. Set traps and poison for chuckers. Worked out a rota for the morrow – shorter shifts, more frequent role changes; message carrying, food and drink fetching... Designated toilet areas – try out the extruder and make a toilet screen and containers for chuckers – dammed little rodents would be undermining the terraces, given a quarter chance.

'If we soak some seed in Pythrene, it might slow the growth down...' was the best idea I could think of.

'Or plant some deeper...'

'Hold off on the irrigation later...'

'Vary the fertiliser strength and amount...'

'Plant more on the north-facing slopes...'

'Or the patches of clay... the sandy section near the peak...'

Great. We were full of stupid ideas, 'So let's do them all,' said one called Sylfi. 'Anything to spread the growth period out. You want a sixty-day harvesting period?'

At least they liked the food. They ate it, anyway. I put DayMia in charge of meals – which foodstuffs, which days; amounts. They all spoke with each other, quiet and serious. And stared at me and said nothing for days on end.

I only had the one big shelter, so we all slept together – them down one end, me in a far corner. 'We'll extrude some more separating panels when we have time,' I told them.

They organised a rota on repairing, cleaning and everything else, except speaking to me. Apart from DayMia, and I usually wished she'd take a vow of silence, too.

Already weary by noon, as always, I helped myself to a platter of Basic Finel gunge and crackers with a cup of water. They all stared at me sullenly, as if I wanted to spit-roast one of their children.

'Where's the rest of your crew?' DayMia asked. 'Why have you been working alone?'

'I murdered two of my partners when they irritated me.' I gave her a warning look – might as well tell her straight. 'Then I split with Chorky, my other partner. He kept the clearance machinery; I retained the land. I also butchered two people on Digsby.'

'Why?'

Several of them were listening in, pretending to be horrified.

'The two on Digsby? They sniggered at the reconciliation meeting, after they'd supposedly received "re-education". They were responsible for a lot of deaths – sheer greed and carelessness. They were as "re-aligned" as my backside. So I dismantled them. They weren't smirking then.'

'Dismantled? They were mechoes?'

'No; but they came apart just the same, in lots of small, extremely painful bits. I'm here – same as you. Four of us were allocated here, to start clearing. Women and other workers were supposed to join us. Never happened. We worked non-stop, and never thought ahead. So this's much more extensive than we originally intended to clear in the first year.'

'You sliced people apart? Are you threatening us?' The others backed away when she said that.

DayMia wasn't a lot of help sometimes.

We rested mid-postnoon when the sun blazed down, and when the youngsters brought the drinks round, up on Terrace Seven. Squatting together with two of the less anti-me women, I asked, 'You know about me – what about all of you?' They exchanged glances and said nothing, eyelashes waving down like prayer mats. No answer then, but they would sometimes talk if I cornered them, and asked direct questions, nicely. They were really pleasant, actually – a bit shy and reluctant, but these two – Sylfi and Lotti were the ones I spoke with when I didn't want an argument.

At least Sylfi didn't blame me for *all* their woes. She looked up, such wondrous eyes, 'We lived in the warren towns in Deenya, our island-continent on Raffery. We were the Underfolk... Warreners. There was always trouble over living rights, property, equality; then toxic pollution worsened, some of the halls collapsed, and nobody took the blame. We resisted when they tried to forcibly evacuate us. Some of our men were killed. Eight or ten onz ago, we were all taken away, split into groups and shipped out like refugees... criminals... kept in places like that Pen. Sent to penal planets like this one.'

'It's DayMia who's kept us together. We're supposed to be grateful they didn't kill us.'

'We end up in slavery instead.' Sylfi's ears drooped for a moment.

'If you were slaves, you'd be— Never mind. So DayMia's your leader, huh?'

'Derris, her Life Partner was. He was the P.U leader.'

'Probably what landed you into bother,' I dared to suggest, 'if he was over-stroppy with your authorities.'

'The system's no different here. We're merely the means of production – dispensable.'

'With DayMia challenging all the time, it's scarcely a surprise Huldrik stopped feeding you.'

'We've never been outside as much, in the open air, as we are here,' Sylfi said. 'It's quite frightening.'

'We have no rights.'

'None of us on Segotta has rights,' I told them.

'But you're a killer. DayMia says you don't deserve rights. None of us has ever harmed anyone.'

'You should try it; it's great fun.'

'I think you'd be top of DayMia's list.' They looked at me joylessly, as though rehearsing their gruesome options.

'Ha. That's almost a comfort,' I said, but it wasn't; not really. I was thinking that Sylfi would be top of my list... my list of beautiful people.

But it was time to get back to work... and they rose in unison, nodded silently and headed towards the wash point in the shade of the Jessmina tree. I sighed, 'Hi ho,' wishing they could bring themselves to be a tad less distant. One of them had left her tally-pad and marker behind. I picked it up... thought... and drew a swift sketch on the palm-sized pap-pad. 'Jipps, but Sylfi's beautiful, such a neck... eyes...' I gazed at it in surprise – I'd never drawn anything before. Ever. Crude, but for two mins' idle play, I thought it had captured her.

'Is that my tally-pad?' A delicate hand appeared.

'Er... Yes... I'm sorry, I...' handed it to her.

She looked. 'It's me.' She blushed. I didn't know they did that. 'It's... it's... One eye's bigger than the other... and that ear's not right...' She was gone, clutching the pad.

With a huge amount of effort and goodwill, we set the irrigation system up for the first three terraces that would need it. Then set about trying to stagger the growth rate, and timing of the harvest – the fertiliser diluted to four different concentrations. Plus the degree of pruning that slowed or speeded growth; even at the risk of small fruit on some plants. Amount of watering... amount of pythrene on each batch... A pseudo-random system for monitoring the results. It was all down to Tonya and Sylfi: they had minds like digitalics, and they smiled, too.

'You often come up here, don't you?' Three of the Ladies joined me on the peak of The Hill towards dusk. 'Surveying your domain, are you?'

I truly didn't want company just then, but they'd purposefully come to see me, so I had to be welcoming. 'Yes. I need the complete picture in my mind; it helps with planning the next few days' tasks.'

'And beyond? The freedom to go where you will?' Sylfi had a wistful little face.

I stared out over all the thick greens of the forest, spreading as far as the eye might wander. 'Me? Free? Never going to happen. The Fed owns me, body and balls, if not heart and soul. Same with you, really: I can't stop you leaving. We're all free to go anytime, though where we'd go, Kimse alone knows. What we have is an arrangement whereby I feed you if you do the work for me. You're doing it for yourselves.'

I don't know if they believed me, but we started the walk down to the shelter yard together.

I left them to their chattering and playing with the little ones, and settled to my usual quiet evening alone with the planning or repairs or extruding or chemick mixing or...

Some stock was missing. The wall panels damaged. Food packs opened and scattered. There was no possibility that it was one of us. Never crossed my mind – it was totally against their nature – even the children, who had minimal mischief in them unless I teased and goaded it into them. We fixed the panels – not *too* well – and I slept in the storeroom.

Then DayMia insisted on having another go at me, contending that it was her Highraffs who were taking all the risk, doing all the work, getting all the pleasure, after one of the Ladies had an accident with a chucker trap. She was interrupting my daily routine of electro-bolting the trapped chuckers and skinning them, which DayMia and the others assumed was mere pleasurable practise for skinning them – because I once said their skin was beautifully pearlescent in the sun.

I didn't like being disturbed because I get into the swing of it, burying the awful mood that comes to me, closing my mind to what I'm actually doing. I straightened up. 'Me getting all the pleasure? The food's the same for all of us – same bedding – same clothes – I'm in the field in all weathers. Pleasure? Y' think I enjoy sleeping in the store, waiting for a break-in? Spending half the night planning rotas, and mixtures for fertiliser and poison? You want to spend dawn every day emptying chucker traps, killing them, skinning and tannizing them?

'You want to be on the same hock block as me? I'd welcome the company. Maybe we'll be able to tune our chips into each other, when Huldrik fits yours? You'll be able to poke into every thought I have. And Huldrik'll do the same with you and Heeria... Sylfi and Sovin... Lotti, Jimmya... all of you. Same risk; same joys, like having your brain melted if Huldrik flips a switch when you set a dainty little hoof – sorry – foot, off The Hill.'

She pulled a face, but her snarl didn't come over too threateningly. Most of the Highraff had front teeth that were a fraction over-large, and it made them look so appealing and innocent, whatever they did.

That was my only consolation some days.

The storeroom was no less comfortable than the group shelter, though colder, without the overall body warmth from the crowd. It was around the fifth or sixth night that they came, splitting the panel open again. They had prise bars and a cutter. Two of them; murmuring and under-breath cursing. An electro-bolt will kill a chucker, but they just stun humans. Stunned these two, anyway.

The Ladies were incensed with these two cringing thieves, 'They've already stolen or spoiled food enough for an onz and a half for everyone. That's enough to feed one person for a year. And now they've returned with knives, prise-bars and sacks, intent on grander-scale thievery.

'Indeed,' I joined in. 'They're stealing the food from your mouths. How much more were they coming for? Intent on starving you?'

That was when I thought they *did* know how to look very menacing, and I decided not to be around the shelter yard that day.

I didn't expect anyone to come looking for them, or Huldrik to blow my head apart, but you never know – best if my head doesn't go into melt-down in front of them, so I made myself scarce for the rest of the day. 'I'm going to check for footprints, perimeter fence damage, trails into the forest, and fix the damage to the store. You lot have the day off. I don't want to see a trace of these two ever again.'

I've no idea exactly what *they* did that day, but *I* toured the perimeter, combined with a berry-picking and fence-checking expedition. See if there were any trails into the forest...

When I returned, the Ladies were in a subdued-excited mood, and there was a patch of disturbed soil beneath one of the Jessmina trees on Terrace One.

'On Raffery,' DayMia began, 'we had a favourite food for celebratory occasions, an open-fired meat dish with stewed fruits.' I waited – she had probably worked herself up into a mood to eat my arms. 'The chuckers you skin? We wish to roast the carcasses for our special evening. Tonight.'

'Go ahead. Anything. Here – I collected a couple of bags of wild berries along the woodland edges. There's also the bewilder-berries on the terrace faces. I'll try some with you.'

She froze.

I stopped. 'Or not? I've clanged again? It's private, huh? Koh, just get on with it. I don't own you.' I sank. Again. They have these special evenings sometimes. Family festas, or religious parties, I dunno. They just tighten up if I ask, and say it's no big mystery, nothing to concern me. 'Just let us do it, hmm?' These times are strictly "Highraff Only" evenings. Great. Here we are, twenty-two of us, isolated almost a day from anywhere, but deep down, it's still them against me.

I cried that night.

*** Heeria ***

'Heeria, my young sister, is coming of age and into season.'

'Eh?'

'She needs to partake in sex within the next thirty days or she will not mature internally. She would become a Preserved.'

387

'I wondered why you were edging round like a three-legged crabb. I presume that's not good?'

'Noooo.' DayMia was very certain of that.

'And you're telling me because...?' As if I couldn't guess, being the only male over the age of ten within fifty clicks travel. 'You want *me* to have sex with Heeria? Really? You're not taking the shine, are you? With *witnesses*? You're jesting. Wouldn't a sworn affidavit be sufficient? Or... whatever internal changes take place, you'll be able to tell? You're going to holo it? What? From the inside, I suppose? To make sure it really happened? No, no. If that's how you— Yes, of course I have some experience – three years I was trothed. Anyway, I thought you lot hated to be seen naked? Shy about your colourant skin patches – like opals, some of you...'

'You've seen?' That look of shock was worth its weight in iridium.

'I chike.'

'She'll stay covered. It'll be dark.' DayMia had all the rules worked out.

'Not with me in there – I don't like the dark. Besides, it might be anybody you substitute. Listen, DayMia, Huldrik can tap in to every thought and sight I have, and the same for every other crim on Segotta. He took great delight in showing us his monitoring board all lit up when we arrived. He could be watching for gruesome deaths, wildly adventurous activities, exotic sex, or anything else he takes a fancy to observing – and selling recordings to the Cheevy Channels on Deadhole or Somesuch Planet. I must be the most boring one on his charts, but he can follow me anywhere, anytime, and see through my eyes, or blow my head off.

'We need to do this.' She was adamant. 'Thus, it must be in the dark.'

'So how are you going to make a recording, then?'

In truth, they didn't exactly watch or record, and it wasn't all that dark. we made my sleeping area slightly more private by erecting panels to form a corner room, plus similar ones for themselves.

Then, I suspect they just kept an eye on us under the covers, checking how many times, and how long they lasted and if there was any variety. Whatever. But I could feel their eyes on us.

It was five alternate nights. Heeria spoke a few times, mostly about the fields and the weather and which terrace was due for an extra dose of Pythrene because it seemed like it was slowing the growth. And hoped it wouldn't taint the flavour of the fruit when it grew – or make it poisonous. She liked one of the extra foods I'd brought… and was getting used to being under the open sky so much…

She even said a few things about her old home. And her parents; and the former planet; things they did as kids; how the night sky was different from Segotta.

She was shy; completely unaccustomed to any intimacy previously. And not too sure about it afterwards, either. But she didn't say a single word about what we were doing in the bed. Not one. In five nights of almost rampant sex. Rampant by my standards, anyway.

My bedding corner was colder after she stopped coming.

The only thing that kept me warm was the thought that I'd made a breakthrough with my Ladies of Raffery. I felt so... *honoured.*

Not all that honoured, though – DayMia never gave it a rest. There was no suiting her. It was all for her people first, last and in between; and not a single word in my favour. At least I knew where I stood with her. It merely became boringly irritating when she objected to *everything* I tried to set up. Not once did she even say, "Thanks for fucking my sister."

'Skyke-it, woman. I'm not the enemy here,' I rounded on her one morning. 'There is no enemy here, except yourself. Nobody cares enough to have enemies: not Huldrik, or The Penal Department or the Fed. It's just how things are – meaningless.

'Except you. You treat us like slaves. We'd be free without you.'

I had a fleeting vision of them dead and rotted in the Farside Eramaa camp, and decided it was a case of "Least said, least worsened." So I left her to it.

Three totally uneventful, routine, work-filled, exhausting days later I was disturbed one night, not long after I'd crawled under the covers and turned on the dimlite. Someone was edging in with me. Obviously, one of The Ladies, but which one? I jiggled thoughts of several possibles – Heeria was top of that list. There was also a little list of ones I hoped about. Sylfi was top of that list. But, whoever she was, she didn't speak, just started touching me and murmuring; they all had that silken caressing voice.

It was really awkward in the morning – I couldn't be sure who it had been; she'd slipped away before dawn.

Mid-morning, Sylfi sidled to me at rota change, took my hand, and led me to the drink and hand-snack tray that one of the kids had brought up the terrace. I couldn't do much more than gaze in awe at her: she was the one I really liked; and she was usually a friendlier go-between than DayMia.

She chattered and smiled all round at everyone. 'Laying your claim, are you, Lady?' I rather hoped so: she was awesomely soft and gentle, and was one you'd notice in the crowd. No, I didn't *rather* hope so – it was more like I was aching for her to want to be with me.

She joined me at the evening meal and two of the others sat with us, even spoke to me, and the underage kids played in our corner. All firsts.

I was on Mount Maior that night – way above the clouds.

'You're prejudiced against us. When you first saw us in the Pen at Central, you thought, "I can make a profit from these creatures." Didn't you?'

'Fruggs on Fire, DayMia, give it a day off. As I recall, I thought, "Maybe we can do each other a bit of good". How could I be prejudiced? I had no idea who or what you were. I thought you looked very, er, attractive. You had beautiful hair in long, tied-back tresses; almost striped golden and brown. You all looked so graceful and sad. Huldrik said he had no more food for a gang of crims, malcontents or refugees, so I paid him for your food, and you insisted on getting your snouts in the trough before you'd earned a spoonful of it. Koh – so *snouts* was undiplomatic of me. Alright, it was

391

unpleasant of me. But it's a very nice snout. Besides,' I called after her as she went to tell the others what an inhumanist scuffer I was, 'it's figurative, not anatomical.'

Ah, well – Some you lose, and others just beat you.

Sylfi came to my bed most nights. She was a joy, so welcome. Quietly intense and beautiful: the down of her skin was brushed velveen. Undemanding, she seemed to know me and what I wanted, or was in the mood for. I usually didn't know myself. No-one said anything, or looked askance at us; just accepting it. Encouraging, even?

I was happier to have her with me than I would have been if the harvest had come to my bed.

*** Cojji, Mimmi, Gabbsy and Tonya ***

One mid-afternoon break, I was showing a couple of the children how to dig a hand's depth around weed shoots, and pull them up. They were great; they loved doing something, and took satisfaction in seeing a patch of clean ground ready for seedlings, and burning the heap of shoots. 'I like it outside under the sun, Uncle Davvy,' Cojji confided.

'And the rain,' Mimmi said.

'And burning things.'

'And running all the way down the hill.'

'The food is better than we had before.'

'Especially the Fishy Pie Basic.'

'My mum says it's tastier than we had at home.'

'She wishes Dad was here… on The Hill.'

'Really?'

'Yes. She likes it here.'
'So does my mum.'

That same evening, one of the boys went down with a fever. He'd been bitten by a chucker, and his hand was becoming gangrenous with the fleshrot. They were desperate, fussing, mumbling and clueless.

I interrogated my head chip. Yes, the drugs were in our supplies. But he was too small to take them directly – they would blow his system. I had to guarantee the costs of replacing them before I could open the box. The light came on, the container opened – it had just cost me up to half a year added, depending how much medication I removed.

I let the chip do the thinking and talking in my head, and knew it was going to be pretty awful: there had to be a go-between who would take the pills, and link up with him. And it had to be male: female hormones would interfere with the parinthonic links.

So I took the four pills and the carrier solution. I waited; then they rigged a blood lead between me and Gabbsy – that was what they called him, anyway. He and I waited again. They all fussed round him and fed him and stroked him.

By morning light, he was stabilised. Then improving. The fleshrot was healing, retreating. And transferring – to me. I felt skyking awful after a time, turning a delightful shade of green, my brain cooking on overload. For all the difference it made to them. Gabbsy was their only concern, and the drugs were doing their stuff with him. Jipps! I felt so whingeingly sorry for myself.

After two days they decided he was well enough to be disconnected. I had to disconnect myself and stagger out. Skyke-all had been done on the terraces for three whole sodding wasted damned never-to-get-back days. Another day before I had the strength to roust them, reluctantly, back to work. That was the worst time – knowing for certain they had no thought for anyone except themselves.

'This lot'll inherit all my time debt when I die,' I despaired to the King Jessmina tree. 'Or Huldrik'll throw them out, as a pack of alien crims served their purpose. Like I care a fart about any of them after this. When I die? That'll be soon enough if I keep feeling like something the chuckers chewed. I gather the principle of the drugs is to spread the load of the flesh-rot, and triple the drugs' fighting front. So that worked, huh?

Sylfi hadn't come any of those nights; it was a bit crowded at times, I suppose. But a couple of nights later, she did, sliding in with me, a murmur and a gently seeking hand. Head so close, I reached and held her... There was a different something... texture, scent, configuration? I dunno. 'Sylfi?'

'No,' she whispered. 'It doesn't matter.'

Even as I stroked her, I wondered if I should feel guilty, betrayous, or if she was Gabbsy's mother or something, assuming Sylfi knew, or approved, maybe. But, if it's meant to be, who am I to go against their will any more than I have to?

She remained in my bed after first light. I did know her. Of course: Tonya was a Terrace Leader, not Gabbsy's mother. Taller and slimmer than most, with lighter brown eyes. Always pleasant, with a lovely smile. Gorgeous, opalescent sheen over her body, too.

One day in the middle of the whole frantic pruning, shaping and weeding season – that's all the time – they wanted the day off. Something religious. 'You had a day off once before and did nothing,' I pretended to protest, but they didn't know how to take jokes. Iron-face DayMia looked as if she'd made a special effort to ask nicely. There was no chance I was never going to turn her down. 'Sure. Look in the blue-labelled boxes. There're some different food packages – not just Basic. Treat yourselves.'

So much for the intended work – re-laying the whole irrigation piping system. Fret not – I could make a start on the pipework myself, reset the plastic extruder and run it in fifty-yat lengths. They'd be easy enough to take apart and move when we needed to. I checked the motor, inlet filter, fuel cells, plastic solvent… We had plenty of raw material in the heaps of chopped timber and scrub that Chorky and I had stacked up, but it needed more plasticiser. A selection of different-shaped nozzles for the extruder would be useful, too.

I had a good day on my own, concentrating and getting it done. It was most satisfactory to survey the results when I packed up as the shadows came over The Hill. The night was warm enough, so I stayed out on the northside, far from any hymn-singing, incense-burning or sacrificing they might wish to indulge in. And I had food in my small snack pack.

Come dawn, I started laying the next section of pipework, thinking the Ladies would have the gumption to realise they were on trust, and would come out on their allocated tasks at the usual time. But, no sign of them. I didn't want to check up and be the bullying Super, so I gave them until mid-morning, then went round the west flank.

Congregated in the yard in a panic, something had occurred. Seeing me approaching, they calmed for a moment, then burst out with it. 'Sandya and Lotti have gone! There are footprints – big ones – boots. They've been taken. You must do something.' A frantic, demanding, huge-eyed clamour.

A section of fence was down – it's only a post-and-wire marker line, not substantial enough to deter anything from coming through. A freshly trampled trail led westward into the forest. 'Get the cab and trailer ready. If I'm not back by mid post-noon, then leave: go to Central; find Supervisor Huldrik and tell him what's happened.'

I leaned to give DayMia a peck on the check – it was automatic, to offer comfort, but she shied away in distrust. Or disgust. 'Hi ho.' I shrugged for the trillionth time, packed the electro-bolter and the plastic-cutter in my backbag, along with half the meddy-box, hefted a hooked prise-bar and set out down the trampled trace of a track to find them.

To call it a forest is easy. What it really is, is dense, primeval *Tangla Yungri*. Someone had determinedly hacked a way through. This was the awful stuff Chorky and I had spent a year clearing, mashing, terracing.

The further I followed that trail, the more incensed I became. I could feel myself boiling up inside, and wanted to scream and shriek and kill: someone had disrupted our haven. It *was* a haven. For me. For us.

Whoever they were, they had no right on my land. Nobody outside the Twenty-Two had rights.

It was only a farr or so to the second hill to the west, past Millop Peak, but I was getting more and more cold-boiled inside. It was rough going, and I oughtn't to be there on foot: there were too many active creepers, dart-thorns and poison leaves; without even thinking about the wire snakes and drip-lice. But I *was* there, and I knew what I was doing. I even spotted the alarm tag, placed amateurishly on a fence post where there had never been a fence before. A stretch had been slackened to let people through.

This was new – someone had started up a clearance programme here – very crude clearing – the trees left in fallen tangles, some burned. Terracing barely started. Imagining it was where the two earlier thieves had come from, I worked round the perimeter, and saw their base.

An open gateway, open yard, three buildings – one leaning over without enough support struts. Two clearance machines stood in the yard; they should have been out on the slopes, working.

Electro-bolter – set on max – in one hand; iron prise-bar in the other, I strolled into the yard unnoticed.

Noises were emanating from one building. I checked the other two first – no-one about. Hadn't seen anyone on the cleared area. Means they're all in here... peering through the part-open door – a spread-out dorm room. Five men. Naked or part-dressed. Two of them massive thugs, one with arms full of tattoos. Laughing and calling, drunken joking.

And sobbing... crying... begging...

Fuckitall to the Pit. Lotti was naked, sitting near the entrance. Three of them were around a body on the floor.

That had to Sandya, under the snarling, laughing threesome… 'Oh shit shit shit. Be calm. Kill them slowly…' I kept telling myself as I eased in unseen. One of them manhandling Lotti. She was struggling. The other laughing and reaching to restrain her. The other three didn't look round – one was raping Sandya.

To the Gods! I felt so cold and hating. One swing of the bar had Lotti's first assailant tumbling face-first, as the electro-bolter rammed into the open mouth of his accomplice. The full charge had him falling, mouth smoking, eyes bulging in agonised horror.

One of the threesome saw me, but tried to alert his fellows instead of coming at me. They were busy. He was flying back, neck burned and stinking. The other one – holding Sandya down – looked up just as the twenty-weight bar crashed down. And he dropped on top of his companion and Sandya… Pinning them down.

The trapped one, still engaged in his rapine activity, roared his fury, with no idea that his world was about to be utterly destroyed. I was so tempted to ram the electrode end into his thrusting backside – but Sandya would get that, too – so half-a-dozen smashes to the back of his knees had the required effect – roaring, struggling, heaving to get his unconscious friend off him, he rolled – face of rage and shock and pain – and a bloodied erect penis.

Absolutely incensed. Gonna burn that thing off him—

Roar behind me. Shoved forward. Shouting. Tattoos was grabbing up at me. Stumbling over him. Another man – behind me, shouting. Trying to spin to see. The electrodes ramming into Tattoos – the shock hit me, too, and I'm smaller than him, so I copped it worse. Can't

398

breathe. Fuckit ⌐– I screwed it up. Desperate to stay conscious, roll away.

Tattoos is trying to come after me – had to laugh – he wasn't going far on those legs. New guy's reaching for the bolter – huge grin. Blur behind him. Bar crashing down. Head splurted... splattered. He's down on his knees. Amazed look.

Lotti was there, slender and bloodied and naked and wielding the heavy bar at him again, teeth clenched. Then Tattoos saw it coming at him. Let go of me. Arms up to grab or defend. Too late. Couldn't stop the bar smashing his raised forearm.

It took us long sobbing moments to get kneeling up and together... All sobbing and mumbling... patting each other... keeping an eye on the scattered moaning writhers around us. Eventually, we struggled upright, hanging on to each other. How can I be so perverted? I saw their bodies Sandya and Lotti. I was jealous! Just for a second. Shame flooded me – that I'd seen. And thought. Even so fleetingly. 'Sorry... sorry... sorry,' I was going. 'I didn't take enough care of you... My fault. Come on... let's clean you... Get you patched. Are you cut? Need any meddies? In my bag...'

I couldn't do enough. I'd felt that instant want. A pang of what the men had been thinking... doing... So ashamed. We washed, dressed wounds, and dressed my Ladies. Sobbing still and clutching each other. I had no intention of trying to join them, hold them or anything – they had each other.

And I had six new diversions... scattered around.

'Suppose we see if there's any food here, Ladies? and you take it to the middle building? There's a vehicle in there. Try to eat... see if it'll start and we'll get you

399

home.' I saw the looks on their faces, 'Koh, not *home*. The Hill, anyway. I'll clear this mess up.'

We shuffled round, found food packs, looked at each other and the six. 'You want to help?' I offered the electro-bolter. They shook their heads, quietly left.

I hated the crawling crying creatures – doing this to my Ladies. And rousing such feelings in me, too. Big Tattoos first – well conscious and threatening, so stupid he still didn't know he was already carved-up and dead.

Gazing at them in their burbling trussed-up agony, I could have left them merely battered.

No, I couldn't. And I could have done it quicker. But I didn't. I knew the electro-bolter and plastic-cutter would come in handy – and fingery... and toesy... and penisy... So I did my Digsby, vengeance-style medium-best torturing; then garrotted them, hanging against the wall, seeing the scene of their crime.

Equally, I could have done it much worse, and much longer. But I must have a thing about not cutting eyes or tongues out. I couldn't. And I could have burned them alive. And *so* much more. But Lotti and Sandya would be waiting – the wagon had revved up some time ago. The Ladies needed to be home... But The Hill would have to suffice.

They didn't ask what I'd done. I didn't say.

They sobbed and held each other. I said nothing and feared they'd all be on the next trailer back to Central.

But it's not the way it went. Half an onz later, someone new was in my bed, silent and unassuming. I did my duty. And the situation continued...

I absolutely did nothing to encourage, or discourage, the Ladies' intimacies with me. Sylfi didn't volunteer anything, and when I very tentatively attempted to open the subject, she put a finger on my lips, smiled and nuzzled into my neck. Jipps! The way her neck can twist and writhe!

They didn't seem to require any encouragement: it was as though they had a rota for nights. And were noticeably warmer during the days, as well. Jipperty! I just loved them all. I even wondered if they put some Rafferian spell on me. Or medicated my food, hypnotised me? Perhaps some ritual of their own? I rather hoped so. For now, at least, they all seemed to be comfortable with the arrangement, including Sylfi, and I certainly didn't want to upset that particular fruit-wagon.

'I'm so skyking lucky to be with these Ladies of Raffery,' I told the King Jessmina tree whenever I meditated there. 'They are so... just *everything*. And I think there's been four to my warm my nights since Sylfi's first coming.'

*** Huldrik ***

Two onz later... I couldn't put it off any longer. Guilt propelled me to Central compound, to confess my waywardness at Six-Four-Four.

Huldrik's Depot was in the middle of the expanding compound, with several new double-storey buildings, and a communications tower that bristled like a pregnant sea-kyamma.

I took two of the Ladies with me, so they could carry the supplies back: I wasn't expecting to return with them, in view of the six deaths at Four-Four. I'd been expecting a head pain, blackout or melt-down ever since, and I had to get it over with.

Huldrik sat back, uninterested. 'Don't come bothering me, Davvy from Digsby. The monitors noted six cessations, following two earlier ones. It's unusual, so I tapped into a couple of them. Saw what they hadn't done on Four-Four – scrappy mess, not real clearancing; wasting their time and my equipment.' He shrugged, 'So, what are you going to do about Six-Four-Four? Lot of my gear and supplies there. Doing nothing now.'

'You must have something in mind, or you wouldn't be asking.'

I saw him laugh for the first time. 'I might just have a proposal, Davvy Six-Four-Six: Clean the machinery; seal it against the weather. Same with the buildings. Do that, and I'll knock you a year off.'

'Two years,' I said.

For the second time, he laughed. 'You learn fast. Fine; do it for two, then. If you feel up to keeping the vegetation down on what they've already cleared – Skyke of a job they did, though – I can make an offer according to what you do. If—' He shut me up. 'If you don't allow the completed parts to revert, you can make me an offer to farm the whole of Six-Four-Four next year.'

We stared at each other. 'Now, push off. I'm busy. You've had your ten mins.'

'Five,' I protested, though I can't imagine why I wanted to stay any longer: he might change his mind, or remember the corpses at Four-Four.

'I spent five checking their monitors while you were outside. It's decided. Suppose you contact me when you want to propose something? Or I'll tell you at Year's End.'

I felt pretty good on the way out: Central had no interest in my disposal of the Four-Four sixsome. I should have been executed for such barbarity – especially as it was exactly what I was sentenced for in the first place. But no-one was interested. And Huldrik said I could put in a bid for working Four-Four if I wanted. Did I?

Outside, the Highraff ladies were waiting, not relieved or happy for me; just neutral. In a sudden burst of relief, I thought I gotta cheer them up, too. 'Let's go in the Stores. I want all sorts of stuff. And you – Buy anything you want. Things for yourselves.'

DayMia was suspicion itself, *'Anything? Why?'*

'Whatever'll keep you happy. No, that was a joke – I know you'll never be happy.'

Sylfi understood, and waved me away, but DayMia was instantly on the attack, accusing me of cushioning my pockets. 'Where's your cash coming from? Why would Huldrik give you money?'

'Money? For me? My money is time added. My luxuries? Like replacement fuel cells, filters, indoor and field lights? Teecon seedlings for the steep slopes; solvent and plasticiser for the extruder; non-work clothes; traps for the chuckers? Extra food? Bedding? And whatever "Sundries" the Storesman recommends, I expect. I can't pay for them with money I don't have – it adds another year and a half on my sentence – I'm well over forty years in life-debt now. There's no way I can ever pay it off. So I can afford it.'

Her look of total disbelief could have triggered a ground-quake.

'If you know where I'm stashing it, DayMia, please tell me. I could do with some.'

She never believed anything that came out my mouth, and she wasn't going to start now. 'And you don't care a pee in the pond about Lotti and Sandya.'

Great! DayBloodyMia has to bring it up now, when I'm trying my doodist to make'em all feel good. 'Oh, Lady... They lay low and avoid me. How I might care about them any more, I have no idea.'

So Huldrik, of all people, puts me in a good mood. And DayMia puts me out of it. I was glad to leave them to it. *Women!* It could only get worse – they were in a Stores! The first one they'd seen in probably a year; full of stuff that would be alien to them, though. I'd wanted to tell them about my escape from Huldrik the headblower; how I was really, really relieved, and practically happy. Ah, well... Another time, maybe. 'Spend what you want,' I parted from them and wandered away.

There was a bar called Yadack's. Shows how much Central Compound had come on – enough population to keep a bar alive. Standing ten paces from the entrance, wrinkling my nose at the aroma, my mouth was watering at the taste that could explode, feeling the atmospheric warmth, and shaking with longing. 'Froo-skyke, I *need* a drink, after the day I'm having, and all the worrying since Four-Four.'

'Daren't go in? Too tempting?' said the too-perceptive storesman's boy. 'Make your own. We sell three flavours of starter packs – Beer, wine and spirit. Mix one into any fruity or grainy mush – follow the guides on filtration, fermentation periods, strengths – added flavourings. You interested? Once it's up and

404

running, it's self-perpetuating. Within reason,' he added, seeing the look on my face.

'I'll think about it,' I told him, 'I have to see somebody…'

In the Governorship side office, a man called Mr Ma'Doff introduced himself as "The Accountant". He asked about the Palma crop – what proportion would be perfect for ripening? How much wasted to pulp?

We chatted, as much as Admin types know how to chat. It seemed that Palma fruits were fetching very good prices this year, so we needed to maximise the output of perfect fruit, with individual wrappings, packing and delivery. The depot would collect if we had a trailer full. 'We should manage that every onz,' I hesitantly predicted. 'It's looking like our harvest will be spread over four or five onz, what with all the measures we took. Skyke, it's been a nightmare getting it sort-of right.'

'If you have the labour, you can mash the overripes for brewing, or filter it for plain, flavoured and alcoholic regional drinks. They're considered very smart. Make sure you have enough containers and some way of mashing the fruit – and filtering it. You go to it, Davvy Six-Four-Six. We'll have you in profit in six or seven years.'

Peering at the screen, he pulled a few faces and furrowed his brow, tutted a couple of times, 'Superintendent Huldrik says you have an eye on Six-Four-Four as well?' He peered at a screen. 'Looks like there's a riverside flatland included. You could make even better money there – irrigation would be cheap for growing amaraze and bluecorn – good market price there, too.'

He flipped through some plazpaps, checked on a screen, frowned. 'That plot could be spoken for, though. There's always someone interested in picking up part-started projects on the cheap.'

So, was that a hint to make my mind up pfq? Or a heads-up that it had been taken already? I nodded and left, promising to keep him up-to-date.

Sylfi and DayMia were all a-tremble when they came out the Stores, carrying a bag each. 'Are you sure we can have these?'

'Course. You want to show me?' Er... No, they weren't into sharing anything with me. 'You've bought something for the others as well? And the children?'

They stopped. 'Can we?'

'Of course. That's what I meant, something for *everyone*. Little gifts – fripperies. And more extras on the food front – spices and the like.' I don't know why, but I suddenly felt more alive – aware – than I had for yonks. It was nice to feel able to do that.

So back in they went.

*** Tonya ***

We were late leaving Central. Late getting back. Total excitement, they were in tears when they burst into the sleeping shelter. Unwrapping and shrieking being the orders of the night. Five mins, and I left them to it. I needed to check the extruder for making wine vats, barrels, containers and pipes. And find out how to mush the over-ripe fruits that were bound to occur.

A night of great joy for the Ladies, and alcoholic anticipation for me. It felt pretty good. Sylfi slipped in towards dawn, lying with me for silent warmth and comfort. That felt awesomely good, too.

I didn't want to spin a noose for my own neck over this, so I mentioned it to Sylfi first. 'Sylf? I've been thinking – yes, I know, dangerous stuff, eh? I was wondering if we look like making a profit, and I can take some as cash instead of time off... I could pay the Ladies— No, no; not for *that*. For the field work and everything. So they can have their own money to spend when we go to Central. Do you think they'd want that? Or would DayMia object?'

In the darkness, I could tell she approved even before she spoke, for she glowed a degree or two warmer when she was pleased.

'Same for everyone?' I suggested. 'Perhaps save something into an account every onz?'

'I think they'd prefer it,' she snuggled close, 'as hold-in-the-hand coin-cash.' So that was decided upon.

Our period of environmental trauma stemmed from the previous year's clearancing work with Chorky, changing the land from deep, tangled sub-humid forest to a hill that looked like a badly-shaved teenage scook-head, with ridges, and clumps of pale purple – the terraces and the scattered Jessmina trees in full flower. But now, there seemed to be some complex inter-relationship between the Cunyuk birds, the fruiting process of the trees, the periodic swarms of insects, the chuckers – or their dung, or burrows, and the bewilder-berries we were trying on some of the steep facings, and the Palma plants that we were cultivating all over the flattish, terraced slopes.

If we'd known all the pitfalls, we probably wouldn't have started, but we had, and now we were trying all ways of pruning the Palmas to slow or speed growth, but mainly to make them parasol-shaped and less than head-height, so we could harvest them more easily by hand as well as by machine. But the birds ignored the insects, and the insects went for the budding fruit, and the chucker dung wasn't plentiful enough to give off the deterrent odour. I would have to re-think the whole ecology thing next season, and not rely on expensive chemix – maybe we'd need to tolerate more chuckers and try different creepers to stabilise the terrace walls.

But we had a couple of charming balmy evenings parading the terraces with Odor-Lites that seemed to deter the insects, and we picked a few ripe Jessmina fruits. They were good. We wondered if there was a market for them. Something else to ask about, next time we went to Central.

I explored my head chip, and decided to build some fake burrows for the chuckers, using the extruder, so we wouldn't have to kill them, and they wouldn't erode the walls. Some of the weed plants were essential for the predatory bugs that fed on the insects at night, and the bewilder-berries tasted different every time we picked any.

An onz of solid, siling rain didn't help the crops, the chuckers or us. We cut down on the rotas because it was too tiring in the mud to do long shifts. At least, the Ladies were more or less speaking to me most days, and the kids didn't edge warily round me, and Sylfi often came to me at meals, as well as bed. Jipps, I worshipped her some days, lost to her warmth and beautiful eyes, and things she said. She was easily the nearest to a

408

kindred spirit since Theadora had died, back on Digsby. Skyke-it, still so raw in my head.

We played with the plastic extruder and made air-filled cushiony things to make the bedding more comfortable. We'd need yet more plasticiser, so that would be another day wasted going to Central. Maybe not wasted if some of them came with me, and enjoyed a long day out. 'If we go in a few onz, I can find out about the possibility of another harvester; we'll never harvest the fruit if it all ripens together. And an extra shelter so we can all have more space.'

'But,' said Tonya, 'what about the shelters at Four-Four? And there's a harvester there?'

Thinking about the six bodies I'd left hanging there, I suggested not looking, but they said, 'We know you killed the men. It was in your eyes when you brought Sandya and Lotti back: it really won't upset us.'

So DayMia, Tonya and a couple of others went to see.

They came back that evening with all the parts and panels for a second dormitory shelter. I was really afraid that it would be one for them, and one for me, but they decided it would be best to have the children in one, with mothers or carers – permanent or temporary – and keep the whole arrangement flexible for cooking and eating and cleaning and relaxation in the evenings. So that suited me as well as them.

My birthdate, near as I could reckon, crept up on me. It was also the date we found who'd been responsible for all the deaths on Digsby, so it was somewhat of a mixed day. No, I kid myself. In fact, I lie: it was an all-shit day. Mostly, I wished I hadn't been born. Finding out who'd killed several hundred people, including my wife and two children, hadn't brought any joy that day. Even killing them hadn't brought lasting pleasure, just weird vengeance-satisfaction.

I suppose I still nurtured that feeling; I owed it to the dead to remember what happened. That was why I could never have taken re-alignment. I brooded sometimes, and tried to think of the positives – which, to be honest, were increasing of late: the Highraff – No, The Ladies… my Ladies – were a great bunch of people, beautiful in mind and form, and I really loved them all – as a group. And Sylfi more and more. Even DayMia. I think she was seeing it as not quite the worst situation in the universe; for now.

To muse alone, I took a brightlight out on Terrace One in the early evening, and sat with it under a Jessmina tree, remembering into the night.

'I come here some nights,' a voice murmured from the edge of the darkness. 'To remember my man. We often sat together beneath a Muulinda tree in the Arbora near home on Raffery. The night sky was so much brighter than here. Such swirls of stars. May I join you? Share your light?'

She was already sitting, anyway. We leaned against the soft bole of the tree and said little else, as I recall. 'Tonya?'

Her head twisted right round. That was so weird, almost un-nerving. But their necks were so long and flexible, and to see a group of them together was heart-warming sometimes – so smoothly sinuous in their movements, like dancers in harmonic movement. She was staring at me – those huge eyes and long lashes. On DayMia that look would have been the Death-Stare, but this was Tonya, and we'd shared a bed on occasion.

But sitting there, holding her hand for a time, I knew I wasn't one of their community; even after helping Gabbsy; and retrieving Sandya and Lotti. Only today, I heard them saying something about a transbreed. I gained the impression that it was me and Heeria they were talking about.

Even though five, perhaps six, of them frequently came to my bed for comfort, they spoke little at the time, or during the days. We entwine with such gentleness sometimes, or urgency and passion, lie together and murmur, stroke, contented for a time. Sylfi says she doesn't mind about the others, and she comes when others don't. I think I'm in awe of Sylfi. I don't dare admit it, though.

Not to her. Nor DayMia. Nor anyone else. I think it's a lot more than just liking her. They would be unbearable if they learned of it.

The Ladies drew lots to see who would accompany me to Central: Mariti, Lotti and Tonya, with one of the Littlies, Peetrilya, or something like that. I could never pronounce his name. Peety was near enough. They wore the clothes that we'd bought, and things that DayMia and Sylfi had added.

By The Hill! They looked so smart! Ladylike. I was so proud of them all.

Mainly, I'd gone so I could talk with Huldrik and Mr Ma'Doff, the Accountant, about forecasts and possibilities, the stability of prices, and if I tried Plot Four-Four with the riverside section, how much would it cost for the optimum crop seeds?

It all sounded possible, and the family were in there with me, so they'd know I wasn't under-dealing, and we

411

worked out the framework of an agreement about their terms as well.

That was when I first wondered what the legal basis was for their confinement. I should have challenged Huldrik there and then, but I didn't. If it turned out there was no lawful basis, he'd have to let them go, and I'd be left with a farm and an unharvestable crop of Palma fruit. In my defence, it was the most fleeting of thoughts, and I was in the middle of asking if there were any other helpers I could hire or partner, perhaps other Highraff. I'd already spoken to DayMia about the possibilities of some of the team looking after the Riverside Land. Just negotiating and exploring possibilities.

Huldrik was very complimentary about my threesome. He was right, they did look very much the "Ladies of the Moment". We practically paraded around Central. It was all so new to them, and growing fast: at least two new buildings in the last few onz. Tonya had their shopping list – nothing huge, matching their savings. But I felt pleased and relieved; the market forecasts were favourable; we'd already tidied up the machinery and buildings on Four-Four; we'd toured the part-cleared property and had some ideas of what might be possible. Things were so looking up.

'Hey. You. Zooman.' I turned to see a big man in a one-piece prat-suit and a stupid grin. 'You watch yourself. This's your one warning. Keep off Six-Four-Four. We're having that. It's fixed.'

I was in instant high-forid mode, and extremely calm – well, fairly calm, anyway. 'Koh, *Moron Mouth:* First, you get down on your knees, lick all our boots, apologise, and beg forgiveness.' It was how I felt when I'd trailed to the yard at Four-Four – incensed, and blind to everything. It almost frightens me how fast it comes on. 'How dare you?'

His confident sneer about sub-breed animals just peeved me. I straight-fingered his eyes. Deep. And then his under-throat. He went down and I was on him. I really lost it, ranting at him and chopping. Two others onto me. *Huge. Thugs.* Saying they'd teach me something or other. 'Eh, *Zooman?* Think your livestock'll stay with you now, eh? Four-Four's ours.'

Skyke, I took a hammering, and a booting, and a carving – one of them had a bayo blade. I heard the girls shrieking and saw them pulling and go flying back. And Peety, too. I struggled up on my knees spitting blood, feeling at my ribs, and groping for a grip on my chucker knife. I stabbed one's kneecap; the other's groin.

Then it went blank.

And I'm waking up Pits-knows how long later. Chained. Yes! *Chained!* Locked in a cell. I knew it was a cell: it's not like it's the first one I've been in. No door, no window, nothing to sit or lie on, except the floor and a skyke-of-a-headache, hand-ache and everywhere-else-ache.

It seemed ages that I lay there, remembering and worrying more about Mariti and Lotti and Tonya and... and... whoever the Littlie was. What had happened to them? And me? And my hands? My head? Food and drink slid through a flap, too far away to reach with the chains on. Especially with my hands stitched and glued, plas-skinned and sealed in C4 bags. One eye was swelled to Sator and back; so I couldn't see or think much, anyway.

413

Two men came in, one Mr Ma'Doff. The other didn't say, but his clothing was a blue-grey uniform style. Probably chief jailor, so I watched him closely.

'We're charging you with triple murders, Davvy Six-Four-Six.'

I tried to look at them. 'Who've I killed this time? The twilliats who came for me? They can't be dead.'

'Bled to death. All three.'

I don't believe it.

'Groin wound cut the femoral artery. Knee wound slashed the poppy artery. And the man in the one-piece – the carotid. You have an eye for arteries, huh? That'll sound like you're a professional.'

'It'll sound like I'm lucky. Or your medics're incompetent. And what's it got to do with an accountant?'

'I'm *The* Accountant. I hold people to account. When events have a financial motive, as the killing of a rival partnership for Hill Six-Four-Four clearly has. This gentleman is Mr Stonebridge, the Security and Enforcement Officer for Segotta.'

'This time, you're dead.' The SEO began our relationship on a low note.

'Where are my Highraff people? What happened to me? How come those three died?'

They smiled a lot, and said I was downed by an electro-bolt in the back of my head. 'It part-fused your mind-chip, so you won't be too much aware of what happened.'

'Nor will anyone else. Your execution date and the like.' The baster pair chuckled their way out.

That was a skyke of a time – trying to remember anything, and wondering what to worry about most – My Ladies and the kids? The Palma fruit? My execution? The Hill? Skyke-it, I had that place coming on fine. Ish.

A Skugg-of-a-lot of nothing happened for a long time after that. Days or hours, I dunno. I think I kept drifting off.

Huldrik came, a bag of bluster and bluff. 'You nearly lost your hands – one stabbed through four times, and the palm slashed across. Defensive wounds, they call them; and one gouge across your wrist that pumped blood out like a rithma having a crap.'

I still couldn't see or feel my fingers, what with one eye buried in gauze and my hands in plazskin. And lying flat on my back on the floor.

'Your Highraff are koh: it's only been four days since—'

'Four days?! I gotta get out of here… the Ladies… my farm…'

'You're going nowhere.' His foot stomped on my chest. 'Not charged with three murders.'

'Oh yes? I'm charging you with Inhumanism, dereliction of duty, incompetence in a Fed Official Position, crookedness, thievery. And which useless MediOff let three scarcely-scratched dirt-brain dilberts die?'

That took him back a strap or two. 'Huh?'

'Ha!' from my position of huge supine strength, I went on the attack. 'Making out you know nothing about anything. The Unhuman things they called my family, like they were animals – that's Fed-Forbidden Language. And *you're* covering it up. It's all on the monitors. And anyway,' I was in a high-stropps mood

415

by then, 'they said Plot Six-Four-Four was theirs – fixed and paid for. What's that about? Who they paid, Huldrik? You? Ma'Doff? That other Crud in Blue?'

That conversation came to an abrupt end when his boot slid off my chest and onto my throat.

Onz mins later I was dragged out to a yard. The Ladies were there – Jipps! What a welcome sight, with Tonya, Marita and Lotti... and Peety and the cab and trailer, all gibbery and panicky and crying and hugging me. 'We didn't know where you were. What's happening? We've been kept in a Pen...'

'Skyke-it, Huldrik!' I shouted to the bare walls behind me. 'You baster. Crookedness in Fed Office; Inhumanism; Cruelty...' I ranted on and the Ladies got worse and I had to shut up when two black-coats stuffed me into the cab. One of them started the motor and pointed to the opening gate.

'Go. While you can. There's still three murder charges hanging over you, remember.'

'There'll be one over you lot as well if you carry—' I think that was when his fist closed my other eye and Tonya took the drive bar.

The journey back to Six-Four-Six was a non-joy event – the pain-killer wore off, and Mariti and Tonya weren't the greatest drivers. They kept sobbing, and looking at my face and my hands like it was their fault. What a skyking mess. What the Pits was I going to do for'em now? I was all in turmoil, including about where might I find weapons to defend ourselves. Or lose myself in the far forest in the hope that Huldrik'd leave the Ladies alone? Or find someone decent to take over and look after them?

Someone decent? On Segotta? Yeah, and lead bricks might swim. 'Maybe if I keep my head down, and say nothing, it'll all go away? Sure it will – three more deaths to my list? That makes an onz on Segotta, never mind the others on Digsby. I don't count Aldri and Bendax – they're officially accidents.

*** Marita ***

It was the most relief I ever felt, to arrive home. And see all the familiar faces – the family. Skyke – I didn't exactly feel safe and saved, but it came pretty close. What I really, desperately, needed was to hug them all, and maybe somebody hug me. Yeah, that'd happen. I crawled up to the King Jessmina tree, and communed with Theadora.

Mariti woke me up at dawn. She gave me a little hug – really spontaneous. 'For Peety,' she said.

The Hill was doing pretty well: the rotas had been kept up, and they'd worked the usual hours, desperately worried that we'd run into trouble. My injuries didn't elicit much sympathy – I was still the enemy, though perhaps not in capital letters now. Even Sylfi would choose them if came to a toss-out. But she was all over me after a few days – a mite tearful, thinking I'd been dead inside the wrappings, I suppose.

Things did settle down for a time. We worked the terraces like Ten-Year Togans with a year to go; and we pretended to forget about the threat of Huldrik and Cronies hanging over us.

'Did you really threaten him?' Sylfi wanted to know. 'But he didn't laugh, sneer and leave you in the Pen? He could have.'

'Actually, he looked a mite shocked that anybody dared speak to him like that. I was surprised he chucked me out so quick.'

Evenings became a rivalry between terrace groups – percentage of plants surviving; weight of weed pull-ups; number of chuckers caught, killed, skinned. Sharing of field news and ideas; the extruded pipes and troughs for swift downhill delivery of fruit. Sometimes they held a chucker-roast and sing-song, especially after Mariti had bought a music chip that was reminiscent of their home music. It disappointed me that I was never invited, not even by Sylfi, not even for the first half-hour, or the last bit, before bed. They have this word, mojaki. It means alien. I asked Mariti if I'd heard right. 'No,' she said, 'the word was moyaki – boss.' The Pits it had – her ears had blushed.

Somehow, I still had the idea there were more goods than bads in our little community, as long as I didn't look for too much from anyone except myself. At least my hands and face healed swiftly, so I had no excuse to dodge the work – as if I'd want to. Besides, harvest was coming into play and the teams were figuring out the rotas on the different terraces and patches – the poorer soils, the sun or shade facings, the growth-delayed ones. Mostly, though it was a matter of looking along the terraces each morning.

My principal contributions were, they told me: First: not ordering anything to be done. 'You let us see and figure it out for ourselves.' And Second: alcohol. I'd never drunk *the middle option* in my life, the so-called wine. But we had plenty of fruits and berries available, and I thought the others might like it. So that was the one I mashed and pressed and stored and fermented and stilled-up. I sprinkled the accelerator into the open barrel after three days, and it all started fizzing. It frothed up, and went clear as a Ragellian preacher's sermon.

I containerised it. Four newly-extruded plastic tubs with open tops. 'It's time,' I told a baffled Sylfi, 'to try the ultimate middle option. Chucker-roast night, is it?'

Yes, it was. 'Matsuri Home,' she bafflingly said. I took one container, about enough to drown a dozen chuckers, and wandered into their private Raffery-only festival night, ignoring all eyes in my direction, and the open, disbelieving mouths. I simply wandered round filling cups and beakers and saying nothing. They were polite, pretended I wasn't there, and went a touch frost-faced at first. But Mariti tried it, pulled a face, sniffed, tried again, and emptied her cups. The chatter tempo went up, and nobody bothered with cutlery when the chucker roasts were ready. The cups seemed to refill themselves and I was even more completely ignored and that was great – just one of the crowd.

Sylfi snuggled close and stroked me, sipping her third or fourth beaker of the fizzy, fruity, intoxicating nectar. DayMia started up the music. I joined in with some of the songs: I'd heard them so often. Mariti got me "dancing", also known as "standing and swaying, drunkenly, propped up by an unending succession of long-necked dazzlers".

Maybe we wouldn't get much work done on the morrow, but that was little price to pay for being a tad more accepted.

We eased into the harvesting gently – a few early-boosted patches to practice on. Everyone geared up with picking machines, delivery troughs, containers. And two days of careful, measured picking and packing, learning how to hold, twist and pull, the same as the machines did – but the machines were too slow to do it all on every terrace. We needed two per terrace, not two in total. But we soon managed the wrapping and packing after a few errors that would have to go to "the masher" – also known as "the trough where we trample barefoot and have a laugh". Two days increasingly busy, increasingly competent, then four with scarcely a break throughout the day. We rigged lights up over two patches so we could have an overnight rota. And shades over two more areas to keep the sun from ripening them too soon. That plastic extruder was worth its weight in platinum.

Six days, and I had to contact Central. "Need trailer collection tomorrow."

Five days earlier than we'd thought. We had a trailer full. Couldn't believe it.

A cab turned up mid-morning the next day, swapped our filled trailer with a new one. 'I'll be back in four days at the rate your packs are piling up. And I'll bring a spare trailer, in case.'

Skyke! We slept alright, too exhausted to eat, almost. But so happy – it was all coming to fruition. Literally.

The mash tubs needed to be emptied every day, and filtered, allowed to settle, and drained into containers.

Some was for the pressed fibrous mass, and most for the drink, which was a plummy-orange colour in eleven-cubit drums. The children mastered the art of making it in two days, and wanted payment for it – a dangerous precedent, that, at their age. So I put them on converting half of it to the alcoholic versions, and promised to let them try it.

*** Amazan and Anakku; Nekhii, Chingis, Tuya and Precious Flower ***

Time for our third visit to Central. Sandya and Heeria came with me, plus two of the others and toddlers Jack and Billie. It's a long trip – half a day in each direction, so we all took turns "driving" for the fun and the experience. It was a booster day-out for them, on top of the main practical reasons of obtaining supplies, including an extruder repair pack; work and leisure clothes. And, of course, we'd worked on proposals for clearing and cultivating the fertile Riverlands at Four-Four. I needed to go over them with Huldrik and a pair of his officers.

But it was Mr Ma'Doff the me-hating Accountant who was there, very snappily confirming all the costs and availability of seeds and equipment. He struck me as being more pessimistic than previously: costs had risen and market prices had dropped. I wasn't feeling any trust for him, the way he'd been last time we met, plus the way he tutted and head-shook over every proposal I made.

Nothing was said about the murder charges, or my earlier threat to charge them all with Malfeasance in Federal Office. Instead, they insisted on replacing my

421

back-of-head chip so they could tap into me. But it had been giving me a lot of pain since the electro-bolt had blown it, and it was valuable for the information it linked me to, like the chemix and the medix.

While we were in Central, I also wanted to check out the market for the fresh juices we'd produced in four flavours, and for "wine extract" in three varieties. We had containers of each as samples. Several merchants and the barman at Yadacks were interested in trying them. '"Posh Local Plonk", we can market it as,' the barman grinned when he tried the second beaker.

Jack and Billie were an absolute treat, swan-necking through the streets, more excited and laughing than I'd ever seen the adults – apart from the chucker and wine night, of course. Jipperty! I loved'em. Happy as clownies, we headed for the Stores, and I could go see Huldrik later.

'Can you hold their hands a moment, Davvy?' The ladies did a sharp right turn, leaving me in the middle of Main Row. It was Central Clinic down there.

We wandered round. A couple of passers-by smiled. You know – nice smiles. That felt good.

The Littlies loved the cream in a biscuit-basket that I bought them. We sat in the sun and it was great the way they chattered and I was Uncle Davvy. I was more than a bit nervous when a hound came sniffing past, interested in the cream suck, but they were naturals with it – the first one they'd ever seen. Clucking and petting and laughing, they offered it fingers with dollops of cream. The hound's owner chattered amicably, and I complimented him on the hound. 'Beautiful animal, so friendly.'

'Yes. So are yours.'

That stopped me dead.

He went, eventually. Is that what people think? Billie and Jack were my pets? I was empty inside, echoing. My pets? The children? I *never* thought of them like that, but I felt so guilty in case the man was right.

Is that how the Highraff see it? That I treat them like pets or pack animals?

They were back, Heeria and Sandya excitedly bright. 'We have news. It's definite that Heeria's pregnant and it's yours, of course.' She looked a touch wary about how I'd be about it – as though I might be ashamed. But I was delighted and hugged her. She wasn't too keen on that in public, but was really pleased overall. So I felt a lot better and she said Sandya had seen the clinician as well, about her baby...

'Her baby? From the... *episode* at Four-Four?' I had no idea how to react to that; it would depend entirely on how she felt, and I'd agree with it.

She wanted to keep it, and would love it dearly, exactly as any of the others. Babies were practically holy beings. It was unthinkable to do anything other than see it as a precious treasure. So that was fine, too: it chimed with me.

Billie and Jack were so excitedly telling them about the hound that I wondered if they'd like one? If it was possible? I thought they were going to say something like, 'Why? Aren't you happy with us?' But they didn't, and were astounded at the thought of owning such a breath-taking creature. 'Actually us? Have one of our very own?'

They needn't have been quite so over-the-top. I went after the man and asked where it was from. He'd brought it with him, he said, from Suttor Twiel. 'I brought seven;

to see if I could sell them here. I'll show you, if you're interested.'

We were. He did. Billie and Jack loved one at first sight, a beautiful male. 'You'll need the fundamentals – winter coat, lead and harness, starter food pack, medications and injections, bedding, toys.' I knew I was being taken on a ride with that lot, but I didn't care. What was another year or two?

'I'll get it ready as soon as the payment's been made.' Excited, we waited at the Central transfer unit. No sign of Huldrik – he was either "Busy" or "Away", depending on who I asked. So we sat and waited, with bad memories of the place. One hour later, Cedrik from Suttor Twiel brought the hound in. It was gorgeous – a touch more purple-choccy coloured than the others, but the same long, intelligent face.

The drive back seemed so quick, everyone thrilled, though I let a grumpy corner of my mind hope that the hound wouldn't lead to a drop in work-rate.

He acquired the name of Amazan, a mythical figure in Highraff legend. His presence seemed to give them a meaning: to be responsible for such a creature. Chasing with the children, or coming to me for a mock fight, Amazan was a huge triumph. His mind-communion with me – head on my lap, and staring at each other – elevated me in their eyes. That felt good, and I was glad he was with us.

Amazan's addition to our numbers was quickly followed by Heeria's gorgeous little girl, Nekhii, who'd be a heart-breaker in any society. Sylfi had scarcely swelled at all: her child was tiny, a boy who brought much delight and wonder to the community with his light blue eyes. They were a total mystery to me as well as everyone else: my eyes are a muddy green, and all the Highraff are a deep, serene brown. A portent of something great, they seemed to believe. Little Anakku's birth was almost embarrassingly swiftly followed by Chingis, Tuya and Precious Flower, with more to come.

Skyke-it – I was in tears at every birth, so beautiful, and me so proud of my three daughters and two sons. And... just everybody at Hill Six-Four-Six.

*** Donna'yiecki ***

Three more onz and it would a year since the Highraff had come with me. The harvest had been gruelling in terms of solid days working, the summer heat, sparing maintenance staff onto Plot Six-Four-Four, baby births, and preparing trailers for despatch.

And our guests. Gabbsy came running up the terraces one noon, 'Some people have arrived and they aren't well. Heeria and Tonya are looking after them as well as the babies.'

They were in the Home Shelter when we returned to the base yard: five of them; humans, and in a right state. A man, older than me, a younger woman who was emaciated, and three under-tens like skeletons. The Ladies had started feeding them on baby milk-foods, and tried to wash their skin, but it flaked and was going raw. My chip said it was caused by a parasite, so we all had to take the stoppers, and smear cream all over them, and keep a lookout on ourselves. I think I was the only one to wonder if they were worth it. But then, I was the only

425

one who was paying for all the medication – half a year every time I opened the drug box.

The Kingtons were a family from a small settler-commune ten days' walk to the east. Set up two years ago, same as me, it had failed because of strife over work-loads, origin dislikes, planting failure and diseases. Six of their group had gone into survival mode –hunter-gatherers with subsistence farming and no ambition to do otherwise. The family had trudged along the rough track, heading for Central, until they saw our cultivated hill.

'For Central? On foot? It's at least another twenty days on foot. You'd never make it. Best stay here till you're better, then we can take you in the cab. The woman was Donna'yiecki, originally from Suntorna – apparently one of the older over-populated Empire planets, and the mother of the three kids. The old man was her father – quiet, good with machines and repairs. I reckon it was her guilt about being a burden that endeared her to the Highraff. Almost pathetic, she tried to do everything for everyone, not caring for herself. 'Not my type at all,' I told Sylfi.

'Huldrik must know about them,' I told the others, 'and not be bothered, if he's done nothing to help or prevent.' We helped them as much as we could, but, with the harvest at its peak, it was yet another critical time on the terraces.

Two days, and the scrawny kids with unpronounceable names were playing with Billie and Jack and Gabbsy and the others. Three days, and they were carrying messages, snacks and drinks around the terraces.

Although a shatteringly busy time for everyone, especially with losing five of the ladies to birth and baby matters, Jipps! we completed the harvest! Successfully in, ninety-odd percent of it as fresh, individually packed fruit. So pleased, so exhausted, we had a huge, spiced chucker-roast and wine evening to celebrate the last trailer-load. The cabs had come twice an onz, and we'd produced about ten times more fruit than we'd ever expected – with the wine and other drink stuff as well. 'Now's the time for the land to rest, to recover from its growing pains and strains,' the Highraff said. 'And for us, also.'

We thus allowed ourselves three onz – thirty-three days – rest, repair and recreation. Even the weeds had taken a break, so I didn't need more than a quick look around each day, though that was for security and contemplation time as much as anything – such as firming up some thoughts about the riverside areas of Six-Four-Four.

We talked over endless possibilities for the future: Not mine – I'm a justly sentenced murderer who earned his right to be nailed to Hill Six-Four-Six, nevermore to move. But the Ladies saw themselves as wrongfully-detained refugees… hostages. Whatever, we decided to stick together; not really certain if we had any choice.

Our newcomers: the older man tinkered with the machinery, and his daughter was permanently keen to help with anything. The kids – Zippy, Squeaks and Boy – had simply merged in with the Highraffs and I never saw an askance glance between any of them. Nor among the adults, either.

So, after a few starter-discussions about the next year's proposals and preparations, the newcomers were included in the planning. As Lotti said, 'We are a true community now. We cannot, and must not, break up what we have here.' Of course, that had me crying as well, and they all tried to calm or console me. Sylfi was most successful.

*** Mr Ma'Doff ***

It was time for yet another visit to Central for our End-of-Year Summation, with updates on sales and prices from the past year; and possibilities about taking on Plot Four-Four long-term, as well as Four-Six. It was decided that DayMia and Sylfi would go with me, with Anakku. It was also decided that *everyone* would be equal – in payments, and visits to Central – children and humans included.

Sylfi kissed me. Just like that. It was amazing how good it felt. So did Donna'yiecki. Not so good, but pretty satisfying, all the same.

I felt uncomfortable, seeing Mr Ma'Doff, but he was the one in the Land and Labour Office, with SEO Stonebridge close by. They looked as though they wanted to throttle us all, but controlled themselves, each nodding and confirming what the other said.

'The final market chips are in,' he told us. 'You made a good profit: five years credit off your sentence.'

It *sounded* great – five years off. But I thought about it, and said, 'Five years credit? From two years' work, including the one with Chorky. That's actually disappointing. All the extras and on-costs have added twenty-eight.' I stared into blank faces, 'So in two years

428

I've managed to get twenty-one years deeper in time-debt?'

I insisted on seeing the figures on screen, and having a plaz printout. 'Huldrik hasn't even deducted the five years for taking care of Four-Four. Pitsofalot of extra work. We all earned payment in one form or another for that alone.'

'The Highraff?' SEO's eyes sneered over my companions, 'There's no time credit for them. They're all on indefinite detentions. So adding or deducting wouldn't make any difference.' The look of triumph was enough to deserve hanging by the ballerinas.

'No! That's inhuman.'

'So're they.'

'No, they're not. We interbreed,' I risked a glance to Sylfi and DayMia. 'That makes them officially Humanic – equal entitlements to everything.

'You'd need a D-Oxy test to prove it, for every child so claimed; and there's no facility for doing the test here on Segotta, and no mechanism for altering anyone's Humanic status.' Mr Ma'Doff and Stonebridge had this worked out in advance; both looking smugly concerned.

'It's obvious. This is our son, Anakku.' I was furious: we were being set up – saw their sideways glances, a slight nod. Something decided. Stonebridge was suddenly on his feet.

'We're calling your sentence in.' He waved a plaz-pap at me. 'A recent Fed ruling tightens up on non-re-aligned criminals who re-offend. We studied what you did to the colonists at Six-Four-Four, and that's far too serious to be ignored or re-aligned.'

Mr Ma'Doff was having his piece of me as well. 'For eleven murders since your arrival here, you're to be transferred off-planet. Today.'

'The Highraff'll get what they deserve in the Eramaa Disposal Camps.' They smirked and sneered at My Family.

I went for them, and I'm fast as well as brutal. But I crashed into the table – I'm not as fast as an automatic-electro-bolt. I was down in less than a beat.

A long, vague awareness of phantasmal time passing – Abruptly awake in sheer raging panic, smelling the oxiric gas on my clothes, from the electro-bolt – powerful enough to kill as often as not. Still on the floor in the L'n'L Office. Familiar chains round my ankles, wrists and neck, I struggled and fought and snarled, but barely managed a twitch in reality while the SEO stood over me, directing a pair of black-coats to tighten the chains and give me a dose of parala. 'Time for you to go, eh? Davvy the Crim? We can't have animal-humans gaining rights and property on Segotta, can we? Say Hello to the vacuum in High Orbit for me, hmm?'

I was in a real shuddering panic then. What about Sylfi and the others? Couldn't speak, scarcely move. Lifting me and half-carrying me. I must have been the most feeble struggler they'd ever dealt with. But I did put a vast amount of effort into it.

Huldrik was the other side of the door, with two more black-coats. 'Ah, SEO Stonebridge, perhaps you'd be so good as to release Four-Six? All charges are rescinded.'

The black-coats dropped me – another Pitsofathump head-first ono the tiles, and Huldrik said something like, 'You might escort the SEO to join Mr Ma'Doff?'

Stonebridge was a lot more violent and foul-mouthed than me when they grabbed him, until he came crashing down next to me like a wall collapse. One of them loosened my bindings and pressure-jected something into my neck. Pulled from under Stonebridge, I sat up, feeling gruesome, head hurting like glass in a cracker.

*** Harator ***

'You cracked your skull,' making it sound like it was my fault they dropped me. We tottered into another office. DayMia, Sylfi and Anakku were there, confused and near panicking, especially when they mopped blood off my jacket and out my hair.

I couldn't pay a lot of attention when Huldrik sat us down, shuffling his fingers while I received the crypel treatment a while longer.

'Mr Ma'Doff and the SEO have been running a small scheme to help themselves and their partners. Small, tolerable. I told them you were off-limits, but they carried on.'

My head was swimming in glitter-treacle. 'What?'

'Depending on enquiries, I'll probably threaten them with conspiracy in Federal Office. If they agree to mild re-alignment, they can be allowed to continue here. Otherwise, it's a posting to a Farside Eramaa Camp.' He shrugged; then straightened up, big fake smile. 'That's it, Davvy Six-Four-Six. Go. Count yourselves lucky this time.'

Again, my first pang was relief that we were koh, and The Hill was still ours. But... 'Hang on – *Lucky?* My head's split open – again, and I've doubled my sentence. And the Highraff have been told they're nothing –

431

prisoners forever? Not skyking likely, Huldrik. What about Four-Four? We all put time and effort into that plot. We've brought proposals for next year.'

The baster looked bored and I lost it with him. I blew, and ranted and demanded all sorts, and my head about burst again, the Ladies trying to calm me down. Then two black-coats *insisted* I calm down. I was washed out by then anyway, and flopped back, furious. 'You devious cheating Shigra.'

He laughed! Course, that started me off again and I really wanted to rip off that stupid grin. I like to think it took all of them to pull me back, but it was probably just Anakku, really.

'Oh, Davvy, Davvy, Davvy...' That hateful patronising repetition! So I gave him my best snarl, and that made my head spasm up, so I decided not to do that again.

'Allow me to tell you something... Segotta was only discovered ten years ago. It was eventually designated as a Pioneer settlement after five years of surveying – that means it's for convict colonies and private settlers, not major corporations. I started here two days later, as on-the-spot governor with onz-onz staff.

'It was intended to be slow, monitored development, but they sent five hundred criminal prisoners in the same ship that I arrived in. With enough equipment and stores to clear half the continent, we began with this compound, cleared land and sent groups out to start satellite communities. The Crims worked or they didn't get fed.'

Taking all this in was straining my mind. My Ladies and Anakku looked equally uncomprehending. What's it got to do with me?

432

'Within the year, we had two even larger prisoner arrivals: all sorts, gathered from more than an onz planets. Mostly, we sent them out to whichever plots they preferred – mines, forestry, fishing or – mainly – clearancing for farming, and did what we could to support them. Part of the support was offering the idlers and recidivists the choice of deep re-alignment, or re-location to an island we call Farside. Only a quarter survive more than onz days on Farside.

And that's how it's been since… Another year and our numbers doubled again, with a few more staff and settlers.' He gazed greasily over my ladies again, sounding so devious. 'There may be a way forward for you...'

That rang alarms in my head, trying to figure out what he was saying. But everything was going black and swirling… I heard him saying, 'Let him go. He's out his skull. Get him treatment.'

Someone was there, fussing, injecting, mopping and tutting all over me. 'Koh. Give him another jab and he'll be capable of listening. Tell the Super he'll be ready in five.'

Huldrik was back, and had the nerve to look concerned. 'You koh now? You had a bad turn. Your head's patched up.' Scruggit! That smirk again. 'Now, we were saying… a way forward. I don't have time or inclination to monitor everybody on the planet – I delegate. But there's never enough capable staff, so a couple of years ago, I began looking for likely Crims to step up. You with me? Good.

'We chose two-onz possibles, you among them, based on your psych profile, your previous line and

433

because you'd opted to retain full memory of what you'd done. We had hopes for you and Chorky, maybe taking over a district. That didn't work out – though you separately surpassed expectations – him with the machines – the most anyone's ever cleared.'

'Yesss… Chorky loved his machines too much to bother bringing in women, families, helpers, getting set up. He only wanted to clear land with his cutters and grabbers, dozers and grubbers.'

'He's still the same. But you, Davvy – very complex, perfectly balanced across the psycho-personality traits. No deficits or extreme biases. *Reasonable*, you might say. Persistent, too. And that set me thinking you might be a section leader without him, hmm?

'Then one day, out the black, a contingent of over five hundred rebellious evacuees arrived here from Raffery – that was you lot.' He nodded to Sylfi and DayMia. 'No notice, no possessions, no information, no time to divide you nicely into groups. And no extra funding to provide food, clothing or shelters. The first thing I knew, you were herding down the gangways.'

He paused… pondering… 'Come see… all of you.' He fiddled with a screen control. 'Ahh, yes…' A wall panel came to life with a zooming-down shot onto a land of smokes and fissures. The camera landed, panned around.

'That's Cyamma,' DayMia blurted out, 'Highraff Parliament! It's… *ruined.*'

The camera explored deserted streets and buildings, underground malls and wreathing vapours. Horrified, the two ladies gasped at each new sight. Sylfi hugged Anakku as though he would be equally traumatised.

'This began three years ago,' Huldrik intoned. 'A mining operation to dissolve the Pharim Shales resulted in ground expansion from nitroid gas production. Vapour escapes fissured the ground... see! Started a chain reaction: regional collapses are destroying the continent.

'Ahh... *This* is a new collapse pit that virtually swallowed a city half a year back. The Fed pulled out as many of you as they could, but a lot of your people resisted evacuation, refusing to believe it was happening. You know – yet another Evil-Fed Plot.

We watched the awful scenes roll by. 'The resistance was self-defeating. So many – *watch this* – fought against the Fed officers. Ah, here, this clip is from an onz ago. Eighty percent of Deenya is uninhabitable, and the Feds are mostly waiting for the last few hundred stragglers to come to the collection stations for off-planet evacuation. It's that, or suicide by remaining. Around half the population has died.'

Sylfi and DayMia took it how you'd expect – horrified-to-the-core badly. 'It's *impossible*,' DayMia said incredulously. 'We were a hundred thousand people...' I pulled them close, held them both, shaking and mumbling wide-eyed. Distraught didn't come into it. We clung to each other, watched, and heard the commentary, stats, projections...

'Raffery,' Huldrik stopped the vid, 'was one single crisis out of the dozen catastrophes that the Fed deals with every year, spread across the Empire. After the first year, there's no more funding for any of them: as far as the Fed's concerned, it's dealt with, no longer a crisis.

'Nobody actually wanted mix-humans then; especially in batches five hundred strong. But, in my job,

I needed to know if Highraff and humans could do more than merely survive together. Thrive, maybe? I had you possible group leaders, so I set up twenty-odd units from that first shipment – different ratios of Highraff to humans.

'Two failed completely – needed rescuing, re-allocating; three more are fading. The rest are doing alright-ish. You were the last one in, Six-Four, and the least promising – as you were on your own by then. That left you with the tail end – the remnants. What? You think it was chance the Highraff were there when you arrived for your review?'

His giblet gaze drifted over DayMia, Sylfi and Anakku. 'But – Look at you now. Despite everything, you're doing well, so I had been wondering about expanding your role? Taking over the plot of land between you and Four-Four? I thought you might become Davvy Four-Four, Five and Six? Hmm?'

'Eh?' That sank in slowly. I blinked a lot, trying to concentrate, and look to my trio for inspiration. 'You're offering me Millop Peak as well? Three adjacent plots? What – as long as I keep the Highraff out there, slaving away, totally isolated from their own people? You know where they all are, perhaps even their own family men—'

'Their best choice,' he waved me to shut up… the two black-coats tightened their grips my shoulders, 'would be to remain where they are, and for you to take this offer. More workers could be allocated to you, including Highraff – plus the seed for almost any crop, with targeted fertilisers; and machines for planting, harvesting, even lumbering. With all the info and training you need in the head-chip... You'd be Super over all three plots, for, say, two years?'

'No. I gotta help my Highraff. You're playing some twisty game here, you scheming shiko.'

'Careful, Six-Four-Six, and get this straight: you have no rights. You're a convicted killer, so don't get difficult with me, or *you'll* find yourself on Farside. The Empire governs, but the Fed *rules*. And on Segotta, *I'm* the Fed.'

I really had to smile at that. 'Didn't take long to get from bribes to threats, did it? It won't work, Super: I've not cared about myself since my wife and kids were killed on Digsby, and I'm not going to start now. Even the Empire isn't stupid enough to scatter fifty thousand evacuees in tiny groups across a hundred planets. Far more efficient to concentrate them on a select few locations: so you must have dozens – maybe hundreds – of Highraff groups. You know exactly where they are – or can fast-find them. So, what's your game? All that vid is a fake? To cover a land-grab?'

He tried to laugh. 'That vid is absolutely genuine – that's occurring right now. Suppose you took the three-plot offer for one year, and I re-designated your Highraff. I change designations all the time – Staff might want to become Settlers, or a dishonest one becomes a Detainee. Or it could be when a Highraff is granted freedom. Your group can officially become Settlers within the hour. As free people, they'd still see their best choice is to stay with you.' That repulsive creeping sneer. He was going to die as soon as these black-coats took their hands off me.

'What's so important about this triple plot? Free or not, the Highraff would still be trapped out there with nowhere to go except the plot next door. They need their own people,' I was shaking, furious with him, I don't know how I dared to talk to him like that. *The Supervisor* of the whole Criminal Colony.

Sylfi and DayMia clutched at my arms, not believing what I was saying to him. 'Davvy, no... You'll antagonise him more—'

'Shut up and listen Four-Six. You're in a hole, cease excavating, or everybody else will fall in with you.' Huldrik sighed with exaggerated patience, 'You're right, of course. This past year, I've received two more consignments – sixteen hundred HEDs – Highraff Evacuated Detainees. Yes, Ladies – there's a lot of you here. Plus onz-onz other mix-humanic refugees from somewhere called Weaver's. And around a thousand more self-financed settler-folk like those who turned up at your place a few onz ago.' He shrugged. 'We do the best we can to give our Crims a chance. Even so, a quarter don't survive their first year, but the Fed isn't interested, as long as I don't raise any alarms – they really don't like alarms of any kind. The survivors do well, but I'm now needing them to mix more – we're receiving too many different groups to stay segregated.'

He stood, walked round, looking out the windows, staring at us. 'In Year Two, you had record production, and no fatalities or desertions; in fact, your population increased by fifty percent, including the human incomers. That's unprecedented with a mixed-humanic group.

He was edging again, deciding... 'There's a developing Empire *Redlight Policy*, "Harmonic Mixing of All Humanics". Soon, it will be designated as a *Primary Concern* for the Fed. That means it will be the next *Must Comply* target for planets like Segotta. So I've been preparing to introduce, and enforce, the resulting compliance policies. Which was why I was ear-marking twenty-some potential mixed-community leaders, including you. My thought was that I might push them up, give them more responsibility – like these three adjacent plots – to give you all better awareness of each other. Expand your thinking. You know... gain the wider picture.'

'Me?' This all had me spinning. Sylf and DayMia's heads swayed – which is quite a sight on top of flowing necks.

Huldrik was studying us, like he was deciding how much to say. Another of his deep sighs. 'That was the situation up to two onz ago, when I received a new contract. The survey of a newly-found planet has recently been completed. Harator, they've called it, probably after some Empire Councillor's Ladyfriend. Drier than here, less oceanic. Its Pioneer status will be declared sometime: it could be in two mins, or possibly in two years – that's Fed decision-making for you. Within a day or two of that declaration, the Fed'll transfer me there. Same job – fresh skies – as per my new contract.

'They'll have me doing the preparation work in anticipation of the move – that might take me away from Segotta for periods.

'Thus, priorities have suddenly become different, and more pressing: I have to make sure Segotta will be in capable hands. Sure, I have deputies, but they're desk-riders...' He was fiddling with some plaspaps. 'And I wonder – considering the timescale and the new priorities for assimilation of large numbers of Highraff and other humanics – if it could be you who's the next Superintendent?'

I sat there, flabber-brained. Sylfi turned to stare at me, so sinuous... graceful... huge-eyed.

'Yes, yes, it really does work as quick and easy as that – The appointment is up to me. I send a name in. Segotta's still a very new and small-change project. There's no big money, no powerful interests and influences, no strategic importance. It's all backvac economics and politics while it's getting on its feet. Everything's done on the quick and cheap by the on-the-spot experts. Yes, even the future of whole, virgin planets. Relatively speaking, Davvy Six-Four-Six, you're the local expert – you have the most successful track record in this multi-humanic circumstance.'

I didn't have the wit to ask or interrupt, and DayMia and Sylfi didn't so much as splutter. Anakku did.

Huldrik gunned on. 'Close your mouth, Davvy Four-Six. To be absolutely honest, up to this morning, I wanted you to take this three-plot posting to lure you in closer, train you up, see how you took to it. But I'm increasingly sure I'm right about you, so the offer is for you to become the Super-in-Waiting, splitting yourself between the Triple-Plot Posting and gaining the wider picture, higher skills, feeding you the contents of my own memo-chip – it's all prepared for my successor. The sooner you agree, and start, the better: I could be gone at any moment.'

He was waiting for an answer, 'Do you think your Highraff could manage The Hill, with your oversight? And maybe the other plots as well? Would they want it?' He looked at DayMia, 'Would you? I'd provide humans and Highraff people from other units where they haven't settled well. See if you can meld them together better. All the seed, fertiliser and equipment you'd need...?

'In the interim, Davvy, you could perhaps manage a region... have oversight of existing strugglers? Plan expansion phases with mixed groups, including the group of Weaver's personnel? You seen any Weavers? Look like us with feathers and a jerky walk? Ease into the bigger role and start thinking planet-wide. There'll no doubt be at least as many contingents again each year. We would both be extremely busy. How does that sound?'

Pitfire! It sounded like an avalanche dropping all over me. My tiny safe-zone was exploding. I clutched sideways for Sylfi.

'Take some early responsibilities: *you* could be the one to grant the Highraff their Settler status, all of twenty-one hundred of them, I imagine. Create a Screen Network for them to contact each other? Allow movement? Exchanges?

This was a "don't breathe or they'll get you" situation, so I said nothing.

'It sounds big, yes – a whole planet. But get it in perspective – eight thousand population at this morning's count; a quarter of them Highraff. That's a village-full, spread out, though it'll double in a year. Who would you want running that? You could appoint an admin officer – there are several already around here who're perfectly capable – and stick to the hands-on, in the field, executive-decision type of governorship for yourself, hmm? This is early dribbles time: we'll need someone in at the beginning, someone with the inside feeling.'

'I... I...' Not me, I was thinking. I couldn't... Sylfi was groping for my hand... DayMia, too. I was frozen inside again... 'I...'

'You'd have no say in who comes to Segotta, but I suspect that if you were making a go of it, there'd be increasing consignments of Highraff, male and female. Probably Weaver's, too – they have eggy babies, by the way. Under such guidance from you, this could become a Highraff-dominant planet. But whoever came, within a year or so, you'd have all the say in where they were posted, and how they're managed. The Fed don't want to know details. You could tick the boxes a year in advance and they'd be grateful for avoiding the last-min rush.'

'*Me?* Why me? Just because I fumbled by on Six-Four-Six?'

'Exactly. The way you've been with your group, you'll mesh in perfectly with this next priority – there'll be Target funding for the next phase. Do you want it in the pockets of folk like Stonebridge – or into the food, shelter and machinery banks for newcomers? I want you to say, "Yes". "Yes, please" would be nice, but I'd understand if the "please" wasn't there.'

Damn him. He was waiting for the answer again. So much rush... too much thinking to do... consulting with The Family...

'Think about what you really want, Davvy. And you, Ladies. You could organise anything however you wished – your base, staff, time spread, priorities. You've been good at all those things, and turned in unprecedented profits as well as survival rates.' He looked triumphant.

I never swallowed that hard before. I was hollow. How total-shocked can you be? We could... and I could... and DayMia certainly could... if only Sylfi and me could...

I knew I'd have to twist my head round to look at the Ladies eventually. Suppose they didn't think it would work? Wouldn't do it with me?

Might I do so much more if I were Supervisor? Could we help so many Highraffs? *And others?* Could we make a difference for them?

'Say "Yes",' DayMia whispered.

Unbidden, my eyes swivelled towards Sylfi; my head followed. I never told it to. I looked at her. Huge lashes fluttering, she squeezed my hand. 'Yes,' she said. 'Yes, yes, we can. And say *"Please".'*

Trevor is a Nottinghamshire writer with many publications to his name, including reader-friendly books and articles about volcanoes around the world, and dinosaur footprints on Yorkshire's Jurassic coast. His short stories and poems have frequently won prizes, and he has appeared on the television, discussing local matters. In the 1980s, his research doctorate pioneered the use of computers in the education of children with profound learning difficulties.

Fourteen years at the chalkface; sixteen as headteacher of a special school; and sixteen as an Ofsted school inspector to round it off, his teacher wife regards their marriage as "Sleeping with the Enemy".

RECENT AND PENDING PUBLICATIONS BY THE SAME AUTHOR

Book 1 – Of Other Times and Spaces.

Published in eBook and Paperback in Feb 2020

Thirty-nine highly entertaining and thought-provoking Sci-Fi short stories filling over 400 pages with "The best and most varied stories in the universe", according to eleven alien species and the author's mum. Starting with snappy three-pagers such as "Air Sacs and Frilly Bits", in increasing length up to the novella-sized "The Colonist". From the laughs of "I'm a Squumaid", "Cats, Cucumbers and Cabbagunkins" and "Friday Night in Somercotes", to the tears of "The Twelve Days of Crystal-Ammas". Could you watch the Scurrugs? Or contend with an encounter of the 4th Kind? Could you ride the Observatory on Belvedere? Or meet the Face in the Rock? With 20+ illustrations – monochrome in the paperback; colour in the eBook.

445

Book 2 – Beyond our Times and Spaces.

To be let off the leash early 2020.

Explore the oddities of time in "Go for a walk, Oscar, dear" and "I'm ten, Daddy". Wonder about the future of homo sapiens in "Coupla Yumans", "A time to be culling" and "Pondkeeper". Muse what happens when we find they're among us, in "Kalai Alaa", "Puppetmaster", and "Hygiene was a mite slack that day". Or immerse yourself in the trials to come in "It isn't easy being a hero", "Nice" and "Holes aren't my thing". Rounded off with two dozen other stories, and a pair of poems – "Anyone's Guess", and "Mirador", plus continued adaptations from "Realms of Kyre" and "A Wisp of Stars". Half the stories with quirky and illustrious illustrations.

Book 3 – Further Spaces, Times and Places.

Due to take flight mid-2020.

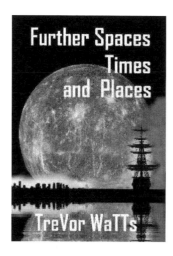

Laugh, wince or cower through the conflicts of "Donya's Tale", "What's the Point", and "Hoist on my own History". Check if they're in our midst in "Herpetor"; "The Ice Cave," and "The Jolly Small Club". Or are we the aliens in "ZeePeeCee", "Reality" and "I keep having blackou—"? Suffer with them as they cross "The Lily Pond" and the "Radiation Lands", or join the doubters in "How much training does a pin get to burst a bubble?" and "An Affair with a Tangerine?". Before realising how futile it all is in "Shall we tidy up?" and "But not as we know it". Still deciding on the final line-up of yarns and legends, a pair of poems, and two dozen ilexic illustrations.

Of Twists and Turns.

Due for publication summer 2020.

The first anthology of short stories from around the world, when the here-and-now takes a turn for the better... or the worse. Complete with illustrations and a pair of poetic indulgences.

From the delightful Japanese "Festival" and "Haiku Man" to the desperation of walking "The Kalapana lava flow", or surviving the Appalachians in "Bigfoot and the Bottle", or northern Canada in "God and the Meteorite". Try "My LGBGT Sandwich" for a laugh, and "United" for a footballer's point of view. Or the dubious joys of "Temmer Harbour", "Anyone for Dominoes", and "Facing up to it". Whether you're into driving, flying or jogging, this is the must-read collection.

And an Anthology of Poetry in a Pear Tree.

The World of Wonders Poetry Book

For publication asap.

Collected poems that everyone
Can see themselves reflected in,
Of flower-strewn girls, of ponies gone,
A ranch-hand wreaks the deadly sin.

Filling up the parting glass;
Of cats and men and ladies, too.
World War One and graves en masse;
Of dynamite and the Devil's brew.

Machu Picchu and Galway Town;
Whoever said, 'Old Men Don't Fall?'
From Java's mud to nature's gown,
The pages here unveil them all.

Minimum arrestable delinquency;
The haggis that truly took my heart;
In elegant idiosyncrasy
I take my leave, I must depart.

Novels waiting in the wings:

"Realms of Kyre". Written, but not yet prepared for public consumption, this is the Epic Fantasy Trilogy+.

"A Wisp of Stars". The awesome Science Fiction Trilogy+ chronicling the rise and rise of Blissen's Empire.

449

CREDITS, NOTES AND THANKS

Part 1. Coffee-Break Quickies

Well Met by Moonlight was inspired by many such
    nights at sea, and prompted by a flash fiction
    competition title. The illustration is adapted (using
    ACDSee) from a painting Sailing-at-night, with
    permission, by Carlos Ramos
    http://stock.adobe.com/contributor/206704460/carlos

Worse Things Happen in Space; based on a collision I
    was involved in in the Antarctic Ocean, between a
    ship (The Fram) and the face of a glacier. It was the
    joke that went around the very relieved passengers
    afterwards, 'Worse things happen at sea.'

Air Sacs and Frilly Bits is from a party game that the
    kids really didn't understand.

Eos, from waking up in hospital and briefly wondering
    what was happening (24th June 2016 – Brexit Result
    Day). The illustration is adapted from two images
    from Canstock and Shutterstock.

Pinball. I thought how much we are at the mercy of the
    Gods of Chance sometimes. Picture based on Public
    Domain images from NASA – many thanks.

Friday Night in Somercotes, based on encounters late
    on weekend evenings in this small Derbyshire town,
    after convivial visits to The Curry Lounge. A picture
    wouldn't do them justice.

And on the Seventh's Day sprang from a visit to General Custer's Little Bighorn battle site, and subsequently reading accounts of the US Seventh Cavalry's ignominious role in conflicts from the Indian Wars to Vietnam.

A Lovely Sunny Day is wishful thinking for a youngster I once saw on holiday, entertaining himself by killing ants.

Second Thoughts was an idle hour one afternoon, inspired by drifting dreams.

There's Something in my Pond was definitely inspired by the disappearance from my pond of five huge koi carp and two dozen smaller ones, courtesy of a heron and a large grass snake. A version of this won a short story competition.

I'm a Squumaid was a wondering venture into how we might relate with exotic aquatic aliens. The picture was created from several Internet images.

Number 16 Bungulla is based on the true story of a trapdoor spider at Bungulla, Australia.

Thank you, Mellissa is loosely based on a few very bright children I've encountered in my career in education. The picture based on a freebie from Pexels.com.

What happened to the Moon came about when I was
photographing the moon one night with a 1200 zoom
on the camera. I thought, 'If something happened up
there, I'd have a ringside seat.' I took the picture,
and adapted it with ACDSee.

Part 2. Linger Longer over Lunch

Cats, Cucumbers and Cabba-gunkins was inspired by
idiots who post shrieking images of themselves
tormenting cats on the Internet. If only...

Cactus George came from meeting several people who
are dedicated to their cacti, and my own painful and
spiny experiences with them.

Above the Parapet arose from an idea for a chapter in a
book I was writing (but left out); combined with a
challenge in a writing group to write a short story in
future tense.

The Spoyocks developed from the thought of how huge
decisions can be made over a cup of tea, or a pint of
beer – such as battle tactics in WW2, or the English
National Curriculum for schools. The picture is an
amalgamation of images from Pixabay and NASA.

I have a Woman on my Mind was sadly prompted by a
traffic incident at a major city junction we crossed
daily when we were in Arizona. My heart went out
to the family of the deceased biker.

The Plasma Storm on Belvedere owes everything to
   The Cliffs of Baccalieu, a Canadian folk song
   written by Jack Withers, about sailing past the shores
   of Labrador in a storm. I did the picture.

Mansfield will never be the same again is based on
   wishful thinking when bellowing men, loud ladies
   and howling kids are out in force. The background of
   the picture is by Duncan.flickr,
   https://commons.wikimedia.org/w/index.php?curid=
   36550680. It was adapted by an alien that came on
   the scene.

Mrs Atkins came to me in a waiting room in a
   Liverpool Hospital. Or she walked past, actually.
   The illustration is a combination of several free
   Internet images.

Fat Cat is a reflection on some people I've met who are
   utterly self-serving, obtuse and arrogantly
   demanding; plus memories of Chapel Point,
   Cornwall, sixty-plus years ago. The illustration is an
   adaption of two free Internet images.

Four Onz grew by itself. I had no idea where it was
   heading, even 9/10ths through.

A Face in the Rock arose from a large piece of tiger eye
   rock we bought at the Tucson Rock Show. The
   illustration is adapted from a photo I took of it –
   guess which part.

My 7th Grade Science Project is a combination of ideas
from a camping trip around Alaska, the 1964
Alaskan earthquake, and how brilliant some
American children's science projects are. The
illustration is a free, adapted image off the Internet.

The Cat's Away arose from seeing an abandoned ants'
nest that had been part of a school project. It had
simply been tossed out at the end of term. And I
wondered... If that was scaled up...

Daisy is based on a delightfully precocious little girl we
encountered whilst looking round the amazing
murals on the walls Exeter, California. The picture is
a composite I made up from free Internet images,
because the miseries at the Exeter Chamber of
Commerce never bothered to reply to my requests to
use one of their images.

Plot 51 came from a holiday – sorry, vacation – in
Alberta, Canada; combined with the story of
Canadian copper surveying in the Thirties; and Area
51 in Nevada, where we visited in the 2010's.

Part 3. An Evening In

The Silversmiths was written after seeing a stall selling
beautiful silver jewellery on a stall at the Ste Marie
Fossils and Minerals Fair in Alsace, France. At very
good prices.

The Light Switch came from a thought of how some
tiny observation or inconsistency can radically

retune a person's thinking. I made up the illustration from a freebie on the Internet.

In the Unlikely Event of an Emergency came from a trip along the sea front and river in Cardiff in a sight-seeing boat that was almost tubular, and festooned with a multitude of warning signs. The illustration is my combination of two NASA images (Many thanks to NASA and ACDSee).

A Little Cooperation came from an idea (about an incident at The Eagle comic offices in the 1950's) for a short poem. Acorn-like, it grew.

Of the 4th Kind was inspired by a news film of a tornado in the USA, with bins and other debris flying through a Mid-West neighbourhood.

The Twelve Days of Crystal-Ammas was originally titled "Boldly Gone". I began it with the intention of exploring how the survivors of a crash-landing on an unfriendly planet might cope with each other as well as their environment. It took its own unexpected direction. The picture is a merging of free web photos.

Watching the Scurrugs started as the story of an adventurous young risk-taker pushing his luck and enjoying his life on the up, or on the edge. Half-way through, he and I were ambushed; events took their own direction, and continued from there. I adapted the picture from Shutterstock24276211.

Kyre? is an adaptation of the first three chapters of my novel trilogy, "Kyre of the Realms". The picture is based on a copyright-bought one on the Internet.

Discovery is adapted from the first book of my novel trilogy, "A Wisp of Stars." The illustration is a combination of artwork from a brilliant Californian movie artist and modeller, and a NASA background image.

The Colonist had been in my mind for some time, in one form or another. It grew, developed and came together over a period. The picture? Literally two minutes on a Post-it.

***

Printed in Poland
by Amazon Fulfillment
Poland Sp. z o.o., Wrocław

59571633R00260